War Among Ladies

ELEANOR SCOTT

BRITISH LIBRARY

First published in 1928
This edition published in 2022 by
The British Library
96 Euston Road
London NW1 2DB

Copyright © 1928 The Estate of Helen Magdalen Leys
Preface copyright © 2022 Alison Bailey
Afterword copyright © 2022 Simon Thomas

Cataloguing in Publication Data
A catalogue record for this publication is available from the British Library

ISBN 978 0 7123 5462 2
e-ISBN 978 0 7123 6830 8

Text design and typesetting by JCS Publishing Services Ltd
Printed and bound by CPI Group (UK), Croydon, CR0 4YY

Contents

❦ ❦ ❦

The 1920s

❦

❦ **1920:** E. Hilton Young MP chairs a committee on school scholarships and recommends that the proportion of free places at secondary schools should be increased from 25 per cent to 40 per cent. (The Education Act of 1944 would eventually provide free secondary education at state school for all pupils.)

❦ **1921:** The census shows that there are approximately 1.7 million more women than men in the UK – a figure that had scarcely changed by the 1931 census.

❦ **1921:** The Geddes Axe, recommended by a Committee of National Expenditure chaired by Sir Eric Geddes, seeks to save millions of pounds in government spending – including teaching. Among other measures, teachers' salaries are cut, and attempts to raise the age of compulsory education from 14 are shelved.

❦ **1921:** The average life expectancy for women in England and Wales is 59.6 years (and 55.6 for men).

❦ **1922 (July):** Rhondda Education Authority fires sixty-three female teachers because they are married. The teachers take the case to court, but lose.

❦ **1924 (January):** Ramsay MacDonald takes office as the UK's first Labour Prime Minister. In *War Among Ladies*, Miss Barr blames 'The Rise of Labour, the Tendencies of the Modern Age, the painful lack of Really Nice Girls' for the state of discipline in her school.

❦ ❦ ❦

❦ **1923:** The Teachers' Pension Scheme is set up to complement the existing superannuation policy provided by the government.

❦ **1926:** New legislation enables women to hold and dispose of property on the same terms as men. In practice, however, women are routinely denied mortgages without a male guarantor.

❦ **1928:** The average age of women at marriage is 26.6 years, and the average age for men is 29.1.

❦ **1928:** *War Among Ladies* is published.

❧ ❧ ❧

Eleanor Scott (1892–1965)

❧

Eleanor Scott was one of the pseudonyms of Helen Magdalen Leys, born in Hampton in 1892 to John Leys and Ellen Holligan. She attended Somerville College, one of the first two women's colleges at the University of Oxford, during a period in which women were allowed to attend lectures but before they were able to gain degrees (this wouldn't happen until 1920). As a student, she would have been chaperoned whenever in the presence of a male student. Following the First World War, Leys became a teacher and, later, the principal of a teacher training college in Oxford.

Leys' father was a prolific writer – following an unsuccessful career as a barrister – publishing eighteen novels in his later years with titles such as *The Black Terror* and *The Missing Bridegroom*. Leys followed in his footsteps, publishing her first story 'The Room' in the *Cornhill Magazine* in 1923, under her own name. This story about a haunted room would later be included in *Randalls Round*, a 1929 collection of ghost stories published as Eleanor Scott – a moniker that would first appear on the cover of 1928's *War Among Ladies*.

It was the first of eight books published under this pseudonym, including two works for children – 1933's *Adventurous Women* and 1939's *Heroic Women*, featuring potted biographies of figures such as Mary, Queen of Scots and Florence Nightingale. When she branched out into mystery novels with *The Bolt* (1929) and *The Death Film* (1932), Leys used another pseudonym, P.R. Shore. It was suggested in *The Author's and Writer's Who's Who and Reference Guide 1935–36* that the author's full name was Peter Redcliff Shore, educated at Oxford University and with an interested in rock-climbing. Leys obviously had fun creating an alternative persona.

Like many of the teachers in *War Among Ladies*, Leys remained unmarried. She lived with her mother in Clapton-in-Gordano, Somerset, during her writing career, and later moved with her historian sister Mary to Devon. Leys' final novel, *Puss in the Corner*, was published in 1934; all of her books appeared within the space of eleven years. She died in 1965, at the age of 72.

❦ ❦ ❦

Preface

❦

Set in a girls' high school in the Midlands in the 1920s with a staff of single women (the ladies of the title) what seems at first a light-hearted satire turns into something darker. With a weakened Head, declining exam results and consequent threat of school closure, tension between the women rises. For some, the changes in curriculum, teaching methods and student behaviour have become too much. Yet for financial security they must continue, not only trapped personally, but also condemning others to see their hard work turn to dust. Misunderstandings, allegiances and plots arise as a consequence. Into this maelstrom steps English teacher Viola Kennedy – newly appointed, determined, enthusiastic and optimistic – learning the hard way to negotiate staffroom politics. Will her desire to 'educate, not merely to teach' survive?

Amid the clashing cultures of the 1920s, the legacy of the First World War is still palpable and is referred to frequently by the Head. The social disruption and the loss of so many men contribute to a narrowing of options available to these women. The original dedication to the unknown male train passenger with his ill-informed criticism of teachers (reproduced here on page 2) is perhaps a steer that this is an indictment of the system rather than the individuals caught up in it. Reflecting the author's own knowledge and experience of teaching and teachers, it provides a fascinating glimpse into a precarious and

❧ ❧ ❧

claustrophobic world with little privacy or economic stability and only limited choices.

Alison Bailey
Lead Curator Printed Heritage Collection 1901–2000
British Library

Publisher's Note

The original novels reprinted in the British Library Women Writers series were written and published in a period ranging, for the most part, from the 1910s to the 1950s. There are many elements of these stories which continue to entertain modern readers, however in some cases there are also uses of language, instances of stereotyping and some attitudes expressed by narrators or characters which may not be endorsed by the publishing standards of today. We acknowledge, therefore, that some elements in the stories selected for reprinting may continue to make uncomfortable reading for some of our audience. With this series, British Library Publishing aims to offer a new readership a chance to read some of the rare books of the British Library's collections in an affordable paperback format, to enjoy their merits and to look back into the world of the twentieth century as portrayed by their writers. It is not possible to separate these stories from the history of their writing and as such the following novel is presented as it was originally published with minor edits only, made for consistency of style and sense. We welcome feedback from our readers, which can be sent to the following address:

British Library Publishing
The British Library
96 Euston Road
London, NW1 2DB
United Kingdom

War Among Ladies

PART I

Summer: Miss Cullen

CHAPTER I

The Hub

The hub of the universe is not, as you might fancy, always in the same place. Some people believe it to be in Geneva; some would put it in No. 10, Downing Street; for others it is behind the door with "Private" on it, after you pass through the outer office; others believe it to be in, say, Paquin's *salons*; some can persuade themselves that it is in a dusty suburb, in the kitchen or nursery of a house called "Fernlea" or "Balmoral"; some, still more unfortunate, place it in a University or College, or even in one room of a college; a few innocents might plump for the House of Commons, others for the Stock Exchange, or even a racecourse.

The people of this story all believed it to be in the same place. Even though they denied that it did, they all thought so, really. It lay, they thought, in the building known as the County Education Offices in the uninspiring Midland town of Stamborough; and it had a kind of deputy (if a hub can have a deputy, which seems doubtful) behind the white-painted door of Miss Barr's study. As the faithful receive the words of the Bishop who is instructed by the Pope, so did the Staff of Besley High School receive those words of Miss Barr which had their origin from the August Unknown at Stamborough.

The analogy does not hold altogether; for the Besley Staff, while receiving with unquestioning submission—(almost, one might say, with complete resignation, as of the immutable decrees of Fate)—the *dicta* of their Sovereign Pontiff at Stamborough, had begun to show a distressing doubt with regard to those minor declarations which emanated directly from his deputy. In other words, they did sometimes, and with increasing frequency, doubt the wisdom of Miss Barr's commands. Sometimes, on personal matters, they even questioned them, which is another proof of the social disruptions caused by the War. Sometimes Miss Barr felt that the world really needed readjusting very badly. She wasn't accustomed, she told herself with an attempt at head-mistressly hauteur which her natural diffidence rendered abortive, to being questioned or doubted. But some are born to be doubted, as others are born to be believed; and, if she had known the truth, Miss Barr always had been. The only real novelty was that she now realised it.

Miss Adela Barr, M.A. (Dublin), Hist. Trip. Camb. (and she always hoped, with a kind of wistfulness tempering the vanity, that people realised the significance of the last three words, and how superior they made her to the ordinary Dublin M.A.) now sat in the white-doored room. It was the eighth week of the Summer Term—an awkward time, as all the Profession know. It is near the end of a tiring year, but the end is not yet. Half-term has gone, and the end of term is not well within sight. The weather is sometimes hot, and always unsatisfactory. Examinations are near. Tempers are short and nerves strained, both with girls and Staff. A bad time for any Head Mistress, and still worse when she is aware of other rifts within the lute. Miss Barr had a gift amounting to genius for closing her eyes to unpleasantness of any kind—a gift that was once praised and cultivated as Womanly Refinement; but this year it had really been impossible to take this comfortable line.

First, there was the ever-present trouble about Miss Lexington. She had to be made Second Mistress; she had excellent qualifications of every kind, and had been on the Staff for eight years. Also she was most efficient. On the other hand, Miss Parry had been on the Staff for twelve years, and had certainly expected the position; but a Welsh degree, and not a very good one, and not much High School experience … Miss Parry had not been pleasant about it, and she had never forgotten it. Miss Barr recognised, in spite of the closed-eyes theory, that things must have been very uncomfortable for Miss Lexington. In her inmost heart she was grateful to her for sticking to her post with so little fuss. Perhaps, though, she hadn't minded much. Such a *hard* woman, Miss Barr thought plaintively—and after all it was three years ago now. Perhaps it had blown over. ... But Miss Parry was difficult—very difficult. So odd in some ways, and so easy to offend. And it did not do to offend Miss Parry.

Then there was the bother over discipline. Miss Barr could not quite discover how this arose, but there could be no doubt that it did. Sometimes she gave the blame to the War, and that was satisfactory, because you could speak about it openly; sometimes she thought the Staff was not doing all it might—all these odd, upsetting new theories about freedom and so on; and here, if she were speaking to one of the Old Guard, Miss Lexington or Miss Fergusson or Miss Parry, she would add: "Of course, these young modern mistresses have not the same training we used to have. They have so little sense of responsibility to their work"; or, "Poor Miss Spiller, she is really *too* refined to deal with girls of this type"; or, "I'm afraid poor Miss Harries is losing grip a little"; or, "Of course, Miss Cullen—one can hardly wonder that the girls rebel against *her*"—and a timid glance would be added to see how the Old Guard took it. Or she might blame in good set terms the Rise of Labour, the Tendencies of the Modern Age, the painful lack of Really Nice Girls, and the deplorable increase of Free Place girls from the elementary schools; but here again she had to go warily, because even with the Staff you never knew. ... People took such *odd* views nowadays, and she did so hate anything approaching a wrangle. It was characteristic of Miss Barr that she always gave this name to arguments which were ably conducted and in which there was a good deal to be said on both sides.

She sat, on this Wednesday morning, in her large and pleasant study. It was a good room, one of the best in the building, but badly arranged. Miss Barr belonged to the type, once very common, though now fast disappearing, that believes that no room can be really Businesslike that is also really comfortable. She was strong on the businesslike atmosphere; that was why she disliked Miss Gilbert's geographical models and Miss Reeve's sheets of pictures illustrative of history, both executed by small children in the Lower School. She would never say in so many words that she disliked them, since to do so even to herself would be to confess herself a reactionary; but she "must confess that she liked a nice *businesslike* class-room." Her own desk was neither neat nor businesslike;

and it is probable that she realized this, since she was now engaged, in a more or less desultory fashion, in arranging the surface of its contents. She looked quite ornamental as she sat there. She always looked her best when sitting, since her abnormally long body then gave an impression of height and dignity which was lost when she stood. Also her head, with its beautifully arranged grey hair, bent gracefully from the long neck, looked refined, pleasant and calm. Her hands, another good feature till you looked at them closely, fluttered prettily over the papers. She was altogether rather like an attractive but somewhat undistinguished portrait in the Royal Academy of 1904 or so.

A knock came at the door, to which she responded by pressing a little knob. The result of this was not apparent inside the room; in reality it caused a small brass plate on the outside of the door to revolve, displaying the command, simple yet dignified, "ENTER." Miss Barr hoped rather wistfully that this device gave a certain *cachet* to her presence. The Staff scoffed, stormed or chuckled at it according to their individual temperaments. In justice to Miss Barr it must be added that the arrangement was installed by her predecessor; but it must also be admitted that, while she would never have installed it herself, she rather liked it. So she pressed it now; and the door opened to admit Miss Lexington.

The Head's heart sank. Miss Lexington was always so deplorably efficient and alert, and she nearly always had something unpleasant to say.

The first thing you noticed about Miss Lexington, in these days of slouching walk and formless lines, was her taut erectness. She was, above everything, what North-country folk call "trig." Her clothes, admirably tailored, contrived to express this characteristic despite their modern cut. She carried herself with conscious firmness. Her very walk said, "Don't think you can trifle with *me*." Her dark shingled hair was rigidly neat. Her face no one could describe fully, for its handsome, worn features were always guarded. The eyes, vividly blue, watchful, alert and bright, had the inscrutable expression of one who walks warily; the mouth, a firm, thin red line, smiled as constantly and as inscrutably as the Sphinx. As the Staff said, Miss Lexington was an enigma. She never gave herself away, not for a second. She could not afford to.

Good mornings were courteously exchanged, much as fencers salute, and then Miss Barr said hastily:

"Is it anything important, Miss Lexington? I have rather a lot to attend to—"

(She felt a little thrill of pleasure as she remembered that she had clearly been engaged with papers which might quite well have been important ones.)

"I'm afraid it is rather," said Miss Lexington firmly, seeing through the untold, almost unintended, lie.

Miss Barr sighed.

"Yes?"

"There are two or three things I want to ask you," began the Staff Mistress with deadly briskness. "To begin with, there's the question of games. You know, Miss Barr, the present arrangement is not at all satisfactory. Miss Rowan is Games Mistress, and I'm sure she feels that all games matters should be left entirely in her hands. As it is—well, Miss Fergusson is—she hardly makes things easy. She—"

"Oh, Miss Lexington! You *know* I can't take away any games work from Miss Fergusson. She has had charge of the School games for eleven years, and I can't possibly ask her to resign everything to Miss Rowan. After all, Miss Rowan has only been here just over a year."

"Does that really matter—the length of service, I mean? Miss Rowan is a trained games expert. Isn't the question rather which of the two is the better fitted to organize the games?"

"Oh, of course Miss Rowan is a qualified games mistress, and I don't doubt that she can *play* games better than Miss Fergusson. But I hardly feel ... Can't they work together? That was the intention."

"I gather that Miss Fergusson is unwilling to collaborate with Miss Rowan. She—well, to put it bluntly, she doesn't care to play second fiddle to a younger woman."

"It's very natural," pleaded the Head.

"Perhaps; but that's hardly the point. The position is that Miss Rowan, who was appointed here as games mistress, feels that she should have full control of all games matters; Miss Fergusson doesn't agree. Yesterday she rearranged the tennis fours, and Miss Rowan, who wanted to try Nellie Beamish for the third couple, put the girls back in the order she had originally given. Miss Fergusson resented it, and—well, things were most uncomfortable."

"I see. ... I will see Miss Fergusson, Miss Lexington; but I cannot take all her games work from her. You must see that. She has organized the games here for so long—"

"I know she has." Miss Lexington tactfully refrained from adding that none of the Staff could imagine why. "And I'm sure Miss Rowan would not in the least wish to deprive her of a share in their organization. But she does feel that they ought to be under her control, and that she ought to have the final word."

Miss Barr looked annoyed, doubtful, plaintive, disturbed and a little embarrassed. Miss Lexington foresaw a return to the eleven-year *motif*, and switched off as speedily as might be.

"So you will see Miss Fergusson. Thank you so much. Then there was something else. ..." She glanced at a paper in her hand. "Oh, yes. May Masters. Really, Miss Barr, that girl is getting beyond everything. She has a most degrading influence on other girls. She ought not to be in the school at all."

"Really, Miss Lexington, this is very astonishing! I have always found May very polite and obliging. What exactly is the charge against her?"

Miss Lexington flushed ever so slightly.

"She is thoroughly low-minded," she replied firmly. She almost added, "Naturally the Head wouldn't see it"; but prudence supervened. Instead she added, "She has low ideas, thoroughly vulgar habits."

"But I can't expel a girl on a charge as vague as that," protested the Head.

"I don't suggest immediate expulsion; but you could ask her people to remove her at the end of the term. We shall never get a good atmosphere in IVb until she leaves."

"IVb. I'd forgotten May was in IVb. That explains it, I think, Miss Lexington. I've always thought Miss Cullen had a dislike for poor May. You know how it is when a Form Mistress takes a dislike to a member of her form. Everything that goes wrong is the fault of that particular girl. No, unless you, or—or any other member of the Staff—has anything definite against May, I can't take any steps. I can't take the responsibility of ruining the child's whole career without very serious cause."

"Just because the father's a Governor," thought Miss Lexington savagely—and, as it happened, unjustly. Aloud she said:

"I think we all feel the same about her. She is a thoroughly bad type—a disgusting type. We all think so. As to a definite charge—I think Miss Cullen did show you the paper she found in May's French grammar?"

"Miss Cullen again! I really can't say I attach much importance to her discoveries. ... Is there anything else, Miss Lexington?"

Miss Lexington bent her head over her list to conceal her anger. She knew, none better, what would happen in IVb. ... Aloud she said:

"One other thing. I wanted to ask you—I suppose you couldn't reconsider the question of duties? Some of the Staff feel them very heavily, especially at this time of the year, with examinations and the heat—"

"Oh, Miss Lexington, *please*! You *know* it's impossible." The Head's voice was almost pleading. "The Staff has done these duties for sixteen years, ever since the school was opened, and there have never been complaints until lately. I see no reason for change."

"The school has grown so much, and the work is so much heavier. Some of us have no free times at all, and the forms are so large—"

"I know. I am so sorry. I will see what can be done, but ... It's very difficult; you see, the discipline is not good in any case, and I am very loath to relax what little hold we have over the girls. ... I will see what can be done, but—"

"That means No," thought the Staff Mistress bitterly. "Why can't she *say* No, and have done with it?"

"Have you anything else—?" hinted the Head politely.

Miss Lexington had, a good deal, but she realised that the moment was not propitious. She withdrew.

Miss Barr sat on at her desk, and if she had been asked she would still have said that she was at work on the documents that encumbered it; but in reality she was only fretting. She was very much perturbed. Every point of Miss Lexington's complaints perplexed and annoyed her. Miss Fergusson was one of the Old Guard; she could not take any step that would alienate her. On the other hand, Miss Rowan was a determined young woman, and it was quite on the cards that if she did not get her own way in this matter of authority (and Miss Barr had to admit that for Miss Rowan it might be a matter of some importance) she might leave. And that would be a calamity. Miss Rowan was very efficient; then the Staff had changed so often—so very much too often. That was partly how the disciplinary trouble arose; besides, it meant discomfort in the school and talk in the town when there were so many changes. ... It really was most inconsiderate of people to make all this fuss, thought the Head plaintively.

"But I'll put my foot down over this question of duties," she thought with a pleasing sense of decision. Like many another in her position, she really thought that to refuse to listen was to come to a firm and wise decision.

Another knock—and this time Miss Barr recognised it. Only one member of the Staff knocked in that aggressive way, and she particularly did not want to see Miss Parry. She hesitated; but eventually the brass plate was made to revolve, and Miss Parry entered.

Her appearance was, in its way, good. Most people thought, when they first saw Miss Parry, that she was a well-preserved woman in the early forties. As a matter of fact, she was not yet forty, and she mistakenly believed that she looked very much less than her age. For a shrewd woman, she was singularly dense when contemplating other people's attitude to herself. She was short, plump, and rapidly getting plumper, but had a certain trimness due to the expensive nature of her clothes and the careful selection of her corsets. In fact, all her clothes were carefully selected; she failed in her aim of looking well dressed by being too well dressed. Her face, good-looking in an impressionist style due chiefly to a healthy skin and pretty, still dark, hair, was becoming marred by flesh and by a continual discontent, which gave to her features a kind of sullenly watchful, almost greedy, expression.

Miss Barr's attitude to Miss Parry was a strange one. Miss Parry had been at the school rather longer than the Head herself, and the ostensible relationship was one of devoted loyalty on the one side and friendly gratitude on the other. But, though both thought they believed this, it was mere theory. In her heart Miss Barr knew that if she gave Miss Parry an inch of ascendancy it would grow to a goodly ell; therefore she, half unconsciously, made a point of refusing any requests or suggestions her subordinate might make—plausible refusals, but none the less definite. And Miss Parry on her side, though the role for which she was cast was that of the Loyal Friend, and though she really made herself remarkably useful in more ways than one, never lost an opportunity either of publicly airing her grievances, which were many, or of criticising with some gall the injustices and mistakes committed by the Head. Between the two there was not enmity, hardly even an armed truce, for neither admitted the real situation. It was one of those subtle, idiotic, and heart-rending situations that do occur between women who are growing old in a life of unnatural relationships, unnecessary labours and repressed instincts and desires.

"I'm sorry to disturb you," began Miss Parry, insincerely. "I just wanted your advice."

Miss Barr's face cleared. She realised from this gambit that Miss Parry had come in the role of faithful reporter rather than that of discontented employee.

"Do sit down. What is it, Miss Parry?"

As she spoke she threw a cautious, almost furtive, glance towards the door. She lived in dread, which she never even half admitted even to herself, lest the Staff should discover that Miss Parry played the part of communication file between them and the Head. Miss Parry probably knew that they at least suspected it. She was a good deal shrewder than the Head.

"It's Miss Cullen. She's *hopeless*. I went by her form room yesterday morning, and it was real pandemonium. And it's getting worse, Miss Barr. What the examination results will be I can't imagine. And it's really rather hard on me. You know how easy it is for her to make an excuse for her results—she'll say it was impossible for her to get the girls through because I hadn't prepared them properly on the lower forms."

"Oh, I hardly think—" murmured Miss Barr tepidly.

"Oh, *wouldn't* she!" Then, realising that too much of the natural vulgarian had escaped, she went on in a voice stiff with refinement: "I 'shaw you she is capable—*more* than capable—of sayin' so, to inspectors or *any* one. 'V cawce I know it's awf'ly bad fawm to say so to you, but—!" The whole voice, manner, even the face, altered as she uttered her shibboleth "form."

Miss Barr fidgeted.

"What can I *do*? I know she's not—well, she's incompetent. Let's be frank. She's incompetent, we know. What can *I* do?"

Miss Parry's face was expressive. The Head realised the mistake of asking a purely rhetorical question that might receive a literal answer. She hurried on:

"We must just hope for the best. Miss Harries has resigned, you know. … It may occur to Miss Cullen …"

Their eyes met in a long and expressive glance. That look said infinitely more than had their whole conversation. In it they told each other all they thought of each other, of Miss Cullen, of the whole situation caused by them and by Miss Cullen. Miss Parry seemed to think it satisfactory. It closed her interview.

"Is there anyone else waiting to see me?" asked Miss Barr with rather conscious weariness as the other rose to go.

"Well, as a matter of fact, there *was* someone. … Who was it, now?" She affected to think. In reality her own interview had been wrested from the waiting Miss Cullen by a manoeuvre which she considered the height of diplomacy and Miss Cullen the depth of trickery. "Oh, I know. It was Miss Cullen."

"Oh-h-h. … Oh, it's sure to be something trivial. … No, ring the prayer-bell, please, Miss Parry, as you go out. And," raising her voice for the benefit of ears outside as the mistress reached and opened the door, "would you ask anyone else who may be waiting to see me to be kind enough to come later? It's five to nine now. …"

With satisfaction she heard the sharp tap-tap of Miss Parry's heels and the clod-clod of Miss Cullen's flat shoes fade away into the distance of the corridor. She was safe for the moment, anyhow. She could think of another excuse afterwards. ...

Five minutes later Miss Lexington, Miss Parry, Miss Cullen and the remaining ten members of the staff and three hundred odd girls were kneeling while Miss Barr, in gown and hood, invoked a blessing on "the teachers and pupils of this school. Help them in the work which Thou hast given them to do. ..."

It was to be hoped that someone would.

CHAPTER II

Monstrous Regimen

Miss Cullen laid down the chalk with trembling fingers. Never had it been quite as bad as this, though coming, she knew, coming for months. The June sunlight, cruelly strong, bathed her as she stood on the little *estrade*. Plain she had always been; and now she was withered, battered. Every wrinkle was clear, every grey hair—and there were many now—turned to glistening silver.

She was an ugly figure standing there in the fresh sunlight, rows of young impertinent faces ranked before her. Her hideous home-made dress of brown casement cloth strained across her square, sturdy body and hung in ungainly folds above the thick ankles and flat, broad shoes. It was an odd face, as so many faces are when you look into them. The skin, reddened and rough, and slack now from want of exercise and years of unhealthy life, stretched tightly across the high, narrow forehead, where no stray line of hair softened the angularity, and sagged beneath the eyes and long, weak, protruding chin. The mouth, set a little open, smiled perpetually, anxiously. The restless eyes, behind strong spectacles, darted suspicious glances, or stared defiantly; they were uneasy, alarmed, defensive. It was a face that sought, in the fashion of thirty years ago, by strained hair, steel-rimmed glasses and protruded jaw, to appear strong; and it was, in every line, weak, distrustful, afraid. Her very voice as she began to speak was self-consciously pedantic.

"Now that is hardly an easy phrase to render into English. It has the true Gallic flavour. *Dénouement imprévu, qui était bien l'écroulement.* ... Who can suggest a translation? ... Girls, attention, if you please. *Dénouement imprévu ...*"

Her voice died away. What was the use? Not one of them was listening.

Not one was interested. Not one—bitterest of all—not one liked her. …
The pause of her voice had not even been noticed in the general buzz of
conversation. … She pulled herself together.

"*Dénouement imprévu*—Hilda, can you suggest a good translation?"

A surprised stare from Hilda. No other answer beyond an insolent
grin.

"I know it is rather difficult. Can't anybody guess? You know the
context. Ruth, what conclusions do you draw as to the meaning?"

"I don't know. I can't draw at all."

Delighted titters greeted this sally; a flood of ribald comment was let
loose.

"Oh, Miss Cullen, may we draw? How *nice*! Girls, Miss Cullen says we
may draw. On the blackboard, may we, Miss Cullen?"

"Certainly *not*. Answer me at once, Ruth."

No reply.

"Girls!" Her voice had the ring of despair. "Girls, will you *attend*?"

A few yawns; an audible comment of "No, old bean, we won't!" to
which the goaded woman dared pay no heed.

"We'll try a little further on. Line fifty-two. Mary, you begin. What
does *cuir* mean?"

Mary sighed the sigh of boredom.

"Leather, isn't it?"

Another voice broke in.

"'Tisn't, then—it's cook."

"Cook? Can't be."

"'Tis, I tell you."

"Same thing, in school dinner."

"Oh, *funny* joke!"

"Silence!" Her voice trembled with fatigue and futile rage. "Your ideas
of the humorous are on the level of the low music-hall stage. No doubt
you get your jests from the—ah—the Jewel Picture House."

"Oh, *yes*, Miss Cullen, we *do*. Have you been this week, Miss Cullen?
Didn't you *love* the kissing scene in 'Baby Blue-Eyes,' Miss Cullen? Oh,
wasn't it *sweet*?"

"*Silence*! I will not have this chattering. Juliet, what are you writing? (What shall I do if she doesn't answer? I can't make her. Pretend I didn't speak, no one heard.) ... Come, girls, don't be stupid. Kitty, you're generally bright." An ingratiating smile accompanied the words. "Don't *you* see what it means?"

"No, Miss Cullen." A wide yawn. Then Babel again:

"Hilda, lend me your comb. My hair's like a mop since gym."

"Trix, what did you make of that Latin? What does *lapis* mean? Rabbit, doesn't it? I've got 'mossy rabbit.'"

"Where's my rubber? Joan, have you pinched my bunjy?"

"Oh, say, have you heard about Gwen Richards?"

"No, what?"

"She cheeked old Earwigs."

"She *didn't*! She *never* cheeked *Earwigs*?"

"Honest, she did. Like this, it was. ...."

They had all left their desks to hear the tale of crime. What should she do—what *could* she do? No voice could be heard above that pandemonium of girls' voices, talking, laughing, two whistling a fox-trot, others slinging missiles about the room. Suppose someone heard? Thank Heaven the ventilators into the corridor were shut! ... Suppose Miss Fergusson, underneath in IIIb, were to hear and complain? Suppose the Head came in? ... In spite of the warm sun her hands were cold and damp. She felt a little sick. Then—thank Heaven!—the bell. It was over—for the moment.

She began to gather her papers together.

"Put away your books."

(She must make them do that, or the next mistress would see the mess—might guess. ...)

"*Girls*! Put *away* your *books*."

No one heeded. Then a gay voice, clear as a flute:

"Bell's gone. Chuck 'em in."

Desks slammed, books were thrown about; talk, talk, endless. Celia Robertson got an apple out of her desk and began to munch, loudly, defiantly, staring insolently at the mistress, challenging her. Miss Cullen looked out of the window. She pretended to be absorbed in the beauty of the line of poplars edging the vivid playing-fields. She dared not take any notice of Celia. ...

At last the books were in. She walked to the door. No one opened it for her. She knew that it was someone's duty; Connie's probably. She hesitated; then she told herself that she could not spend any time in making a fuss over such a detail. ...

In the passage stood Miss Lexington, waiting. Miss Cullen flushed.

"So sorry to have kept you," she said with her broad mirthless smile. "We've been having rather an amusing lesson, and we got so absorbed we weren't ready for the bell. I hope you won't find them too excited. They've been so happy!"

Miss Lexington merely smiled, quite pleasantly, and went in.

"She doesn't believe me," thought Miss Cullen. "Cynical brute. Why shouldn't she believe what I say, I'd like to know? Does she think I'm a liar?" And she stumped in righteous indignation to the Staff Room.

"IVb," she muttered to herself, going down the stairs. "Anyhow, they can't be worse than that *awful* IVa. ... They're my own form. They *must* attend. I'll *make* them attend."

She collected books. Others were there—Miss Rowan, the gym mistress, "free"; Miss Lovell, hastily collecting text books and lexicon; Miss Jessop, her hands full of botanical specimens. It was to Miss Jessop—kind, young and inexperienced—that she began to speak in that curious, hard, self-conscious, would-be humorous voice.

"Ah, dear! It's a hard world for the wicked!" she sighed. "Do you teach IVa? No? I've just come from them. Interesting, and so lively! They enjoy life so thoroughly it makes one feel quite old!"

Miss Jessop smiled politely. She was in a hurry to get to the lab. before her form arrived there. Why *would* Miss Cullen talk so much between lessons?

"I believe they are rather a jolly lot," she murmured, and escaped.

Did she know? Had she heard? Miss Cullen wondered anxiously; and she went to her next lesson determined to be ruthless.

"I'll make 'em sit up! Wipe the floor with them," she muttered, stumping along the polished corridor with her flat, broad feet. ...

Peace fell in the pleasant Staff Room. Miss Rowan, her gym. tunic falling comfortably up to her waist, her long, shapely legs disposed at ease on a second chair, took up *Punch*, idly enough, for the copy was a week old. Miss Reeve, the history specialist, red pencil in hand, frowned over a pile of exercise books. At the window, a long, pleasant row, fluttered blue linen curtains; outside a drowsy bee mumbled among heavy-scented pinks. A mowing machine whirred from the tennis courts. The Staff Room was, as the Staff often murmured, too good to last; soon, as the school increased in numbers, it would become a classroom, and the Staff would spend its rare moments of leisure in some small, dark room, cheerless by reason of its aspect, while a riotous Form disported itself in this pleasant room. Not that they, as a whole, grudged it; children, one knew, needed the best; only in a life like theirs it did seem a little hard. ... Anyhow, they would take the pretty hangings with them. They had subscribed for those among themselves.

There was no sound for some minutes except the flicker of the curtains in the tiny breeze, the hum of the mowing machine, the bumbling of the bees, the yawns of Miss Rowan, and the vicious grunts with which Miss Reeve emphasised the digs of the red pencil. Then Miss Rowan flung aside her paper.

"What a swot you are," she drawled in her pleasant South country voice. "Don't you ever take your free times *as* free?"

"Can't. Haven't time. Must get the damn kids through somehow, though God alone knows how." (Yes, quite a lot of High School mistresses talk like this. Many of them are still quite human.)

Suddenly there came from overhead an appalling crash. It sounded as if a desk had been overturned. But it was no accident, apparently, for smaller explosions, bumps, rattlings, scurryings, followed, and a wild burst of laughter.

"Good Lord!" exclaimed Miss Rowan, startled out of her composure. "What the dickens is going on in IVb?"

"Need you ask?" inquired Miss Reeve sardonically. "A French lesson, of course. Cullen taking her own form. Jolly, isn't it?"

"They'll have the ceiling down, that's all," remarked Rowan. "Chuck it, Reefer; you can't correct books through that. Chuck it and be sociable."

"Sociable!" snorted the other, throwing down her pencil and tilting back her chair to a precarious angle. "*Sociable*! I feel more like murder. The damn fool. Why can't she resign before it's too late?"

"Too late for what?"

"Too late for everything—for the school, for herself, for the exams., for every blessed thing. It makes me see red. Here's this woman, drawing the maximum salary under the scale—half again what I get and twice what you do—and she's utterly incapable. What chance has anyone else got with IVb next lesson?"

"*I've* got 'em," said Rowan grimly. "I'll make 'em sweat, never fear. Rags they'll be when I've done with 'em. … Good Lord!" as a crash before whose violence any previous effort seemed mere playful mirth, shook the Staff Room. "What *can* they be doing?"

"Any old thing. What they like. My God, Rowan, doesn't it make you *sick*? That's a *French* lesson—do you realise that? That's a Form preparing to take the Senior next year. What'll happen?"

"That's easy. They'll fail."

"Of course they'll fail—just as this year's lot will fail—just as last year's did. What else can happen? And—don't you see what that means to the rest of us?"

"Can't say I do. How can it matter to you and Lexo and Parry and the rest if Cullen's results are bad?"

"Matter!" snorted the irate historian. "It matters just this much, my dear. If they fail in French, *they fail the whole exam.* D'you get that? If they plough in French they plough altogether."

"*What*?" gasped Rowan, sitting up. "D'you mean that if a girl—if Mavis Reed, say—gets distinction in Maths, and honours in history and every other blooming subject, but ploughs in French—"

"She'd fail."

Rowan whistled long and low.

"Jolly system, isn't it?" asked Reeve bitterly. "Five mortal years has that woman had us at her mercy. Results are bad—the Staff is bad, say the inspectors. You can point out till all's blue that the results are due to one subject; they don't listen. We're damned, all of us. Isn't it enough to drive you to drink?"

"Mmmm." Rowan pondered. "I see. I've always thought you people were a bit hard on old Cullen. Now I see your point of view. ... It is pretty damnable. ... But look here, Reefer, what can the poor old blighter do? She must be near pension age. She'd never get another job. How *can* she resign?"

"I don't suppose she would get another job."

"Yes, but then—if she didn't serve out her full time——"

"Oh, she'd forfeit her pension, of course, to say nothing of all she'd paid into the fund. ... Oh, I know it's hard on her, damnably hard. But it's just as bad for the rest of us. It would be the same thing for Parry, or Lexo, or even for me, I dare say, if we all get fired. Only *we* shan't have deserved it."

"They *couldn't* fire you—on another woman's results!"

"*Couldn't* they?" Reeve's voice was grim. "They do. They *will*. ... I tell you, Rowan, the position's hopeless—hopeless! If the Head weren't so weak she'd have got rid of Cullen terms—no, years—ago. She's sorry for her. So'm I. So are we all. It means the end for her. She'll never earn again, and she'll forfeit her pension, as well as all she's paid into the Pension Fund. But I'm sorrier for the people who suffer the same thing for her faults. Parry'll find it as hard to get a job as Cullen will; so will Lexo. Who's going to take them, at the maximum salary, when there's dozens of young sparks fresh from the university ready and eager to begin at the minimum? I grant you it's rough on Cullen to get the boot at her time of life; but it's a damn sight harder on the rest of us, who don't deserve it."

"The whole thing sounds to me like the arrangement of a lunatic," said Rowan. "Whose was it?"

"Lord knows. It *was* a lunatic, probably. Most people who touch education are lunatics—or become so in time. ... Well, only five minutes more." She rose and put her unfinished pile of books into her locker.

"Va—where's that book of notes? … There's the bell—and there's IVb coming down to gym. Wish you joy of them, Rowan!"

"*I'll* deal with 'em," said Rowan, lifting her lazy length from the wicker arm-chair. "I'd better begin now," she added, as a mad rush of feet sounded on the staircase.

Reeve, collecting her books, smiled grimly. Rowan had left the door open, and the voices came clearly on the hot, still air.

"IVb, turn and go back to your form room. Then line up and come downstairs *quietly*. And the whole form will stay in for me for a quarter of an hour after school."

Silence, but for the subdued patter of thirty-two pairs of feet retiring in decorous order to the form room. Then came Miss Cullen's voice.

"Oh, Miss Rowan, I beg your pardon. I—I—they misunderstood me. They thought I had given them permission to run, as we were late. Otherwise, of course, I would never have *allowed* them to make that noise."

"It's all right, thanks," said Rowan a little brusquely.

The three women's thoughts were almost audible.

Rowan: "Liar."

Miss Cullen: "She thinks I'm lying. How dare she think I'm lying?"

Reeve: "Well, if she's got to lie, she might do it better than that. She *must* think us fools."

IVb, subdued and demure, marched quietly past the three mistresses into the empty gymnasium.

CHAPTER III
Portrait of the Heroine

It was ten minutes to six. Miss Cullen lay, hideously asleep. The stiff nightdress, with its heavy breastplate of tucks and linen frills, was buttoned closely round her withered neck. Her mouth fell in a little, for her false teeth ("such *obvious* ones, she must have got them at one of those quack American dentistry places ") lay in a glass on a table beside her. They looked, in their red and white vividness, like bits of raw streaky bacon in the greenish water. Her face, sallow among the white bed-linen, was relaxed and infinitely tired. A few wisps of thin greyish hair straggled away from the tight little braid. The mellow light of the young, fresh sun picked out her ugliness as mercilessly as the children at school picked out her oddnesses.

The faint clear note of a church bell trembled on the dewy air. It was light, airy as a magic bell; as if in response to a charm, she awoke. She yawned enormously; her tired eyes, sunk in her head, opened slowly, slowly, and shut again. Then one shrivelled arm, decorously clad in a white thick sleeve that ended at the wrist in a featherstitched band and frill, extended to the table and fumbled for a watch that lay as if guarding the teeth. It seemed as if she *could* not be awake enough to read its face; but she was. She knew she still had a quarter of an hour.

As consciousness returned to her, a horror that was almost physical descended upon her. Another day. ... Another working day. That meant. ...

She shuddered a little, and turned her face, burying it deeper in the pillow. She felt like some culprit of the Middle Ages, awaking to a new day of torture, ridicule and shame.

Slowly it all came back to her. How horrible yesterday had been! The bored Sixth, yawning, fidgeting, idling; that defiance from IVa—she shuddered again, and her face grew hot, hidden in the pillow. Celia Robertson—how she had stared at her as she ate that apple, openly, against all rules. ... And Miss Lexington *must* have heard. It was mean, horribly, incredibly mean, to wait outside like that, listening, spying. ... She knew, really, that to wait outside a classroom till the end of the last lesson was school etiquette; yet this thought gave her the courage of anger, and she turned her head, rolling over to lie on her back.

IVb. Ah, that had been awful. No one, she thought, could ever guess what she had endured in those interminable forty minutes. She winced visibly as she remembered it, her eyelids pressing together for an instant, as you wince under a knife thrust or a probed tooth. Shame and humiliation and anger and pain surged in her heart. ...

Then, to-day. She turned it over in her mind. Early service—that meant peace, anyhow, and quiet, and warm gratification of her starved affections. Then would come the hurried breakfast, the hot, uphill walk to school, and then work. ... It *must* be better to-day. It must, or she simply could not endure it. ... She would go home to lunch at midday. It was twenty minutes' walk, and her feet ached in this hot weather, but the brief escape was worth it. She never took long over meals; it could just be done. ...

Her mind wandered, and her heavy eyelids drooped. Faint wisps of sleep stole back across her brain. A few more minutes, just a few. ... Then habit, and a kind of grim determination of which she was at times capable, overcame the tempting mistiness. She sat up and pushed her legs over the side of the bed. The sun lay in two broad bands across her feet; odd, they looked almost grey outside the warm ribs of light. ... Her head nodded forward, heavily, hopelessly. Her opened hands lay helpless, the fingers limply carving on the crumpled sheet. ...

This would never do. She would be late, and she hadn't been late for Early Celebration at St. Bede's for over a year. She got up and moved, heavily, like a sleepwalker, to the huge slate sarcophagus of a washstand. Hot though the sun was, she shuddered as she splashed chillily, damping her down-rolled nightgown, gasping hoarsely.

"I'm getting old," she told herself. "Feel the cold so much now. ... Urrhh. ... Cold baths I used to take. Old now. ..."

She began to dress with speed, accuracy, and entire lack of interest, like an automaton. She took up each garment from the neat pile in exactly the same order in which she had taken them for years and years. It never occurred to her to make any change in her costume that was not demanded of her by cleanliness or the season. On the first of May she put on "summer underlinen"; on the first of October she put on winter clothes. She would make the change in the middle of a spell of hot or cold weather, simply from a devotion to routine. When one knew this one began to understand why, twenty-six years ago, she had "gone in for" teaching, and how the clerkly side of the profession, the registers and lists and markbooks, enthralled her.

She never looked in the mirror. Her style of hairdressing rendered this unnecessary, and she felt no interest in what she saw there—no gratification, no depression even. It simply did not matter. With closed eyes—closed from a dim kind of sensuous enjoyment—she swept the comb through her hair before she knotted it up and clamped the knot to her head.

Her fingers moved with the precision and speed of a machine. Tapes—buttons—click, click, those things on corsets—buttons again. Handkerchief—gloves—Missal—purse. There.

The sleeping house smelt like a village shop, of cheese and cloth and dead flowers. She crept softly down through the sunny stillness. The sunlight lay in bars across the gaudy linoleum, as if she were shut into a golden, quivering cage. By seven she was on her knees in the damp, heavy-scented coolness of the ornate church.

She felt happy now, peaceful, quiet, soothed. This hour was her one really happy time in the long day. In the stillness, the hushed voices of the minister and server, the tiny silvery tinkle of the bell, she found a satisfaction, partly real and partly sentimental, that somehow fed her starved soul enough for it to endure the day. She could never explain this to the common-sensible people at school who tried to dissuade her from the abominable practice of early rising. They simply wouldn't—couldn't—understand how she needed that hour. She was *wanted*, there. ... To the very end she never knew that the church was ugly, the vestments tawdry, the music sugary, the whole service imitative, artificial, in the worst possible taste. ...

It was later than usual this morning when she came out into the hot, bright day. She blinked at the white street, the vivid trees and brilliant sky. Her good time was over. She must hurry, hurry, or she would be late. She felt ill. The heat, perhaps, or the lateness last night. It had been nearly one o'clock. ... Even to herself she would not admit that it was fear that gave her that odd quaking at the stomach. ... If only it wasn't Thursday. Thursday was such a heavy day—such big classes, such a full time-table. She sighed, and thought, "I mustn't give way to depression." She always called it depression.

She tried to keep work out of her head until after breakfast. She thought things always seemed better then. She never ate much after she had been to early service; but she drank tea, four or five cups, scalding hot, and that put vigour into her. Things didn't look quite so hopeless after that.

At eight-thirty she was on her way to school; and now, as she set off with her short-stepping, flat-footed, ungainly walk, she ran over the day's programme in her head. Then, suddenly, she realised it. Third lesson—IVb. She couldn't. She simply couldn't. Not after yesterday. It had been too ghastly. She had meant—with all her strength she had meant—to control them; and they had been like demons, yelling, shrieking, openly and insolently flaunting before her their fearlessness and her own incompetence. Her form, flouting her in her own form room. ... They despised her utterly. ... Her face burned as she thought of that scene. She felt as if it were seared on her. She could never forget it, never. Slow tears, tears of self-pity, welled up; her eyes smarted; an ache came in her throat and the tip of her nose grew hot and damp. She so wanted them to like her—her own form. ... But no; she couldn't go through that again—not so soon, anyhow.

"I *can't*!" she breathed in a kind of panic. "I can't. No one can make me. I won't. ... I *can't*. ..."

Terror seized her. Absurd though it may seem to those who do not know, that is exactly what happened. In spite of the hot June sun blazing on the brown stuff that stretched across her shoulders, she felt cold. Her feet were icy, her hands clammy. Her heart beat in hard, heavy thumps. ... There was the school, red against the big elms. ... Girls everywhere, laughing, chattering, running along to the pav. to put away their tennis racquets and cricket bats. ... IVb. ... She *couldn't*.

Someone greeted her. She pulled herself together. Miss Reeve, fresh and neat in a frock like a Kodak advertisement, was just ahead of her. Miss Cullen noticed with a pang that two girls, one Celia Robertson and the other Miriam Davis of her own form, were squabbling over the privilege of putting away her bicycle. ... There was Miss Lexington, neat in dark-blue linen, and that flighty little Miss Pearson looking like a shop-girl going out on the river, in flowered voile and a ridiculous hat. ... And girls, girls everywhere, all looking so fresh and demure, but fiends really, fiends waiting for her, to torture and humiliate her. ... She felt horribly sick and cold and weak. ...

Then, with another spurt of that odd determination of hers, she set her jaw at an aggressive jut. IVb, indeed! *She* would deal with IVb. The sight of Miss Rowan—Miss Rowan, who had added to yesterday's humiliation— talking to a knot of IVb girls, decided her. She'd show them!

She swung into the school on a gust of defiance. ...

Miss Rowan always came to tea with Miss Reeve on Thursdays, before going on with her to the town swimming baths. To-day conversation had flagged all through tea until the end was near; then both began to feel a desire to talk.

Miss Reeve looked inquiringly into the teapot.

"Have some more tea?" she asked hospitably.

"Is there any?" Miss Rowan's tone was a happy blend of hope, doubt, renunciation and greed.

"Of sorts."

"Don't want it strong, thanks, 's long's it's wet. ... Don't give it all to me."

"I've finished, thanks. Smoke?"

"Better not. I'm in training."

"Oh! What energy the woman's got. Mind if I do?"

"'Course not. Carry on. ... I say, I thought you'd asked Parry too?"

"I did, but she cried off at midday. Said she wasn't fit to do anything but swear. I didn't break my heart."

Rowan grinned.

"Can't say I do, either. But what was biting her?"

"Oh, same old thing. It *was* rather hard luck, losing her one free time in the week, but she does make a song and dance about it."

"Why did she lose it?"

Miss Reeve stared.

"My dear old bean, where were you at break? Where've you been all day?"

"Running off heats for the sports. What's the row *now*?"

"Why, Cullen gave over. Reported sick."

"She came to school all right. I saw her."

"'Course she did. IVb-itis was what *she* had."

"*What*? She *funked* 'em?"

Miss Reeve nodded, her face inscrutable.

"Well, I'm ... *Sure*, Reefer?"

"Rather! It was like this. I came up the drive with her. I thought she looked queer then."

"She always does," grinned Rowan.

"Oh! yes; but I mean—squeamish. Looked as if she'd been across the Channel and tried not to be sick all the way. I felt sort of sorry for her, I must say. Heat does try some people, you know. Well, I soon spotted it wasn't that. That little ass Miriam Davis took my bike, and Cullen looked as if she wanted to bite her."

"*What*? Why?"

Miss Reeve shrugged.

"Oh, well, Miriam's rather gone on me, you know. Oh, yes, I know what rot it all is, you needn't snort like that. But, believe it or not as you like—I admit it sounds too futile—Cullen was jealous. You see, Miriam's in IVb, and she hates Cullen, as they all do in that form. ... Anyhow, I could see with half an eye that Cullen didn't like it."

"Well? What's that got to do with Cullen malingering?"

"It has really, in a sort of way. You see, Miriam knew it would feed Cullen—and it did. So when she went up to her form before prayers she was out for their blood."

"Jolly good thing too."

"Yes—if she could get it! But she can't, and she knows it, so of course they all know it. They just love her to get the wind up. Well, of course there was an unholy din in IVb before prayers; and—well, Cullen funked it."

"How d'you mean, funked it?"

"Jessop told me. She went in and talked to Jess in IIIc. No reason to—nothing that wouldn't have done after school, or next week—or never, if you come to that. And there she stuck, till the prayer-bell went, just making talk, with the devil and all going on in IVb. She didn't tell Jess she felt ill, though," added Miss Reeve pensively.

"When did she cry off, then?"

"End of first lesson, I think it was. She went and told Lexo she was ill. Gil took her second lesson, and Parry third—IVb."

They were silent for a few minutes.

"What I can't understand," said Rowan after a pause, "is how the woman can be such a *fool*. Naturally the kids are a bit above themselves; anyone would be, with an ass like that knocking about, and I must say I don't think Harries and Spiller are much better. But to *funk* them—! Good Lord, I wish I was their form mistress! They'd soon sit up and take notice."

"Of course, you know," said Reeve, thoughtfully lighting a new cigarette from the stump of the last, "it is a bit different for her. Your subject's popular; and you're young, and we both teach in the new way. She was brought up in the old school—same as the Head—blackboards and keep silent and learn-by-heart-and-never-think-for-yourself and walk quietly and always behave like a lady. ... And she *looks* so odd, Rowan. That puts kids off."

"Nothing to do with it," answered Rowan sturdily. "She's not a patch on the old dear who used to teach us maths. at Priors, and she had us all eating out of her hand before she'd done with us. Lively lot we were, too."

"Well, I don't know how it is, because she usedn't to be so bad. She wasn't as bad as this even last year. Of course, she was always odd, and that precise voice is enough to drive you to drink—but I don't believe her discipline was worse than Harries' or Spilly's, or even poor old Murchison's. But the point is—they all admitted it. Murchison left, and Spills and Harry are both going. ..."

Another short silence; then Miss Reeve exclaimed:

"Oh, I say, Rowan, an awful thing happened to-day! I'd quite forgotten. You know what a *frantic* voice Pearson has. She doesn't mean to yell, I suppose, but you can hear what she's saying a mile off. Well, she and Jess and Moore and I were in the Staff Room after dinner, and Moore said something about Cullen—you know how sort of innocent she is. She said she was so sorry Cullen was ill and that, and Pearson shouted, 'It's a very *useful* sort of illness.' Moore just *looked*—(she *is* a fool, poor ass, though I don't suppose she can help looking like a fish)—and she said, 'I'm afraid I don't quite understand.' So Pearson went in off the deep end, and she was making such a row I thought I'd better check the flood; so I said something about how the girls weren't learning anything, and how hopeless exam. prospects were and that; and Pearson yelled, 'Of course she can't teach! She can't even keep the wretched kids moderately quiet. She's the most hopeless fraud that ever took a screw for a job they can't do.' And then—Cullen came in!"

"My hat! Did she hear?"

"She couldn't *help* hearing, Rowan! You know what Pearson's voice *is*! My only hope is that, as we didn't mention any names just then, she mayn't have spotted we were talking about her."

"My dear ass, she *must* have spotted *that*! Who else could you mean?" Miss Rowan's grammar, never very strong, always collapsed under stress of excitement.

"She *might* have thought we meant Spills."

Rowan snorted, and the other went on:

"It must be rotten, you know, Rowan, to be Cullen. Good at her job years ago—and hopeless now. Hating it worse every day, and can't chuck it. And always afraid she may be told to go, and lose her job and all hope of the pension she's worked and paid for. ..."

"Yes, rotten, I know. But, as you were saying yesterday, it's still harder on perfectly good women like Lexo who suffer for her sins. I never knew how foul the whole game was before; but Cullen does, I expect—and she jolly well *ought* to go."

"I know she ought. I've said so for terms and terms. But it's beastly hard, Rowan."

"Life is hard—for schoolmarms," said Rowan philosophically.

But it is easier to say that life is hard than it is to face the reality. That is what Miss Cullen was doing that evening. Not really facing it—few of us ever have the courage to do that—but dimly acknowledging it, trying in vain to keep it out of her mind as she dealt with the piles of exercise books before her.

"*Et là il viva*—oh, Dorothy, my dear child!" She drew a neat line in red ink. "Can't teach ... can't teach ... what do they know about it, girls like that, new to the profession? *Je le pense extraordinaire que rien tourne dehors.* ... What nonsense is this? Oh, no, no, you silly girl." Another red line, and some corrections written in—corrections that the child would never bother to read. "Children like that—mere girls—how can they know? Years of experience—splendid testimonials. ..." Suddenly she fumbled for her handkerchief. "Must get on—must get on. What does it matter what they think?"

She finished the book before her; then, quite suddenly, she laid her head down on it.

"It does matter—it matters horribly!" she cried half aloud. "How could they talk about me like that—how *could* they?"

Then began one of those queer dialogues that some lonely women hold with themselves. Two different women inhabited the spare body of Miss Cullen. You could almost see them—one speciously bright and false, the other beaten, cowed, horribly sincere.

"Perhaps they didn't mean you."

"I know they did."

"Much more likely they meant Agatha Spiller. *She* really *is* incompetent, and always has been."

"Perhaps. ... No, they didn't. They meant *me*."

"Well, suppose they did. What do they know about it, chits like that, so conceited and ignorant?"

"Ah, but they were right! They were right!"

"*Were* they?"

"Well—I don't know. Were they? *Is* it true that I'm a fraud—that I can't teach?"

She faced the problem, sitting upright now, staring before her, unblinking in the crude light of the gas.

"I *can* teach. I've got girls through exams, for over twenty years. Of course I can teach."

Then, suddenly, the Second Self took the other side. You never know what side she is on.

"Yes—you *could*. Can you now?"

Again, helpless, bewildered, she faced it.

"If I could once I can still."

"Ah, but conditions are changed. You're old-fashioned now. Exams are so different. Your methods are out of date."

"Are they? Am I really out of date? Oh, God, don't let it be true!"

She thought, profoundly. Her chin sank forward, the weak, narrow line of the bone showing hard and shiny above the pouch of skin. Her hair straggled untidily from its tight little knob. Her eyes, dark and tragic behind the steel-rimmed glasses, brooded hopelessly. Unconsciously she tapped her pen on the blotting-paper before her, making a neat row of red dots. The gas fizzed and plopped in the quiet room.

"It's *not* true. I *can* teach. I'll show them that I can. I'll make them take it back. ... *Suppose I can't?*" She pondered, her pen idly tapping. "Of course," she thought, her head still bent in thought, "of course the obvious thing is to resign. But suppose I do. I have no chance whatever of getting another post. None. '*I left because my examination results were bad.*' That's what I'd have to say. Need I say that? Couldn't I say the climate didn't suit me? ... No, not after six years here. Or that the work was getting too heavy? I might say that. It's quite true. Only, all posts seem to be heavy now. Still, I might say that. ..."

A moth whirred in, flopping stupidly. She rose to put it outside the window. When she returned to her seat she had, quite unconsciously, made up her mind that not only could she say so, but that it would be the genuine and only reason for her hypothetical resignation.

"But there's the question of salary," she went on, less agonised now, looking at it as a practical possibility. "There are disadvantages in being at the maximum. Economy at any cost, no matter how great a cost." That rather pleased her; she thought it had an epigrammatic flavour. But anxiety soon claimed her again. "They never realise that experience is *worth* the extra money—worth it twenty times over. How can girls fresh from college know the ropes as I know them—all the examination dodges, the little tricks of school routine?"

And then, quite distinctly, she heard the voice of her second self:

"*Do* you know them? You knew the exams. of thirty years ago. Do you know them now?"

And she knew the answer was No. ...

For a moment she was panic-stricken. She stared round her wildly, almost as if she saw the crowd of tormentors closing in upon her. A failure too expensive and too ignorant for anyone to want her no hope, no chance. And in four years' time a pension would be hers to claim—no more work, no more worry, just a peaceful old age. ...

Four years! Surely she could manage that? Surely she was not bound to forfeit the pension she had looked forward to for over twenty years?

"I can't," she groaned aloud. "I *can't* give it up. It can't be expected of me."

And "Fraud!" said her conscience. "Cheat. Fraud."

She thought again, deeply. Suppose she did give it up—the work, the hope of a pension, everything. What then? What could she do, a woman of fifty-odd, trained for no other work, with no private means and no influence? She had a sister who had reached the lofty rank of an Inspectorship; but she knew that even inspectors are not wealthy; and, besides, one can't just ask to be kept. ...

"I may live on for another twenty years," so ran her thoughts. "I haven't saved enough for that. I can't and won't ask Ann to keep me. I shall never get another post. *No.* I won't resign. Nothing shall make me. I shall get over this weakness next term, when it's cooler. I'll show them what I can do when I'm roused. … Anyhow, come what may, I won't resign. If Miss Barr thinks me incapable she can ask me to go. I'm probably over-sensitive. Anyhow, I *will not* resign!"

On this resolution she shook herself. Her eyes lost their simple, troubled look and became their usual selves—alert, aware, a little suspicious, the eyes of a person who is alive to danger and anxious to conceal it. She had thrust away into a dark corner of her mind that knowing, bitter, sharp Second Self; but all the time she worked she was aware of her, lurking, ready to pounce out and torment her again with doubts and fears. And for this she quite unjustly blamed Miss Pearson and Miss Reeve, asleep in their respective beds. For no one likes to be called a fraud, even if it is true.

Lying in her not-too-comfortable bed, she was worried and stung by the old problems as by flies. Resolutely she shut them out. She wouldn't think of them. She must sleep. She'd think of something pleasant—her old life at college, her friends, all scattered now. … Fraud. That's a dreadful word. I've never been that. I've always been honourable. I've lost grip, I know—it's the heat, and I'm not as young as I was. And they don't help me, nobody, not even the Head. *Especially* not the Head. … If only somebody liked me and believed in me. … I'm not well. I must get some of that powder—tasteless in tea, they say it is. I'll soon be myself again. Fraud—no, that's *not* fair, it's not, it's not! … The Senior's very near now. If only the girls do well! I'll pray for their success. A Novena, perhaps, like the Romans. … *Is* it a fraud, if I can't do the work? *Was* I shamming this morning? No—no, I wasn't. I did feel ill, I did. And it's not fair to count that. I *can* do the work. I can, I will. …

And so, late in the night, she fell asleep.

CHAPTER IV
The Senior

Like many another county high school of its type, Besley was a centre for the Local Examinations of one of the older Universities. Like scores of its counterparts, it was annually stirred to its depths by the magnitude of this event. The gymnasium, which was also the assembly hall, became temporarily one large examination-room; desks were ranged, each an accurate number of feet and inches from its fellows; blotting-paper, foolscap, "rough" paper, nibs and ink were laid out with the solemnity of some ancient religious rite.

It is not quite as absurd as it looks, this solemn ritual of the examination room. Sometimes the issues are quite important. To the girls, of course, they are always this, and sometimes a future may really depend on the work done in that familiar hall, hung with trophies and boards containing the names of departed girls whose prowess in games or the less valiant field of books their school for some obscure reason sees fit to commemorate. But it does not often occur to the ambitious maidens, bending their smooth heads over the puzzles before them, that their personal success is the least part of the war they are waging. They seldom guess that by their success or failure they may make or mar the life of a woman who can take no personal part in a struggle on which her very existence may depend.

All the Staff at Besley were anxious this year. A school lives or dies in the eyes of Authority by its examination results, and Besley High School was in a parlous state indeed. Steadily through the last five years the honourable roll of "Distinction," "Honours" and "Passed" had dwindled; every year had the examiners, those remote and awful beings, dreaded as fiends, as capricious, as implacable, damned a larger number of Besley girls with those mystic hieroglyphs which to the initiated mean: "Ill-taught—incapable—uneducated—failures." And they knew that by this year's results the school's fate would in all probability be finally decided.

It was, then, no wonder that in the Staff Room faces were pale and haggard and nerves taut on that hot July morning when "the Senior" began. Each woman who had prepared pupils for that examination felt afraid—afraid, even if she knew that in her subject the girls were well grounded and capable of doing good work. You can never tell what follies a girl may commit in an examination; and, besides, as Miss Reeve had pointed out, each stood or fell by the work of another mistress—a mistress whom they all either disliked or despised, and in whom they quite justly had no shadow of confidence.

How much of this Miss Cullen knew, no one could guess. Whether she still had confidence in herself, or was concealing her sinking heart behind a front of brass—whether she feared or hoped—was ignorant of their peril or merely ignored it—not one of her colleagues knew. She herself could hardly have told them. She knew the position was desperate; she knew what it would mean to all the staff if the school were closed down on account of the inefficiency of its teachers; but like many of us (if the truth were told, like nearly all of us) she did not face the issues at stake. She dared not; and her dread was so instinctive that it was unconscious. She honestly did not know that it was fear that forbade her to examine the future. Once indeed, in a moment of rare courage, she had taken a list of the candidates and had put a mark against the names of those who were safe to pass the French test. There were thirty-two candidates; her list had only five marked names. Her heart sank; she went over the list again with scrupulous care. No. Only five safe. ... She tore the list into innumerable fragments and tried to forget that she had made it.

Two days dragged heavily by. The first French paper was over. It was the grammar paper—the critical one for results—and she had not seen it. No one had offered to show it to her, and she had not cared—or was it dared?—to ask. It was, in a way, her warrant for life or death; she felt she *must* know what it was like; and she could not bring herself to ask a girl to show it to her.

It was six o'clock. The last paper of the second day was over. Miss Cullen stood in the Staff Room, staring out with unseeing eyes over the gay flower-borders and sweep of lawn. They were out now, standing in excited groups, showing each other papers, asking for translations, parts of verbs, all the conundrums set by the ingenuity of the examiners. If only she could know! ...

The door opened, and in a moment her mask was on. She turned round, her mouth ajar in that odd, nervous, self-conscious smile that so soon and so inevitably got on the nerves of her colleagues. It was Miss Lexington who had come in. Her upright, incredibly neat figure was even straighter than usual. A dusky colour glowed on the high, sloping cheek-bones that made her face so individual. Her firm mouth was set tightly, the usual polite, wary smile vanished. She obviously had herself under strong control. Always she had the air of a person to be reckoned with; now she looked positively vindictive. Out of sheer nervousness Miss Cullen spoke.

"Another day gone!" she said, stretching her arms affectedly. "Don't you find this heat very trying, Miss Lexington?"

"I find many things very trying," said the Second Mistress. Of a less dignified lady one would have said that she snapped. Miss Cullen's heart sank.

"Have they had your paper yet?" she asked. Like a nervous skater, she could not avoid the thin ice.

"Yes."

"Was it good?"

"Quite. ... Have you seen yours?" There was something almost ominous in the way in which the question was asked.

"Not yet. I can't say I'm interested. One gets so used to examinations that they seem to matter very little."

"*Matter very little!*" Miss Lexington opened her mouth to wither the casual lady; then she closed it very firmly. After a pause she said, stooping down to her locker as she spoke:

"I think you had better get someone to show it to you."

"Why? Have you seen it?"

"Yes. And I have heard what Janet Smith answered, and Daisy Riddell."

"Yes?"

Miss Lexington stood upright and faced her colleague. Miss Cullen felt like a creature at bay.

"Did you expect either of those girls to pass?"

Now Daisy Riddell had been on the list of the certain five; but Miss Cullen felt that something was wrong—badly wrong.

"Oh, well," she drawled, "that's never a very safe thing to say of any girl, is it?"

"One generally has some idea. You filled in the paper."

Miss Cullen's mind leapt to that paper—that document of prophecies, so often unfulfilled, demanded by the implacable Board, of what mark one's pupils are likely to get in a forthcoming examination. She knew she had put Daisy high—third or fourth, anyhow.

"Oh, as far as *that* goes … Yes, unless she lost her head, Daisy should have done fairly well."

Miss Lexington turned back to her books. Miss Cullen could bear it no longer.

"Did she seem to think she had done badly?"

"It wasn't a question of *thinking*, Miss Cullen. She simply couldn't *do* the paper. She had tried three questions; she had, I believe, finished half of one answer."

Miss Cullen opened her mouth once or twice, but no sound came. She felt stunned, numb; but the sight of her, ugly, ridiculous, incompetent, maddened Miss Lexington. She knew what the results of that fatal paper would be, and how they would probably wreck her own blameless career.

"It seems a pity that she should not have known just a little of the ground she had to cover," she said coldly as she turned away.

Miss Cullen stood there in the sun. The jolly sound of a cricket bat smiting a ball came to her ears; shouts came faintly from the Ten-Acre Pitch; on the drive outside someone was telling a story, punctuating it with giggles. The heavy scent of lilies hung in the air and mingled with the smell of ink and the odd foreign scent from the linen curtains. She looked round the room vaguely, noticing, as a stunned person may sometimes notice, tiny irrelevant details—Miss Rowan's blazer lying dangerously over an inkpot, loose scraps of paper, an empty teacup. ... It couldn't be true. Daisy—one of her best, sometimes *the* best. She must see that paper. She must know the worst.

She summoned all her courage. Slowly, with an air of careless ease, she strolled out on to the drive.

Knots of girls still hung about, comparing notes and chattering. With a pang painfully acute Miss Cullen realised that if it had been Miss Pearson, Miss Rowan, Miss Reeve, even the unapproachable Miss Lexington, who strolled down that gravel walk she would have been surrounded by an excited mob, anxious for her opinion, her help, even her mild criticism. But she—they ignored her. Her criticism was quite indifferent to them. They had not the least desire to hear her opinion. They did not believe in her. If she wanted to see the paper she must ask for it.

Accustomed as she was to rudeness and neglect from her pupils, this was a hard thing to do. She could hardly bring herself to do it. Yet she felt that she must know the worst. She strolled on, summoning up her courage and quelling her pride—past the girls, back to the school, back again, trying to look as if she were taking a constitutional. Then she saw a ray of hope. Nellie Beamish, a girl so sweet-tempered that most people thought her affected, and so gentle that most people thought her silly, was coming down the drive. Kitty Thompson was with her—and Daisy Riddell. Daisy had obviously been in tears.

"Well, Nellie," said Miss Cullen, with her wide, false smile, "how did you like the paper?" (Nellie, she knew, would be polite. She had never failed her yet.)

"Oh, I *couldn't* do it, Miss Cullen!" moaned Nellie, opening her big baby eyes. "I *never* thought it would be like that!"

Daisy sobbed audibly.

"Dear me! Have you got it there?"

Nellie produced the fatal paper. The eyes of all three girls, wide, reproachful, hurt, were fixed on her as she read.

"H'm. ... It's not such a bad paper. A little beyond the syllabus." She invented wildly as she read the questions. "Yes, *not* quite fair—decidedly not fair. Have you got your answers, Daisy? Did you have time to copy them out?"

Daisy gulped.

"I had lots of *time*," she said, "but I couldn't *do* them. I only did 2*a*, and I'm sure that was wrong. It didn't make sense. My long translation was so silly I tore it up."

"*Daisy*! Did you only send in *one* answer?"

"Only half one. I couldn't do 2*b*."

Daisy's eyes met the mistress in a stare half defiant, half frightened, wholly miserable.

"And Connie? Helen? Annie?"

"Doris did best. She did four, and tried one other."

The mask was off for a moment. All four stared at one another in silent consternation, helpless, hopeless. Then Miss Cullen recovered herself.

"Oh, I don't expect it's as bad as you think, you know," she said with her nervous half-laugh. "May I keep this just for to-night, Nellie? I have a collection of papers, and I should like to copy this out to add to it."

Nellie handed it over, quite willingly, but without enthusiasm. Miss Cullen recognised the difference from her usual manner and sighed.

"Well, cheer up, girls. I'm sure you've all done better than you think," she said as she turned away.

But it was a lie, and she knew it was; and the girls knew it too, and she knew that they did. For the paper was a modern one, and Miss Cullen taught by the methods of thirty years ago. The collection of papers was a myth, too; she wanted time, time to study those conundrums that demanded original thought and not the reproduction of textbooks. Not that it mattered now. Nothing could help her. She had failed, and she knew it; and she also knew that, for her, failure meant—the end.

CHAPTER V
In Search of an Ally

When Miss Cullen knew that the worst had happened, she shut her eyes; she did so instinctively, very much as one might if overwhelmed in deep waters, only opening them now and then as she sank to cast an agonised glance round for help however slight or frail.

The last few days dragged on interminably. Only a week, and the examinations would be over; another, and a day or two more, and term would end. Each day seemed hotter, drearier, longer, than any human day could possibly be; each evening the Staff laboured over piles of foolscap brought to them by girls who escaped public examination in favour of "school exams."; each night passed like a hot and evil dream, too soon merging into a day wearier, closer, more interminable than the last. Each morning faces looked a little sallower, eyes heavier, hair duller, dress more careless and jaded; each evening nerves were a little more rasped, tempers a little shorter, reason a little more obscured. And as each day passed Miss Cullen realised that the danger was so much the nearer, and that she had done nothing.

Only eight days of the term were left. It was during "break" in the middle of the morning that she, as it were, came out of the stupor into which she had fallen. She had been superintending a form examination—a calm occupation enough, and one which she would as a rule have used to work off a little of her own arrears of work. To-day she had sat idle through the forty-odd minutes, not thinking, not planning, merely allowing her dazed and terrified thoughts to buzz about her brain like frightened birds, in a cell, dashing from one point to another and recoiling in alarm from every contact, falling stunned into silence.

She was early in the Staff Room. She took her unobtrusive place at the far end, and watched the Staff assemble. Miss Parry was first, her expression lowering, her full mouth sulky. She marched straight over to her locker, slamming books in crossly. Then, together of course, Miss Gilbert and Miss Baldwin, deep in "shop." They went over to the open window and remained there, Miss Baldwin standing and idly swinging the tassel of the blind—a dark relic of war days—and Miss Gilbert perched on a table. Then came Miss Pearson, a pale, dark girl of twenty-four with no claim to good looks, taking a chair from which she could, from her long, dark eyes, steal sidelong glances at her reflection in the clear glass of the window.

"And that was the *Sixth*," she was saying to Miss Reeve, in a voice unwittingly harsh and strident. "I told Margaret Moffat—"

"They're all alike," said Miss Reeve. "It was Margaret who invented that wonderful phrase about the cardinals parading about in their chimeras."

"I don't mind that kind of howler," cut in the usually silent Miss Lovell. "It's so perfect in itself. One can see the cardinals doing it. What I object to is their literalness. Esther Price, for instance, who has just translated 'for me' by 'nam ego.'"

"Well, it was Margaret who said that Ben Jonson—"

The door opened again and Miss Lexington entered. She crossed the room and took a seat near Miss Parry, who immediately joined her, talking in low, eager tones. Miss Cullen sat on in her frozen isolation. With a fresh sinking of the heart she saw the confidential attitude of Miss Lexington and Miss Parry. If those two, once such bitter foes, each in her own way so powerful, joined forces, it would be a terribly strong combination. So far, though Miss Parry, who had the Head's ear, had been against her she had also been against Miss Lexington; and though she knew that she could by no means count on the Second Mistress as an ally, she also knew that she bore her no active animosity. But if these two powers united—if Miss Parry drew Miss Lexington round to her side—she was lost indeed.

A kind of panic seized her. She must do something at once—take some step to avert this disaster. She gazed round the room, rapidly summing up each mistress in turn, in pitiful search of an ally.

Miss Lexington. You couldn't count on the Second Mistress; besides, she was so efficient, so—so inhuman, such an enigma. Everyone found her a puzzle. No possibility there, she thought, looking half enviously at the firm mouth, the inscrutable expression, the keen blue eyes; no, she would be, if anything, on the side of efficiency and order. She would have no sympathy for failure.

Miss Parry, of course, she passed over without a second thought, and Miss Fergusson, the close friend of Miss Parry for over ten years, could not be anything but an enemy. Anyhow, Miss Cullen disliked her, as did most of the Staff, for her sentimentality and aggressive self-assertion. She could be counted out.

Miss Reeve sat next. Her face was turned away, but Miss Cullen's heart sank at the very look of her upright, virile body and red, shingled head. She was a fighter, hard with years of struggle—a gallant warrior whose own courage had never taught her anything but contempt for the feeble fighter. Miss Cullen remembered that overheard conversation. She knew that Miss Reeve despised her. ...

Miss Rowan. She was standing in a characteristic attitude, the square, boyish face with its halo of soft, short hair bent a little forward on the strong neck, the candid eyes looking up from under level brows with a gaze that somehow gained in directness from the odd, downcast tilt of the head. Her hands were clasped behind her, her feet placed well apart. The whole attitude was confident, strong, and just a little stupid. She would never understand—could never understand. Yet Miss Cullen put her down as "possible" in her mental category. She would at least be fair— perhaps kind, too.

Miss Pearson she passed over almost at once. She had no idea how the pale, dark-eyed, dark-haired girl, flaunting her bright, cheap, ugly, fashionable frock, regarded her personally; but, even if she had never heard that raucous denunciation of three weeks ago, she felt that she could never have made an ally of Miss Pearson. She was— well, Miss Cullen's mother would have said that Miss Pearson was not a gentlewoman; Miss Cullen, had her principles not forbidden it, would have called her common. Miss Cullen had a strong instinct for refinement; she was fastidious about her friends; and though, if Miss Pearson had been in trouble or in need of help, Miss Cullen would have gone to her assistance at once, she would not choose her as an ally in her own need. That was a very different matter, she thought, unconscious of patronage.

Miss Harries—useless, almost in the same position as herself, save that she was leaving to enjoy a life of leisure on a small income lately inherited. In any case, her support would have been worse than useless; "birds of a feather," the Staff might have commented in thought, if not openly. The same applied to gentle, flaxen-haired Miss Spiller, who might have done at a pinch, but was in any case leaving to enter on the religious life in an Anglican convent where the sweet austerity and gentle piety of the rule appealed to her nature as if created for it. Miss Cullen looked at the smooth, fair head, the strongly marked arch of the high crown falling into a straight line at the back of the skull—that line tell-tale of amiable weakness and obstinacy—and sighed. Miss Spiller would have done well as a confidante, if not as an ally. Too late now, though, and too late, too, for Miss Jessop, who was leaving to prepare for her wedding. Anyhow, she would never have really understood. What should a girl of twenty-three, leaving to marry, guess of the fear and pain and bitterness dragging at the heart of an old maid of fifty-six who had failed at the task at which she herself had succeeded?

Then there were the Inseparables, Miss Baldwin and Miss Gilbert. Miss Gilbert had rather attractive green eyes under her straight, shingled mouse-coloured hair. She looked jaded, of course, but she also looked serene. She might do. She would listen, anyhow, and Miss Cullen felt that she might—just *might*—take her side. Miss Baldwin would be the obstacle. Her mouth was hard, and Miss Cullen had the feeling that her irritable expression was not entirely due to "end of term." If she was against her, Miss Gilbert would be too, as a matter of course, since she was Miss Baldwin's shadow. ... Still, she might try.

Who remained? Well, there was Miss Moore, the art specialist, who lived entirely in the clouds, and who had been known to walk to school with the head girl of her own form and ask her, as a topic of polite conversation, what her name was and what form she was in. Miss Moore did not have a form to manage now. She would be friendly, Miss Cullen was sure of that; but her friendship would mean nothing, because it would be absolutely blank and impersonal, and because it would be extended equally sweetly and equally vaguely to the vulgar, vain Miss Pearson, or Miss Harries, or even Miss Parry.

There remained only Miss Lovell. She was not in the room—she seldom appeared there, her absences in keeping with her whole mysterious personality—but Miss Cullen could call up vividly her image—that curiously impassive, ivory-white face, in which the emotional scarlet mouth seemed to lead a caged and independent existence. A puzzle. Miss Lovell always seemed to look down on the petty struggles and rivalries of her colleagues from a kind of Olympian height. She was not particularly superior, or conceited; she simply did not appear interested, except in a curiously detached, almost scientific, way, as an entomologist is interested in beetles. Miss Cullen knew that if she appealed to Miss Lovell she would listen with perfect politeness—as the entomologist might listen to the brrrr of an insect—would murmur a phrase or so whose meaning would be a little ambiguous, a little ironic—and that would be all. If Miss Parry called on her next day she would receive precisely similar treatment. No, she could hardly count on Miss Lovell. That meant, then, only Miss Rowan and Miss Gilbert as possible allies, with Miss Baldwin and Miss Lovell as dim, almost negligible, hopes.

Miss Cullen was "free" during the next lesson, and, as it happened, she had the Staff Room to herself. She knew that there were three piles of examination papers waiting for her to correct, and numberless reports to be filled in and initialled; but just now her own affairs occupied her too completely to allow her to take up the usual routine. Like many of her kind, she could never think clearly unless she had all the factors of a problem written out before her. If she had ever read "The Wrong Box" she would have had the greatest sympathy with Maurice in his list of "Good" and "Bad." Indeed, she proceeded to take much the same step herself. She took a sheet of paper and began to write.

"Resignation," she wrote at the top, title-wise. Then with a ruler she drew two neat perpendicular columns. "*Pro*" she headed one and "*Con*" the other.

Pro.	Con.

1. I am unused to modern methods.
2. My discipline is falling off.
3. My examination results are not good.
4. My colleagues are uncongenial.
5. I am not just now physically fit to do the work required of me.

She paused before filling in the second column. Then she wrote: "I cannot afford to go." That was all. There was nothing else to say.

She sat looking at her work. Even now she would not admit, even to herself, that she had seriously understated the case in the column marked "Pro." Still, she realised that the case was grave; she felt, more than ever, that she needed help, sympathy, advice. Where was she to turn for this? Miss Rowan—Miss Gilbert; Miss Baldwin, Miss Lovell. Four possibilities. That was better than nothing....

She put her paper carefully away in her attaché case, together with sheets of notes, loose scraps of extra work from special girls, her spectacle case, part of a cake of chocolate of a hard and nutritious kind, a bottle of aspirin tablets, and her fountain pen. She felt that she had taken a definite step towards the solution of her difficulties by writing them down and thinking over possible allies. She felt braced, cheered, almost self-satisfied, as if, by making out that list, she had really begun to put matters right. Perhaps she had. That feeling of vigour, of hope, was something.

"*That's* done," she said to herself, triumphantly snapping the double locks of the shabby case; she felt she could hardly wait to begin her campaign on her possible supporters.

She caught Miss Gilbert first. She would be a good person to start on, she was so placid always; and then, when she felt safer, she would go on to the more doubtful ones, Miss Rowan, and perhaps—if she had the courage—Miss Lovell.

"Oh, Miss Gilbert, I wanted to see you. I've so often tried to catch you, but somehow I never succeed. Can you and—er—Miss Baldwin come to tea with me on Sunday? It would be so nice."

It was out, and, she felt, skilfully out. She might have killed two birds with one stone; by securing the pleasant Miss Gilbert she might have secured the less approachable member of the firm of The Inseparables.

But Miss Gilbert looked a little doubtful, a little embarrassed, almost.

"I'm not quite sure," she hesitated. "Miss Baldwin may have arranged. … May I let you know this afternoon? I don't quite know—we'd half promised—"

"Certainly," beamed Miss Cullen with her wide, anxious smile. "But *do* persuade Miss Baldwin. I should so like to have you both."

And pinning her aged hat securely to her knob of hair, she walked away.

As soon as the flapping sound of her flat-footed walk had died away, Miss Gilbert sought her crony, on duty outside the cloak-room.

"I say, Cullen wants us to go to tea on Sunday," she said, just low enough to avoid being heard by the girls.

"Oh, damn, Gil, we can't. Not at this stage of term. I couldn't bear it."

"Couldn't you, Jingo? It—She'd like it so awfully."

"Margaret Westrup, you were speaking. Fifty lines.—D'you *want* to go?"

"*Want* to? Good Lord, no! Only she does have a rotten time. And she'd like it so much if we did."

"Mmmmm. … Yes, Joan, what is it?"

"Please, Miss Baldwin, 'twasn't Margaret's fault she spoke. I spoke to her first."

"Did you? Then *you* can take fifty lines," snapped the overwrought Miss Baldwin.

"Instead of Margaret?"

"As well as Margaret."

"Oh, but, please, Miss Baldwin—"

"*I* spoke *first*, Miss Baldwin."

"It was my fault, really, Miss Baldwin. I pushed Joan on to Margaret."

"Listen to me. You will each of you, Phyllis *and* Joan *and* Margaret, do me fifty lines before break to-morrow. Perhaps you will then remember that it's no excuse for breaking the rule to say that somebody else broke it first. *No* one may speak in the cloak-room. And if you speak again, even to me, I'll double it."

The three girls slunk back with sullen eyes in which there was a kind of unwilling admiration.

Miss Gilbert returned to the charge.

"Well—shall we go, Jingo?"

But the encounter with the talkative trio had laid the last touch on Miss Baldwin's rasped and irritated nerves.

"No, we won't. I couldn't stick it, Gil, truly. I'd do something awful. Cullen's frantic voice and toothy smile yammering at you when you might be quiet in a field. No, I won't, and you can tell her any old lie you like."

Thus it was that Miss Gilbert met Miss Cullen with apologies in the afternoon.

"I'm so sorry, Miss Cullen. It seems that Miss Baldwin has already fixed up an engagement for us on Sunday afternoon. I did tell you, didn't I, that I wasn't sure. I'm so sorry."

Miss Gilbert, never a really proficient liar, was bungling so badly that even Miss Cullen saw through it.

"*So* sorry," she said, with the "toothy smile" that had partly, at least, caused the rebuff. "Some other day, then. ..."

The afternoon went by, not too badly—or else she was so preoccupied with her plans that she didn't see. She was engaged over the remaining possibles. Miss Rowan—Miss Lovell. Which should she try next? ... Finally she made a compact with herself. She would ask the one she saw first after prayers.

The last lesson on Friday was not a "taught" lesson. Mistresses sat in charge while the girls "got on with" the heavy preparation set for the week-end. Thus it was that Miss Cullen had time to think; and thus it was that her courage began to ebb. Should she give it up—avoid the risk of another snub by bearing her burden alone? But no; she had made that bargain with herself, and, with her odd, unexpected, unnecessary determination, she decided to abide by the compact.

At last the bell sounded.

"Put away your books." (That command, at least, was always obeyed!) "And quietly ... *quietly*, I said."

And because the form was a very low one, only IIb, silence fell at once. Her courage rose again, warm and comforting.

"All nonsense, my discipline's *good*," she thought, looking with triumph at the bent heads and busy hands before her; and she ushered the form into the assembly hall for prayers in a glow of pride. She hadn't felt so well, so happy, for months. ...

But it was that very confidence that proved her undoing. On the crest of the wave she sought the abyss.

It was in the Staff cloak-room. Hot, jaded, tired, irritable women, worn with the work of the week, a heavy weekend's work before them, were herded together, pushing politely, stretching for hats, waiting for a turn before the inadequate and distressingly unbecoming mirror. Resentful eyes were fixed on Miss Parry, leisurely trying different angles for her coquettish hat; they became hostile when Miss Pearson dallied there, out of her turn, fluttering her eyelids at her own reflection, sliding her long, dark eyes sideways, posing, posturing. It was all they could do to keep from open comment. As it was, Miss Baldwin whispered, Miss Gilbert smiled in reply, Miss Rowan fixed weary eyes on the ceiling and softly whistled. And they all wondered crossly why old Cullen stuck there, taking up space in the congested room. She couldn't want the mirror, with that face and that hat.

Miss Lovell waited, cool and aloof, until they had all finished. Then she approached the mirror; and it was then that Miss Cullen plunged to her doom. Buoyed still by her tiny triumph over IIb, she took advantage of the empty room to say, almost as casually as if she were conferring a favour:

"By the way, Miss Lovell, are you engaged for either to-morrow or Sunday? Or can you come to tea with me?"

Miss Lovell turned slowly. She was even whiter than usual, and, to the observant, her eyes would have spoken of deadly fatigue and pain. But her hot, red mouth smiled a little, coolly, almost insolently; her lids drooped a little over her heavy eyes. For a moment she did not answer; and then:

"No, thank you," she said deliberately, still smiling a little.

Miss Cullen was startled. It was as if she had a grudge against her—as if she *meant* to hurt. ...

"Unless," said Miss Lovell, turning at the door, "you are leaving this term. In that case I might *make* time to come in—to say good-bye, you know. ..." She paused, as if for an answer. Miss Cullen opened her mouth once or twice. No sound came. "No? I thought not. ... Then you must excuse me."

And with her long, indolent, graceful step Miss Lovell went down the corridor.

Miss Cullen stood in the tiny cloak-room, one hand at her mouth, her eyes as wide and hurt as a child's behind her thick glasses. She said nothing.

Outside the girls on the cricket pitch shouted as they played.

CHAPTER VI
End of Term

At Besley, as at many county high schools, there was an institution, loathed and dreaded by the Staff with emotions which custom staled not at all, called Dinner Duty. At some schools this is a duty in name only; at Besley, as at some schools, it was the name for an hour which, coming at the end of a tiring four-hour morning and preceding a wearisome afternoon, was little short of torment.

Two mistresses, changed weekly, shared this time of trouble. One sat in the Assembly Hall from the end of morning school at 12.45 until a quarter-past one; the other relieved her then, and was enthroned until twenty to two, when the girls dined, with both these unhappy ladies in charge, on a meal which in summer seemed invariably to consist of Irish stew and suet pudding. No one knew why the children were immured in the hall instead of being out in the grounds, or why, if immured, they had to be policed; at school one gets to accept these laws as unquestioningly as one accepts the great laws of nature. One accepted, at Besley, and only hoped that one was on Second Duty, which was not only five minutes shorter than First Duty, but also allowed a breathing space between the end of morning school and the wearisome minutes on the dais; one snatched at those few minutes' relaxation and quiet as Dives might snatch at Lazarus' proffered drop of water. You can face things again after that half-hour; but it is not so precious when it comes later, and dinner, steamy and noisy, is imminent.

It was Tuesday. Term would end on Thursday, and the rush and scramble must be known to be believed. Reports to sign, lists of marks from "school exams." to be copied out in triplicate, examination papers to be arranged for the Head in order of merit, with detailed accompanying lists (no one ever looked at either papers or lists; Miss Moore had been known, in a fit of absent-mindedness bordering on mania, to destroy every paper she had received, and the seventeen sets were never missed from the staggering pile that went in to the Head; but that was no reason for not arranging papers and making lists); there were reports to copy out into the "Form Report Books"; marks to add, percentages and averages to strike; textbooks to take in and check; exercise-books to look over and return to the stationery clerk; term marks and examination marks, honours marks and lines, to add and arrange in every possible order—every form mistress knows the weary business, and how, in those last two unspeakable days, one moves with one's head in a fog of meaningless, futile detail, one's nerves at shrieking point, one's body heavy with sheer fatigue, till one wonders what will give way first. No one is tolerant in those last two days; they try friendship to the utmost and put the last touch to enmity. And it was in this week that Miss Lexington, in a moment of forgetfulness amounting to insanity, put down Miss Cullen and Miss Parry to take dinner duty together.

Miss Cullen, by virtue of her senior rank, took her choice of times, and of course selected Second Duty. Everyone who had the chance did that. Miss Parry, murmuring into Miss Fergusson's sympathetic ear that it was rather hard on her, mounted the dais in the hall. Miss Cullen took a deck-chair into the garden.

Miss Parry, sitting on the platform in the hall where the air had been exhausted by the morning's gymnastic classes, watching the restless interned girls with the eye of a hawk lest any should attempt to sneak out to the fresh wind and calling sun, saw her colleague move out into the garden with inward rage. She was tired out, too, in spite of her comfortable mode of life and complacent mind. The shouts and jabbering by which eighty girls sought to relieve their spirits confused and irritated her unspeakably. She could have choked any of them with the greatest delight. However, in ten minutes she would be relieved—and then *she* would use that deck-chair.

The hands of the big clock crept on—incredibly slowly, but they did move. One-fifteen. The woman was due. … One-eighteen—she was late.

... One twenty-five—one-thirty—one-forty. The dinner-bell rang, and still Miss Cullen sat peacefully in the garden. *She had never relieved her colleague at all.*

Miss Parry felt certain she had done it on purpose. She came down from the platform with fury in her heart—black, seething fury. In a voice trembling with rage she mustered the girls in a line, pouncing with vicarious wrath on any child who spoke to a neighbour.

The bell stopped. The file began to move. And then the door burst open and Miss Cullen, looking both distraught and alarmed, rushed in.

"Oh, Miss Parry, I *am* so sorry!" she gasped. "I *absolutely* lost sight of the time ... I am *so* sorry. ..."

Miss Parry answered not a word. As she said afterwards, recounting the scene to her sympathisers: "I looked at her. That was all. Just *looked.*"

It was enough. Miss Cullen understood. In a quite disproportionate misery she took her place at the head of the table allotted to her.

The thing worried her all through the hot, noisy meal. The windows were all wide open, but even so beads of moisture formed on the panes, and clouds of vapour hung clammily on the close air. Miss Cullen ladled out potatoes and parsnips mechanically, brooding in a fashion suited to great tragedy over her fatal error.

"She'll never forgive me," she thought with melancholy certitude. Then an idea struck her. "I'll offer to do double to-morrow," she thought, cheering up a little.

Coming out from dinner, ready with her offer to make amends, she saw Miss Parry already in converse with a little group—Miss Fergusson, Miss Pearson and Miss Baldwin—and knew that she was relating the story of her wrongs. She could almost hear the burden: "It's rather hard on me. ...

"I'll put it right," thought Miss Cullen; and then she heard the fatally loud voice of Miss Pearson:

"I should make her do double duty to-morrow."

"Oh, of *course* I shall do *that*," answered Miss Parry, "but it isn't the same thing. ... I'll let her see she can't play fast and loose with me like that." And Black Care settled once more on Miss Cullen's back. Her offer was anticipated, put in the wrong light—it would be worse than useless to make it now.

The thing bothered her all the afternoon, as she struggled, first with a restless, bored, impudent Fifth Form and then with a Lower School class. If you have not experienced it, you would never believe the gigantic proportions such an incident assumes at the end of term. It is like a real disaster; you can think of nothing else, though you know you can do nothing about it; it makes a gloomy background to the whole day.

As the minutes drew on towards 4.30 Miss Cullen became more and more convinced of one thing: she could not, and she would not, face her hostile colleagues in the confined space of the cloak-room which had been the scene of that other cruel rebuff. She was too sore, too self-conscious, too miserable. Earlier in the term—even a week ago—she would have carried it off with a jest—("My mind must be going—*have* you heard what I did this morning?" or "Miss Parry *have* you forgiven me my *awful* crime?")—but now she was past it. And she made up her mind that, for almost the first time in her Besley career, she would cut afternoon prayers—sneak down to the cloak-room, secure her hat and case, and be gone while the Staff prayed.

She did it. Like a thief she crept out from the school buildings, her heart actually throbbing with anxiety lest she should be seen. With a feeling of mingled shame and triumph she reached her lodgings.

❦

Flatter and flatter went the voices as the dreary hymn dragged its slow length along.

"Tone and a half down," sang Miss Reeve to Miss Baldwin. The Staff, standing in a row against the painful ridges of the rib-stalls, did thus communicate occasionally during the hymn.

"A-a-at least," sang back Miss Baldwin. "And she's pla-aying all wro-ong," she continued, as the weary pianist, agitated by the baleful stare of the music-loving Head, dropped out a few sharps.

"A-a-men," sang the school.

"Let—us—pray," stated Miss Barr. The school sank on its knees, heads reverently bent, brains vacant, or busy at work elsewhere, behind the decorously closed eyelids.

"… be upon us and remain with us for ever.—Amen. Stand."

With a rustle and a sigh they stood. The nervous pianist began a march.

"Sixth Form—forward."

Sudden agitation ran like a ripple down the line of the demure Staff.

"*Who's on cloak-room duty?*"

"*Don't know. Not me.*"

"*Ask Lexo. No one's gone.*"

Pause.

"*Lexo says it's Cullen.*"

"*Well, she's not here. Where is she?*"

With weary boredom Miss Rowan detached herself from the line of Staff and lounged down the corridor.

"Stop talking there. Next girl who speaks gets no games to-morrow. … No, you *mayn't* go to your form-room. … (Lord, I'll have Cullen's blood for this!) … Maud Ashley, no games. … You did. I saw you. Don't play? All right, a hundred lines, then, for lying. … (Will the damn kids *never* go?)"

Miss Lovell came up.

"I'll take over now if you like," she said indolently.

"No, I don't mind. I haven't all the extra jobs you people get at the end of term."

"You've had them—sports and all that. Go on, Rowan."

"No. You'll be doing lists and things all night. I don't mind. They won't be long now."

Miss Lovell turned away. Her head had ached intolerably for the last two days, and she really couldn't argue.

"*Can't* you girls buck up?" inquired Rowan resignedly.

"Just going, Miss Rowan." "Good afternoon, Miss Rowan." "Good afternoon, Miss Rowan."

"Good afternoon, Mary. …'Afternoon, Janet. … You the last, Millicent? Good, I'll lock up, then. Good afternoon."

Miss Rowan never took long to prepare for the street. In three minutes she was cycling down the drive, recklessly breaking the law by so doing.

At that very minute Miss Cullen, sitting down to her horrid tea, remembered that she had been on cloak-room duty.

❦

Last day but one. All books to be counted and put away. Girls to go to the Head one at a time (see list). Form mistresses to keep their forms occupied without definite lessons. No buns at lunch-time. Girls in a turmoil of excitement. Each form mistress faced by a restless, surging mob of girls with no books, no work to do, no interest left in anything but the holidays, and told to keep them quiet and occupied while the Head sends for them, one at a time. Four mortal hours of this between breakfast and dinner; two more in the summer afternoon, with girls now weary, hot, tiresome beyond belief.

A few fortunates who were not official Form Mistresses sat in the Staff Room. Miss Lexington collected various futile statistics for the benefit of Miss Barr, who would never read them. Miss Moore was still signing reports which should have been done two days before, only she hadn't been able to fit them into her muddled fourteen-hour day. Miss Spiller was preparing books and registers to hand over to her successor. Miss Rowan was painfully making out the list of subscriptions to the School Sports Fund and the Staff charity which supported the orphans of indigent clergy in a refined parsimony.

"Wish I could add," she groaned. "I say, I couldn't get a penny out of Cullen for the Clergy Children. What d'you think of that? And she's at the maximum."

"Perhaps she sends hers separately," suggested Miss Spiller, with whom charity in speech as well as in cash was almost a profession.

"H'm. P'r'aps," said Miss Rowan. "Her name's never on the published list of subscriptions, though."

"It may be sent anonymously."

She did not believe it, though she suggested it; and yet it was the exact truth. Miss Cullen always kept her left hand in strict ignorance of the movements of her right. Miss Rowan simply scouted the idea.

"Don't see why she sh'd be so beastly elaborate," she muttered. "Anyhow, she hasn't given *me* anything for it. … There! Now I s'pose I'd better write up the cricket results for the mag., hadn't I?"

"Oh, please do," answered Miss Lexington. "The printers are waiting for them to bring out the magazine."

"Right. I'll do them now. How d'you spell Wednesday, somebody? That's a thing I never know."

There was silence as they all worked intently on their various tasks. Then Miss Lexington said:

"When you've finished what you're doing, anybody, would you go and relieve one of the form mistresses? They must be nearly dead by now. Not the Fifths, perhaps, but anyone from IVa down."

"I did go in to Miss Jessop," said Miss Spiller, "but she had her children entranced with a game about nature study. She said she didn't need any help."

"Of course," hesitated Miss Lexington, "the person who really *should* be relieved is Miss Cullen, with IVb. …"

No one spoke for a moment. Then Miss Rowan said:

"Well, I don't want to be nasty, but she did get out of a good bit yesterday."

Again no one spoke; also no one made a movement to go. Then Miss Lexington came over to Miss Spiller.

"I wonder if you could do this for me, Miss Spiller," she said. Murmured explanations followed. "Thank you so much. Any time this evening will do." And she walked out of the room.

"She's gone to take over from Cullen," said Rowan. "It's a rotten shame. Poor old Lexo, she has a dog's life at the end of the term anyhow. Shall I go? I could post this to the printer, I suppose?"

"I shouldn't change again," murmured Miss Spiller, knitting her brows over her task. "Miss *Lexington* won't have any trouble with IVb."

As she spoke, Miss Cullen entered. Miss Spiller blushed hotly.

"All busy?" asked the new-comer brightly.

A grunt from Miss Rowan was the only response. Miss Cullen sat down, picked up a week-old paper, put it down, went to her locker, did something quite unnecessary there, walked over to the window, returned to her chair. Too nervous to remain silent, she began one of her endless, meaningless monologues, biting off the words with that curious precision characteristic of her speech.

At last the absent-minded Miss Moore looked up.

"I've just written 'obsolete theories' instead of 'Very Fair' on Edith Ewell's report," she remarked mildly. "*Would* you mind not talking, Miss Cullen?"

Miss Cullen, reddening slowly, fell silent. A few minutes later she left the room.

"Good thing, too," growled Rowan. "Now we can get on—and p'r'aps she'll go back to her job and let poor old Lexo get on with hers. Can't stick people behaving like that."

And Miss Cullen, who had gone to breathe the air on the drive under the window of the Staff Room, felt yet another pang. Odd, she wouldn't have thought she *could* suffer much more. ... Miss Rowan, too, one of her few hopes. ... But she didn't go back to IVb. That was impossible. ...

The last morning. Chattering in the cloak-rooms, on the stairs, in the corridors—lawful chattering, since it was beyond the power of woman to stop it. Then Assembly—girls in decorous rows in the hall, the Staff tardily and grudgingly provided with chairs by contemptuous prefects. Then silence during the Reading of Lists—endless, interminable, inaudible lists of marks, percentages and position of each of the three hundred and ten girls, while the Staff, outwardly prim, inwardly fidgeting, sat, eyes on the clock, thoughts on the minutes flying and the punctuality of trains. ...

A homily. Will the woman *never* stop? She said all this last term—says it so badly, too, so feeble, so unconvincing. ... May Masters passing a note to Vera Wilson—no good, can't do anything now. ... Janet talking—catch her eye—that's stopped her. ... *Glory and honour of the School—what's* that? Exam, results? Lot of glory there'll be about those. ... Holidays a time of healthful recreation ... holiday work done with all your might—likely, isn't it? ... Train goes in twenty-five minutes. ... Ah! Hymn at last.

"*Lord, dismiss us with Thy blessing.*" Silly, how that idiotic scooping tune and sickly words get you, every time. It's because one's so desperately tired, I expect. ... "*Those returning make more faithful tha-an before. Amen.*" Dismiss.

Crowded corridor. Girls wanting one's address. Queue outside the white door to say good-bye politely. Let Reefer go first, she'll never get her train. Good-bye. Good-bye. Have a good time. ... Good-bye, Jess; best of luck, old thing. ... Good-bye. ...

And so, at last, the train. And Miss Cullen, sitting on the hard, carpet-covered seat in the dusty railway-carriage on her way to the solitary boarding-house holiday, was making a resolve:

"It *must* be all right next term. It *shall* be. I will be strong—firm with them all. They shall see they can't treat me as they like. ... Oh, yes, next term will be better. It *must* be."

It could, whispered her inmost self, hardly be worse. ...

PART II

Autumn: Viola

CHAPTER I
A Clean Slate

The Autumn Term is always more interesting than the others. Whatever changes are made on the Staff and in the general organisation of the school generally come then. People are fresh from a long holiday. There are new sets of girls to be prepared for examinations, and one always hopes however futilely, that they may be an improvement on last year's lot. Friends on the Staff meet with the pleasure caused by absence. Everyone is in better health, better looking, better tempered, most people have some new clothes. The very building is clean, and smells pleasantly of soap and furniture polish.

The Besley Staff, like most staffs, assembled on the day before term for a Staff Meeting, nearly always both long and futile, and this term often unpleasant, since tradition held that examination results should be openly enlarged upon by the head mistress—an arrangement disliked intensely by the Staff, and loathed and feared by the Head, who was nevertheless credited by her assistants with taking a fiendish joy in this public execution. This symposium was (again by tradition) held at 4.15—an hour which meant that one either had to arrive in Besley before lunch, hours too soon, or appear at the meeting tealess and breathless, having arrived at 4.7. Most people chose the latter alternative. Only the very prudent, or the unfortunate Staff Mistress, who had to be in Besley two days before anyone else on account of the Entrance Examinations, arrived both early and fed.

This term three new arrivals were among the prudent—the successors to the Misses Spiller, Harries and Jessop. They eyed each other very much as do strange dogs who are too well bred to growl, each wondering whether the other two were also new or were old Staff, all a little shy of asking. The arrival of Miss Fergusson, Miss Parry and Miss Lexington (two prudent, and one from Scotland by the only available connection) solved their problem. Miss Lexington began to effect introductions.

Miss Wilson, a thin, anaemic, well-dressed girl in the late twenties, was, it appeared, to take Miss Harries's place; Miss Jervis, short, round-eyed, rosy, with thick shoes, aggressive tweeds, and silk stockings, had Miss Jessop's botany; and Miss Kennedy, a tall, pleasantly fresh-faced girl of twenty-five or so, took over the English with which Miss Spiller had struggled with such small success. The rest of the Staff, finding time in spite of their late and breathless arrival to eye the new arrivals, felt a faint spasm of hope. Miss Kennedy at least looked capable, and Miss Wilson "interesting." An improvement, they felt; but something must be wrong somewhere, for them to have come to a school with the reputation of Besley at all. ...

They sat around the bare Staff Room table, each with a notebook and pencil, the meek new-comers positively struggling for inconspicuous seats and earnestly hoping that no one would say to them: "Friend, go up higher." There were not enough chairs—there somehow never are at Staff Meetings; Miss Kennedy found herself precariously balanced on the edge of a chair more than sufficiently filled by the robust form of Miss Jervis, and felt acutely grateful to the kind neighbour who edged up to support her unseated left leg. This was Viola Kennedy's first experience of teaching, and she had much to learn.

They rose reverentially as Miss Barr entered, and anxious looks passed from face to face as they saw the ominous gravity with which the Head regarded the lists that she held in her hand. There would be an interval of trivial details, and then the thunderclouds would burst. ... You could almost hear their anxious hearts beat as they tried to guess the contents of those fateful detailed examination lists.

The very first words were minatory:

"We will allot the forms first," said Miss Barr. "Unfortunately, owing to what I can only call the *disastrous* results of the Senior, the Fifths remain practically unchanged, except for those unfortunate Pupil Teachers whose time has expired and who therefore leave, perforce, their whole future ruined. There will now be three Fifths, in order to accommodate the girls from IVa. Miss Lexington, will you take Va as your Form?"

A gasp came from the Staff. It was unprecedented for the already burdened Staff Mistress to have a form. However, the Fifths were beyond most people. ...

"Miss Parry, you will have Vb. Miss Reeve, Vc. Miss Kennedy, will you take IVa?"

Another shock—Cullen's form given over to a new-comer!

"Miss Lovell, IVb. Miss Baldwin, IVc. Miss Wilson, Remove. Miss Gilbert, Lower Remove. Miss Moore, IIIa. Miss Jervis, IIIb. Miss Fergusson, IIa. Miss Pearson, IIb. Miss Newton, of course, keeps the First Form."

Miss Cullen involuntarily bit her lip. She was not to be entrusted with the care of a form, then? Even that dreamer, Miss Moore, had one; but she was passed over, left out. ... It meant less work, of course; but the sting was there.

"And now," went on Miss Barr, after a mass of seemingly interminable detail had been discussed and re-discussed, "now I come to a very unpleasant part of the evening's work. We have had bad results before— unfortunately; but we have *never* had results like these."

An indefinable sound ran round the table. Consternation was in it, and awe, and a kind of terror.

"Of all the thirty-four girls who took the Senior," said Miss Barr in impressive tones, "only *four* have passed."

They gasped. This was terrible—almost incredible.

"Those four are Doris Canfield, Marjory White, Annie Day and Mary Simonds. All the rest have failed."

Miss Lexington ventured a remark.

"Then Mavis Reed and Daisy Riddell and Nellie Beamish—?"

"Failed. They failed in French, and therefore, of course, in the whole examination. Though their work in other subjects seems to have been excellent."

"May we have some details?" asked Miss Lexington.

"Certainly. In mathematics we have nothing to be ashamed of. Your results are excellent, Miss Lexington. History is very good, too, though not quite up to the high mathematics standard. Geography—as good as can be expected, I think. English is very weak—eighteen essays marked Bad, none above Moderate, and textbook work poor. You will have your work cut out for you, Miss Kennedy."

Miss Kennedy smiled, rather nervously.

"Science is not what it might be, either. Of course, Miss Baldwin, I realise that you found the subject in a very bad state last year, but even so, things should be better than this."

Both the Head and Miss Baldwin blushed in miserable embarrassment, and everyone else studiously looked elsewhere. The new-comers glanced at each other. They had not been prepared to see their seniors thus publicly laid low. They could not know that Miss Barr yearly tortured herself and her Staff thus from a genuine sense of duty.

"But the French—well, words fail me. It is, of course, the French that has caused this catastrophe. If they had been able to clear that, twenty-six would have passed instead of four. As it is, all our best girls—Mavis and Daisy and Helen Andrews and Nellie Beamish—all fail. I have never in all my experience seen such a list as the French Grammar paper has produced. Never. I don't know what to say. ...

"Well, I dare say you all realise what this means. It means that, in the next three terms, the whole atmosphere of the school must change. We must pull up the discipline all through the school. We must get real hard work out of the girls. And, if I may say so—we must *all* make ourselves thoroughly acquainted with modern methods and modern examinations. ... That does not, of course, apply to everyone," added the Head in a kind of jerk that the Staff thought vicious but was really due to the effort with which the words were said—"but I feel that it is necessary to remind some of you that educational methods have greatly changed in recent years. ..."

The voice went on, but few of the Staff listened. Angry as they might be over this disaster, they had no wish to see and hear the public humiliation of Miss Cullen as she sat, speechless and impotent, under the scourge.

And they had plenty to occupy their thoughts—visions of the future, when this catastrophe should come to the notice of Authority, and when anything—*anything*—might happen in consequence. ...

The Staff Meeting broke up in unwonted gravity. Little knots formed, talking in lowered voices. Only Miss Cullen, alone, wounded and alarmed, crept away, the sound of Miss Barr's voice still ringing in her ears, the knowledge of the drift of her colleagues' whispered conversations chafing her sore heart.

The new-comers, not quite grasping the baleful import of the news, walked down the drive together. The chief impression made on the virgin mind of Viola Kennedy was one of unpleasantness, together with an impression that, if the meeting was typical and the examination bogy so feared, educational methods hadn't perhaps changed as much as Miss Barr seemed to think. But she preserved a prudent silence on these matters of state. Round-faced little Miss Jervis, who did not seem to know the meaning of the word shyness, babbled as they went.

"D'you know what I heard one of them saying? Miss—is her name Lexham? The Staff Mistress?"

"Lexington, I think."

"Yes, well, it doesn't matter. She said to the little fat one, 'I shouldn't wonder if this means the end of the school.' And the little one said, 'D'you think they'll close it down?' and Miss Whatsername just nodded."

"Oh, I don't think that can be possible," Miss Wilson struck in. "Not on the results of one examination. Though I must say I never did hear of *any* school getting results like that."

"Ah, but it isn't only one exam.," said Miss Jervis, solemnly nodding her round head. She was one of those people who seem to absorb, not always accurately, all the news and personal gossip of a place as soon as they arrive. "It seems they've been going down and down, and this is just touching bottom."

"Still," said Viola Kennedy, "they'd never *close* a school, would they, for such a trivial thing as examination results?"

"I don't know," answered Miss Jervis. "I'm only telling you."

"What a ghastly idea it is to call the Staff over the coals in public like that," said Miss Wilson, who had what is unjustifiably called an Oxford voice. "I felt sorry for that poor French woman."

"Miss Collins," put in Miss Jervis. "Yes, so did I. But what a freak she is! Did you *ever see* such clothes? Shoddy, and so rottenly cut, and her *hat*—"

Miss Wilson and Miss Kennedy seemed to take no interest in "Miss Collins's" clothes, and Miss Jervis was (temporarily) checked. A few minutes later the trio arrived at Miss Kennedy's rooms, and she detached herself from the others and went in to unpack and prepare for her first day's work at school.

Viola Kennedy had never been "on her own" in rooms before, and she had the romantic pleasure of the very young in the new experience. She took pleasure in putting out her books and small possessions, in giving to the stiff "apartment" something of the home-like air that her room in college had possessed. But, as she ranged books on the very inadequate shelf, she found herself thinking continually of that curious Staff Meeting, with its decorous surface and its conflicting undercurrents. For Viola was what is very vaguely called "sympathetic," and the tides of feeling moving about the table had not passed her by untouched. She wondered what it all meant—that hostility, that speech of Miss Barr's, those references to discipline, that urgent "We must make these girls *work*." ... It was such a prehistoric way of looking at things, she felt, this insistence on examinations as the be-all and end-all of education! Surely it couldn't be the Head's criterion of things. ... She felt that more must lie beneath the surface, and wondered, half idly, what it could be. ... Her enlightenment was to be rapid and complete.

Your first entry into a school is always rather trying, unless you are one of those fortunate beings (if they really exist?) who honestly did not know what it is to be conscious of one's self. Certainly Viola Kennedy was not of them. Neither was she particularly self-conscious; but the open stares and half audible comments of the girls who thronged the drive made her cheeks burn.

"Ill-mannered little brutes," she thought viciously, as she cycled up the drive in the wake of three obviously senior girls.

She followed these ladies round to an open cycle-shed, already fairly full, and secured a niche for her machine; and then she made her way to the main entrance she had used last night. To her surprise girls stood there—tall girls, mostly wearing prefects' badges—and they made no attempt to move.

"Will you please let me pass?" asked Viola, her eyes sparkling a little as she spoke.

"This is the Sixth Form's door," answered a lanky girl, looking her coolly over. "The Staff use that little one round by the cycle-shed, where those juniors are."

Viola felt angrier than the occasion perhaps warranted; but she obediently sought the inferior door where the younger girls buzzed like flies round a honey-pot. It seemed odd, she thought, that the Sixth should have even a tiny privilege not accorded to the staff, and she wondered whether it had been a rather ill-mannered jest.

She found the cloak-room. A selection of the Staff were already there, preparing in grim silence for the day. As Viola finished her small arrangements and left the tiny room, she found someone close beside her—the odd-looking woman who had been so severely dealt with at the meeting the night before.

"You *are* Miss Kennedy, aren't you?" said this lady. "I thought so. My name is Cullen. I used to have the form you are in charge of now, and I thought that, if you cared, I could show you all their different lists and registers and so on. These small matters of detail are rather confusing at first."

"Oh, thank you very much," answered Viola. "I should be awfully glad if you would."

They walked on down the corridor, both supremely unaware of the shrewd glances that followed them and the shrewish whisper of Miss Parry, "She's sucking up to the new Staff already!"

"And—do you mind my telling you?" continued Miss Cullen. "Staff aren't supposed to cycle in the drive. Of course you couldn't know."

"But I saw some girls doing it. I just followed them."

"Ah, senior girls have many privileges which are denied to mere Staff," said Miss Cullen with her wide smile. "I saw your little encounter with Rose Byham. No doubt she put you in your place?"

Viola flushed.

"She was very rude," she said shortly. "I must say," she added on an impulse, "I should think that that sort of thing accounted for a good deal of disciplinary trouble."

Miss Cullen's eyes gleamed.

"You see—" she began eagerly, and broke off abruptly as Miss Lexington and Miss Parry, in close conversation, entered the Staff Room. Viola, looking expectantly at her to hear the end of her sentence, saw with surprise a fleeting look of consternation in the alert, suspicious eyes behind the thick glasses. For Miss Cullen another blow had fallen. There was obviously to be a truce between these two formidable antagonists; and who could say what the combination might not achieve? Her doom was sealed indeed.

CHAPTER II
A New Leaf and a New Broom

Viola Kennedy, had she but known it, owed her present engagement to the fact that she had never been to a training college, and was therefore theoretically worth a little less than her colleagues. In other words, she was cheap. Also, her lack of this extra qualification and of any experience went against her with better schools. All the three newcomers had something against them, for the good scholastic agencies no longer sent their best clients to Besley; some agencies would not accept Besley notices at all. So it was the unwanted who got positions there. Miss Wilson had a heart which caused frequent breakdowns; Miss Jervis had left her university hurriedly and without a full degree—no specified reason given; Viola was cheapish, and technically not as well fitted to teach as her colleagues. She began to wonder, as she entered the form-room allotted to her, how a "trained" mistress would have dealt with the situation.

IVa (the dread IVb of last year) was enjoying itself. The noise was such that no human voice, not even Miss Pearson's, could possibly have made itself heard. Girls talking, shouting, banging desks, stamping, all looking at her with merry, challenging eyes to see what she would do.

She did nothing. She simply stood, a slight and purposely ironic smile just curving her lips, and looked at them with the detachment of one watching the antics of a curious exhibit in a museum. Occasionally she made a note on a piece of paper. She seemed interested, faintly disgusted, perhaps, as one might be when dissecting a frog, but thoroughly absorbed.

The girls were puzzled. They did not like her air—she actually seemed to despise them. And some of the gusto went out of their humour when they saw that she didn't seem to mind in the least. After all, there isn't much fun in shouting and banging unless you annoy somebody by doing so. Gradually the clamour began to die down. Still Viola Kennedy took no notice whatever of them. Soon there was complete silence; and then, at last, she spoke.

"You know, you're awfully silly," she began in a perfectly friendly voice. "I know nothing about you—nothing whatever—except what you choose to show me. You're in the same position about me. But I'm not such a fool as to come in here and let you think, by my behaviour, that I'm a raving lunatic. If I am a lunatic, you'll find it out quite soon enough without any help from me—I'm not going to give myself away. You must find out about me for yourselves. But you haven't the sense to make *me* find out about *you* for *my*self.

"Now, get this straight, please. I've not heard a word about you—any of you. For all I know you may be the meanest set in the school—or the most sporting. I shall only know what you show me. I shan't ask anyone what your reputation is. And that's true of each girl, too. I don't know who's the black sheep, or the head of the form, or the best at games, or anything else. *And I don't want to.* I want to find out for myself, just as you'll have to find out about me. I don't know how you'll like it, but I mean to enjoy it!

"We'll have to know each other's names. Mine's Kennedy—Miss Kennedy. Will you tell me yours, please?—in alphabetical order, if you can manage it."

There was silence except for a few whispers as the names were given. For the moment, anyhow, she'd got them. ...

Books were given out, time-tables made. Viola never seemed to imagine that they might not accept the one or make the other. One girl—a red-headed Jewess named Rhoda Stein, who longed to usurp May Masters' place as acknowledged leader of the form—tried to annoy by pretending to be deaf.

"Please, I can't hear. What comes after Mystery on Fools' Day?"

"You really ought to be medically examined," said Miss Kennedy seriously. "I'll make a note of it. Deafness may sometimes be a sign of mental trouble," she added low, as if to herself.

Rhoda flamed scarlet.

"Mental trrrrouble!" she shouted. "I will tell my father that is what you have said!"

"And what will you tell him?" asked Viola sweetly. "That deafness is a sign of mental trouble? Do. I'm sure he will like to know. But do tell him, won't you, that he needn't worry about you, since your deafness is so very—er—spasmodic. If you feel it coming on again, come right up here to my desk so that you'll be sure to hear."

The girls glanced at each other. She knew too much, they decided. … Peace reigned while the writing continued.

If only they had known how hard and fast Viola's heart was thumping under her pretty jumper, pandemonium, joyful, heartfelt pandemonium, would have broken out. As it was, they were undecided. Should they take the opportunity for turning over a new leaf? After all, there was that beastly old Senior in view. Or should they continue their career of vice so happily inaugurated last year? The latter course seemed a little doubtful; it didn't seem certain that it *would* be as joyous as it had been last year. First day of term had always been one long rag under old Cully; certainly they'd never been forced into writing out time-tables. This one knew too much. … They decided, in the strange, voiceless, signless way that a form does decide, that they would leave it till break and see what May Masters thought. …

The bell rang, and Viola, flushed with both anxiety and triumph, with rather the feeling that she had at home when she'd steered the *Spindrift* round a particularly tricky place, or won an especially hard-fought game of tennis, walked sedately to the Staff Room. The first two "periods" always went in the arrangements of forms on the first day of term; after that you began to teach properly, and gave a lesson before break. Now, Viola had to face the Upper Sixth.

She collected books, and wondered to see the room so empty. Only Miss Reeve was there.

"Am I horribly early, or horribly late?" she asked in some trepidation.

"Neither," answered Reeve, smiling. "Just about right."

"I thought, as no one else was here—"

"Yes. You see, strictly speaking, we aren't supposed to come in here between lessons—only at break and when we have free times. The rule was made at the end of last term. The idea is that we must live in a whirl, and we may even stop to chat if we meet here between lessons. Think how awful that would be. Life is real, life is earnest. No, we must eliminate the risk of chat by carrying all the things we want round with us from form to form."

Viola looked at the humorous face under the red thatch of hair.

"You're joking, aren't you?"

"Never more serious in my life. It's a serious subject."

"Do I really carry my Middle English lesson notes to the Second Form, and 'Tales from Malory' to the Sixth?"

"You do."

Viola laughed. "How perfectly priceless!" she remarked.

"'Tis, rather, though one doesn't always see it. … You going to the Fifth?"

"The Sixth."

"Oh, then don't bother to go yet. They make a point of being late, to show they don't care a damn for us. So we make a point of being later, to show we don't care a damn for them. Soon there won't be any lesson left at all, which will be no loss."

Viola Kennedy flushed ingenuously.

"It seems to me that the Sixth need to be taught their manners more than anything else," she remarked.

Miss Reeve laughed.

"If you can teach them *that*, I'll put up a monument to you with my own fair hands," she declared.

Viola went to meet the redoubtable Sixth, determined that, monument or no, she would at least begin to teach them this important lesson. …

The Senior English mistress has very few free times—if any—in most schools of the Besley type. Viola did not again that morning go in to the Staff Room, for at break she was occupied with two girls over a little matter of a passed note and an open lie; and so, during the last lesson, Miss Reeve, who had an easy day on Wednesdays, was able to discuss her with Miss Baldwin.

"That girl Kennedy seems to have some sense," she remarked. "What on earth possessed her to come here?"

"Her first job, and she's not trained. Yes, I went by her form-room this morning, to save her life if necessary, and they were *quiet*."

"Help!" gasped Reeve. "Cullen's old form quiet, on the first day of term! What had she done? Doped 'em?"

"She seemed to be giving them some sort of pi-jaw."

Miss Reeve's face was eloquent of admiration and commiseration, as of one who sees a daring martyr walk into a den of lions.

"And she went to the Sixth with the full intention of teaching them their place," she murmured. "Well, I don't know about the other two—that little boot-button woman looks too awful for words—but I should think we've struck oil in that girl."

"Wait and see," said Miss Baldwin in gloomy prophecy. "Lot's of 'em *begin* well."

And Miss Reeve nodded in sage agreement.

Viola went through that day like a general fighting a campaign. A good many defeats had variegated the bright colour of her early victory, but she felt that on the whole her score was *plus* rather than *minus*, and she found herself actually pining for the next day's fray—a spirit that, had Miss Reeve known of it, would have strengthened that lady's sentiments of admiration, for, as she often said, she "did love a good fighter."

One thing Viola learnt at once. She saw, in her first five minutes, that her best weapon would be variety. She must never try the same game twice—at least, not until it had been forgotten. If she was to succeed, she must haunt and startle and waylay—and especially startle. And, as she walked home one evening, she was busy planning means of achieving this desirable end when Miss Cullen caught her up.

"I live up this way too," said the older woman, "so I thought we might walk up together—if you don't mind?"

The humility of this, coming from a member of the Senior Staff, was not entirely appreciated by the novice; she murmured a response, polite but not cordial. Miss Cullen proceeded:

"And how are you getting on with my old form?"

"IVa? Oh, yes, I'd forgotten they were yours last year. They'll be quite a nice lot, I think, when they get a bit more used to me. I suppose they're all a little gay for the first few days, especially with a new mistress. But I like them, quite, so far."

"Yes. … There are one or two rather—well, bad characters. You'll soon find them out."

"Well, as a matter of fact," said Viola a little doubtfully, "I meant to ask their old form mistress when I knew who'd had them—Did you ever have any serious bother with a girl named Masters—May Masters?"

"May Masters? Has she begun already? Yes, I regret to say I had. We all have had, I think, at one time or another. Has she been rude, or—?"

"Oh, I don't mind rudeness—I can deal with that. No, it was—I caught a paper being passed round—a cutting from one of those fearful low-down rags one vaguely knows of and never sees. You know?" Miss Cullen nodded.

"I got the thing from a girl called Gladys Toms, who didn't own it, I feel sure—in fact, I don't think she'd had time to look at it even. It was—well, vulgar's far too mild a word. May denied that it was hers, but she looked at me so challengingly, and the others looked so startled when she denied it, that I feel sure that it did come from her. What would you do about it?"

"I shouldn't do anything just yet," answered Miss Cullen after a short pause. "I should try to get certain proof that it was May who circulated it, and then go to the Head—no, to Miss Lexington," she corrected herself hastily. "But don't do anything till you are absolutely *certain*."

"That's what Miss Parry said," Viola admitted a little doubtfully. "She was there when I opened the thing after morning school, and she didn't seem to think much of it. She said—" Viola broke off abruptly. She had just remembered Miss Parry's final remark, "They'll soon be all right now they have a sensible form mistress. Their last one was *hopeless!*"

Miss Cullen guessed at this, and her face, too, flushed. She had a strong, almost overpowering, impulse to ask Viola to come into her rooms with her, and, once there, to pour out everything—all her troubles and perplexities and griefs. There was something about the girl that appealed to her. She was young, but not too cocksure; she looked kind and sympathetic and candid. ... She would be sure to listen, Miss Cullen felt. ...

Then she changed her mind. It wasn't quite fair, perhaps, to influence a new-comer. She must discover for herself the weaknesses of the Head, the injustices of the Staff, the meannesses of Miss Parry. She must see and draw her own conclusions. She was "a lady" in Miss Cullen's mother's sense of the word, and she was fresh to it all. Miss Cullen determined, with a chivalry that many of her colleagues would never have shown and some would not even have understood, not to take advantage of her powerful enemy by securing this young ally by means even a little unfair. Surely the girl would judge aright!

So, with an effort that cost her a sharp pang, she let the chance slip. Viola noticed something a little wistful in the expression of the faded eyes as they parted; she felt that there was something to come, and she paused a moment to give the older woman the opportunity to speak. But she said no more, and they parted in the soft September sunset, each feeling oddly attracted to the other.

"She might stand by me if things go wrong again this term," thought Miss Cullen. "She looks as if she'd be a good friend."

And Viola, going on her way up the golden-flooded, ugly little street to her lodgings, thought:

"Poor old thing, how ugly she is, and what a *maddening* voice! ... but there's something about her—something—what?—pathetic? wistful? She looks unhappy. ... So *she* was their old form mistress! Of course, I remember now, that first morning, she told me she was. ... And there was something at that appalling Staff meeting. ... This *is* a queer place!" she concluded, as she let herself in to the linoleumed passage of her stuffy rooms. "As soon as ever I've been here long enough to get a testimonial of sorts, I'll move on somewhere else!"

CHAPTER III
To the Rescue!

The days went by. Viola Kennedy felt as if she were in a dream—a queer, mad dream compounded of noise, tea-parties, work, duties, triumphs over rowdy girls, contests with rebellious ones, arguments with silly ones; of lessons leaving her with varying impressions of interest gained and held, of fruitless striving with stupidity or vulgarity; of new acquaintances on the Staff; of painful acquirement of silly rules, tiresome duties, foolish, hampering regulations; and above all and through it all the knowledge that she was succeeding.

She enjoyed it all, even the most tiresome bits of it, as a keen recruit in time of war may enjoy wearisome "fatigues" or meaningless drill. She used to stand in her place at prayers before the Head came in and let her eyes, with the lust of battle in them, wander over the ranks of faces before her.

"They'll be *keen* before I've done with them!" she thought, with the gallant arrogance of untried youth. "They'll love the stuff for itself—*want* it. Not just yet, of course, nor for some time; I'll have to leave the upper forms wallowing in examination cram; but with the younger forms. ... They'll have a chance to get at the real thing before the exam. bogy gets them. ..."

And then the piano would strike the opening chord of some hymn—generally, if the morning were particularly gloomy, "All Things Bright and Beautiful"—and no time was left to think. In school there never is. One is not expected to.

There was something about the school, all the same, that baffled Viola. She felt as if she were walking in a forest where strange and dreadful savages hunted, stealthily, invisibly, a monstrous and unseen quarry. She felt as if all about her were traps, lurking hunters, hiding prey; all the exciting, palpitating thrill of a hunt. And she wanted to see—to understand—to see the hunters and the hunted, to take sides, even; but it was all too impalpable, and she had only the vaguest ideas as to the reason of the strife and the identity of the combatants. There is something appalling in this warfare, silent, secret and unrelenting, that is waged by polite women with smiling faces and gentle manners, against one another. When you realise it, it takes your breath and leaves you horrified by its stealth and its malignity.

The weather had surprisingly held fine for the first few days of the autumn term; and still more surprisingly Viola had managed (by a miracle, some said; others of a less child-like faith declared it was by accident) to get the Head's consent to hold some of her less rowdy classes in the school garden. She had a special spot, a corner near the botany lab., which was isolated from the main building save for a long tentacle of corridor, where she used to retire with an orderly form and make them begin, at least, to enjoy the sound of lyric poetry. As a rule, nothing disturbed the serenity of that class; but on one Tuesday morning, just as work had begun, Viola realised that someone was taking a class in the botany lab., generally empty at that time. It wouldn't matter, she thought; she was a good twenty yards or more away; her voice couldn't possibly disturb the mistress in the lab., and even if they had all the windows open she would hear no more than a faint hum from the other class.

She was soon undeceived. The buzz became a noise, and soon noise became Bedlam. Catcalls and shrill whistles broke out presently, and then a rhythmic *thump*-thump, *thump*-thump, reminiscent of her own first interview with IVa.

A glance ran round Viola's form, and a smile that seemed to recognise a familiar jest. Viola thought she understood.

"Excuse me a moment," she said, rising. "That form's been left to itself,

I imagine, and they think they won't be heard in the botany lab. I'll be back in a moment. Just read on."

As she hurried away the smile on the faces of Vb grew yet broader.

"Scullion, of course," murmured one.

"Course it is," answered another. "Gee, wouldn't I like to be there when she goes in! ..."

Viola hurried, but she was light on her feet; as a matter of fact, if she had stamped along the passage to the lab. no one in that room would have heard her. She threw open the door and walked in, her eyes alight with anger.

"I suppose you're expected to be *working*—" she began in fine scorn. And then she saw Miss Cullen.

She was standing in an attitude almost of defence, close up against the blackboard, as far away from the yelling horde of girls as space could put her. Her hands, clasping and unclasping convulsively, hung at her sides. She was flushed, a dusky, unbecoming red; and Viola saw, with a pang of acute pity, the terror with which she turned on the opening of the door.

For a second Viola hesitated. She could say nothing the only possible thing to do was to go at once, putting a decent face on it if possible, pretending she hadn't seen—and yet it was awful to leave her there, to face it, with that hunted look on her ageing face. ... Hurriedly she invented a lie.

"Oh, Miss Cullen, I wonder if you'd mind," she murmured, approaching the desk as if to confide something of real importance. "You said you could give me a copy of last year's register of my form. I can't get my ages quite right. *Could* you be so kind as to get it for me? I'll carry on here till you come back."

The relief in the other woman's face was patent and pitiful; but she dared not acknowledge it.

"Why, certainly, Miss Kennedy, if you're in a hurry for it," she returned graciously. "The girls have plenty to do for a few minutes. I shan't be more than that"

As she departed Viola, thinking of the unguarded Vb, felt a qualm of fear. She could see them from the window. They were sitting as good as gold, quietly reading. If only no one came by! If only no one of importance—the Head, or Miss Lexington—spotted what she'd done!

However, in for a penny in for a pound. She'd plunged, and she'd go on plunging. Before the door was well closed on Miss Cullen's broad back the gallantry that was so big a part of Viola's nature carried her to a rash decision. She meant to "give them beans"—she, a new-comer, in support of one of the most senior members of the Staff. ... Only Miss Cullen must never know.

"I suppose you think it's rather sporting to behave like that," she said, trying hard to control her voice and breathless with indignation and daring. "As a matter of fact, it's the rottenest thing I think I've ever seen. Perhaps you can't see that Miss Cullen is ill. I'll give you the benefit of the doubt, though I can't imagine how you've been so blind. And for thirty healthy people to go for one ill one is too sickening for words. ... I don't want to speak to you. I'm too furious, to think there are thirty such—such cads—in the school. ... Go on with your work."

One girl stood up.

"We didn't know Miss Cullen was ill," she muttered.

"That's because you're too selfish to *look*," snapped Viola. "You don't expect her—or anyone else—to come to you and *say* they're ill, do you? You should keep your eyes open. ... Now mind you make it up to Miss Cullen for this—and, whatever you do, don't let her know that I told you she was ill. *She's* a sportsman, anyway, and she won't take any odds, even if they're fair ones."

At that very moment the unmistakable clop-clop of Miss Cullen's tread could be heard. The form bent diligently over its books.

Viola returned, triumphant, to the garden. She thought, as she approached her own form, that it looked rather repressed—*too* repressed. And then, as she came close, a figure—short and grey-haired—rose from Viola's chair.

"I have been taking charge for you, Miss Kennedy," said the Head, rather too politely.

Viola flushed to her ears.

"I am so sorry, Miss Barr," she stammered. "I had to go in just for a moment. I could see them—" hastily she altered her intended speech— "see they meant work," she substituted lamely. It would never do for Miss Barr to know where she had been. She felt generously glad, though, that she *had* been there—that Miss Barr had found an unattended form in the garden rather than a riotous one in the lab. ...

"I shouldn't leave them alone *ever*, Miss Kennedy," said the Head in what she believed to be an undertone. Vb exchanged indignant looks. "And I don't think," she added, "that you had better work out here now. It grows chilly as autumn draws on."

Viola looked at the deep sky and mellow sunshine and tried hard not to smile. She was not very successful.

"Very well, Miss Barr," she replied quietly.

Miss Barr moved away over the grass, and her thoughts were—very justifiably—angry.

"Impertinence!" she thought. "Calmly tells me that she went off and left her form—gives no excuse—and smiles in that horrid sarcastic way right in my face when I refuse her leave to let them be out here, with their eyes all over the garden, just idling! Really, I don't know what the teaching profession is coming to!"

As a matter of fact, Viola's intervention had done very little good. It did secure Miss Cullen a little—a very little—peace; but girls are heedless creatures, and these had the habit of "ragging old Scully" so deeply rooted that it would have taken far more than a lecture from a mistress they hardly knew to make them change. In other ways, the interference did positive harm. Such a thing cannot be kept dark in a school; Miss Parry's charge, "sucking up to the new Staff," seemed to her colleagues to be justified, and they began to bracket together Viola and her elderly *protégée*. And Viola herself began, as the day went on and the incident recurred again and again to her memory, to doubt the wisdom of that impulsive rush to the rescue. It might have hurt Miss Cullen far more deeply than rebellion itself could do to know that her weakness had been laid open to a junior member of the Staff; and she must have known—she couldn't help knowing—that her rescuer had seen her trouble. ...

At the end of afternoon school Viola made up her mind to yet another daring deed. She escaped as early as possible from prayers, and, taking up a post of vantage in the corridor, watched for the departure of Miss Cullen. She was determined, against all precedent, to join the elder mistress and try to "get square."

Her manoeuvres succeeded. Blissfully unaware of the meaning glances of the Staff, Viola approached Miss Cullen, who, owing to many rebuffs and humiliations, had not that fine sense of dignity which many Senior Staff possess. She allowed Viola to join her with positive affability.

When they had walked a short distance the girl opened fire.

"I'm so glad to get this chance of speaking to you," she began. "I have wanted all day to apologise to you for bursting in on you as I did this morning. I—I was in a hurry—I didn't stop to think—"

"No. Let's be frank," said Miss Cullen in a voice at once infinitely weary and unusually attractive. "You thought the girls were alone. You went in to quiet them."

Viola made no reply.

"I'm glad to have this out," Miss Cullen continued. "I want you to know the truth. I—I've taken to you so much—do you mind my saying so?—and I should like you to know. I should like you to tell me what you truly think. I haven't been quite myself lately, and I—I can't always control the girls. That's why I have no form. But I feel sure that my weakness is only temporary. If I can just get fit again it will be all right. I've had so many worries—and people don't understand. ... But you don't think, do you, that it's my duty to resign—to leave?"

Viola was profoundly ignorant of the laws by which the ordinary Secondary School is run. She had no idea of the effect of Miss Cullen's failure on the rest of the school.

"Why, no," she answered, in some surprise. "Surely not, if it's just a passing weakness? Do you think of resigning?"

"I don't want to," confessed Miss Cullen. "It would be a very serious matter for me, you see. At my age and at my salary, I should hardly get a new post; and that would mean, if I failed to get a position for four years, that I should have to forfeit my pension and all I have paid in to the fund. I should get no work and have no pension. So if I could keep on here, just for the four years more—consistently with my duty—just long enough for that—"

"Oh, surely you could!" cried the girl warmly. "It's not as if your—your trouble—were serious enough to undermine school discipline altogether." (If Miss Cullen flushed Viola could not see it in the glow of the evening sun.) "As a matter of fact," the girl went on, "I thought all this repressive discipline was a thing of the past?"

"It is," said Miss Cullen eagerly. Although she personally had neither tried nor believed in the new ideas of school government, the fact that the Besley discipline was old-fashioned was certainly a handle. "Oh, of course it is. No up-to-date schools retain it. And that makes it so difficult, when one is used to the new type of discipline. But new ideas don't go down here."

"It's difficult to know what to do quite," said Viola slowly. "I don't believe one bit in all this dogmatic 'Do this,' 'Be silent,' 'Sit straight,' 'Don't speak' business. I thought no one did nowadays. Nobody learns self-restraint if someone else is always restraining them. But, on the other hand, if the Head wants it, I suppose it's our duty to enforce it?"

Miss Cullen saw opening before her a wonderful new way out. She did not know in the very least that she was untruthful as she plunged eagerly into it.

"Well—I don't know," she said. "It's a question, isn't it, between one's loyalty to the one and to the many. If one definitely thinks it's wrong to repress children, ought one to try to do it?"

"Don't you think," suggested Viola, "that one can manage a sort of happy mean—I mean make them not *want* to be noisy and silly? They aren't such a bad lot really."

Miss Cullen sighed. The new way wouldn't be altogether plain. ...

"*You* may manage it," she admitted, "since you're new to the place and haven't anything very bad to contend with. I don't think it's possible for anyone who's been long on the Staff. Only, take my advice, Miss Kennedy, and *always stand up to the Head. Never* give in to her. Then you may succeed."

Viola walked home turning this conversation over in her mind with mixed feelings. She wondered—first, whether that collapse could really be due to Miss Cullen's endeavours to let the girls try self-government. Somehow she couldn't help doubting it—it had been so complete a pandemonium; her own small efforts had had no such disastrous result. Secondly she wondered whether she ought to adopt the Head's disciplinary ideas. Thirdly she wondered what Miss Cullen had meant by that cryptic utterance about standing up to the Head; and lastly—for she was shrewd enough to notice small indications—she wondered what it was that underlay the whole episode.

CHAPTER IV
The Other Side

Miss Lexington had done her duty (with a little less reluctance than usual) and asked Miss Parry to tea. Being a very conscientious woman, she made a point of asking every member of the Staff to tea at least once during each term; she considered it her duty, as Staff Mistress, to perform this small act of courtesy, especially as the Head very rarely invited any member of her Staff to a social function. Miss Lexington, bitterly, if secretly, resenting the time spent on these entertainments, used to attribute this remissness on the part of her chief to various causes, none of them the true one.

"It's her job to do it, not mine," she would think, bending her brows over the selection of her party. "Slacker, she is. Never seems to think I want free week-ends as much as she does."

Or—"I do believe the woman's too mean to ask them. She grudges the expense."

Or—"Thinks it's beneath her to invite the likes of us, I suppose."

Not one of these suppositions came within a league of the truth. Miss Lexington could never have understood that the Head was painfully shy of most of her own Staff. They were of a different generation, a different tradition, from her own. She had no idea of what went on in the heads of, say, Miss Rowan or Miss Gilbert. She knew nothing of the strange interests of Miss Pearson or Miss Fergusson. And it says something for her that she knew this. She did not know them—was sure they could not want to know her. Both she and they would far rather be left free to go their own way, uninvited and unfettered. So she left them so, half hoping that they recognised her friendly intention in doing so, half fearing that they would think her stiff and unsociable. Never did she dream that her failure to entertain was commonly attributed either to snobbery or to stinginess. Still less did she imagine that Miss Lexington, silently, stoically doing her duty, shouldered this, too, of her Head's burdens and was doggedly polite in her stead.

Miss Parry's entertainment was always the one that Miss Lexington particularly dreaded. Conversation with that lady was often edged and always difficult. But this term she was genuinely anxious to have a quiet talk with her *bête noire*. Miss Parry might be common, but she was also extremely shrewd.

She gathered, from the alacrity with which her invitation was accepted, that Miss Parry was as ready as herself for parley. She made none of those patently insincere hesitations with which she was wont to enhance the value of her acceptance.

"I should *love* to come, thank you," she had breathed fervently. "I want to have a *good long* talk with you."

And she had let her pretty dark eyes rest on Miss Lexington's steady blue ones in a most meaning way. Miss Lexington then knew that the council would be one of grave import.

Even in a state of revolution Miss Lexington would always preserve the decencies. Though both she and her guest were burning to begin on the topic that obsessed them day and night, not one word of it—not even of "shop"—could be breathed while the teapot, that symbol of social as distinct from professional relationships, still adorned the table; but when it had been removed and cigarettes were lighted, the atmosphere became more genial.

"I suppose you know," Miss Lexington began, "that Miss Gilbert will be leaving at Christmas?"

"I heard a rumour. She's very wise to go while she can."

"Isn't she? How I wish I could!"

"Ah! ... But it's too late for us. I—well, if you'll *promise* not to breathe a *word,* I'll tell you a secret. I made some enquahries last holidays, just to see. ... You see, I knew of course what was goin' to happen in the Senior, though 'f course I didn't guess *how* bad it would be. And I knew that when the fuss began to be made by the Education Committee, *she* would be sure to blame it on to me—say the girls hadn't been prop'ly prepared in the lower forms and all that."

Miss Lexington nodded.

"I know," she murmured.

"And it isn't *true*, Miss Lexington!" cried the small lady, sitting bolt upright in her eager indignation. "You know yourself that they're thor'ly well grounded up to the Lower Fourths. ..."

"Yes, I know. You're most thorough with them."

The plump little figure relaxed.

"Yes. Well, where was I?"

"You thought she'd attribute her bad results to you."

"I *knew* she would! So I went to one or two agencies—just to see, you know, if there'd be a chance. ..."

"Yes?"

The dark head shook despondently.

"Not an earthly! They all said the same. 'We can't hold out any hopes,' they all said. 'You see, you're at the maximum salary, and we have plenty of young teachers on our books ready to begin low down the Scale. Besides,' they said, 'it looks bad to leave a school in the winter, after twelve years' service.' And it does, you know."

"I know," sighed the other, worried. "It's the same for me, of course, and for Miss Reeve and Miss Lovell and Miss Fergusson. ... But you know, Miss Parry, what I'm afraid of is that soon we shall have no choice. We'll *have* to leave."

"You mean—?"

"I mean that this is our very last year. If results are as bad next year as they were this, it means the end of the school—and the end of *us*."

They brooded in sombre silence for a minute or two. Then Miss Parry burst out:

"It's not fair—it's not *fair!* Our results would be all right if it wasn't for *her*. Why should she drag us all down with her? She's responsible. She deserves what she gets, that's what I say. And I tell you, Miss Lexington, I for one won't stand it! I'm not goin' to sit down and twiddle my thumbs while she steals my work and my salary and my pension away from me! I tell you I won't *stand* it!"

"How can you prevent it?" The quiet, restrained voice was in itself a rebuke for the other's angry volubility.

"I can do it all right!" stormed on Miss Parry. "We could do it if we all worked together. We could *make* her resign."

"Ask her to, do you mean?"

"We could do even that, of course. What I meant was, we could make her life a misery to her till she does."

Miss Lexington flushed a little. Torture did not appeal to her as a method of persuasion.

"I think her life is probably a misery to her now," she said quietly.

"I hope it is! Then she may change it."

"Well, you know, Miss Parry, it's not altogether easy—"

"Easy? 'F course it isn't easy. But it's no easier for me—or you."

This was unanswerable. Miss Parry drove it home.

"I can't see why you and I should lose everything just because Miss Cullen has to."

"No. I know what you feel. She is bound to, of course. Even if she struggles through this year the end will come then."

"'Course it will—and too late for us! Her discipline is as bad as ever—worse, I do believe. It makes it very hard for anyone who takes a class after her."

A short silence. Then Miss Parry broke out again.

"She's so *mean*, too—so underhand! You know what I told you weeks ago—that she'd make up to the new Staff? Well, I was right. That Kennedy girl's hand in glove with her already."

"*Is* she? I'd have thought she had more sense."

"She can't know, of course, what the truth of the matter is. She's heard Cullen's version, you see—you can imagine what tale *she's* told, can't you? How we're all so horrid to her, and she feels so ill, and she's so hardly used—yach!"

She positively bounced in her chair in her disgust.

"It's a very great pity, for Miss Kennedy's own sake, if she's really getting intimate there," said Miss Lexington thoughtfully. "It'll damn her with the Head, to begin with; and she has no experience—knows nothing of what school discipline is, or should be—"

"The Head doesn't like her anyhow," declared Miss Parry.

"Doesn't she?" The Second Mistress fixed a thoughtful eye on her junior. Miss Parry, realising how very nearly she had given herself and her relationship with the Head away, blushed slightly.

"I've noticed one or two little things that make me think so," she said, nodding wisely. "You keep a look out and see if you don't agree."

"It's a great pity," said Miss Lexington slowly. "She seemed so much the sort of girl we needed. A nice girl, too, I thought."

"I know ... I wonder ... Of course, if she's only heard Cullen's side. ... Hardly fair, is it, to let her hear only one side when it's such a serious thing. ..."

"You mean, she ought to be told the whole thing? I don't think we can do that quite." Miss Lexington flushed a little as she spoke. There were very great disadvantages in having to form an alliance with a professional grabber, who snatched at weapons, fair or not, as she snatched at every other advantage. In her heart Miss Lexington knew that Miss Cullen was really far more akin to her than this, her chosen ally.

Miss Parry flushed too.

"Oh, I don't mean anything *nasty*, you know. Only just to let her see there *are* two sides. ... It's so unfair to the girl to let her get herself mixed up with a person like that with her eyes shut. ... I owe her an invitation. ..."

"I don't think I'd say anything if I were you," counselled Miss Lexington anxiously. "After all, Miss Cullen may not have told her—"

Miss Parry snorted. There is no other word for it.

"Of *course* she has! She knows she hasn't a friend in the place unless she gets hold of the new Staff who don't know the first thing about it. Of *course* she's told her her side—and a nice tale she'll have made of it, you may depend!"

"Still—"

"It's the girl I'm thinkin' of," Miss Parry pleaded eagerly. "She'll be in such a false position. ... I'll be very discreet, I promise you. I'll just ask her to tea, and—and be very nice to her, you know" —with a little conscious glance—"and show her we all want to be friendly with her, so she needn't stick to one. And I may drop just the least little teeny hint. No more, I promise you."

Miss Lexington felt, and looked, embarrassed. Miss Parry's ways were not her ways. Still, she couldn't exactly say so—and she couldn't ask her not to invite the girl, when everybody was inviting everybody else. ...

"Couldn't we have her together?" she suggested. "I haven't asked her yet, either."

"Oh, if you like! Only I thought that perhaps, as Second Mistress, you mightn't care to share invitations. You never have, you know. It might look a little pointed."

There was always a tiny sense of strain when Miss Parry alluded to Miss Lexington's coveted position. The Staff Mistress hastened to reply.

"Perhaps it might. ... Well, I'll leave it to you, then, to do as you think best. Only do be awfully careful, won't you?—and don't say a word if you think she hasn't heard something already."

"Trust me. ... Hullo, here's someone coming in here—Miss Reeve, isn't it?"

"So it is. Excuse me just a moment."

Joyfully Miss Lexington went to the door to welcome this other ally who was so very much more to her taste than the elegant little diplomatist sitting in her best armchair.

"Hullo! Holding a council of war!" inquired the downright Reeve as she saw Miss Parry. "Give me a cigarette, there's a good soul. I've been on train duty. Thanks. Well, what's it all about? Cullen?"

"Of course."

Miss Reeve, inhaling smoke, nodded.

"'Course it is. Well, come to any conclusions?"

Miss Lexington shook her head.

"There aren't any to come to," she admitted. "We're pretty helpless."

"Mmmmm. Ghastly business. I say, I heard a rumour ..."

She broke off, glancing at the half-open door.

"It's all right. My landlady's out."

"Oh! Well, Rowan's got an uncle in the B. of E., you know, and she says she's heard we may have a change of inspector here soon."

"Well?" Miss Lexington's voice was devoid of interest.

"Well—did you know that Cullen's sister is an inspector?"

"*What?*" They were interested enough now. "Is there any fear—?"

Miss Reeve, slowly expelling a cloud of smoke, nodded. She couldn't help enjoying the situation immensely.

"If we get a change from that devilish Mortimer woman, we'll have Miss Ann Cullen," she said grimly.

The others exchanged alarmed glances.

"In that case—" began Miss Lexington slowly.

"In that case," broke in Miss Parry, shrill with excited anger, "we may as well pack. It's not *Miss Cullen* who'll be blamed for the results of the Senior."

"I'm thinking of taking a six months' course and training to be a housemaid," said Reeve grimly. "It seems to me that there *might* be a demand for me then. There certainly won't be otherwise."

Silence fell. They certainly had food for thought. ...

Miss Lexington was the first to rally.

"After all," she said, with more appearance of hope than she felt, "I don't know that anyone could be worse than that fiend Mortimer. *She's* a friend of Cullen's, too. In fact, I believe it might be better for us if the adverse report were signed by Cullen's sister. Someone at the Board *might* smell a rat."

"*Might!*" Miss Reeve rose. "Well, I mustn't stay. I promised to go round to that Kennedy girl's digs and take her to the Town Library, which she wants to join. I like that girl."

Miss Lexington shot a glance at Miss Parry.

"Do you? I'm glad," she said, slowly and meaningly. "Miss Parry was just saying that it was a pity she should be so much with Miss Cullen."

Reeve grinned broadly.

"Think I might be a good antidote? Poor old Cully, I don't blame her for trying to scrape up a pal or two. Anyway, *I'm* not going to try to put

Kennedy off her," she said. "It's a pity, though, for her to get mixed up in our squabbles at all. P'r'aps she won't. P'r'aps she'll find something real to interest her. She's still fairly young."

And, with malicious pleasure in the knowledge that her last words, at least, must have stung Miss Parry through her hide of vanity, Miss Reeve took her airy departure.

Miss Lexington walked slowly back from the front door to the sitting-room. She, too, had been a little stung. … Somehow, as she saw the plump, discontented, self-centred face awaiting her, she was filled with revulsion. Ugly, incompetent, dangerous though Miss Cullen might be, she was at least a lady. … Miss Lexington felt that things were all wrong. It *couldn't* be that she was going to back Miss Parry against Miss Cullen!—And yet, justice is justice, and Miss Parry certainly had justice on her side. …

With a sigh of perplexity and depression, she rejoined her new ally.

CHAPTER V

Miss Parry and Cupid

It was the fashion—rather a pleasant, sociable fashion—at Besley for the older members of the Staff to ask newcomers out in the first few weeks of term—to ask them to tea, take them for walks or cycle rides, lend them books, and generally do what they could to make life as agreeable and ordinary as possible for their bewildered and generally over-driven new colleagues. Viola had been to two or three such parties, and had enjoyed them all—for she was a sociable soul, and made friends easily—when Miss Parry invited her.

They were in the cloak-room, Viola politely waiting for her senior to finish with the mirror, and meanwhile studying with some attention and great interest the considerable skill and care of that lady's attire.

"Ah y' engaged on Wensd'y aft'nune, Miss Kennedy, aw can you come t' tea with me?" asked Miss Parry suddenly, the ladylike stop full on. It was usually allowed full play on social occasions.

"Thank you, I should like to very much," replied Viola with perfect truth. She was more than a little "intrigued" by this small discontented-looking lady who seemed (curiously, it struck Viola, who made something of a study of people) so very intimate with the unapproachable Miss Lexington.

"Ay live at Naneteen Linden Rood—raahther a naice paht," drawled Miss Parry. "Very *good* rooms, maine ah ... But we'll walk up togethah, shell we, aft' school? Wensday—don't f'get."

Miss Wilson entered as Miss Parry disappeared on her way to her good rooms.

"What *is* her name?" she asked casually. "Never can remember names.

Always want to call Miss Lexington Miss Liddell—on account of the lexicon, I s'pose."

"Whose name?" asked Viola, whose attention had wandered.

"Fat woman with a grievance."

Viola couldn't restrain a chuckle. It was so apt a description—and so far from Miss Parry's own idea of herself.

"Oh!—Parry."

"Parry. 'Course it is. Most 'strornary woman. Talks like a perfect lady, 'nd then forgets to. Never met anything like it, have you? You been to tea there yet?"

"Not yet. I'm going on Wednesday."

"You'll enjoy it. I did. Got to mind your p's and q's, though. She'll give you a fringed hanky and call it a tea serviette."

Viola laughed.

"Why?"

"Why at all, or why 'serviette'?"

"Either. Both."

"Same reason. Thinks it's refined. She'll call the slop-basin a tea-bowl. See if she doesn't. Wonderful woman. Didn't know there was such a woman in the world. ... Aft' you with the soap. Wonder why schools never have soap that'll wash? Tow'l's like brown paper, too. No pumice, no nail-brush—'course, they don't 'xpect us to want luxuries. ..."

"They've hung the mirror in the wrong place, too."

"Yes. That's to mortify your vanity. That's why Pearson's lip-stuff always goes wide o' the mark. ... Say, d'you like cycling?"

"Yes, rather. Walking better."

"'Mm, I can't walk, though—nor cycle much. But enough to get out o' this hole every now and then. Care to come one week-end?"

"I'd like to most awfully."

Viola's tone was sincere. She felt very strongly drawn to this casual-spoken, frail-looking girl who seemed to take life for one big joke.

"Right, then let's. Going? No, don't wait; I've got accounts to do."

❧

Viola was both surprised and dismayed to see, on the Wednesday of the party, that Miss Parry appeared at afternoon school in a rather elaborate and very expensive frock of *crêpe-de-Chine.*

"She must be having a regular party," she thought, with the dismay of youth at such a contretemps. She had a momentary wild idea of rushing back to her rooms after school and changing into some garment that would correspond more or less with her hostess's magnificence; but she abandoned the scheme almost before it was formed.

"Can't help it if there's a dozen duchesses all dressed up to the nines," she thought. "If there are, they'll be so taken up with each other's clothes they'll never notice mine. … But Miss Parry might have warned me that it was a 'posh' party."

"Wait for me after," Miss Parry breathed into her ear as they filed their respective forms into the hall for prayers at the end of the afternoon. "We'll walk up together."

So Viola, soon ready, hung about until Miss Parry, beautiful in unnecessary furs and a coquettish hat, joined her.

"I haven't got a big pahty," Miss Parry began as they walked along, Viola with some difficulty accommodating her long, free swing to the little lady's short and rather breathless walk. "Nevah think it's quaite so naice, do you, as just a little coosy cup all t' ahselves? Just you 'n me 'n Miss Ferg'son. Do you maind?"

Viola murmured something polite. She found Miss Parry a little difficult to talk to. Fortunately she did most of the talking herself.

"It's rahthah a lung way," panted the elder, as the tedious walk extended, "but ay alwes think it's worth it to be in a reahlly *naice* paht, don't you? So open heah, don't you think?"

Viola could see very little difference between Linden Road and any other of the rather dingy little streets in which the Staff had entertained her; but she admired it with enthusiasm. Miss Parry somehow had that rather hypnotising effect on people.

"Rahthah naice room, I alwes think," continued the cicerone, introducing Viola into it. Viola, looking in a kind of mesmerised daze at the conflicting colours, the "smart" hangings and livid jazz cushions side by side with numberless photographs in all the horror of plush and gilt frames, with lodging-house "ornaments," with oleographs and shell-framed mirrors, murmured congratulations on the apartment.

"*Soo* glad you laike it," beamed Miss Parry. "I alwes laike people to say just what they *think*, you knoo, but no one evah fainds fault with may taste. ... *Do* sit daown. We won't wait for Miss Ferg'son, naughty girl, she is, late again. ... Oo, theah she is. ... Come along, Trixie. We were just gooin' to staht withaout you."

"*Trixie!*" thought Viola in fascinated admiration, as Miss Fergusson, large, fat and forty, strode heavily in. Viola had the common trick of "fitting" Christian names to people, and "Belinda," called Bell for short, had struck her as the appropriate name to attach to Miss Fergusson's "B," since Blowsabel was presumably out of the question.

The tea was as elaborate as Miss Parry's frock, and Viola, with the frank greediness of the early twenties, rejoiced to see the spread of chocolate biscuits, Simnel cake and other delicacies awaiting attack. She only regretted that the tea was a "polite" one. After school dinner she could have done full justice to that generous catering.

"*Such* nice rooms, *aren't* they, Miss Kennedy?" gushed Miss Fergusson, handing food. "They'd be *rather* nice anyhow, but Miss Parry has *such* taste. That's what I always say—such *taste*! So artistic, don't you think, the gen'ral effect?"

Viola had long ago discovered that all that was required of her at these junctures was a polite and undistinguishable murmur. She didn't need to lie actively.

"And a *treasure* of a landlady, haven't you, Milly?" Miss Fergusson burbled on.

"She is rahthah a deah," simpered Miss Parry. "Devoted to me, you know."

"Oh, *devoted!*"

"She does *ev'rything* for me," Miss Parry continued, turning to Viola. "Looks after m' clothes—does m' little bits o' mendin' for me—shampoos m' hair. She *lahves* it. She's laike a mothah t' me, reahlly she is. ... Pooah old soul, she's gettin' very old and rheumatic. I nevah do an'thin' to give her unnecess'ry trahble, of course."

Viola, remembering the mending and shampooing, felt mildly astonished at this. She also wondered why, in a house presumably her own, a landlady who suffered from rheumatism should live in a basement overlooking a stream.

"I wonder she doesn't use the room behind this one," she remarked, "instead of having to go up and down from the basement."

"Oo, she did at one taime, but she said she didn't feel free to hev vis'tors in—I must be quaite quayet, you know, in th' evenings—and so she desayded she'd rahtah leave me *quaite* undisturbed. Then we *both* feel at lib'ty, you see. ... But she's so abs'lutely devoted to me, she'd do anything I asked. I don't know *what* she'd do if I left! ... Thu' of course, as things are, it looks as if I maight *hev* to. ..." She sighed profoundly.

"Oh, don't say that!" pleaded Miss Fergusson. "The school wouldn't be itself without you, Milly, after all these years. They'd never *let* you go."

"You never know," rejoined Miss Parry, suddenly forgetful of refinement in her eagerness. "What with *traitors* about you, and such ingratitude and trickery as there is in the world—"

Viola felt thoroughly bewildered. No doubt she also looked it, for Miss Fergusson turned from her role of general admirer to that of explanatory chorus.

"Such a *difficult* position, isn't it, Miss Kennedy?" she cooed.

"I'm afraid I hardly know what it is," Viola replied. "I gathered that there was a good deal of—of restlessness and so on; but I don't at all understand why."

"I *thought* you didn't!" cried the now excited Miss Parry. "I said to meself, when I saw you walkin' home with a certain lady, 'She doesn't know,' I thought, 'and it's a shame to keep her in the dark, hearin' things all wrong.' So I thought I'd just drop you a hint."

"Always so thoughtful!" murmured Miss Fergusson.

Viola glanced sharply at her, hoping to surprise a twinkle; but she was perfectly serious. The tone of rapt admiration was no doubt a true index of her feeling.

"You see," Miss Parry began, "it's always been rather difficult here. Of course I ought to've had a very diff'rent position here years ago; but they put a new-comer in over my head. It was rather hard on me; but I hope I know how t' ooverlook *pers'nal* grievances."

She dropped her eyes as she made this avowal. Viola, completely bewildered by the sudden change from one voice to the other, found nothing to say—particularly as the reference was, to her ignorance, so obscure as to be unintelligible. She knew nothing of the old Lexington–Parry feud.

"I always *did* say you behaved like a perfect *angel* over that!" cried the enthusiastic Miss Fergusson.

"Naughty girl!" Miss Parry reproved her fondly. "You mustn't take any notice of her, Miss Kennedy. She *will* say these things. ... Well, as I say, I let that pass." Again excitement overcame gentility in the eager voice. "But now—well, now it's more than a question of precedence. It's a matter of life or death to me! Do you know what's happening here, Miss Kennedy? *One woman, to save her own skin, is plottin' to finish the school.* And I shall be one of the first to suffer."

Viola felt very much startled. For a moment she wondered whether Miss Parry suffered from delusions. But Miss Fergusson seemed as solemn as her idol; and, with all her faults, Viola had seen how shrewd Miss Parry was. Yet it was a most curious remark. ...

"But how can any one woman—except, perhaps, the Head—do that?" she asked.

Miss Parry emitted a bitter laugh. Miss Fergusson shook a mournful head and contemplated the tea-leaves in her cup.

"We-e-ll," drawled Miss Parry, her shrewd eyes fixed on Viola's puzzled face, "you know what ar failure's due to, don't you?"

"I understood it was the French results in the Senior."

"Exactly. And don't you see what excuse will be given when the authorities inquire about those failures? Why, that the girls aren't properly grounded lower down the school. ... And it's very hard on me, for if there *is* one thing I *do* know, it's how to teach French. But, you see, the school doesn't take a junior exam., so I can't prove it; and so that's where the blame will be laid. ... Hev s'm moah tea."

At this point Miss Fergusson, with a glance at her watch, exclaimed in horror that she was overdue at the meeting of the Town Hockey Club, to which she, by virtue of her one-time position as games mistress, was attached as honorary member. Would they excuse her if she ran away now? No, she'd let herself out—no one was to move. "Good-bye—good-bye—such a lovely tea, dear Milly."

"You must thank Miss Jefferson for that," smiled Miss Parry, waving an affectionate hand. "I reahlly *cahn't* cater for m'self," she explained to Viola. "I know I don't look ahfter m'self a bit, but I cahn't help it—I s'poose I'm rahthah ascetic in thoose ways."

Viola murmured congratulations.

"Weel, as I was sayin' … it's rahthah hard on me, you see, this exam. question, because I never have a chance to show my level. So if—a certain lady—I needn't mention names, need I?—likes to say that the girls come up to her so badly prepared that she can't cover the senior ground in the time, she's believed. And so *I*, who've been here over twelve years and never had a failure with any single girl, will be called incompetent and—probably—asked to go."

"But that's disgraceful!" exclaimed Viola. "Are you *sure*, Miss Parry? I mean—it seems impossible that any decently brought-up person should do a thing like that, don't you think?"

"To you or me—yes, quite imposs'ble. But ev'ryone doesn't tehke an hon'rable view of things, not when their own safety's concerned. … Well, there's no good in talkin', I s'pose. …"

She sighed heavily. There was a sudden and most curious likeness, to Viola's eyes, between her and her antipathy, Miss Cullen. How both would have resented her saying so!—yet it was true enough, and Viola felt now for her the uncomprehending and instinctive pity she had so often felt for the other woman. Her affectations and pettinesses seemed momentarily to have dropped from her. Just at this moment, in her genuine anxiety and trouble, a simple and bewildered expression in her pretty eyes, her face falling into the lines of old age and worry, Miss Parry was pathetic, and attractive as Viola had never before found her.

"Let's talk of somethin' moah cheeahful," said Miss Parry, brightening up. "Ah you int'rested in photos?"

Without waiting for a reply, she rose and proceeded to hand various efforts of photographic art to Viola, who, like most of us under the same circumstances, vainly racked her brains for appropriate comments. She wondered irritably as she did so why anyone thinks that the portraits of people, unknown even by name, can conceivably be of interest to a stranger. One cannot even say "That's a good likeness," or "What a libel," or any of the other silly things one says when one knows the original.

"Heah's *rahthah* a naice one," said Miss Parry, handing a portrait evidently cut from a "high-class" magazine. "I wanted to hev one uv him in unifawm—a navy man, I alwes think you can tell, don't you, even in mufti—somethin' so feahless in the express'n—but I couldn't get one. He's a peeah—ay'd better not give his actchal taytle, even to you, but an Ayrish peeah … West Ahland, soo romentic, I alwes think, don't you? I maight have been a peahress to-day if I'd've said so … but I alwes think merrige soo hollow, don't you, without true lahve?"

"I'm afraid I don't know. I've never tried."

Miss Parry ignored the levity. Probably she didn't hear.

"Yes … pooah boy, he felt it very much, I'm afraid. … I sometaimes wish I'd've said yes. … But it was a queschun of principle with me. I'm Haigh, you know, and he was a Nonconformist. Soo I sent him aweh. …"

She sighed. Viola found nothing to say beyond an inane:

"How romantic!"

"It wus, wusn't it? Yes. Pooah boy. He nevah got oover it. They say he died with may name on his lips."

Viola jumped. She felt as if the correct response was, "Dead, Mr. Peggotty?" but she merely said:

"Oh! Is—is he dead?"

Miss Parry bowed a complacently mournful head.

"He jahst couldn't beah laife withaout me. … You understand, don't you? … Of cawce I nevah tell anyone his name."

Viola reflected that, if she had been curious, it would not have been difficult to discover the name of a Nonconformist Irish peer, especially if he held a naval commission and (presumably) committed suicide. But she wasn't curious; and besides, she had strong doubts as to the existence of this impetuous and improbable nobleman. She felt sure that she had seen that magazine picture before; she dimly connected the regular and insipid features with the stage.

"This," said her hostess, handing her yet another picture, a real "studio portrait" this time—"this is *such* a deah boy. Trevor, his name is—sweet name, ay alwes think."

"He looks very young," said Viola incautiously.

"Oo, yes—well, oold enough to know what he wants!" said the charmer with a conscious smile. "But I woon't give him an ahnswer yet. I alwes think it's soo difficult to reahlly know one's own haht, don't you?"

Viola longed to giggle. She knew so well what she was required to say—what Miss Fergusson would have said positively lusciously. The photograph was one of a mild youth in the very early twenties—Viola felt sure that he must be younger than herself—and Miss Parry! ... Viola did her the usual injustice of putting her down at forty two or three. ...

"It's a very great responsibility," she said solemnly.

"Thet's what I alwes feel. Two laives—perhaps *moah*, you nevah *know*, do you? But ay doon't know. I may take it on. I hev a very strong sense of duty. ... Oo, must you goo already? *Soo* naice hevin' you. I alwes knew you'd understand, if you reahlly knew how things weah. ... Rahthah hahd, don't you think, not to be able to put one's self raight? ... Yes, ... Well, g'dbay. See you t'morrow."

Viola felt extraordinarily relieved to be out in the open air. She grinned from ear to ear as she thought of Trevor and the anonymous peer; but it wasn't, she told herself, altogether a grinnable matter. It told rather a dreadful tale, that craving of this woman in middle life for the romantic excitements that belong, if at all, to passionate youth. And she had room, too, for sympathy with the real anxiety and bitterness that underlay the idiocy and selfishness and conceit. She wondered, as she swung on her way with a rapidity that gave vent to her long-repressed impatience, whether it could be true that Miss Cullen would do a thing like that—let an innocent person suffer—and suffer so cruelly—for her fault. Miss Cullen had seemed a decent sort, Viola had thought—queer, of course, but straight and kind, nothing mean about her. ... But Miss Parry was very shrewd, and the fact that Miss Lexington was clearly on her side spoke strongly for her. Already Viola had a great respect for Miss Lexington's judgment. ... It was all very odd and rather beastly, she thought, as she settled down to four solid hours of corrections and preparation for the next day. Even as she opened the first book a chuckle escaped her at the memory of the victims of Cupid in Miss Parry's collection.

"I wonder if she spotted it when I grinned," she thought. "If I see much of her I'll have to practise saying the things Trixie does without a quiver. ... All the same, the school part is *rotten*." And she sighed deeply.

She had, of course, no idea how much more profoundly that sigh was echoed by Miss Cullen, who had seen her emerge from Miss Parry's rooms rather later than the customary hour for departing after a tea-party, with a beaming smile irradiating her face—and who naturally feared that she had lost yet another friend in her coming struggle for existence.

CHAPTER VI
Round Robin

"Lexo and Parry seem to be getting very chummy," remarked Miss Rowan one Thursday morning as she struggled from her "civvies" into her abbreviated gym. tunic. "They're walking to school together to-day. Passed 'em on my bike."

"I know," rejoined Miss Reeve. "Unholy alliance, what? I always said if ever those two *did* combine we should see stars. But I never thought they could." She threw an uneasy glance round as she ended her incautious speech to see whether either of the two ladies in question, or Miss Cullen, were within hearing. She was only just in time. The next moment Miss Lexington and Miss Parry entered the tiny cloak-room; and it was patent to the blindest that their recently finished conversation had been a momentous one.

Miss Lexington also threw a general's eye round the assembled company.

"Can you all stay for a few minutes after school to-day for a quite informal Staff meeting?" she asked. "Don't say anything about it, please, even to each other—we don't want any discussion. And—and people who are free this afternoon won't be wanted."

She flushed a little as she said this; and the astute Reeve immediately ran over in her mind the names of those mistresses who were off duty on Thursday afternoons.

"Moore—those two new ones, Jervis and Kennedy—and old Cullen," she thought. "Something to be kept quiet from Cullen, then. The others don't count."

The obedient Staff said not a word; but all that morning there was an atmosphere of suppressed excitement, and mistresses, encountering each other in corridors or the doorways of class-rooms, exchanged looks of grave import. So you might imagine a Cabinet Minister might look when dissolution is in the air.

After school that afternoon they congregated in the Staff Room with much more alacrity than the usual Staff meeting evoked. Something was in the wind—something serious. This would not be a meeting to discuss girls' chances in examinations or to arrange some new distribution of duties. Here, their own fates would be discussed by themselves. ...

Miss Lexington opened the meeting.

"I don't want this to be a long or a formal meeting," she began, "but some of us feel that we ought, as a body, to discuss the situation caused by this year's exam. results, and—and try to take some step to safeguard the future. You all know, I expect, what the general position is; but if you will allow me, I will just go over the main points that arise.

"First, we all know that the school is in as dangerous a position as any school can well be. Our efficiency is judged by our examination results, and our examination results are unspeakably bad. That means, to the Board of Education, that all of us—*all* of us—are unspeakably bad too. And that means—well, it means the end for a good many of us. ...

"We can't keep things dark, of course. Already no decent agency will look at our requirements. Only those who have no choice at all would take a post here. And of course that means, normally, that we shall get an increasingly bad and inefficient Staff; and then our failures won't be due—as they are now—to one person only."

A significant glance went round. They knew that now she was getting to the crux of the matter. Miss Lexington went on:

"Things are no better this term than they were last. Last year's IVa and IVb aren't going to get through the Senior this year. How can they? We all know their attitude to—to certain members of the Staff. They won't work for people they despise. Well, the conclusion's obvious. Next year's results will be as bad, or worse, than they were this year. And that will mean—the end of the school."

They had known it—but they could not restrain a gasp when their secret fears were thus bluntly spoken.

"Now, I don't want to be hard on anyone. I know how hard life is for us all; I think I may say that I have a more intimate acquaintance with circumstances than perhaps any of you realise." (The Staff exchanged glances. Each was wondering exactly how much Miss Lexington knew of her circumstances, and recognising that she probably knew a very great deal.) "But what I feel is—that things are hard for us all. We cannot afford to take risks. And, in this case, the many are clearly suffering for the one. If the school is closed—and I *know* that that is more than a possibility—is it likely that we shall get new posts—any of us? Do you know that in a small country High School in the west the other day, four hundred people were in for one English post, and over two hundred for a science one? And we're dear—all of us. We're all above the minimum salary. We're a drug on the market. When Governors can take their choice of hundreds, is it likely that they'll take expensive people from a school that's been closed for inefficiency? And even if that doesn't happen—if it's only those mistresses who have trained girls for the exams. who get their *congé*—that means that seven of us at least must go—seven, whose work is admittedly efficient. We all know what that will mean for those seven. They will never get another teaching post—not with that behind them, and a salary above the lowest. They will forfeit not only their salaries but their pensions, and not only their pensions but all the sums they have compulsorily contributed to the fund. ..."

"Well, that's the situation. What do you advise?"

"The *solution's* obvious," drawled Miss Parry.

"Yes. But how is it to be effected?" asked Miss Reeve. "*We* can't suggest to other members of the Staff that they might resign."

"Well, but look here," broke in Miss Rowan, "it's clear that if the incapables don't go before next term we shall *all* be in the soup. And if they don't see it we must make 'em."

"But that's just the point—how *can* we?" asked gentle Miss Gilbert. "It's clear enough now, to anyone who looks, what ought to be done. ..."

There was a little pause. No one quite liked to take the next step. At last Miss Lexington spoke again.

"I feel this so strongly," she said, "that I've been to Miss Barr about it.

I—I didn't ask, in so many words, that she should dismiss—any of the Staff; but she couldn't help knowing. ... Well, she said that she didn't feel that she could ask anyone to resign. She pointed out that if any mistress who is at the maximum salary were asked to leave it means the end of everything for that mistress. ... Of course, it does. And it will next year, for all of us who are at the maximum. The Governors won't consider us as the Head considers—one of us."

"Whut ay suggest," said Miss Parry, beginning in her most refined voice, "is that we wrayte a letter to Miss Barr, saigned bay us all, telling her how we all feel ah futchah endangered bay one member of the Staff, and requestin' her to ahsk that member to resaign."

Miss Rowan emitted a soft whistle.

"Bit thick," she muttered. Miss Parry heard her.

"It'd *have* to come next year," she said, refinement immediately forgotten in anxiety. "It only means two terms sooner for her, and perhaps never for us. Reahlly," with a rapid recovery, "ay doon't see the point in sparin' *one* for jahst two terms at the cost of soo much."

This was true enough. Then the silent Miss Lovell spoke.

"What would you say in such a round robin as you suggest?" she asked.

"Oh—well, what would you suggest, Miss Lexington?" Miss Parry snatched eagerly at the sign of weakening.

"Something like this, we thought." The honest Miss Lexington immediately overthrew the suggestion that this idea was an impromptu one. "That the Staff, seeing the gravity of the situation caused by the examination results, and seeing no prospect of improvement under the present *régime*, request the Head Mistress to consider the wisdom of asking—a certain lady—to tender her resignation."

They considered this.

"Too mild," opined Miss Pearson's harsh voice. "Miss Barr wouldn't pay the least attention."

"Perhaps you're right." Miss Lexington tried some sentences on a sheet of paper. Miss Pearson's dark eyes stole sideways to catch her reflection in a glass-fronted bookcase.

"You do all think this a good move?" Miss Lexington suddenly asked.

The Staff exchanged glances.

"Would you all give your opinions, starting here, at my left, and going all round the table? Miss Lovell, what do you think?"

"Yes. I think if she won't go herself she ought to be asked to. As Miss Parry says, she would be dismissed next summer in any case, and—it would mean the rest of us, then."

"Miss Gilbert?"

"Y-yes, I suppose so."

"Miss Parry?"

"*Yes.*"

"Miss Rowan?"

"Oh, I—suppose so. Rotten business," muttered that lady.

"Miss Reeve?"

"I agree with Miss Rowan in every respect."

"Does anyone oppose?"

No one spoke.

There was a short pause. Then Miss Lexington said: "Then—we'd better do it. This is what I've written:

Dear Miss Barr,

The undersigned members of this Staff, having considered the extremely grave situation caused by the examination results of this year, and seeing no prospect of improvement under existing conditions, have decided to take the serious step of asking you to request the resignation of the lady to whom those results were due. The Staff consider that the future both of the school and themselves is gravely endangered by the present state of affairs; and they feel that if their request cannot be acceded to they must ask you to receive their resignations.

Is *that* strong enough?"

A few alterations were proposed and made; and Miss Lexington proceeded to make a fair copy.

"Here it is," she said a few moments later. "Will you all sign, please?"

One by one, with grave faces and troubled eyes, they did so. They felt, most of them, that they were signing Miss Cullen's death-warrant; but then, as Miss Parry had said, that was merely a question of time; and, by signing hers, they might save the lives of the rest. ... Still, reason is not a comforting poultice to a sore conscience, and it was a very silent group that signed the letter.

The school premises were supposed to be closed to the Staff at five. This rule was made out of regard for the caretaker, whose duty it was to lock up the school, rather than for the Staff, who had to carry home their loads of exercise books instead of correcting them on the spot. Miss Barr told herself, and made herself think, that it was so *much* better for the mistresses not to be eternally on the school premises, and that she had their interests in view as well as those of the caretaker, in permitting this mandate to be passed without one dissentient voice. But since both she and the caretaker himself had more consideration for the hard-worked Staff than the Olympians who had (without the smallest personal knowledge of the school or its work) framed the code of school laws, it was generally possible to get the door opened for one or locked after one if one simply had to break the rule.

Thus it was that when Miss Cullen, starting on her preparation for the next day's work, realised that she had inadvertently destroyed, along with some waste paper, a sheet of valuable notes for her Sixth Form lesson, she thought she would go up to the school, despite the lateness of the hour, in case the Staff Room had not yet been put to rights and its waste-paper basket emptied.

She got in easily enough, and Carson, hearing her tale of woe, offered to let her stay as long as she liked and lock up later. Had she known it, Miss Cullen had a strong potential ally in Carson, who, as he said to his wife, "did know a lady when he see one, if she *was* a bit rum."

"The other mistresses 'aven't bin gone so very long, miss," he informed her, unlocking the door, "so you'll find the Staff Room as it was left."

"That's very late, surely?" said Miss Cullen. "Was there a Staff meeting, Carson, do you know?"

"Something o' that, miss, I dessay. They was all 'ere, Miss Rowan an' all, so it must've bin a meetin'. ... Shall I wait, miss, or come back again after?"

"I may be some minutes looking through the basket. I'll tell you, Carson, when I'm going. Thank you so much."

There was a good deal of litter in the waste-paper basket, and Miss Cullen soon found that the only way of retrieving her lost page of notes would be to look over every scrap in the collection. A tiresome job, and it would take up a good deal of her precious time, but it would be quicker than thinking the whole thing out again and looking up her examples and quotations. It had taken over an hour to prepare that lesson.

She had not got very far, and she certainly had not found her notes, when she stopped looking. She held in her hand a sheet of paper on which someone had made various attempts at an address—or was it a letter?

This Staff, considering ... gravity of the situation ... request the resignation ... exam. results. ...

A Staff meeting after school—held secretly. A Staff meeting to which she had not been asked. ... There was only one construction to be put on it. ...

Slowly, for she felt quite stunned by the magnitude of the catastrophe that had befallen her, she put two and two together. They had held that meeting about her. They had asked the Head to make her resign. ... This was indeed the end.

She carefully put the paper back into the basket and walked out of the school with the precision and care of one half blind.

"I've finished, Carson, thank you," she called mechanically as she passed the door leading in to the caretaker's premises.

"Thank you, miss. Found the paper, miss, I hope?"

"The paper—oh, yes, thank you. ... Yes, I found the paper. ..."

❦

She walked home in a kind of bewildered anguish. She could not plan anything—could not even think clearly. She reached her lodgings in the same helpless, stunned state of mind that the discovery of the draft of the Round Robin had left her in.

Presently, sitting in her own room, her thoughts began to clear. She could look at the thing squarely. With the danger so imminent, she must act—act vigorously and at once.

"There are only three courses open to me," she concluded at last. "One is to ask Miss Lexington not to present that letter. To tell her everything, and ask her for her help. That I will never do. She knows enough to know how I am placed. I *will not* appeal to a friend of Miss Parry's. Or, I might resign myself, before they present that letter. That—no, I've thought that over often enough. I can't do it. I must avoid going if I possibly can. And the last course—I don't like it—it hardly seems. ... And yet, it's not as unfair as what they're doing. It would only be asking for an unbiased opinion. I have every right to make an appeal. ... I'll do it."

Hurriedly, almost furtively, she rose and went to her desk. She took a sheet of her very best note-paper and a pad of rough paper on which to make drafts of what she would say. For this must be the best, the most convincing letter she had ever written in her life.

"They dislike Miss Barr at Stamborough," she thought as she dipped her pen. "And how very fortunate that it is Miss Mortimer who is inspecting in this district just now. Miss Mortimer knows dear Ann so well. She'll be glad to hear what I have to tell her. ... But it mustn't be too personal. I want it to have the official ring about it. ..."

She began to write. As she did so her indignation, and a kind of righteous wrath, kindled her imagination until to herself she really seemed the victim she wished to be thought. She forgot that she had ever admitted any kind of weakness. She was a scapegoat, a victim to the selfish panic of her colleagues, who had taken the underhand step of asking the Head to dismiss her. ... Her eyes positively flashed behind her glasses as she composed the letter.

She wrote several drafts before she was satisfied; but at last she achieved a letter that suited her. Critically she read it through.

Dear Miss Mortimer [she read] *I cannot but feel some hesitation in writing to you; but I feel that I owe it, not only to myself but to the school I serve, to ask you if you can, without great inconvenience, pay us a surprise visit of inspection with the special aim of investigating certain conditions in the school.*

I am aware that it is, to say the least of it, a little unusual for an assistant mistress to correspond on such a subject with His Majesty's Inspector; but your acquaintance—I might almost say your friendship—with my sister, Miss Ann Cullen, the Inspector, encourages me to draw your attention to certain facts which have been concealed from you.

I feel sure that, during your last year's visits of inspection after the deplorable results of that year's examinations, you realised that under existing conditions no mistress here can do the work required of her with satisfaction to herself or value to the school. The organisation is, as you know, faulty, and all representations to the Head Mistress are ignored; the preparatory work is, in my subject, at least, neither thorough nor accurate—a fact which is not apparent, since no junior or preliminary public examination is taken, so that the bad results in the senior forms are naturally attributed to one who is not entirely responsible for them.

(During the many drafts of this masterpiece, that sentence had been erased and replaced innumerable times; but now, feeling herself the oppressed rather than the oppressor, and knowing Miss Parry to be behind the intrigue against her, she permitted it to stay, and silenced a protesting conscience ruthlessly.)

You are, I know, aware of the almost impossible conditions under which some of us are expected to work. I think that in all probability you have realised that the personal element increases the difficulty, already overwhelming, against which I personally have to contend. Not only is every obstacle put in my way, but the work I achieve is ignored, my abilities questioned, my protests about the conduct of children dismissed, and my position generally rendered almost intolerable.

("That'll fetch her," thought the scribe, quite unconsciously, as memory of the feud between the Head and the Inspector recurred to her.)

I am convinced that if you will, at your earliest convenience, pay a visit of inspection with these facts before you, you will see to it that justice is done. That is all I ask.

She signed it with a distinct feeling of pleasure. It was, she told herself, *true*—true in every word. No one could deny what she had written. All she wanted was justice, impartial justice, and that she would never get, either from her colleagues or the Head. ... And she liked the tone of the letter; it seemed to her to be both independent and courteous, warm and yet restrained.

She felt a glow of triumph, almost of virtue, as she dropped that epistle, heavy with the fate of the school, into a pillar-box.

It was not until she got into bed that she remembered that the notes for that lesson had never been retrieved. ...

CHAPTER VII

Intrigue

Miss Barr always made it her boast that she was the first person to arrive in school. Whether she had any special task or not, she was always in her study at 8.30. If she had been asked what she did there, she would have replied, with a kind but weary smile, that no one who had not held the post could imagine the host of small tasks that fall to the lot of a head mistress. This is quite true, of an efficient head mistress; of Miss Barr it was not. But she did not know that it was not, and she liked—(as many of us do; I do myself)—to feel the importance of being what the Scotch call "throng." She felt then that she was giving herself, body and soul, to the sacred cause of Education.

There was a considerable pile of correspondence awaiting her this morning; a note from a parent complaining of a child's detention—another complaining of her girl's home work—another complaining that Juliet was very backward in arithmetic and "seemed to have no heart in her work"—another requesting that Ada might have individual attention in drill—another asking that Hilda might have special coaching in French out of school hours. Just as, to parents and children, school teachers seem a race apart, so, to the average teacher (and especially to the average Head) "parents" are a species differing from the rest of mankind—a strange, irritable, unreasonable, powerful, maddening race, to be alternately bullied and cajoled—a race from whom one extorts cash, and on whom one occasionally, on Speech Days and such *festas,* lavishes food and compliments. I don't know what parents think, for I never was one myself; but I know that a child of ten, whose mother took paying guests, once, in round-eyed astonishment, reported to the rest of her form, that Miss Jones (who was her own form mistress and her mother's boarder), "ate *meat*, just like an *ordinary* lady." The form could hardly believe it. ...

Miss Barr threw aside the communications of the Accursed Tribe. They irritated her, and she was already tired and anxious enough. Her secretary could answer them on her own initiative. What else was there?

There was a square envelope addressed in an unusual, upstanding, determined hand—Miss Lexington's hand. What could this be? Miss Barr, as she looked at it, had a horrid fear that it might be a resignation.

The Round Robin did not take her entirely by surprise. It annoyed her extremely; but she had thought yesterday that something was in the wind. Head Mistresses, if they are sensitive at all, become exceedingly sensitive to the atmosphere about the Staff. Miss Barr was far too consistent to swear, but that is what she would have liked to do had it occurred to her. This really was too dreadful. ... She could not ignore it; she could not refuse; she hated having to yield to such a request. Had she not thought a hundred times of taking this very step, and refrained every time when she considered what it would mean to that unfortunate woman whom she so much disliked and pitied? ... She sat tapping her desk, pondering.

She hated the thought of asking Miss Cullen to resign. Her motives were mixed, of course—motives nearly always are—but the two chief ones were quite genuine and sympathetic compassion, and a hatred of "unpleasantness." It is true that the second of these was the stronger; but, to do her justice, the first was quite robust.

"What could she do if I dismissed her?" she thought. "Poor thing, no one would ever *look* at her for a respectable post. I couldn't in common honesty give her a testimonial. ... She would simply go under. ... And how very unpleasant it would be to tell her she must go! How *very* unpleasant. Most distressing. I really don't think I *can*. Really, the present Staff is most overbearing and inconsiderate. ..."

Was there a loophole? She looked through the objectionable communication again. "Future, both of the school and themselves, seriously endangered. ..." How absurdly exaggerated! ... "If their request cannot be acceded must ask me to accept their resignations. ..." It sounded quite determined. ... Well, of course, better one than all—especially such a one. But how very unpleasant, and what a scene there would be. … She must convey to Miss Lexington how very much she disliked these violent coercive methods. …

Still, under all her irritation and discomfiture, her chief feeling was now one of rending pity for this necessary victim of the god Efficiency. Miss Barr was, as timid, deprecating women often are, highly imaginative. Generally this vision was personal—a sympathetic comprehension of the attitude of others towards herself, and an instinctive correspondence to the requirements of the situation thus caused; but now she could see and feel entirely for another person—could feel the humiliation and distress, the growing despair which must inevitably follow on the sentence which justice and expediency alike demanded she should pass. …

There were minor irritations, too. It would mean a visit to the County Education Office at Stamborough, and they were so very—well, inhuman—there. She hated going. She hated seeing Miss Cullen. … At that moment she hated the Staff, the school, the children, the life, the very word Education.

She'd have to see Miss Lexington at once, she supposed, and give her some sort of answer. There would be a conversation in which Miss Lexington would be sure to be aggressive. She would have to promise to see Miss Cullen before the day was out. She did so hate to be *rushed* into things. …

Suddenly she had a bright idea. She rang her bell.

"Mrs. Carson," she said, as the caretaker's wife appeared, "I shall not be here to dinner to-day. I have to go to Stamborough. Miss Lexington will be in charge."

"Excellent," she exulted as the woman withdrew and she seized on a time-table. "I can think the whole thing out in the train, away from the conflicting elements here. And I must go to Stamborough sooner or later. After all, I needn't say anything to them to-day about this distressing situation. If I get an idea of some way of dealing with it, I can speak; if I don't, I need say nothing—yet. If the Staff like to think that my reason for going is connected with this effusion of theirs, they can. I am not deceiving them in the very slightest degree."

She rang again. If Mrs. Carson looked annoyed, Miss Barr did not, as she commonly did, notice it. She was too delighted at having discovered a temporary refuge.

"Will you ask Miss Lexington to come to me, please?" she said, still tracking from column to column elusive trains that took incredible hours to get from Besley to the twenty-mile distance of Stamborough.

Mrs. Carson went out in grim silence. She was the type of servant that dislikes and despises a "considerate" employer but will slave for a tyrant. Miss Barr was always considerate to her maids, and Mrs. Carson made her pay for it. But she obeyed her in outward things. In a few moments Miss Lexington appeared; and Miss Barr, probably because she expected it, thought her air disgustingly eager and self-assertive.

"Miss Lexington, I want you to take charge here today," began the Head. She paused an impressive moment before adding, "I find I have to go to Stamborough—on very important business."

Their eyes met. Miss Lexington flushed a little, partly with embarrassment, but chiefly with triumph.

"We've scared her," she thought. "She's going to move at once. ... Very well, Miss Barr," she replied aloud.

"There's nothing of importance to tell you, I think," continued the Head, looking at her diary. "No, nothing that won't keep till I can deal with it myself. (*That'll* show her if she can run the school!) Thank you, Miss Lexington. Perhaps you will take prayers? I have only just time for my train."

Miss Lexington was delighted to take prayers; not that she liked the actual performance—she loathed it, though preferring her own version to the Head's; but it meant that Miss Barr was in action. She had never expected so swift a reply to the Staff's challenge.

The Second Mistress returned to the Staff Room with a sparkle in her eye, and, drawing Miss Parry aside, confided to her the glad news. After all, it was her right. She was more affected than anyone.

It spread with the rapidity of all news in a congregation of women. Faces brightened with the joy of battle and the dawn of hope. At last a definite step had been taken. At last a little progress had been made.

The most immovable obstruction to the school's chances might soon be removed.

The "new Staff" felt, of course, that something was in the wind—something rather pleasantly exciting. Two of them retained the reserve proper to their condition as newcomers; but Miss Jervis's curiosity and desire to be "in it" overcame all such propriety—if, indeed, it ever occurred to her. Miss Pearson seemed to her a good source from which to get information. Miss Jervis hoped already for Miss Pearson's friendship; for though each thought the other "common," and so spoke of her to the rest of the Staff, there was enough likeness between them to make them both dislike each other and fly to each other for a sympathetic point of view. Soon, no doubt, they would be as necessary to each other as Miss Parry and Miss Fergusson.

"I say, Miss Pearson," whispered Miss Jervis hoarsely, "what's the excitement? What's happened about Miss Cullen?" For although she had been studiously omitted from yesterday's meeting, Miss Jervis was quite shrewd enough to guess that the French mistress was the stormy petrel.

Miss Pearson threw a wary glance round. She was torn between a desire to snub Miss Jervis as an inquisitive new-comer and the longing, which most women know, to impart an exciting piece of news. The latter was on the whole the more attractive.

"Why," she breathed, an anxious eye lifting for the approach of any other mistress—she did not want to gain the reputation of a "blabber"—"don't you know? Oh, no, of course, being *new*, you wouldn't. We—the senior members of the Staff—are in such a dangerous position through Miss Cullen's incompetence—"

"Oh, I *know*!" burst in Miss Jervis. "*Hopeless*, isn't she? It's disgraceful!"

"Well, we knew that results wouldn't be any better while she's here—and if they're not, it'll mean the end of the school."

Miss Jervis's eyes really did resemble the boot-buttons to which Miss Reeve had likened them.

"*No*! Would it *really*?" she breathed.

Miss Pearson, delighted with the impression she was making, nodded solemnly.

"So—you won't repeat this, will you?—we sent a Round Robin to Miss Barr to ask her to make Miss Cullen resign, or we would."

Miss Jervis positively licked her lips. This was indeed a plum.

"And," Miss Pearson lowered her voice as far as she ever could, "*Miss Barr's gone to Stamborough at once.* Gone to get their leave to dismiss her, you see."

They gazed intently into each other's eyes; and Miss Pearson suddenly felt a little alarmed. Miss Jervis was so obviously gloating over this story—so clearly thinking already of the effective way of telling it—and it simply *must not* reach Miss Cullen's ears. That poor woman was clearly quite unconscious of the blow about to fall on her; she had seemed absolutely bright in the cloak-room.

"You won't say a *word*, will you?" she warned her colleague anxiously. "Miss Cullen, of course, must *never* guess."

"Oh, I *won't*," vowed Miss Jervis.

❦

Viola Kennedy, coming into the Staff Room a few moments later, also wondered what was the matter. Everyone wore an air of suppressed excitement; Miss Jervis was positively bursting with repressed information; Miss Cullen had a curiously elate air—she looked, thought Viola, trying for a simile, like a person lost in a maze who has suddenly seen the way out. Had she but known it, this was the exact truth. That is precisely how Miss Cullen felt—as if she had at last found a way out and taken the first step to freedom.

Having paid her brief visit to the Staff Room, Viola went, according to the curious rule that existed in Besley as in many High Schools, to sit in her form-room before prayers. Some head mistresses think that you "make friends" with your form by doing this; some think that you keep them quiet; some think that your presence "prevents bad tone"; some just like you to do it because it is done in other schools. In reality very few form mistresses fulfil any of these ideas. They just sit, and try, by busily opening drawers or writing imaginary entries in note books, to pretend that they have some real business to perform. Both Staff and girls know that it is a pretence; both are ignorant of what the effect of the ritual is supposed to be, but know that it has none beyond making both mistress and girls a little more bored with each other than they might otherwise be.

Viola particularly hated these barren minutes. She had nothing to do, though plenty awaited her elsewhere; the girls never approached her to speak—("and why should they?" she thought. "I wouldn't in their place, with lots of friends to talk to")—and she felt obtrusive and unnecessary, a symbol of that discipline she so much disliked. It was almost a pleasure to her when the door opened, even though it was Miss Jervis who entered.

She approached Viola's desk with an air of mystery.

"I say," she whispered, "don't say I told you—better not repeat it at all—but *do* you know what's happened?"

Viola, a little confused by this cryptic utterance, shook her head.

"The Staff—the *old* Staff, I mean—have sent in a request to the Head for Miss Cullen's dismissal, and Miss Barr has sacked her."

Viola flushed hotly.

"How rotten!" she said aloud. "I do think that's a mean thing to have done. What business is it of theirs?"

"Hush! The girls will hear. ... Well, you know, the Board has threatened to close the school if the girls can't do better in the Senior, and of course they all fail in French whatever they do in other subjects, so you can't wonder, of course I'm sorry for her we all are but you've got to consider yourself in this life haven't you and she *is* a scream. ..."

The voluble stream flowed on, but Viola hardly heard it. It was true, then, that dark hint of Miss Parry's. ... But poor Miss Cullen! How perfectly awful. ... Probably the Boot-button had got her facts wrong. She often had.

"There's the prayer-bell," remarked her informant. "I must go. Good-bye."

"Good-bye. ... Stop talking, girls. Form up. Alice, I said stop talking. If you speak again you'll do me twenty lines. Ready? Carry on."

IVa marched demurely down to pray. Viola, keeping a sympathetic eye lifting for Miss Cullen, saw that lady standing in her place with a triumphant mien and a glint as of battle in her eye. Again the simile of the found wanderer in the maze occurred to Viola. What had really happened? Clearly, not that horror that Miss Jervis had related with such unholy glee. Whatever it was, Miss Cullen didn't seem to mind. ...

CHAPTER VIII
May Masters

Intriguing though it was (and in a school these small mysteries are very intriguing), Viola had, as it happened, not much chance to puzzle over the situation presented to her by Miss Jervis and the elated mien of Miss Cullen. One's own affairs are generally more exciting than the greatest thrills that happen to one's neighbour; and before the morning was over Viola had a matter of her own to occupy her mind.

Ever since that morning—(could it really only be three weeks ago?)—when she had secured the objectionable document from Miss Gladys Toms, Viola had kept a sharp eye on May Masters. She had never found her out in anything worse than mild cheating and rather pronounced vulgarity and insolence; but she felt intuitively quite sure that there was something more than either in some of the covert glances and whispers that she "spotted" with considerable frequency. She had nothing direct to go on; but a woman who is at all sensitive to what is vaguely called "atmosphere" has a very shrewd idea of what is mere folly or bravado and what is definitely "wrong" in girls whom she sees daily.

For some days now Viola had felt that the "wrong" atmosphere was rapidly strengthening; and on this morning, when the whole school seemed charged with excitement and secrecy, she got her proof.

She looked round suddenly from the blackboard to see May Masters put something into the back of her slipper and thrust her foot back under her seat. The girl sitting immediately behind May—a sycophantish spectacled creature named Lilian Burton—stooped forward, her hand ready to fumble at May's foot, her shallow mistrustful eyes on the mistress at the board.

Viola spoke at once.

"Lilian, sit up. May, what are you stooping down for? Put your feet under your desk."

"I was only pulling up my slipper. It slipped."

Feeble giggles greeted this sally. Viola ignored them.

"Do you need help from the girl behind you to put on your shoe? Lilian, why were you bending down?"

"I wasn't, Miss Kennedy."

"Oh, *don't* be so idiotic. A stupid lie like that has no excuse at all. Answer me, please. Why were you bending down?"

No reply.

"May, stand up and come out here. No, keep *both* your shoes on your feet. ... Now take off your left shoe and give me the paper inside it—yes, the paper you were trying to pass to Lilian. ... Quickly, May, I'm waiting."

There was a short duel of looks. Viola won, but only because she was fully determined on her course of action and May was not; the child had not yet had time to make up her mind as to the line she would take.

"Thank you. Go back to your place. I will speak to you later."

Viola put the missive in the pocket of her coat. She had already learnt the unwisdom of opening a doubtful document before a class. You have to take instant action, before you have really been able to get the hang of a case or take an unprejudiced view; besides, a little suspense is a very valuable deterrent. So the note went into safe keeping until the mid-morning break.

May's suspense could hardly have been greater than Viola's own. She might find the note a mere piece of folly; it might be a request for assistance in school work; it might be a proof of that subtle poison which seemed to emanate from May Masters, and which was certainly spreading rapidly throughout the form, where pasty faces and heavy eyes and leering glances seemed to multiply every day.

At last break came, and she was able to look at her find. It was brief, but to Viola it was quite long enough.

Dear L [she read], *I have arranged to meet Him, you know where, and we won't half have some larks, like proper sweethearts, not only just canoodling. He will bring a nice boy for you if you will come too. Dare you.—M.*

It was also embellished by sufficiently striking illustrations.

Viola read it—flushed—paled—flushed again, as the drawings caught her eye. This was almost more than she had expected. She must act—and at once.

She remembered what Miss Cullen had told her three weeks ago—that in such a case it was useless to appeal to the Head, and that Miss Lexington was the best person to go to. Miss Barr's absence at Stamborough certainly made it possible for her to appeal to the Second Mistress; but at the moment she was not in the Staff Room.

Viola glanced round.

"Do you happen to know where Miss Lexington is, Miss Cullen?" she asked, speaking to the mistress nearest her.

"Yes. She is engaged with the doctor and Molly Hall. Molly fell and hurt her back, and Miss Lexington thought it necessary to take firm steps."

Miss Cullen's voice sounded even more clipped and odd than usual. It did, when she felt brisk. Then, seeing Viola's doubtful and troubled expression, she altered her tone a little.

"Can I help you at all?"

Viola hesitated a moment; then she decided to speak.

"Well—it's this." She lowered her voice. She was so absorbed in the matter that she did not realise how this intimate tone linked her, in the eyes of the furtively watching Staff, with the object of their pity and wrath; perhaps she would not have cared if she had. "You told me at the beginning of the term that if ever I got any proof of May Masters's bad conduct that I'd better take it to Miss Lexington rather than to the Head. Is that really so?"

Miss Cullen looked at her a little oddly.

"I should, if I were you—if you really have something to go on."

"Would you mind telling me why?"

Miss Cullen hesitated. Her code of loyalty, even to such a Head as Miss Barr had shown herself to be, hampered her badly. She felt she couldn't, to a new-comer, say "The Head won't listen." So she fumbled, half opened her mouth in that irritating way of hers, hedged—and made a fatal mistake.

"My *dear* child," she exclaimed in her most humorous voice, "don't you know that we *all* prefer to approach Authority through an intermediary? I'm *surprised* to find how little consideration you have for the dignity of a Head Mistress. *Of course* one approaches her through the proper diplomatic channels."

Viola flushed with annoyance.

"As this happens to be rather important," she said stiffly, "I prefer to go straight to the Head—unless there's any *real* reason why I shouldn't. I gather that there's not. Thank you."

And she walked away.

"Silly *ass!*" she thought savagely as, to escape the irritating presence, she stalked down the corridor on an unnecessary errand to the library. "Doesn't she realise what's serious and what isn't? Can't she see that I've got to do something about this at once? Thinks she's *funny!*"

But the passage with Miss Cullen had helped her to make up her mind. Diplomatic channels, indeed! What bosh! No, this was a matter for the Head and the Head alone. It would be idiotic, perhaps absolutely wrong, to go to anyone else with a thing like that. She couldn't help feeling that Miss Barr disliked her; well, she'd have every reason to be really angry with her if she went, in a serious thing like this, to anyone else, even to the Second Mistress. After all, it was worth a day's delay. ... She would go to the Head first thing to-morrow.

What Miss Barr did in Stamborough on that visit of hers never transpired. It is certain that she did not visit the Education Offices. If she had, Miss Mortimer's letter, arriving the very next morning, would not have startled her so badly.

She really got a horrid shock. It was, she thought, a "nasty" letter; besides, inspectors ought to give one longer notice than that. ... She hadn't really got the time-table for the school absolutely fixed yet; only ten days ago she had found that IVc were getting too many English lessons and not enough maths. Why that silly girl Kennedy couldn't have *told* her that she was actually giving IVc four lessons a week *she* didn't know. Surely her *sense* might have told her that that was *far* too much for a junior form in a subject like English that didn't matter. These untrained girls expected the Head to run round after them the whole time, helping them in their work. It really was too bad. And now, in the fourth week of term, she would have to rearrange the whole time-table, and it was impossible to do so and get it running smoothly before to-morrow, in time for the Inspection. ... It really was a shame to have an inspection launched on one like that with no real warning. ... Rereading the "nasty" letter, she felt sure that there was "something behind it."

She was just going to ring to summon Miss Lexington, that she might impart the dire news to the Staff, when she heard a knock at the door. It was not, as she had half hoped, a visit from Miss Parry; she expected a call from Miss Parry *à propos* of the present attitude of the Staff; she badly needed some guidance just now. She paused, trying to identify the knock before permitting entrance; she *would not* see Miss Cullen. ...

At last she risked it. She pressed her knob, the brass plate (presumably) revolved, and Viola Kennedy entered.

Miss Barr felt distinctly irritated. She disliked this girl. She was impertinent, assured, far too self-confident for one just beginning. Rumour said that she was "in" with Miss Cullen. Then there was that bother over the time-table.

"I am exceedingly busy, Miss Kennedy," she began coldly, "although as a matter of fact I want at some time to talk to you about your time-table. You really cannot expect me to pursue you all to find out whether you have your right number of lessons with various forms. Surely your own *sense* might have told you that *four* English lessons is far too many for *any* junior form; and now I find that you have given IVc that number for over four weeks. ... I shall have to rearrange the whole time-table."

"I'm very sorry. I just copied down what I was given. I am only giving less than that in other forms because my own time-table is so full that I can't give more. Three lessons is so very little to cover all one wants to do—"

"Oh, excuse me, Miss Kennedy, there you are quite mistaken. In the lower forms it is ample. *Ample.* All the other mistresses, as a matter of course, work a little English into their lessons." Viola thought, with a shudder, of the guise Miss Pearson's and Miss Fergusson's English instruction might assume—of the accent of the one and the sickly sentimentality of the other. "I will ask them all, if you like, to make a definite attempt to introduce a little literature into those lessons that permit of it."

"Oh, no, thank you," interrupted Viola hastily. "I dare say I can get in all I want."

She wasn't going to have her juniors, her only hope as far as real love of books was concerned, made to learn "If" and "Abou Ben Adhem" if she could help it; and she felt convinced that some of the Staff would make them do so.

"You see, you *can* do it then," said the Head with a smile that made Viola want to swear. "And, as I am on the subject of your lessons, I presume you know that you have given III Remove a reading book of which there are not enough copies to go round the form?"

"Oh, I wanted to ask about that," said Viola eagerly. "There are thirty-five children in that form, but the only book of which there are thirty-five copies is Lamb's Essays. Of course, that's too advanced for children of ten; it would only spoil it for them afterwards to read it now, before they can begin to appreciate it. In fact, there wasn't much in the book-room that I wanted for them; but the nearest was that selection from the Arthur Cycle. There are thirty-three of those. Does it matter if four girls share two books?"

"*Certainly* it matters. It has a very bad effect on discipline to let girls sit close together like that, with every chance to whisper and play. I cannot possibly allow it. Is there no other book?"

"There's an edition of 'Treasure Island,' which they'd love, of course; but it's awfully small print, and their room is so dark."

"No, Miss Kennedy. I cannot allow children of that age to have as coarse a book as 'Treasure Island.' They are not old enough to appreciate the beauties which, to older readers, compensate for the speech of the characters."

Viola bit her lip convulsively. Otherwise she restrained herself.

"Then—?"

"The Lamb, of course. It's the obvious book for the form. Get it given out at once, please, and take in the copies of the Arthur stories. Yes. And I will change the lessons in IVc as soon as I can do so. It is *most* annoying."

Viola, concealing her indignation at being blamed for the Head's faulty time-table of work, stood her ground.

"I have something I very much want to consult you about, Miss Barr," she began. "Yesterday I got a very—well, a very doubtful letter which was being circulated in IVa. May Masters was passing it round. I should like you to look at it, if you will. I think you will want to deal with it yourself." And she held out the incriminating sheet.

"Really, Miss Kennedy, you must understand that I cannot be expected to deal with these small disciplinary matters in a form. If you can't manage IVa you must say so frankly, and I will see what new arrangement can be made. I should have thought you might manage to control your own form without coming to me for help."

Viola flushed crimson.

"I believe I can control them," she said as quietly as her wrath permitted her. "It is the morality of this girl that horrifies me. It is dangerous. ... Will you look at the letter?" And she proffered it again.

"I have really not the time, even if I had the inclination, Miss Kennedy, to interfere between a form mistress and her form. The very fact that, as you admit, a letter was being passed round in your form at all surely shows that your control is not as complete as it might be. As I say, I am exceedingly busy. I have just heard that an inspector is coming here to-morrow, and there is this trouble with the time-table to arrange and countless other details to see to. ... If you *really* can't manage May Masters," she added as a safeguard, "I will see you about her at the end of the week. But while the inspectors are here you really must try to be more independent. ... Now, will you be so kind as to ask Miss Lexington to come to me?"

Viola, too angry to speak again, walked out of the room, May Masters's letter still in her hand. She began now to understand Miss Cullen's attitude in the whole matter.

"Impertinent girl!" fumed Miss Barr, re-reading Miss Mortimer's unpleasant letter for the seventh time. "I *never* saw such a mixture of insolence and incompetence. ... Miss Cullen's intimate. It's not surprising. ... What the Profession is coming to!"

And she closed her desk with a distinct bang.

CHAPTER IX

Inspection

One gathers, from reports of conferences and commissions and other bodies or meetings where educational problems are mooted, that one of the chief functions of His Majesty's Inspectors is "to help and advise teachers by constructive criticism, bringing fresh vision to bear on problems which have become invisible or insoluble from intimacy, and giving constructional criticism on matters of instruction and discipline." That is the theory, and no doubt it often is the practice. But there are also places and occasions on which it is mere theory, and, to those who endure inspection, a theory which is too ludicrous to be worth even a bitter smile.

Miss Mortimer was a comparative new-comer to the Stamborough district. She was on her mettle to prove herself efficient, keen-sighted, thorough; and she was one of those women, of whom there are a good many, who believe that to give a bad report on the subject of their investigation is proof of these desirable qualities. Besley was, to her, a plum which, with its gradual declension from favour, merely became plummier. No one wanted her to say a good word for Besley; more, she knew that to say a good word for Besley would be to frustrate her own desire to be considered efficient at head-quarters. She was, as Miss Barr rightly conjectured, out for scalps. Miss Cullen's appeal gave her the requisite moral support. She felt a positive Crusader.

The faces of the Staff, when Miss Lexington broke to them the news of Miss Mortimer's imminence, would have pleased that lady. The startled, apprehensive eyes and agitated exclamations would have been grateful tribute to her power. But they would not have elicited mercy. Miss Mortimer was a Rhadamanthus. Judgment, with her, was never tempered with mercy. In fact the Staff often wondered whether the defiant or the meek were in the end the greater sufferers.

Viola, in her untried innocence, did not quite grasp the full terrors of the situation. She merely thought that an inspector would visit the school with the idea of discovering whether she, among others, could teach. Her lessons might be visited, a few questions asked about her ideas and methods. Well, she didn't mind that. She was still enjoying her work, planning lessons with eager zest, delighting to see interest and pleasure take the place of boredom, and even occasionally finding imagination putting forth tiny buds in unexpected places. And her ideals were perfectly definite. She hadn't rushed into this job, which she loved with all her heart, without having a very clear idea of what she was aiming at achieving and the best means of getting the results she wanted. She wasn't afraid of being inspected. She couldn't think why anyone reasonably good at her job should be, especially experienced mistresses.

She said something of this to Miss Reeve during break. That lady smiled sagaciously.

"Wait," she advised. "If you say that at the end of the week you'll either be extraordinarily blind or extraordinarily lucky."

"But why?" urged Viola. "I don't see what *can* happen."

"Well, I can't tell you what will happen," said Reeve, "but remember this: Don't trust Miss Mortimer an inch. The sweeter she seems the more she'll be out for your blood. And, whatever you do, however much you want to, don't say a word about anything but your own subject—and not about that, unless you're asked direct questions. Don't say a word about the school, or the discipline, or the hours, or the time-table, or the duties, or the Head, or any blooming thing. That is, of course," she added, "unless you want to get a good personal report at the expense of the school. ... She'll pump you, and she's a good pumper. Don't let her draw you."

This seemed to Viola, like much of the advice she received from the Staff, very exaggerated. She was coming to the conclusion that her colleagues, nice as many of them were in most ways, were under delusions about many things. They were all so suspicious. They took such a warped, prejudiced view of the simplest things. They saw mischief and double-dealing everywhere. Perhaps it was the effect of their narrow, conventual lives. ... And then she remembered certain facts ... well, perhaps their wild-sounding ideas were not always so very far wide of the mark. Odd things certainly did happen. She had, even so early, began to repent certain impulsive, outspoken remarks made to Miss Pearson and Miss Jervis. They seemed to have "got round" in a distorted version. And there were certain queer things which could, it seemed, only be accounted for by Miss Lexington's sensational-sounding theory of a "spy on the Staff"; and there was this business between Miss Cullen and Miss Parry which she had at first simply scouted as impossible. ... Still, she felt that Miss Reeve's estimate of the Inspector was probably tinged with the predominant unhappy hue of suspicion that overhung the school. In reality, the lady would come with an open and unbiassed mind, and the feeling of individual members of the Staff towards the Head, towards each other, towards the school, would not be of the least interest to her. She still felt quite calm, though it must be confessed that she prepared her lessons with even more care than usual that night.

Viola was not surprised when, in the middle of her lesson with IIIa, the door opened and Miss Barr ushered in a smiling and charmingly-dressed stranger. Viola had no knowledge of what the etiquette was on such an occasion; she had a vague idea that an introduction would be made, and that she would then be asked to continue her lesson, while the pleasant visitor listened and Miss Barr tactfully withdrew. Like many of her ideas, it was clearly mistaken.

"This is IIIa," announced Miss Barr. The standing girls gazed at the visitors with round-eyed solemnity. "May they sit, Miss Mortimer? Sit, girls. Dorothy, dear, get a chair for Miss Mortimer. ... Thank you."

She drifted away. Miss Mortimer sat down composedly.

"Just go on, please," she said to Viola over her shoulder.

With something of an effort—she would never be one of those to inherit the earth—Viola obeyed.

It was a grammar lesson—work which Viola did not wish to teach, but which was insisted on by Authority; and, since it had to be taught, she had invented various dodges for making the children take an interest in it.

One of these was a kind of match between teams, "picked up" by two small grammar-fiends, who posed each other with grammatical problems and scored marks on the blackboard for correct answers. IIIa loved "grammar matches," and were allowed one periodically, both as a reward for good work done in "learning" lessons and as a test of memory.

Viola wondered whether she should explain the aim and principles of the contest to the lady who now sat with her shoulder so pointedly turned to her and a bright smile fixed on the thirty-three awestricken faces of IIIa. She decided she would.

"Now both teams are to prepare questions," she said to the form. "Three minutes to think. Get two questions each, in case someone else has the same as your first." To her disgust, she found that her heart was thumping hard—as hard as it had on that remote morning when she had first encountered IVa. "You may ask anything you've learnt this term," she continued. "Barbara's team will ask first."

Then she turned to the Inspector and began to explain the aim and rules of the match. To her surprise the lady made no reply whatever, but merely wrote down in a notebook every word that she said. When she had finished her explanation, Miss Mortimer looked at her in a pitying way that riled Viola exceedingly.

"Of course it's of no *educational* value whatever," she remarked, "though I realise that it makes a very easy lesson for the teacher."

Viola flushed her ready crimson.

"Oh, pardon me," she said, "I shouldn't give such a lesson if I didn't think it useful. It's a test of knowledge for the children; it stimulates their interest in what they learn; and by the questions they ask and the answers they give I can see better than I could in any other way where they have failed to remember or understand their work."

The Inspector made no reply. The possibility of Viola's inheritance of the earth became even more remote. ... However, she wasn't going to alter her lesson. She'd behave exactly as usual.

"Time," she announced. "Barbara, send someone from your team to ask the question. Mabel, someone from yours to answer."

The two small champions stood up.

"What is a clause?" whispered the challenger.

"Speak up, Maud, I can't hear," said Viola.

The child blushed crimson. Viola, who knew her for an intensely nervous, almost hysterical, creature, hesitated. Should she tell her to sit down, or give her one more shot? Just one, perhaps. ...

"Just a little louder, Maud. Vera couldn't hear you. What did you ask?"

To her horror, the overwrought Maud burst into a suppressed choking between sobs and giggles.

"Never mind. Sit down. Send someone else, Barbara. Yes, Alice will do."

The rest of the match proceeded smoothly. The girls showed their usual zest and intelligence; they asked sensible questions, gave reasoned answers; their behaviour was eager, but quite quiet; and they displayed a most creditable amount of knowledge of a subject which Viola had to confess was a dull one. She was distinctly pleased.

The Inspector left just before the close of the lesson; but the children hardly seemed to notice either her presence or her absence, they were so full of the excitement of the game-lesson. There was a general sigh when the bell announced its close.

Break, that morning, was a gloomy affair. Miss Lexington had been told off by the Head to keep silence among the girls in the Hall—a process maddening alike for her and them. Miss Parry and Miss Reeve were on duty at other points with the same object; Miss Cullen was nowhere to be seen. In the Staff Room there was an atmosphere of tension and gloomy irritation.

Miss Pearson suddenly burst in, her usually pale face crimson, her whole aspect excited and angry. She looked very near tears.

"D'you know what that—that *woman's* done?" she cried.

"Hsssshhh!" hissed everyone. Even if it be true, assistant mistresses may not allude to His Majesty's Inspectors as "women."

"*Oh!*" gulped Miss Pearson in exasperation. "Well, listen." She lowered her voice. "She said she wanted to go all over the Domestic Science

Room last lesson. Well, you know, I generally have the babies—Ia—in there, as Miss Newton hasn't a lesson on, but if that Woman wanted to go poking into cupboards and counting cake-tins, I couldn't. So the H.M. told me to take 'em to the lib'ry. Of course there are only twelve lib'ry chairs, and they're miles too big for the poor little blighters, so I sat 'em down in a circle on the hearth-rug as good and happy as could be. *She* came in. 'Whay ah thoos children on the floo-ah?' she said." (Miss Pearson pitched her harsh voice to a shrill treble drawl to convey her impression of the Inspector's voice and arrogant manner.) "So I explained how it was. 'Oo, they mahst hev chai-ahs,' she said. I said there weren't any. 'They c'n fetch them from the room Ay've jahst been in,' she said. And dashed if she didn't send those little seven-year-olds *upstairs* to fetch down the chairs from the Domestic Science Room!" There was a general murmur. The stairs were steep and the Domestic Science Room chairs heavy. "Well, that's not all. When they *had* got back and I'd fixed them all up all over again and started on my lesson and all the rest of the palaver, she said, '*Du yu knoo you're neahly ten minutes late stahting this lesson?*' I c'd've *killed* her!"

Murmurs of commiseration went round. Miss Pearson, whose unpleasant accent broadened and hardened perceptibly in moments of excitement, and who always (the charitable said on account of adenoids; the others said on account of parentage) had difficulty with nasals, went rapidly on:

"There's somethink in the wind, you see if there's not. *D'you notice who's not here?*"

"Some people are on duty," said Miss Rowan coldly.

"Yes—and some aren't! Some are talking to Inspectors as if they were their dearest friends!"

All eyes now turned in her direction.

"Oh, *I* saw them, the two of 'em, on the upper corridor," went on Miss Pearson in growing excitement. "I wouldn't behave like Miss Cullen does for a pension! If there's anythink I hate it's slyness."

"Hssshhhh!" came the alarmed hiss. Miss Pearson subsided sulkily.

"All right, all right!" she snapped. "Only if there's a row over this inspection, we'll know who's to blame!"

"It's only a rowing over those damn' results, I expect," said Miss Gilbert pacifically.

"*Is* it?" snorted Miss Pearson. "You'll see. ..."

CHAPTER X
The Gentle Art of Pumping

Miss Cullen was not brought up in the school which starves conscience to death almost as a duty. On the contrary. She pampered hers until it was positively bloated with good living, and rode her life like an Old Man of the Sea, effectually preventing her from taking any pleasure in those manoeuvres which would have filled Miss Parry with the unholy joy of the diplomat successfully outwitting her opponents. To Miss Parry her fellows were her foes, and her motto was "Do or be done"; to Miss Cullen they were friends (though not intimate ones—her feeling for them was rather dutiful than cordial) and her motto was the much older one, "Do as you would be done by." Thus it was that the healing ointment of her success contained a large and most unpleasant fly. Her conscience simply refused to allow her to enjoy it.

She had not expected that Miss Mortimer's response to her plea for justice would come so soon. It had seemed to her almost like a miraculous reply to prayer when Miss Lexington told the horrified Staff the dire news of an immediate inspection. She had felt that now, at last, she really had taken the line that would lead her to safety and freedom; and while the rest of the Staff, assembled at prayers that morning, thought agitatedly of their coming ordeal, she had offered up a genuine thanksgiving for the swift answer to her cry for help.

But now, now that the step was taken, she was not so sure. She felt subconsciously glad that she had not had longer in which to make her decision, or her resolution might have failed. She had forgotten how pale and anxious the faces in the tiny cloak-room would look. She longed, on that day of the inspection, to say something to cheer them all up—to reassure them by saying, "It's all right. She's not going to hurt any of you.

She's only coming to inspect my work, to tell the Board that I'm not really as hopeless as you all think I am."

But even as the grotesque idea came into her head, it withered. Miss Lexington and Miss Parry, entering together, had each given her one glance—a glance of such cold contempt from the one, of such virulent fury from the other—that she felt momentarily appalled—appalled as one might be who has laughingly cast friends adrift in a boat and then realises that it is sinking. She did not like to stay in the same room as those two who had eyed her so; and then the pointed silence of the others, their gloomy eyes and marked coldness, distressed her. ... She must escape from them somehow. She hurriedly raked up an excuse; for her self-consciousness forbade her to walk away simply, as if nothing was the matter. It seemed to her that that would be to acknowledge herself wrong, put in Coventry.

"I really *must* go and put the French section of the library in order!" she exclaimed. "If we're to have an inspection we must be in apple-pie order, mustn't we?"

No reply.

"Has anyone got any French books out?"

Still stony silence.

"No? Ah, well, I hardly expected you would. One hasn't much time, has one, to keep up one's enjoyment in literature? What a life for cultured women to lead!"

Silence.

She simply could not carry on this one-sided conversation. Sore, but still forgiving, she collected her possessions and walked out, followed by expressive glances and a half-laugh from Miss Baldwin.

In the library she pulled herself together. Why should she feel guilty? *She* had done nothing to be ashamed of. All she had done was to ask for an impartial judgment on the school and on herself—such a judgment as the Board of Education was bound to have made, in any case, sooner or later. *She* hadn't asked for the dismissal of one of her colleagues! It was for the rest of the Staff to feel guilty, not for her.

She sorted and arranged the books, taking a quite unnecessary time over the operation, for the French section was, as always is the case in such libraries, both small and unused by anyone but the French specialist herself. Miss Reeve had read the books there once, but some time ago she had found that she had not the time to read the classics even of her own tongue.

During prayers Miss Cullen alone of the Staff kept her mind on her God. She prayed genuinely—prayed that her action might be attended with good for all those present. Only her childlike faith in miracles could have inspired such a request; nothing short of a miracle could possibly have answered it.

She knew, intuitively, the moment at which Miss Mortimer arrived. She was not at all sure whether she would herself be visited as she taught; but she knew with certainty that at some time during the day Miss Mortimer would seek her out, and that she would be asked to amplify— and justify—those accusations at which her letter had merely hinted. And she was prepared to do both.

They met, fortuitously as it happened, outside a classroom. Third Lesson had just ended; girls and Staff alike were hurrying to lunch and the momentary pause of "break."

"Ah, Miss Cullen!" exclaimed Miss Mortimer, extending a beautifully manicured hand. "I was just wondering where I should find you. ... Are you free just now?"

Miss Cullen beamed the rare smile of one who is at last understood.

"I am free until the end of the Fourth Lesson," she said.

"Ah! Now I wonder—can we have a nice quiet little talk together somewhere? Somewhere—er—quite private?"

Miss Cullen hesitated. Her honest mind rather recoiled from the implication of intrigue and secrecy. Still, of course one must have tact; she realised that. ...

"The Fifth Form Room will be empty next lesson," she suggested.

"I don't quite like a form room. One can never count on being free from interruption there. Why shouldn't we just stroll up and down here? Then we can see—er—anyone coming. I suppose the form rooms are all empty?"

Miss Cullen reassured her; and the colloquy proper began.

"Now, Miss Cullen, I want you to understand first and foremost that I'm here as your *friend*," began the Inspector; and her tone was so kind and the pressure of her hand on the older woman's arm so warm and reassuring that Miss Cullen felt the hot, unaccustomed tears prick her eyelids. "I feel so much for you," Miss Mortimer continued. "I do so *well* understand your position and how difficult things are for you. You would feel better at once, I am certain, if you only had a better, happier *milieu* for your work."

"Oh, I know! I know that's true!" said Miss Cullen eagerly. She took out her large, usefully solid handkerchief and blew her nose vigorously. "It—you must forgive me," she muttered. "Things have been so hard lately—I'm tired and nervous—and you are so kind—"

"Poor thing!" murmured Miss Mortimer. "I am so sorry, Miss Cullen, so very sorry. I do so wish I had known sooner. … Never mind, we'll soon get things put right for you. Now, tell me—what is it that makes things *most* difficult?"

Miss Cullen hesitated. It was, after all, a little awkward to talk over one's colleagues. …

"You felt that there was need for urgency, didn't you, in asking me to see into things? Had something special happened to alarm or annoy you?"

The memory of those tell-tale scraps in the waste-paper basket rushed over Miss Cullen. She flushed her dusky, unbecoming red.

"I—yes—there was something," she muttered.

"Something personal?—some slight or injustice? Or something definitely wrong in the management of the school?"

"N-no—not quite that—"

Oh, it wasn't nearly as easy as she'd thought it would be! She twisted her large, solid handkerchief between her ugly, ineffectual fingers. How *could* she give them away to Headquarters, her colleagues, once her friends?

Miss Mortimer, shrewd woman of the world, had not gained her present position without some knowledge of how to handle her kind. She saw that there was only one way to make this woman speak. She must be frightened—put thoroughly on her defence. To save herself she would speak. It was fear, she saw that clearly now, that had driven this ugly, loyal woman to make that desperate cry for help. Fear must make her speak again.

She looked at her watch.

"Of course you realise," she began, a subtle change in both manner and voice, "that to write as you did was a most unusual step to take? Only the most unusual circumstances would account for your doing such a thing."

Miss Cullen tugged obstinately at the handkerchief.

"I know," she muttered. She looked desperately round her. Should she, even now, at the eleventh hour, rescind her appeal—say she had taken that desperate step in a nerve crisis? Or was that too dangerous, too revealing of weakness?

Miss Mortimer again consulted her watch. There was just a trace of impatience in her perfectly courteous manner. Miss Cullen felt she must justify herself somehow.

"It—I felt—I had to do something—to put myself right. I—they—I felt I was being made the scapegoat for everything—for all the failures and faults of the school—I was blamed for it all—"

"Of course, the Besley results in the Senior were, even for Besley, quite extraordinarily bad this year," said the Inspector smoothly. "Besley results are notoriously bad, too. And as far as I remember your list was decidedly weak, wasn't it?"

How chilly that friendly voice had become! Was it too late, then, after all? Was her doom already sealed? Oh, no, surely not! Surely this wasn't dismissal! … Sheer panic seized on the wretched woman.

"It was, I know," she broke out, feverishly voluble now. "I have enough experience of examinations to know how very bad that list must look. But, you see, Miss Mortimer, the girls come up to me knowing nothing—*nothing*! No one can get girls up to Senior standard in two years unless they are thoroughly well grounded. The preparatory work must be efficient. …"

This was more like it. There was information to be gained here.

"You think that the Lower School is not up to standard?" the inspector inquired soothingly.

"I'm sure it's not. It can't be. I've got hundreds—literally *hundreds*—of girls through examinations in my time. It can't be my inefficiency that makes them fail now!"

"No, it would appear as if there must be another reason," mused Miss Mortimer. Neither lady gave utterance to her knowledge that this decline had been a gradual one, spread over years, not, as Miss Cullen had suggested, a sudden collapse. Eagerly the mistress snatched at the note of yielding.

"And the girls are so rude, so ill-disciplined! There is even a certain amount of definite bad tone."

"But you should report that."

"I have! I do! But—!" An eloquent gesture ended the sentence.

"You mean—surely you don't mean that no steps are taken?"

Miss Cullen nodded impressively.

"I mean just that," she asserted. "How can any mistress be expected to keep girls in order when they know that appeals to the Head will be ignored?"

The inspector's face was very grave.

"Then you suggest that your own failures, as apart from the general list, are due to two causes—to bad preparation in the lower forms and to general bad discipline throughout the school—bad discipline which there is no attempt to suppress?"

Miss Cullen nodded again.

"And you have tried to get these conditions altered? You have complained?"

"About the discipline, yes. I could hardly go to the Head with complaints of the work of a colleague."

"No, perhaps not. I see that. But you have made representations about the bad tone?"

"Oh—repeatedly."

"And what steps were taken?"

"*None*! On my honour, Miss Mortimer, none whatever. I might never have spoken. The whole Staff will bear me out."

There was a short impressive silence. Then, the way made easy, Miss Mortimer neatly extracted from her unwitting victim all she had to tell.

All the weaknesses of the Head, the failings of the Staff (with especial reference to Miss Parry, for whom Miss Mortimer had long cherished a strong dislike), the faults of organisation and management, the heavy duties, the obsolete systems, together with much that was in itself harmless enough but could be made very effective if properly dressed for head-quarters consumption, were drawn from her, sometimes by direct questioning, more often by adroit inference. Miss Mortimer had nothing to learn in the gentle art of pumping, and she pumped Miss Cullen dry.

As soon as this agreeable task was completed, the interview was gracefully terminated. Miss Cullen left the presence with Miss Mortimer's gentle words of kindliness and warm support ringing gratefully in her ears. She felt safe now. Everything that was needed to damn Besley utterly and irrevocably had been uttered—much of it quite unknowingly—to that shrewd inquisitor who had made her so happy. She knew that she had endangered the future of one, at least, of her colleagues; what she did not realise was that she had imperilled the whole institution on which her own fate, as well as theirs, depended. Once she had served her end, and Miss Mortimer's fame as an efficient inspector was assured, she would disappear with the school she had betrayed. ...

She did not for one moment realise that. To do her justice, she did not realise that the school was endangered by what she had said; but in any case she thought that she was now safe. It brought relief—what relief only those can tell who have passed through an anxiety like hers, a dread of a penniless old age with relations who know that you have your faculties and your training and cannot understand what you have done with all you must have earned. At ease now, she could picture that future which had once been too imminent to face, with the shuddering horror of one who looks over the precipice from which one has been saved.

"I had to do it," she told herself. "I had to escape that. You can't be too fastidious when it's a case of life and death like that. It was a mean thing to do, to get at the inspector behind their backs. Yes, it was, very mean. I should never have done it if they hadn't made me desperate. What was I to do, when they had threatened my whole future like that? They'd tried to take everything from me—my work, my future, my pension, my independence. I should never have done such a thing if they hadn't driven me to it. And, after all, what have I done? I've asked for an impartial judgment, which was due to come in any case; and I've told the truth, no more, to those whose business it is to know. When you think of it, I've done no more than my duty all through. ..."

But, as we said before, Miss Cullen's was a pampered conscience. It had been unwontedly suppressed and generally ill-used. It had its torturing revenge on her that night. Even the Staff might have forgiven her something if they had known.

CHAPTER XI

Opinions

As she walked home that afternoon Viola thought over the day. It hadn't been so bad after all, she decided. Of course, the inspector had been rude; but perhaps all inspectors were. She hadn't, after all, been unbearably rude—at least, not as far as she herself was concerned; of course poor Miss Pearson had suffered, and Miss Parry, they said, had been visited for four solid lessons and slated at all; still, under these conditions, other people's trials afflict you but slightly, and Viola's reflections were on the whole pleasant. IIIa had acquitted itself well. She felt pleased with the memory of their intelligence and keenness. Though nothing had been said to her by way of praise, she felt sure that no blame could possibly be hers over that lesson. She had been lucky, she congratulated herself. Presumably her trials were over until next term, since she had gathered from conversations in the Staff Room that inspections were, at the most, terminal affairs, and Miss Mortimer had certainly gone back to Stamborough.

As she proceeded on her way she fell in with various colleagues. First she met Miss Reeve, who had been "free"for the afternoon, and looked refreshingly care-free in consequence. The lucky woman had apparently been engaged in shopping at the only respectable bookshop in the place.

"Oh, I *am* glad to meet you," she said, drawing Viola aside. "I'd just remembered something I had to tell you, and I was afraid I'd have to stagger all the way down to Holcroft Road, which I could hardly have borne to do. Look here, it's this. I ought to have asked you ages ago. Will you—would you care to join the Town Dramatic Club? Our English specialist generally does, but Miss Spiller didn't care for it—against her principles, for some queer reason—and so I forgot to ask you before. We have quite a jolly time—read a play and then select people to act it and give a show about Christmastime. We're very late this year—the President's been ill—and the first reading is to-night. Do come. You'd like it, I'm sure. You get to know people in the town, and it's a break from the everlasting old school. Do say you will."

"I'd love to," said Viola. "I adore reading plays, especially with new people. But can I, without being proposed and passed and all the rest of it?"

"Of course you can. Our English mistress belongs almost *ex officio*, but I particularly asked about you on account of Miss Spiller never having belonged. So that's that, then. I'll come round for you about seven-thirty, if that'll suit you. Let the work go for one night, or you'll be in your grave before you're forty."

She smiled and nodded and went on her way, leaving Viola pleasantly interested in the thought of a night off and of meeting people who had no professional interest in Results or Inspectors or Head Mistresses or Bad Tone or Discipline or Corrections or Examinations or any of the other dull things which constitute the chief preoccupations of an assistant mistress at the average High School.

Viola next met Miss Lexington and Miss Parry; Miss Parry was pouring a flood of earnest conversation into the ear of the Staff Mistress, who looked both a little incredulous and rather perturbed.

Miss Lexington noticed Viola first, and touched her companion's arm with a warning hand before she greeted her.

"So you've survived Miss Mortimer?" she remarked. "*Isn't* she a dreadful woman?"

"She wasn't anything worse than rather rude, to me," answered Viola.

She rather thought that a queer glance flashed between the other two—mild triumph on Miss Parry's part, acquiescence on Miss Lexington's. "I said so, didn't I?" the one glance seemed to say; and the other, "So you did. I wouldn't have thought it." It puzzled her. It looked—confirmatory, that was it, as if her innocent words proved some theory that Miss Lexington had hardly believed.

"What did she do?" asked the Second Mistress with unwonted curiosity.

Viola related the encounter.

"You escaped lightly," was Miss Lexington's comment. "But don't flatter yourself that you've heard the last of it. She'll have put a very different construction on it to the Head, and you'll probably get a very different verdict from what you expect."

"But look here," said Viola, forgetting, in her interest, the respect she generally accorded to Miss Lexington, "I don't quite see. Do you mean that she may have reported to the Head on my lesson without telling me *anything*, good or bad?"

"Exactly."

"But—that's not allowed. I happen to know that, from a friend of mine, who had a dispute with an Inspector over that very point. No Inspector may say anything to a Head that hasn't been said to the teacher."

"Are you *sure* of that?" asked the Staff Mistress eagerly.

"Practically sure. I can quite easily find out for certain."

"Then do—will you? It would be grand for us if that were so," continued Miss Lexington, turning to her companion. "Morty's broken that rule here ever since she's been inspecting us."

"I'll find out, rather, if you like," answered Viola. "But it does seem only fair, doesn't it?"

The two elders smiled bitterly.

"You'll find fairness has very little to do with it, in the educational world," said Miss Lexington.

"Anyhow," argued Viola, "I don't see that she *could* find anything to complain of in that lesson, except that she didn't care for the method. The children did splendidly."

"To do them justice, they generally do," said Miss Parry. "They seem to know we're up against it when the Inspector comes round. S'pose they can hardly help knowing, the way she rows us before them. Disgustin', I call it."

"All the same," added Miss Lexington, "don't you make too sure. You never know."

"That's right, you *don't*," Miss Parry cut in emphatically. "She was with me last lesson this morning and all the afternoon solid; but d'you think she told me what she thought? 'Course she didn't, because I c'd have answered her double quick if she'd 've criticised me. ... 'Course, it's chiefly me she's out for. It's rather hard, with my experience and all, but that's the truth."

Viola glanced at Miss Lexington to see whether this characteristic remark amused her. Apparently it did not; her face was quite grave, even anxious. *Could* there be any solid truth in it, then?

"Why should she worry about you so much?" she asked.

"*Why*? Because she's here as *a certain lady's* friend!" cried Miss Parry. (Miss Lexington glanced round warily, but the street was nearly empty.) "She's here to damn the school—and us—to put Miss Cullen right. Don't you see through it? Miss Cullen's excuse for her failures is *my* incompetence. *That's* what she's told them at Head-quarters. And now they're out to make out that that's true—though of course it's not. I don't mind saying that my elementary French lessons simply *could—not—be—* improved. I remember an inspector we had here once (that was before your time, Miss Lexington: *such* a naice boy he was, a Mr. McNab), well, he said to me once, 'Well, Miss Parry,' he said, 'if I could teach like you do,' he said, 'or a quarter as well, I'd be satisfied.' That's what he said. 'Or a quarter as well,' he said. 'It's a reel education,' he said, 'to listen to a lesson like that. I feel better for it,' he said. And now this *woman*—!"

Words failed her. The others made sympathetic murmuring sounds.

"Well, we mustn't keep Miss Kennedy from her tea after a day like this," said Miss Lexington; and the small conference broke up.

Miss Reeve was late for her appointment that evening, and they had to hurry so fast to get to the house of the President of the Dramatic Club that conversation was impossible. This was, perhaps, just as well, for, with the passage of the hours, Viola had become less and less inclined for the experience. She was more tired than she had thought by the anxieties of the day, and she wanted quiet more than she had ever wanted it in the whole of her vigorous youth. She walked silently beside the hurrying

Reeve, her mind dwelling confusedly on a dozen different problems at once. Was it true that this inspection had been engineered by simple-seeming Miss Cullen to destroy a colleague? Would an inspector come at the summons of an assistant mistress to criticise a whole Staff? What had been the meaning of that nod and glance that passed between the two senior mistresses when she innocently announced her comparative success with that dreaded inspector? What was she to do about that captured letter of May Masters? ... Like most of her profession, Viola was fast losing her sense of humour and proportion. She felt that these questions filled the whole horizon, so that nothing else, no question of State or religion or personal relationship or anything whatever, was of the smallest importance in comparison. She would far rather have spent a quiet evening in her hideous rooms brooding over these conundrums than have gone forth to meet a whole company of new people. Her head ached, she felt tired, and depressingly knew that she looked jaded and shabby. ... She thought with real longing of her ugly, little silent room and waiting bed, where she would not have to consider appearances at all; she thought with apprehension of the coming day, with its unprepared lessons. ... Suddenly she realised, for one sickening second, the tortures that a bad disciplinarian (Miss Cullen, for instance) must feel when she dreads, not for an instant, but for hours every day, the coming of a new day. ... How perfectly horrible. ...

"Miss Reeve," said Viola suddenly, "I'm so sorry—but do you mind if I don't come after all? I'm tired and stupid, and—and I've a heavy day to-morrow—"

"Both excellent reasons why you should try to forget things to-night," said Miss Reeve as briskly as shortness of breath permitted.

Viola hated her.

"I don't *want* to come," she said petulantly.

"You will soon," said the inflexible warrior at her side.

Viola subsided sulkily. Though she would never have confessed it, even to herself, tears were not far off—tears of sheer fatigue. She hated Besley, hated Miss Reeve, hated the school, hated everything and everybody. ...
With a desire that was almost physical pain she longed for the open sky

and the sea and the silent spaces of a night at home. ... Homesickness such as she had never before known or dreamt of overcame her—sickness for the openness and directness of a life in which there was no intrigue or jealousy or suspicion. ...

"Here we are," announced Miss Reeve, turning in at a large gate with gloomy laurels on either side. "Not so late, either. It's only five past."

The room seemed to Viola's tired eyes to be full to the brim of light and glitter and pink faces and noise. She noticed Miss Parry's plump, pretty countenance above an unnecessarily splendid orange frock; she saw other faces, dimly recognised from frequent encounters in the few decent shops of Besley. She subsided thankfully into a deep chair indicated by her plump and glittering hostess.

"We're doing 'Much Ado,'" whispered Miss Reeve. "Appropriate, isn't it? I brought a copy for you. They're sure to ask you to read, on account of your job. You're supposed to be a pro. If you're asked, mind you do. I *especially* want you to." And she flashed a meaning eye towards the gorgeous form of Miss Parry, who was deep in ogling conversation with a black-haired rather sulky-looking young man with a clever mouth and brooding eyes.

"Latest victim?" whispered Viola to her companion.

"Very much so. Doesn't he look it?" returned Reeve. "Poor thing, he does loathe Parry! and she makes a dead set at him every time. 'Pon my word, it's getting a positive scandal. All the town's talking about it. ... Hush, Mrs. Atkinson's going to give out the parts. Now remember what I said!"

The plump lady rose and "took the floor" completely.

"We are most forchnit," she began, beaming a chairmanly smile on the company, "in havin' amongst us to-night a reel specialist in our great litracher—I refer, I need hardly say, to Miss—er—Miss—er— Kennedy, a new-comer, I understand, to this li'l tahn of ars." ("So *that's* where Miss Parry goes for a model of the refined voice!" thought Viola, listening in fascination.) "I'm shaw we shall all—er—profit by hearin' her render the part of Beetris in the play we're readin' to-night." She paused interrogatively; Viola, Miss Reeve's sharp elbow in her side, made polite

– 154 –

affirmatory noises. "You will? Soo many thenks," beamed the President. "Other parts as follows: Don Pedro, Mr. Aston; Don Juan, Mr. Ellis; Claudio, Mr. Atkinson (yes, George, you must, I've got you down for it); Benedick, Mr. Hyde; Dogberry, Mr. Lawson …" The tide of names flowed over Viola's head. She only awakened to hear "… and Ursula, Miss Parry."

Miss Reeve's thin hand pinched her arm.

"Poor old P.! Look at her face!" she whispered.

"Oh! Did she want Beatrice? Was that why you—? What a shame! I didn't care two straws whether I read or not."

"'Twasn't only Beatrice she wanted—she wanted young Hyde. I wasn't going to have her making an exhibition of us if I could help it; that's why I spun Mrs. Atkinson a tale about your powers. Now the poor lad will get a chance to escape. We sit more or less in groups. … Look how he's cheered up!"

The black-haired youth, with an almost indecent alacrity, was crossing the room towards the new Beatrice. He no longer looked sulky—he looked mischievous, like a naughty schoolboy who may put his tongue out at any minute. Viola found herself smiling too in appreciative sympathy. *She* had felt like that, after that tea-party with Miss Parry. How much worse to be one of the "deah bo-oys" she cultivated!

"This is Mr. Hyde, Miss Kennedy," Miss Reeve introduced them. "Mr. Hyde lives near us, at Linden House School," she added.

"Silence, please, everyone!" cried the still-smiling President. "Mr. Andrews is going to begin."

Smothering a yawn, Viola opened her copy of the play and began to listen. …

Straightway the charm worked. Within ten minutes Besley and all its works and pomps was forgotten as if it had never been; within half an hour she was wandering in a walled town of mediaeval Italy, Beatrice reincarnate. She talked in poetry of love and wit to a Benedick whose deep voice had an undercurrent of laughter in it; she teased and glowed and mocked and softened; she championed a wistful Hero instead of shabby, ugly Miss Cullen, and challenged to duels of words a courtly gallant instead of a smooth-tongued inspector. … She was no longer

Viola Kennedy, an overworked, overstrung mistress in an ugly provincial school; she was made anew in the form of a lovely lady born under a dancing star. ...

The hours sped by all too soon. Too soon came the gay conclusion of the merry dream, and Viola awoke—literally came to herself—in a buzz of congratulations.

Half bewildered still, she listened, flushed and happy, to the flood of compliments.

"Charming, Beatrice, charming!"

"So spirited!"

"Excellent—really first-class, Beatrice."

"Such a lahvly paht, isn't it?" purred Miss Parry.

"And so well suited to you," added the erstwhile Hero hastily.

"Benedick inspired me," laughed Viola.

"Oo yes, Benedick was *wahnderful*, wasn't he, Mrs. Atkinson!" cooed the charmer.

"Oo yes, *wahnderful!*" echoed the President, opening soulful eyes. "Soo fervent he sahnded, didn't he? Quaite laike the reel Benedick must've done."

Miss Parry looked a little disconcerted, a little malicious, and wholly cross.

"Do let me get you some coffee or something," said Benedick's earnest voice into Beatrice's ear. "I can't bear this."

Viola turned a sympathetic face.

"It is pretty awful, isn't it?" she murmured back.

"Let's escape. Come and get some food," he muttered.

Viola rose with alacrity. Now that the fun was over and the spell broken, she realised that her head was throbbing and thumping with fatigue and excitement.

The black-haired young man took her hand and made a profound bow to the clamouring company about them.

"We're overwhelmed," he announced solemnly. "We're going to hide our blushes. No one's to follow us. We want to tell each other how wahnderful we are. Come on, Beatrice."

He led her down the room to a table where coffee and cakes were set out. Skilfully dodging the other questing males, he secured two cups and a selection of food that proved him to be a forager of the ablest order, and then, with equal skill, he piloted Viola into a quiet corner where there were two low chairs and a shaded light.

"You've had about enough, haven't you?" he said quietly, as he settled her to his liking.

"Very nearly," Viola admitted. "Ours is a wearing life, I find."

He looked at her with an odd, half-frowning directness that reminded Viola irresistibly of Rowan.

"Teaching, you mean?"

She nodded; then corrected herself.

"Not so much the teaching—that's all right; it's—the rest."

"What sort of rest?"

"Oh!—friendships and quarrels and plots and putting your foot in it by accident, and parents and inspectors—"

"Oh! I know."

"You teach, too, don't you?"

"Only sort of. I'm a relation of Mr. Glynn—the head crammer, you know. We take backward louts and stuff 'em. I do the games. I'm—just putting in time there for a bit."

His face darkened as he said it—darkened till it was almost ugly. Viola felt a throb of interested feminine curiosity.

"Like Besley?" he jerked out then.

"Hate it," she replied as succinctly.

He nodded.

"Hole, isn't it? Where d'you come from?"

"Polreath—Cornwall. D'you know it?"

"No. I'm from Ireland."

He scowled as he said it. Then:

"Sorry," he muttered. "I didn't mean to chatter. Thought you'd like a bit o' quiet," he added, with a sudden disarming glance like a schoolboy's.

"I like talking, thank you—when it isn't shop. ... At least—I generally do."

He opened his mouth to rejoin, and then, looking her full in the face:

"Like to get off home, wouldn't you?" he said with an odd, boyish abruptness.

"Please," Viola half whispered, rising to her feet.

He rose too, and stood a moment looking at her with the half-sulky, half-straightforward look that reminded her of Rowan.

"*I've* liked it," he jerked out. "I meant—you're so tired, aren't you—?"

"*Awfully*," responded Viola. Her voice was shaky with fatigue.

"Are you—will you—I mean, have you far to go?"

"N-no—Holcroft Road, if you know where that is."

"Out near the gasworks somewhere, isn't it?"

She nodded.

"Good mile—more. Care to run down in my sidecar? I've got my bike here."

Physical relief ran over Viola's weary limbs at the very idea.

"I *should*," she said gratefully. "You're not going that way, though?" she added doubtfully.

He ignored this.

"Have s'more coffee before you go? No? Come on, then. You're done to the world."

Viola realised the truth of this as they went back into the glitter and buzz of the big drawing-room. She had turned so white that, fortunately for her, no one seemed to think it anything out of the ordinary that she should have a lift home. ... She didn't, of course, realise her luck in this. She had not yet really got into Besley ways. All that worried her was the thought of the morrow and its unprepared lessons. Something would have to be done about that. ...

CHAPTER XII

The Morning After

The clock on the black slate mantelpiece had just struck one. The gas fizzed and plopped and whined in the quiet room where the only other sound was the soft, thin scratch of Viola's pen and an occasional deep, unconscious sigh. Then, quite suddenly, in the middle of a sentence, she pushed back her chair and stood up. She had to stand so for a moment, her hands resting on the table and her eyes closed, for the giddiness of exhaustion seized her; and in that moment she looked old beyond belief. Her skin, stretched and shiny across her forehead and cheekbones, sagged under her eyes and below her pretty round chin, and made deep folds on either side of her mouth, drooping into the formless lines of fatigue and depression; her eyes looked small and sunken; her hair straggled in wisps about her brow and ears. There was a sudden and sickening likeness between her youth and Miss Cullen's age. It had begun. ...

Her mouth gaped in a yawn. She turned, put one fumbling hand up to the gas, and stumbled out of the room.

Her rest was broken that night. Dreams, half waking and half sleeping, pulled and worried at her tired brain. She thought of Benedick and Miss Mortimer and May Masters and Polreath and the school hockey prospects and Mrs. Atkinson and Miss Reeve; she worried about Miss Cullen and Miss Parry, about Miss Lexington, about the Head, about her form; she lived again in Verona in the golden days of youth and love. She rose and took aspirin and bathed her face, and went back to her tumbled bed to dream and worry again. Finally, as the clocks were striking half-past four, she fell wretchedly asleep.

She was late, of course, in the morning. She lay, too tired to open her eyes, wondering whether she dared send a message to school to say she wasn't well. She couldn't teach—hadn't an idea in her head; she couldn't remember one word of the lessons she had prepared last night; her head and limbs ached heavily, her throat felt dry and rasped. Should she give in? Should she just stay where she was?...

Will had nothing to do with her decision. She hardly realised what she was doing as she crawled out of bed and went over to wash. There are no bath-rooms for High School mistresses in towns like Besley. They are luxuries, for the rich and leisured. Very enterprising landladies have inefficient geysers at a shilling a time. It is surprising (at first) to find how soon discomfort and economy overcome the habit of a daily bath.

It was a morning of thin blue skies and tingling air—a morning that called you out to brisk action; but Viola only realised that it was cold, shudderingly cold, and that the water, never warm, brought to her to wash in was now barely tepid. In her heavy, depressed mood that seemed to her typical of the coming day, of her coming life. ... She took no interest in her haggard, sunken-eyed reflection; like her forerunner, she dressed automatically, apathetically, careful only by instinct and habit.

She knew, without caring, that she had a bare seven minutes in which to gulp breakfast if she was to be at school in time. The meal had been standing in the cold and stuffy room for over a quarter of an hour, and Viola pushed away the clammy bacon pettishly. She had just poured out a cupful of the chilled and bitter tea when, with a perfunctory tap at the door, her landlady entered.

"You was very late las' night, miss, gettin' 'ome," she began truculently. Viola realised wearily that she meant to be unpleasant.

"I know," she said with some futility. "And I'm late now," she added pointedly.

Mrs. Holmes sniffed.

"Them as is out till all hours can't expeck to be in time in the mornin'," she stated.

Viola said nothing. She felt her fingers "crisp," as the French untranslateably say, in a physical effort to control her irritation, and noticed with detached annoyance that they trembled as she spread her marmalade.

"And I must ask you, Miss Kenn'dy, if you please, not to leave your books and what not layin' abaht fer me to pick up," continued Mrs. Holmes with sudden volubility. "I can't afford the time to go out enjoyin' meself till near on midnight an' then come 'ome on a gent's motor-bike, nor I wouldn't wish to, nor I can't afford the time to go a-pickin' up other folkses mess, 'ardworkin' though I am an' no one's ever said diff'rent, I 'aven't the time nor no woman wouldn't 'ave the time, be she 'oo she may, and so I tell you."

Viola rose and began in complete silence to collect her day's work into the attaché-case, the badge of the profession.

"I suppose," continued the irate dame behind her, her voice rising shrilly, "I suppose as some folks considers it beneath 'em to arnswer when a lady speaks to 'em. If that's the case, all I can say is as they're no ladies, not in what *I* mean by ladies. ..."

She paused, provocatively. Viola, still in complete silence, went to the dusky overmantel and put on her hat. Her eyes were too dim with anger and fatigue to see her own reflection; it was a gesture of disdain.

She collected her scarf, gloves, case and a pile of textbooks. Then she spoke.

"I shall not be requiring these rooms after this week," she said in a voice which no amount of effort could render quite steady. "You had better look out for another lodger. Will you let me pass, please? ... Good morning."

She was out at last—in the air, even though still caged in a street of mean little houses, all alike, with dingy curtains and smutty grass plots. The landlady's maddening voice no longer assailed her ears; and the silence, broken only by the sound of her own impatient steps, was complete and soothing. But the silence meant that she was late—horribly late. She must hurry, hurry. ...

She couldn't. Each step seemed an incredible effort. The weight of her books seemed insupportable. She didn't care if she was late. Nothing mattered—nothing, nothing. ... With a sudden, almost involuntary, decision she swerved from her direct way and struck into a field path. It was a *détour* which she sometimes took on her way home, for it was quiet and grassy; but it was longer, and she knew, at the back of her tired mind, that she was making bad worse. She didn't care in the very least degree.

The long grass was pearled with the melting frost of the night. It clung, heavy and wet and cool, about her feet. The last leaves fluttered in the sharp, tingling air, and then hung, dead, against the thin, pale blue of the sky. From a ditch there came the sharp, sweet scent of water-mint.

Suddenly, with that scent, her stupor broke. Tears stung her eyes and ached in her throat; her chin quivered uncontrollably. That tang, breathing more than any other scent of cool, empty places wet by rain and caressed by wind, brought to her a sudden knowledge of the reality of the outside world—the true world of freedom and the open air. She was like a blind man who, for one instant, is allowed to see.

She stood quite still, her feet in the long, wet grass, the cool wind stirring in her hair and blowing over her parched face. She closed her eyes and stood drinking in the peace and stillness. She was consumed with a desire to lie down there in the cold purity of the wet grass and let the wind pass over her for ever and ever. That would be Life, real life. …

Habit, backed by a well-ordered conscience, is generally stronger than desire or even passion. She opened her eyes, sighed, shifted the books in her aching arm, and walked on.

The school seemed deserted. Silence in the tiled, aloof corridors; silence in the tiny close staff cloak-room, lined with hats and coats, gloves, each pair so characteristic of its wearer, lying on the top of the boot-lockers. They must be at prayers, Viola thought apathetically, changing her damp shoes; and, like a reply, came voices:

"Christian, seek not yet repose!" they choroused; and even to Viola's weariness the choice, after the day before, had its humour. She recognised in it Miss Lovell's selection.

She was at the door of the Hall in time to collect and marshal her first class—a quiet Fifth, she remembered with faint relief, who could read the play in preparation for next year's Senior.

The second lesson, she realised with comfort, was "free." She would be able to sit in the quiet Staff Room and think out the rest of her day's programme. She came out from the Fifth with unusual promptitude.

Miss Pearson was waiting in the corridor to take over. Viola said something—a polite nothing such as form the small change of social intercourse. With anyone else she wouldn't have bothered, but she so actively disliked Miss Pearson that she was always at her politest with her. Miss Pearson shot her a baleful glance from her dark, conscious eyes and walked stonily into the class-room.

Viola shrugged her shoulders.

"What's biting her?" she thought idly. It didn't much matter. Miss Pearson's grievances were so frequent that no one except the very meek paid any attention to them, and anyhow nothing mattered to-day. ...

Ten minutes' peace in the empty Staff Room served to restore her in some degree. She was strong physically, and, with a few minutes' thought, realised how much of her troubles of the night before were due to sheer fatigue. She had no need, really, to bother over the inspection; she'd come out of that ordeal quite decently. She could manage a day's work quite well for once on this half-hour of preparation. She had no need to bother about Miss Cullen and Miss Parry—let them fight it out themselves. As for her landlady—well, she could hardly be less comfortable, wherever she went. With a small sigh of satisfaction she began to make her notes for the day's work.

Two minutes later she was interrupted by the caretaker's wife. Miss Barr would be glad if Miss Kennedy could speak to her in the study for a few minutes.

"Either May Masters or the inspector," thought Viola as she followed; and as she went Miss Lexington's prophecy came into her mind—"Don't flatter yourself you've heard the last of it. She'll have said something to the H.M., and you'll get a very different verdict eventually." Viola dismissed the memory as a mere indication of the Second Mistress's settled pessimism. It could not be possible that she would get into trouble over that lesson with IIIa. She felt curious rather than apprehensive.

She knocked, and almost at once the brass plate gave its curt command. She entered.

Miss Barr remained, as Heads often do, writing for some moments. Then she apparently realised her subordinate's presence.

"Oh, sit down, Miss Kennedy," she said quite graciously.

Viola's hopes rose high. This was not the greeting due to one whom inspectors have banned.

"I just wanted to ask you— You know, I don't believe a *word* Miss Mortimer says about *any* of my staff, but I thought it best just to ask you—*did* you have any serious disciplinary trouble yesterday in IIIa?"

Viola frankly stared.

"Disciplinary? No, Miss Barr—I never have had any trouble with IIIa, and yesterday they were perfect saints—intelligent, too."

"I asked because Miss Mortimer reported to me that a child was shockingly rude—laughed at you to your face—and you simply took no notice."

Viola pondered. Then she remembered the hysterical Maud.

"Oh! I know what she meant," she said, "but it's not true that she was rude. I should have thought that that was quite obvious. It was Maud Jenkinson." She explained.

"Ah, I *thought* that there would be some good explanation!" exclaimed Miss Barr triumphantly. "As I say, I *never* believe her reports on my staff. *Never.*"

This seemed a curious relationship, thought the ingenuous Viola, between the head mistress of a biggish school and a visiting inspector—one trumping up absurd accusations against innocent mistresses, the other making it a rule of life to discredit the reports of the person who was supposed to bring an unprejudiced eye to bear on the faults and virtues of the school.

"I haven't had a moment yet to come in to one of your lessons myself," continued the Head, positively oozing amiability, "but I'm *quite* sure they're *excellent*. And I know how good your discipline is."

Viola, with a vivid memory of her last interview with the Head—only two days ago—had a struggle to conceal her feelings. If she failed, the failure was apparently not noticed.

"Yes. That's most satisfactory," purred Miss Barr. "I congratulate you, Miss Kennedy. It seems to have been a quite excellent lesson. You are a real stand-by. ... Now, I *wonder* if you would be so kind as to undertake a little thing for me? Some of the girls, you know, are going to the lecture on Foreign Missions to-night. I meant to take them myself, but this sudden inspection has put so much extra on me that I simply haven't the time. I *wonder* if you could manage it for me? It will be a most *interesting* lecture—I'm sure you would enjoy it. I shall be pleased to give you my ticket, so that you won't be put to the least expense. I do hope you can manage it."

Nothing was further from Viola's wishes than to go to a lecture on Foreign Missions attended by a tail of High School girls. She had a tottering pile of exercise books to correct, and to-morrow was her heaviest morning. However, she didn't like to refuse the Head, even though she wondered how she could tell beforehand that the lecture would be interesting, and how the inspection, well over now, could still be putting extra work on to her. Still, it doesn't do for new assistant mistresses to be either inquisitive or disobliging. She agreed.

"Thank you so much. Here's the list of girls—a good many of them are from your own form, you see, so that'll be so nice for you. Yes. Thank you. Now I wonder if you could find Miss Parry for me and tell her I'd like to see her for a moment?"

Viola departed, did her errand, and then returned to the Staff Room, now embellished by the forms of the Misses Rowan and Reeve, both free. To them she half ruefully displayed the ticket pressed into her hand by the Head.

"I'm going to spend an improving evening," she said as she explained.

"Dashed if I'd've gone," said Miss Rowan. "Why did you?"

"Well, it's not very easy to say no to the Head, is it, over a thing like that? Besides, she'd just been rather nice—the inspector had slated me to her and she listened to what I had to say and backed me up. I didn't feel I *could* turn round and say I wouldn't do the first thing she asked me. And she says the inspection's given her a lot extra to do."

"Isn't she a cunning old brute!" exclaimed Rowan, half in admiration, half in contempt. "Gets in a new staff—makes her feel more or less under an obligation—pitches some yarn about extra to do *after the giddy inspection's over*—makes a favour of handing on her mouldy old ticket! She *is* the blue limit."

"You oughtn't to have taken it on," said Miss Reeve. "You'll find it's the thin edge—I mean end—of the wedge if you aren't jolly careful. And she'll tell us all how she nobly gave up her ticket for a *most interesting* entertainment in order to let one of her Staff go. ... Oh, well, you'll know next time. She's bound to try it on again pretty soon. You be firm."

"I will," promised Viola, a little bewildered and much amused. It seemed as if the simplest matters concealed unplumbed depths of cunning at Besley High School.

Although they weren't, Viola's ears ought to have been burning just then. Behind the white door Miss Barr was eliciting her informer's opinion of this new-comer, who seemed such an incalculable mixture of innocence and arrogance, conceit and simplicity, obstinacy and efficiency.

"What do *you* make of her, Miss Parry?" she asked as the plump little figure in its new green "woollies" settled into the other arm-chair. "Is she very simple or very deep?"

"*Deep*." Miss Parry's voice was hoarse with emotion. "When she thinks no one sees, she simply *lives* with Miss Cullen. I've seen her actually run after her and tack herself on to her—a new girl like that, with One of Us! ... And Miss Cullen seemed to *like* it. ... And she's gettin' very friendly with the others—tryin' to find out things, I 'xpect."

"But Miss Mortimer was very down on her. I thought that spoke well for her."

"I dessay it was all arranged between them. I shouldn't trust her, Miss Barr, not while she's in with Miss Cullen. I shouldn't wonder if she's a sort of spy of hers, keepin' in with us so's to let her know how things are goin'... You never know with an underhand woman like she is *what* she's up to."

Her own voice, excited, broadened and vulgar, seemed to strike the little lady unpleasantly.

"'F cawse," she added immediately in her most refined accents, "I don't want to prej'dice you agenst her, paw girl. ... I know it's very bad fawn f' me to seh anything, in a weh; but you understend, doon't you, haow 't is?"

"Quite, quite," murmured Miss Barr. "Hm. I hadn't realised that it was more than just the usual beginning of term tea-party friendship. ... Yes. ... So you think—?"

"*She's not to be trusted*," hissed Miss Parry melodramatically.

Their eyes met in one of those long confidential glances that expressed so much between them.

"I have a Sixth Form lesson due now," murmured Miss Barr. "I can't wait. But if you happen to be free this evening, I wonder if you would care to come to supper? I have a lot to talk over with you—"

"Soo d'laighted," cooed Miss Parry. "Oonly—ay doon't know if you remembah—the lec'chah—"

"Oh, I've arranged for that. Miss—er—Kennedy is taking the girls."

Again that explanatory look passed.

"I have a *lot* to talk over with you," repeated the Head, as her satellite rose to go.

CHAPTER XIII

Coventry

The morning did not go so badly for Viola after that. She had regained her confidence, which meant of course that the girls she taught believed in her too. She began to wonder, as the placid minutes passed, whether it was necessary, after all, to work so hard over the preparation of her lessons. She pulled herself up at once. Of course, if she were out only to keep girls quiet and cram into them the dry bones required by examination exigencies, she need never prepare a single lesson; but, idealist and enthusiast as she still was, she told herself that she was out for far more than that. She wanted to educate, not merely to teach; and she had so little time! Still, the temptation was there; soon, as mental and physical fatigue claimed her more and more, she would listen; soon she might fall, as many another enthusiast has fallen, and "English" would be, for her pupils, too, only another "subject" for examinations. ...

She came into the Staff Room at lunch-time feeling much more cheerful. She selected her bun, poured herself out a cup of the pale sweet drink that Mrs. Carson libellously called coffee, and perched herself on the edge of a table to enjoy the few minutes of leisure.

Something was wrong. She knew that in a second. Grim silence held the room, brooding over the munching women like a thundercloud. Miss Cullen, muttering her self-conscious monologue at her locker, did no more to relieve the tension than did the belated fly buzzing under the dusty shade of the electric light. Viola felt that overwhelming desire, which most people have known at some time or other, to break the spell. She felt that she must say something—anything.

"You were quite right, Miss Parry," she said in a voice which sounded even to her own ears false and flippant. "I didn't escape trouble over the inspection. I've just been hearing about it."

Miss Parry sniffed. Miss Pearson caught her eye, smiled significantly, and returned to her sidelong contemplation of her own reflection. Miss Lexington looked stony. No one said a word.

More out of pure contradictoriness than anything else, Viola went on, cocking her chin a little:

"I suppose no one knows of any decent rooms to let?" she asked the world at large. "My landlady had a row with me to-day, and I've told her I'm going."

There was a short silence. Then:

"Was that why you didn't take your duty this morning?" inquired an icy voice.

Viola jumped. "Oh! Was it—am I on cloak-room duty? Oh, I say, I *am* sorry! I absolutely forgot."

Miss Pearson smiled again, an incredulous and bitter smile.

"Who took it for me? You, Miss Pearson? Thank you ever so much. I'll take your next, of course. When is it?"

Even to herself she sounded voluble, unconvincing.

"I haven't another this term. I always plan to get my duties over early in term." Miss Pearson paused, then added meditatively: "Funny, isn't it, how some people seem to forget these things. I never forget a duty myself. I don't see why anyone should. But I remember, last term …"

She stopped, and each member of the old Staff mentally completed the sentence. Another link was forged in the chain that bound Viola Kennedy to Miss Cullen in the eyes of the Staff.

"I'm frightfully sorry," Viola said feebly. No one spoke.

"I suppose," she went on in desperation, "nobody can suggest any rooms? I must look for some at once. I'm leaving mine in a week."

Silence.

Then Miss Lexington spoke, very coldly.

"I'm afraid you won't find any others. *You* gave the notice, I imagine?"

"Yes. Mrs. Holmes was unbearably rude."

Miss Lexington gave a tiny shrug.

"You see," she said, still chilly, "those are Staff Rooms. Certain women in the town always let to the Staff. It's not exactly a right, of course—I mean Mrs. Holmes has no legal hold on you; but she will expect the Head to find her another lodger. She has let rooms to the Staff ever since the school opened. She is a recognised Staff landlady, and looks to the school to provide her with lodgers."

"But that's absurd!" cried Viola thoughtlessly. "I can't be expected to put up with discomfort and insolence just because other people have."

Silence.

"Do you *all* do that?" asked the girl, looking round in despair at the stony, weary faces. "Do you all put up with discomfort and rudeness because these women have established a legendary claim on the school?"

"Except in cases where the Staff has enlarged," said Miss Lexington icily, "we hand on rooms from one to another as we leave. You will find it very hard to get another working woman to take you in. Her friends would consider that she was a—a blackleg."

"*Well!*" exclaimed Viola with vigour. "Of all the hidebound, back-number, *stuck* places Besley seems to me to be the worst!"

Raised eyebrows and down-drawn mouths showed the disapproval of the Staff. Viola realised, too late, the imprudence of the sweeping condemnation. Had not several of her colleagues caught the spirit of the place, and become as immovable as the idiotic traditions that bound them? She felt a second's dismay at her *faux pas;* and then she shrugged her mental shoulders. She really didn't care two straws if she *had* offended. They wanted jolting—*hard*, she added to herself, viciously.

All the same, it wasn't comfortable. Whether you are within your rights or not (and Viola felt a doubt as to whether she was within hers), you always feel on the defensive when a whole group of people—especially the people with whom you are in close contact, daily and hourly—disapprove of you. Viola felt a silly, childish longing to apologise, to put herself in the right again by promising to be good. She felt that that was what they wanted her to do, all of them. Then they would forgive her and be friendly again. …

The day dragged to its weary close. Only one incident broke the placid, heavy calm of these uninspired lessons. Towards the end of the afternoon, when Viola, in a voice sluggishly slow lest it should betray her impatient irritability, was expounding the eccentricities of English grammar to a Lower Fourth form, the door softly opened and the Head appeared. The girls lounged to their feet, boredom clearly written on their sullen faces. They were aggrieved—first by having a dull lesson from Miss Kennedy; then by having to stand at all.

"You may sit," said Miss Barr graciously. Thirty-two bodies slumped heavily into seats.

"I just wanted to see you a moment, Miss Kennedy," the Head continued, lowering her voice to the State Secret whisper in which she, like most Heads, conducted all her public conversation with her staff. "I meant to speak to you before prayers this morning, but you were late, I think?"

She paused, clearly expecting an explanation or apology.

"Yes, Miss Barr," Viola assented stolidly.

The Head gave her a sharp glance. Was this impertinence, or fatigue, or merely bad manners, ignorance? She would give her the benefit of the doubt.

"Yes. … A pity, I think, Miss Kennedy, not always to allow yourself *plenty* of time in the morning. I always like my Form Mistresses to have ten minutes *at least* with their forms in the morning, just to get to *know* them, you know. It means such a *lot* to a girl, a Form Mistress's friendship and influence. …"

Viola had a fleeting vision of the form-room in the morning—that ten minutes when talking was allowed so that this theoretical acquaintance might grow. She saw the huddled mob at the far end of the room, whispering and giggling, while she sat, idle and self-conscious, at her desk. …

"I'm sorry. I was very tired," she murmured.

"Yes. We all are tired to-day, I've no doubt. As I said this morning, the inspection throws extra labour on—on most of us." The Head stressed this last sentence. This girl was not to run off with the idea that Head Mistresses did not suffer, even more than the ruck, from the ills of inspection.

"Yes. Well, I just wanted to see you now, Miss Kennedy, to remind you of the lecture this evening and to hand you the tickets. Three-shilling ones, you see. I never let the girls go in cheap seats when they're under school charge. I like a certain—er—tone kept. And you *will* keep a very strict eye on them, won't you, and see that they—er—maintain the honour of the school? It's so very important that they should make a good impression in the town just now."

Even Viola, weary and preoccupied with her own small troubles, could not miss the intense anxiety underlying those last words. She felt a momentary dart of acute interest, almost apprehension, as the Head's eyes, revealing, pathetic, alarmed, met her own.

"Yes?" she breathed.

The Head's lips parted. She was clearly so consumed by anxiety that she was on the point of sharing it, even with this new-comer. But the habit of caution restrained her.

"Yes. So I trust to you, Miss Kennedy, to keep a very close watch. ... Here are the tickets."

She moved to the door, opened at once by a child too new to be anything but awestricken by the near presence of this demi-goddess; and so drifted away. A few minutes later the bell ended the purgatory of that interminable day.

Not entirely. There were still the final straws of prayers and departure. Prayers were bad enough—the flat, dreary wail of the hymn, the over-emphasis of the Head's voice, raised in the artificial tones so common to those who address their God in public, the toneless gabble of the responses, the final exhortation, the dreadful cheeriness of the march out. But the cloak-room was worse. ... The stuffily-cold atmosphere, smelling of macintoshes and bad soap and wet shoes and Miss Pearson's heavily-scented face-powder; the polite, restrained fury of the tired women struggling for wraps and shoes and a turn before the mirror; the snapped remarks: "Excuse me, *my* shoes, I think"; "*Could* you move just a *little* farther along?"; "Really, I'm sorry, but I can't help it—someone near the door is simply *shoving*"; all made up a whole that baffled Viola's attempts to keep normal. As befitted one in disgrace, she sat on the boot-lockers

and waited. After all, it was easier than pushing in among all that mob. ...
How she hated them! How sick, sick, *sick* she was of it all. Five weeks had
gone, and she was doomed to thirty years. ...

Something like terror seized her at the thought. *Thirty years!* She
couldn't, no, she *couldn't*. No one could. ... She looked round her in a kind
of horror, like a creature caught in a trap, looking at the other victims.

Yes; it could be done. Thousands of women, not as strong, not as
happy, as she, bore their sentence—women who even hated the work
which she, so far, still enjoyed. She looked at them with new eyes. Miss
Lexington carried her burden stoically, grimly even, Miss Reeve gallantly,
Miss Parry resentfully, Miss Wilson apathetically; but they all endured
it. Only Miss Cullen looked as if she could bear very little more—Miss
Cullen and Miss Lovell. It seemed to Viola, looking at that white carven
face and hot eyes, as if Miss Lovell must soon break under the daily
grinding of the mill.

The tiny room emptied. Viola rose, wearily, apathetically, and began
to prepare for the street. She had ceased to feel annoyance or regret or,
indeed, anything for the snubs of her colleagues. She had realised, in that
brief space of time, that they were not normal, any more than the trapped
animals to whom she had compared them. She *knew*; for she, too, was no
longer normal. Perhaps she never again would be quite normal, quite her
old self, as convicts are, they say, never quite the same after their years of
unnatural life are over. ...

She dressed with swift, automatic movements and made her way down
the tiled corridor to the small side door consecrated to the Junior School
and the Staff. She never thought, now, of the fuss she had been going to
make over that significant detail. She was in the rut.

She realised, as she turned out of the building, that someone was
waiting for her; and all her numbed consciousness woke to a fret of
irritation that Miss Cullen should have chosen to-day of all days to attach
her undesired presence to her junior colleague. Her fingers tightening,
Viola told herself that she *could not stand* Miss Cullen to-night—and
knew she would. ...

"I hope you realise, my dear Miss Kennedy, that you've been put in the corner!" began the senior, with her wide, anxious smile. "Very naughty girl you've been."

Viola said nothing. She dared not give a chance of expression to the fury of irritability that seethed within her.

"Oh, my dear, don't take it to heart!" cried Miss Cullen, suddenly dropping the humorous manner as Viola preserved a stony front.

"Oh! I don't," replied the girl shortly.

"That's right! I feared, just for the moment ..."

The relief in the older woman's voice was so patent, so pathetically pleased, to discover that the new recruit had escaped unwounded from the shafts which had pierced her own heart so often, that Viola melted.

"I'm only very cross!" she said, with an attempt at a smile—"Things have gone wrong all day—and the inspector was such a pig—and there's this bother about my rooms—and I've got to take those wretched kids to the lecture tonight. ..."

Even as she spoke, Viola wondered at the change in herself. Once she would never, never have thought of lumping human, individual girls all together as "wretched kids." Had the blight, then, fallen on her too? Would she soon become another in the band who class all girls together, damning them impartially?

"I know—believe me, I do know," said Miss Cullen; and the sincerity and sympathy in her voice somehow comforted Viola's soreness. "And it's so worrying for you about the rooms. It will be so difficult to find new ones."

"Oh, I can't believe it's as bad as they say," Viola declared. "Anyway, I've done it now—and I'm glad I have. I can always go to an hotel or something for a bit—"

"My *dear*!" There was real consternation in Miss Cullen's voice. "I mean—forgive me—but you can't do that, you know, you really can't. Think what talk it would make—"

"Miss Cullen! You can't mean it!" cried Viola. "You can't think that Besley is so far behind the times that it would be scandalised if I spent a few nights at an hotel while I looked for rooms?"

Miss Cullen looked extremely uncomfortable.

"It would be *far* wiser not to," she said almost pleadingly. "Believe me, I do know. You can have no idea of the gossip and—and scandal in a town like this. You see," she added almost apologetically, "they've nothing else—no interests, no thoughts, no tastes—nothing. They live for trade and business and, when that's over—well, their neighbours are the only thing left. ... They must discuss something—must invent something, if it's only scandal. ... You mustn't blame them entirely. They know of nothing better."

"But I do blame them!" cried the girl hotly. "I think it's horrible. No wonder the children have such beastly ideas in their poor little heads. I only wonder they're as decent as they are. I think it's *horrible*," she repeated viciously.

"And I think it's pathetic," said the elder woman quietly. "You see, I'm old. I—I am not impulsive now. ..."

Viola said nothing. She had a sudden, startling realisation of the coming time when she, too, would no longer be young and impulsive. With an unusual spasm of humility, she hoped that she would be as kind, as forbearing, as the ugly woman clumping along wearily beside her.

"Well! I'll give up the hotel then," she said drearily.

"That's right," approved her senior. "You see—we're in the limelight here; and—well, the truth is that the school is rather disliked in the town. The Head has never made herself really popular with the townspeople; she—she's too refined, I think; they don't understand her, nor she them, and so—well, they irritate one another, you see, and each side takes offence where often none is meant. And so there's a lot of unkind talk about the school—there have been so many changes on the Staff, and one or two of the younger mistresses we had last year were very indiscreet—indeed, some are a little indiscreet now. ..."

Viola, thinking of the ogling glances of Miss Parry and the flaunting appearance of Miss Pearson, had perforce to agree.

"But I'll tell you what you *could* do," Miss Cullen continued hurriedly, as one who takes a heroic, but reckless, step. "My landlady has a nice bedroom—her sister has just left home—and—and—couldn't we share a sitting-room? I'm very quiet, always over my books, and they're nice rooms—quiet—"

Viola's consternation was almost visible. Her pity for the poor, plain, unwanted failure at her side made it just possible for her to be reasonably gentle and pleasant in their daily contact at school; but to *live* with her—to live with that precise, pedantic voice, that broad, mirthless smile, that anxious, would-be humorous talk …!

"Oh—thank you very much—it's very kind of you to offer," she stammered. "But—do you think—don't you think it's perhaps a mistake for two of a Staff to dig together? I mean—it makes life even narrower, don't you think, if—" She broke down, stammering awkwardly.

"Well, think it over. No need to decide now," said the elder woman. She could hardly conceal the anxious note of pleading in her voice. She had no wish to coerce the girl; but it would be so pleasant, so great a comfort, to have a companion, a friend, young, kind, to whom she might one day speak freely from her sore and heavily-burdened heart.

"Yes, I'll think it over," the girl assented hurriedly. "It's awfully good of you. … You turn off here, don't you? Good night, and thank you."

And in her relief she almost ran up the road to her rooms.

Miss Reeve and Miss Lexington, talking earnestly at the next corner, watched the parting.

"You see?" said the Second Mistress in a kind of gloomy triumph.

"Mmm. Quite chummy, they looked. Pity. I thought that girl was going to be quite useful. But of course if she's in with *Cullen*—!"

Miss Lexington nodded.

"She must know, of course?" ventured Reeve.

"About the inspection? Of course, if she's a friend of Miss Cullen's, she must. And you remember—she said how light the inspector had been on her. Naturally she was, if the girl's a friend of Cullen's."

"But to-day she said she'd had a bad report," objected Reeve.

Miss Lexington shrugged expressively.

"Yes—*to-day* she did."

"What d'you mean?"

"I mean that Cullen's put her up to it. She knows well enough that all the rest of us would notice it if her one friend was the only person to get a decent report."

"Mmmmm. I wonder. She looks an honest kid."

"Yes. And a week ago I'd have said that Cullen was an honest woman. But you can't deny, Reeve, that it must have been her doing that we had the inspection at all."

"No. It certainly looks like it," admitted Reeve.

"Yes. And I'm afraid we'll have to class Miss Kennedy in with Miss Cullen," said Miss Lexington.

"It's a pity," sighed Reeve, "but I'm afraid you're right."

And so was Viola's sentence passed.

CHAPTER XIV
Girls Are Human

All unconscious that she had been accused, tried, and condemned by the powerful quorum consisting of Miss Lexington and Miss Reeve, Viola returned to her rooms determined that before all else she would get a grip of herself. She would get rid of all this miasma of hints and perplexities, suspicions and dislikes, rumours and intrigues; she would, somehow, anyhow, get back to her old, fresh standpoint, seeing people as live human beings, not as pawns in elaborate manoeuvres or cogs in a machine. She would—with all her will she would force herself to remain *alive*.

Her tea—even chillier and duller than usual—was served by a sour-faced Mrs. Holmes in grim, protesting silence. A sniff accompanied the slam that signified her exit. Viola shrugged a tolerant shoulder. She was in disgrace all round, it seemed! Well, that didn't matter; she'd know how to act now that she knew where she was, and there was only one week of Mrs. Holmes to endure. She almost laughed aloud as she thought of the faces of the Staff when she'd said that she was giving up these horrible rooms. When she was settled and comfortable, she'd ask them all to tea and show them. ...

She had not very much leisure after tea. She had to be back at the school at half-past five to collect her troop of girls and parade them to the lecture. This began at six, and would, she imagined, last till half-past seven or so. Then the girls were to be solemnly escorted each to her own gate—Viola realised with relief that, in a town like Besley with only one residential quarter, this would not take as long as appeared—and she would be back in her rooms somewhere about half-past eight. Then her evening's work of preparation and corrections would begin.

She started early. The morning had shown her what even a few minutes spent in the silence of an empty field may do to restore one's sanity; she meant to have a second such breathing-space before facing the programme before her. The air was cool and blue with the faint mists of late autumn. As she slammed the gimcrack door behind her the thin tang of weed fires met her nostrils. Sounds of children's voices, shouting in play down the street, came to her ears with that curious romantic clarity that autumn gives to the noises of the world. The lamps gleamed like jewels in the misty air; the oranges and blue paper of the little greengrocer's shop at the corner were beautiful. Viola felt that touch of excitement that the romantic young often know with the coming of misty evenings— that sense of adventure, of suspense almost, of a dream coming true, as if something were suddenly to be revealed. ...

She turned into the wet grass. How still it was in the hushed, dewy field, shrouded in the autumn mist. How remote it was from the lights and sounds of the town. How real, how true, it was in its chill aloof silence. She stood and listened to her own hushed breathing. Softly, like a magic bell, the church clock sounded. It was like the prelude to adventure. ...

With a sigh she realised that that note of enchantment was no more than a call back to the world of duty. She walked on up to the school.

The girls were waiting for her, a chattering mob. Interests in Besley were so few that even the prospect of a missionary lecture excited these children. It meant being out at night, and a darkened hall to sit in, and lantern slides. Viola, realising the pathos of it, was suddenly overwhelmed with a gush of affection and pity. No wonder that they grew up with their imaginations half starved; no wonder that, in middle age, they peered inquisitively at the lives of their neighbours to find that excitement and romance which they could not find within their own minds. Miss Cullen's tolerance had been truer than her own impatient scorn.

"I'll *make* them see," she thought pitifully. "I'll show them where to find interest and beauty and *real* life—not the hectic sham they think life is."

And again she felt a gush of warm interest and affection flood through her as she looked at the excited, chattering girls before her.

She called the roll, formed the children into an orderly group. She wasn't going to insist on the obsolete absurdity of a "crocodile." That wasn't the way, she thought, to encourage self-respect.

"Keep close together," she said, as they settled into something like quiet. "And mind you're quiet when you're in the hall—don't disturb other people. I'll sit somewhere in the middle of you. All got your tickets? Right, come on, then."

To her rather touched surprise, Viola found herself instantly secured by two girls—Miriam Davis and Rhoda Stein, both of her own form. Miriam she liked—a gentle, retiring girl, possessed of sudden deep enthusiasms and enormous patience. Rhoda interested her. The passionate, sullen little Jewess had real imagination smouldering under her vulgarities, and an ambition that was almost great by its sheer force lifted her above the ruck of her fellows. Also she had sensibility. Once when, to show them how it should sound, she had read over a speech in the play the form was reading, Viola had surprised tears in Rhoda's veiled eyes and a dark flush on her sallow face. And the child herself, when she forgot her surroundings, could put genuine feeling into the parts she read. There was the real stuff hidden away in Rhoda. ...

They chattered as they walked, Miriam telling her of the various encounters of Besley with the sports teams of other schools in the neighbourhood. Her devotion to Miss Rowan glowed in every sentence. Suddenly, in the middle of a narrative, Rhoda cut in, speaking in a husky murmur for Viola's ears alone.

"Miss Kennedy, I want to read again that poem which you read to us last week. Please, what is it?"

"I don't remember, Rhoda. How did it go?"

"About peace—and music—" The child hesitated, frowning in her effort to remember the lines. "It had a line that is in my head always ever since."

"Tell me the line."

Rhoda shot a scowling, suspicious glance about her. No one was listening. Reassured, she began; and the thrilled beauty of her deep rather husky voice made a sudden catch come into Viola's throat.

"'There is sweet music here that softer falls
Than petals from blown roses on the grass
Or night dews on still waters ...'

"Oh, I forget!

"'Music that gently on the spirit lies
Like tired eyelids upon tired eyes ...
Cool mosses deep ...'

"I cannot remember. ... Please, what is it?"
Viola told her.
"Would you like me to lend it to you?" she asked.
Rhoda shot her a sudden, vivid, unfathomable glance.
"Please," she muttered gruffly.
"You like poetry, don't you?"
The child looked round warily; she broke into a vulgar, affected snigger.
"*I don't think*!" she sang out in a raucous, self-conscious drawl. Two of the others had drawn near enough to hear. ... All the same, Viola knew that the spark would not be utterly quenched. She quietly turned her attention to Miriam, who was ready to talk with courtesy and some humour of that odd hockey match last year when the Staff had played the School. Her story lasted till they reached the lecture hall.

At the door, Viola waited to usher in all her flock. Rhoda Stein was the first, obviously hanging back behind the others. As Viola passed in, she touched her arm.

"Please—I do like to hear and to r-read poems," she whispered, "only I do not like that they should be laughed. I wass afrraid."

"I know. I understand," Viola answered quietly.

"And—the book?"

"I will bring it to school to-morrow. I'll give it to you after school, and you can put it straight into your bag with your lesson books."

Rhoda shot her a quick ardent glance.

"Thank you," she said. Her lips opened as if she would say more; but she closed them again, and in silence they entered the hall together. In Viola's heart was the thought; "If only May Masters would leave, Rhoda would run the form. *Then* we really might begin to do things."

The lecture was all that Viola's fancy had pictured. The speaker had that unfortunate manner which suggests lessons in elocution and "Public Speaking," earnestly studied and laboriously acquired. The usual emasculate jests raised punctual titters at regular intervals. The slides, highly coloured and of a most improving nature, were exactly those suggested by the topic of the "little chat—no set speech, muh friends, just a little friendly chat among ahselves." Viola yawned, thought of other things, listened abstractedly, yawned again. In the grateful darkness (how she blessed the hideous slides that necessitated it!) she closed her tired eyes in a momentary doze. She heard vaguely a whisper at the far end of the row of girls; she didn't blame them in the least. If she had been one of them, with friends about her, she would have talked too …

The inevitable appeal for funds, and the lights snapped up all over the hall. Blinking and half dazed, Viola collected her flock and led them into the thronging crowd struggling down the narrow gangway. She envied them their coming free evening. Their homework had been excused on account of the lecture; hers was yet to come.

From house to house, in the dark streets pricked with orange gas-lamps, she led them, dropping each child at her home. At the end of one street she was aware of a thrill of excitement among the dozen remaining girls.

"What's the matter?" she asked.

No reply.

"Let's see—who lives down here? Vera Wilson, isn't it, and May Masters? Come on, girls."

A lanky figure detached itself from the group.

"I live just here at the corner, Miss Kennedy," said a whining voice that Viola recognised as Vera's.

"Oh, good. Run in, then, Vera. Good night. Come on, May."

No response. Then a timid voice:

"Please, Miss Kennedy, I think May's gone home."

"Gone home? When?"

"I—don't know, Miss Kennedy."

A whisper and a tiny titter came from the remaining girls. Then one, Lilian Burton, who sat behind May Masters in school, and who was her especial crony, spoke.

"She ran across Neville Road, Miss Kennedy, and went straight down home from there."

"Did she? Sure, Lilian? Did you see her?"

"Oh, yes, quite sure, Miss Kennedy."

"All right. Come on, then."

And she continued to restore her charges to their homes.

That night Viola slept like the dead—a deep, dreamless, satisfying sleep that soothed and restored her as only sleep can. She awoke to another cool blue day, thin trails of cloud stretched across the remote pale sky like shreds of torn gossamer. She tumbled out of bed, remembering with relief that the discomfort of these rooms would soon be a thing of the past. Then she remembered Miss Cullen's offer, and frowned a little over it as she rubbed her wet shoulders with a towel like brown paper.

"I simply *can't*," she thought. "I'd have a row with her in two days, however hard I tried to keep my temper. That voice, and that dreadful pedantic manner—! I must try to think up a good excuse."

Her appetite was unchecked by the gloom of Mrs. Holmes's manner and the dreariness of the meal prepared for her. She was full of vigour and optimism. What a fool she had made of herself yesterday!

"All comes of being sorry for yourself," she told herself. "Makes you lose your sense of humour at once. Maudlin, too."

She swung gaily out of the little house—and, at the corner of the street, ran straight into Miss Cullen.

"Good morning!" her senior greeted her, in her heartiest, most "humorous" intonation. "I hope you're going to be good to-day, to make up for yesterday's sins."

"I hope so too," Viola responded a little dryly. "The difficulty is that it's rather hard to avoid people's corns if you have no idea where they are. I can't think why all the Staff were so furious with me yesterday. It can't have been because I forgot a duty. Effects of the inspection, I suppose."

Miss Cullen looked at her—an odd glance, composed of wonder, deprecation, interrogation, sympathy, and other ingredients which Viola could not disentangle. It was as if she had said: "Shall I tell you? Or are you only pretending not to know? I'm sorry for you, but I know you don't want my pity. I'd better not say anything."

A gust of impatience at the absurdity of it all swept over the girl. Unconsciously she hastened her pace in accordance with her feelings. Really, these mysteries and secrecies were too childish! No, she certainly could not bear to live with Miss Cullen. How she hammered on and on, that dreadful pedantic, self-conscious monologue, with one eye always and always on her companion to see what impression she was making! She must think out a good excuse before she was again invited to share Miss Cullen's bed and board. Already she was almost too late.

"I've been thinking," the elder woman began, her voice almost natural in its anxiety; and then she broke abruptly off. "Would you care to come and have tea with me this afternoon?" she tried again. "I do hope you can," she continued, without pausing for an answer. "I—should like to have you so very much." And the wistfulness of her voice, and the pathos of the fact that this elderly woman was almost pleading with her to accept her hospitality broke down the reserve with which Viola had hedged her tender heart.

"I should love to," she replied untruthfully, her impulsive pity and generosity making her voice sound cordial.

"*Will* you? Will you, really?" How eager she sounded, like a child promised a wonderful treat! "That *will* be nice. I'm free this afternoon, so if you will come straight round to my rooms after school I'll have tea all ready. I *am* so glad you're not engaged. You won't forget, now, will you?" she added, with a nervous half-laugh that, Viola knew, concealed a genuine anxiety.

"Indeed I won't," she promised, laughing a little too to keep up the jocular air that robbed their words of their too serious intent. "*Nothing* shall prevent my coming, Miss Cullen."

And, joking though their manner had been, the girl knew that the tiny sigh which her companion uttered was one of relief. Mentally she endorsed that promise.

"Poor old thing!" she thought, with a pity that was not far from affection. "How pathetic she is! I'd be a pig not to go. ... I'll go, *whatever* turns up to prevent me. ... It's a shame that she should have to ask like that, so humbly. ... How desperately lonely she must be, and how people must have snubbed her! *Shall* I dig with her? Could I keep on being nice to her if I did? 'Fraid not, I'm not nice enough myself. ... Shall I try?"

Almost she spoke; her lips were parted on that impulse of generous compassion, when Miss Cullen herself spoilt the chance. Her eye, ever alert, suspicious, watchful, had seen Miss Parry and Miss Pearson advancing from the other direction. She determined to show them that she was not as utterly forlorn and friendless as they imagined. She burst into a voluble monologue, an animated, nervous torrent of conversation, that overwhelmed Viola and left her breathless. Almost against her will, the girl was saved from the consequences of her impulsive charity.

Miss Parry and Miss Pearson pointedly slowed down their pace to allow Viola and her aged companion to draw ahead. It was as clear a drawing aside of their skirts as a gesture could be; and Viola's chin cocked higher as she saw it.

"*Pigs!*" she thought viciously. "Poor old thing! I'll show them."

And she, too, began a furiously animated cataract of talk about nothing. Certainly no David and Jonathan could have proclaimed an intimate friendship more pointedly than did Miss Cullen and Viola as they entered the school premises.

Miss Parry drove a well-padded elbow into her companion's side.

"*See?*" she hissed.

The pale, sulky-lipped girl nodded.

"Oh! *That's* been clear for weeks," she sniffed. "What a fool that girl is."

"H'm. I'm not so sure that she's a *fool*," rejoined Miss Parry. "There's Miss Lexington. I wonder if *she* saw them?"

She had, of course; everyone had. For Viola, in her indignant warmth, had intended them to. She was not at all surprised at the icy reception of her greetings to her colleagues. Being a fighter, she rather enjoyed it.

CHAPTER XV
Trouble

No doubt many people have observed the great truth that when you awake convinced that the day will be pleasant it almost invariably turns out to be particularly beastly. Viola Kennedy had not yet discovered this. She thought that a good beginning meant a good day. If she needed disillusionment, this particular day was well calculated to administer it.

The blow fell during the last morning lesson. Viola was engaged with an Examination Form when Mrs. Carson, that portent of evil, arrived at her door.

"If you please, miss, Miss Barr would like to see you at once in her study."

"She knew that I was with a form, I suppose, Mrs. Carson?" Viola was not going to be snubbed over an abandoned form again if she could help it.

"Oh, yes, miss. She told me where to find you."

"I see. Thank you, Mrs. Carson; I'll come at once." And, setting the gaping girls some work to do during her absence, Viola went down to the white-painted door and knocked.

As she stood waiting for the summons to enter, she thought she could hear voices in the study—male voices, she was almost sure. What could this portend? An irate parent? A new inspector? A governor? An official from the dim and awful Board itself? And why had she, a humble and insignificant junior, been summoned to the interview that Miss Barr was conducting with these masculine invaders?

Even as she stood and guessed, the brass plate revolved and she entered the study.

Yes, males—two of them. One, a kindly, grey-haired, bewildered, embarrassed man of perhaps fifty; the other—Benedick.

"This is Miss Kennedy," said Miss Barr; and Viola knew at once, from the hesitating voice and agitated manner, that there was trouble in the air. Also she noticed that the disturbance, whatever it might be, was enough to make the Head lose sight of her manners. She had not introduced the men to the lady, but had indicated the lady to the men. That meant that the trouble was serious, and that she was involved.

The visitors had risen, and young Hyde was offering her a chair. The other man was looking at her in an embarrassed yet vexed manner, as if he really was very much annoyed about something, but didn't like making a fuss and didn't want to get her into trouble.

"Miss Kennedy," the Head began, "this is Mr. Glynn of Linden House School." The grey-haired man and Viola both bowed politely. "Mr. Glynn has come with a serious complaint—a very serious complaint indeed. ... I thought I made it quite clear to you, Miss Kennedy, when I entrusted the girls to you last night, that you were to be in charge of them entirely—to accompany them to the lecture, to keep them under your own eye when there, and to return each girl personally to her own door."

"Yes, Miss Barr."

"And did you do so?"

"Yes, of course."

"You *did*?"

"Why, yes!—Oh, except that I didn't actually hand May Masters in at her own door. She ran across the road opposite the turning that leads into her road—I suppose because it was so much quicker."

"At what time was this?"

"Oh—nearly nine, I should think. After the quarter to, anyhow."

Miss Barr turned triumphantly to the black-haired Benedick, who looked intensely uncomfortable.

"Now, Mr.—er—Hyde, you must see that you have been utterly mistaken. I *thought* it was most unlikely that any of my girls could behave in the manner you—er—described."

Hyde's face was a study—unconvinced, obstinate, yet relieved, as though he thought, "You're absolutely wrong, but if you like to think you're right, so much the better."

Mr. Glynn fidgeted.

"I understood—you said you were positive, Martin."

The younger man hesitated. Then, with an appealing glance at Viola:

"I am," he blurted out. "I'm awfully sorry—but I'm dead certain."

Viola looked from one to the other in bewilderment.

"Would you mind telling me what's happened?" she asked.

"This gentleman," said Miss Barr, indicating Hyde with a delicate gesture, "is engaged at Mr. Glynn's establishment. I understand (you will correct me if I am wrong, Mr. Glynn) that there has been a certain amount of—er—disciplinary trouble between his students, who are young men rather than boys, and—and—er—girls from the town." She blushed as she mentioned the unavoidable detail. "At eight o'clock last night Mr.—er—Hyde was coming in from a long walk and entered Linden House premises by the side gate which gives on to a shrubbery. There he found—exactly what, Mr. Hyde?"

"I heard giggling and rustling," said Hyde in gruff discomfort. "I went in, and found one of our chaps—young waster, he is—and—and—a girl." He stopped, flushing uncomfortably. Miss Barr flushed too. Viola gathered that compromising details had been given to the Head from which she was to be spared.

"I was savage," Hyde went on. "Mr. Glynn had done a lot for the lad, and he's not so bad at bottom, if he wasn't so weak; I mean, he'd have run straight enough if the girl had let him alone. You see, I—I knew the girl." He broke off again in obvious embarrassment.

"Now that's what I want to get clear," said Miss Barr, clearly hoping to confute the wretched young man. "*How* could you be so certain that you knew the girl?"

"Well! If you want the whole truth," he blurted out desperately, "because she—she'd made advances to me."

"*Really*, Mr. Hyde!" murmured the horrified lady.

"Well, you asked me," retorted the goaded youth. "The truth is, I doubt if any of our elder boys *haven't* had overtures from that young woman. I

– 189 –

knew her at once; and even if I hadn't, she lost her school hat as she ducked through the bushes. It had her name in it—May Masters, plain as possible."

"You see, Miss Barr," said Mr. Glynn, his quiet tones sounding quite urbane after his junior's gruff embarrassment, "if it were a first offence, I wouldn't have troubled you at all—I'd have written to the girl's parents. But from what Mr. Hyde tells me, and from what I have seen myself, this girl is a real—er—menace to our boys; and if she is that, she is certainly a menace to your school. I felt that it was a matter of which you ought most certainly to be informed."

"Quite," murmured Miss Barr, almost absently. Then she turned an icy countenance to Viola. "And now, Miss Kennedy, perhaps you will explain how it is that a girl who was entrusted to your care from six to nine last night was found in Mr. Glynn's shrubbery at eight."

Viola knew that she was on her defence—knew, too, that the Head's hopes, which she herself had raised, of an alibi for the culprit were completely dashed.

"I don't understand it at all," she began; and then memory swept over her. She saw it all.

"*Oh!*" she exclaimed, horror-struck.

The other three looked at her curiously.

"I *do* understand," she said; and there was something touching in the quiet candour with which she faced her judges. The two men, at least, could see and sympathise with the effort it cost her to speak out.

"It was entirely my fault," she said, her limpid eyes fixed on the older man. "I see it all now. I knew May meant to do something like this. I told you, you remember, Miss Barr—I showed you the letter I found in May's possession."

The Head opened incredulous eyes.

"Pardon me, Miss Kennedy. I have seen nothing of the sort. If you found such a document, you certainly never showed it to *me*."

In horror Viola remembered how the Head had refused to look at that letter. She had been too busy. ...

"I tried to," she answered, imprudently candid, "only you said you were too busy to look at it then."

Miss Barr crimsoned.

"And so, because I was engaged at one particular moment—you did nothing!"

Viola was silent. It sounded bad enough. ...

"In any case—was May not in your charge last night? How did she elude you?"

"She must have slipped out when the lights were down for the slides."

(Why, oh, why, had she not inquired into that whispering which had come to her half-dozing ears?)

"But surely you would then have noticed her absence when you saw them home?"

"I ought to have. May—as I told you, May was the only one I failed to take to her door."

"But you said that you saw her go to her house?"

Miss Barr was still clutching at a straw of escape.

"No. One of the others—Lilian Burton—said she'd seen her go. I didn't see her myself, and I oughtn't to have believed Lilian."

"So that it is possible that May could really have escaped from your charge and gone to this—er—this assignation which you knew she had planned, and yet you knew nothing of it?"

"Quite possible. I'm afraid it's what happened."

Miss Barr opened her lips to speak, but words failed her. She turned instead to her senior visitor.

"I can only apologise most sincerely, Mr. Glynn, for the criminal carelessness of one of my Staff," she said. Viola crimsoned, and then grew very pale. "Had it not been proved to the hilt I could never have believed that any of my mistresses could have allowed such a thing to happen while a girl was in her care. That must excuse my utter incredulity when you first mentioned the matter. And I must apologise to you, Mr. Hyde, for questioning your accuracy. I am more sorry than I can say that it was even possible for one of my girls to do such a shocking thing."

Young Hyde made an impulsive movement, as if to interrupt, more than once during this speech. At its conclusion Mr. Glynn rose hurriedly.

"Oh, no apology is in the least necessary, Miss Barr," he exclaimed.

"Please don't think that I came here to lodge a complaint. I only thought that you were probably quite ignorant of the girl's real character—I've no doubt she appears quite pleasant and well-behaved in school—and that you ought to know of her conduct. Such a girl as that must have a most pernicious influence. Also I thought that you would probably deal with her far more effectively than her parents, who, I should imagine, have no control over her at all. It—I really thought it only friendly to tell you. I should be most annoyed if one of my boys did a similar thing and I were not told."

"Certainly. I quite understand, and I am most grateful to you for your sympathy and help," said Miss Barr graciously, extending her delicate ringed hand.

To her quite obvious distaste, after bidding her farewell the master turned and shook hands with Viola.

"Don't take it too much to heart, Miss Kennedy," he said kindly. "I can't see that you were to blame in the very least. Good-bye."

Viola smiled gratefully, but wanly. She knew that her Head Mistress would not take that view; and that Martin Hyde had also guessed it she knew by the painfully warm pressure with which he wrung her hand as he followed his chief.

"Poof! Thank the Lord that's over," exclaimed the junior as the two men swung down the winding drive. "Never felt such a cad in my life—*never*."

"It wasn't the girl's fault, really," said the elder man. "The Head ought to have known it if the child was such a minx as she obviously is. I gather Miss Barr's one of the shut-eyes."

"That won't prevent her from having it in for the mistress, though," growled Hyde. "She'll want to work it off on someone. Did you see her face when she asked the girl to explain?"

"Mmmm. Poor old girl, she knows her school won't take many more knocks. Bound to be condemned soon, you know."

Martin Hyde grunted.

"Can't say I'm wasting any pity on *her*," he muttered. "Inefficient—Lord, Joe, it fairly oozes out of her. It's the girl I'm sorry for."

"Miss May Masters?" suggested Glynn slyly.

"Is it *that* little devil? No, but Miss Kennedy. She's in for a rough time, if I'm not a long way out. I felt like a cad, I tell you, Joe, handing her over to that old woman's mercy."

"H'm! If I'm anything of a judge, she can stand up for herself pretty well," responded Glynn. "Rather a pretty girl, I thought?" He shot a glance out of the corner of his eye at the lowering face of his kinsman. Hyde merely grunted.

"I wonder will she sack her?" Martin suggested suddenly.

"Not she!" said Glynn confidently. "She can't afford to sack her staff; might never replace 'em."

Hyde strode on in gloomy silence. Then:

"Mind if I'm a bit late for lunch?" he demanded abruptly.

"Not a bit. But won't it do in the afternoon?"

Hyde muttered something quite unintelligible, and wheeled about. His senior stood looking after his rapidly diminishing figure.

"If I'm not much mistaken," he said half aloud, "he's off to administer consolation. Can't say I'm surprised—she really was quite a pretty girl. ... It might be a solution," he added thoughtfully, turning back towards his own school.

During the short interval in which Miss Barr had summoned the caretaker to show her visitors out, she had been making a genuine effort to conquer her very pardonable anger. She had, to a stranger, one of her own profession who was in a position to judge, declared her belief both in the character of one of her girls and in the efficiency of one of her staff—and had been refuted. She felt more sheer anger than she had known for days; and the prick Viola had administered in reminding her of that disregarded letter added stimulus to her wrath. She meant, as soon as the visitors were gone, to take full vengeance on the cause of her public humiliation.

She turned back from her position near the door, where she had stood to bid the two reluctant informers farewell; and then something in Viola's attitude—the frightened eyes and courageous bearing, the fragility of her youth and the gallantry of her lifted chin—touched her to sudden softness. She was only a child, after all—a frightened child, waiting for punishment.

"Sit down, Miss Kennedy," she began.

Reluctantly Viola sat. She felt that this was a trick; the looming stander has so much the advantage of the sitter in a painful interview. She felt braver on her feet. ...

To her relief the Head then sat too. There was a short, painful silence, while Miss Barr considered her opening and Viola braced herself for the coming storm.

"Miss Kennedy," the Head began at last, "I don't want to be unjust to you over this—er—this most painful episode. I realise that I may have been—er—lax in my treatment of May Masters. Of course, if I had read the letter you speak of—as I admit I ought to have done—I should never have allowed her to go out at night under school supervision. I was to blame in that she went at all; but since you had read the letter, and knew what was in her mind, don't you think that you should have kept her under your eye the whole time?"

"Yes," whispered Viola; her voice was scarcely audible. "I ought never to have let her get away to the other end of the row. It's—I'm so unused to this—this watchfulness. I didn't realise—"

"I know," said the Head quietly. "I've seen very clearly how all of you younger mistresses chafe over the vigilant system of superintendence that we employ here. You understand now that there is a very real reason for it. ... Well, Miss Kennedy, I'm sure there is no need for me to say more. It is a most painful thing to have happened, and I am sure that you feel it as much as I do."

She paused. Viola could see that, to the elderly virgin, the incident was almost unbearably painful.

"Miss Barr—I am so sorry—so very sorry!" she said a little tremulously. "I do see how very careless—criminally careless—it was of me. ..."

Miss Barr hesitated; then, taking an impulsive plunge:

"I'll tell you something," she said. "Horrible as it is in itself, there are other reasons which make this—er—incident most unfortunate. *Most* unfortunate. We live in the public eye here; we are, as a body, disliked in the town—why, it is too long a story to tell now. Distorted versions of this affair will get about; people will gloat over it and gossip about it.

The governors will hear of it—the County Education Office will know. ... it's another nail in our coffin," she added almost below her breath. Then, suddenly, she remembered to whom she was speaking. The wells of confidence dried up. "You won't, of course, repeat that to anyone—*any* one," she said anxiously.

"No! Oh, no, never!" exclaimed Viola. "Miss Barr—is the school really in danger?" she added on an impulse.

For a second the Head's eyes—unveiled, sincere, terrified—met hers. Viola *knew*, then, what fear had inspired those words, "It's another nail in our coffin." She, Viola Kennedy had, by her careless indolence, helped to thrust this ageing woman—yes, and all her colleagues—down to despair. ...

To the subconscious relief of both women, the shrilling of the school bell put an end to their mutual revelations.

"End of school," said Miss Barr, rising. "Don't be too much distressed," she added kindly, as Viola, still murmuring incoherent words of penitence, left the study.

Viola decided that she would not stay an instant longer on the school premises than she could help. Thoroughly upset as she was by the interview, she felt a dread which only the shy can appreciate, that a word from anyone, friendly or sarcastic, biting or kind, would make her cry. If the Head had scolded her, been rude, unreasonable, angry, she could have held her own; as it was, she only just escaped in time to conceal her emotion.

She hurried down the corridor, her lips bitten to restrain her tears— tears which, she told herself angrily, were due more to her physical condition than to penitence.

"Silly *fool*!" she told herself furiously, cramming her hat down over her pretty hair. "I never used to cry for nothing. ... *Idiot*!" she scolded her reflected image, wavering through a mist of unshed tears.

The hum of voices came from opened doors. The forms were being dismissed. Hastily she fled from the approaching tide of colleagues.

Viola had only one idea in her mind as she hurried through the school gates—to get away to the quiet and peace of the field. She must have that restoration before she faced people again. She could get an hour, anyhow. ...

She got through the street somehow, and turned into the little field path. It was very still. The grey sky seemed to lean near the wet earth, friendlier than any blue. Viola took her hat off and held it in her hand. The damp breeze lifted her hair caressingly. She was alone, utterly, peacefully alone. She could let herself go at last.

She stood with lids closed over her tear-wet eyes, her face lifted to the sky, her lips trembling in little sobs like the faint crying of an exhausted child. Except for the hushed rustle of the withered grass, there was no sound but that tiny sobbing, infinitely pathetic.

A voice broke in on her solitude.

"Beatrice—Miss Kennedy—don't—*don't*," it said.

She knew it was Martin Hyde's voice—only she had never heard it quite like that before, tender, grieving, soft as only Irish voices are soft.

Too tired to care, she opened her swimming eyes.

"Oh, go away—*please*," she whispered with quivering lips.

"I can't. I can't leave you like this. ... Beatrice, I'm so sorry, so terribly sorry. ..."

"It's not—that—altogether. It's only—I'm tired—I shouldn't have cried—for *anything*—once. ... Don't mind me, please. I only want to be quiet. ..."

"Would you really rather?"

She looked him full in the face; and the trouble in his grey eyes made her pull herself together. She fumbled for a handkerchief.

"I always seem to make a fool of myself as soon as I meet you!" she said with a shaky little laugh. "I'm not really a c-cry-baby. Only I get tired, and then I seem to cry easily. ... There! I'm all right again now."

"Indeed and you're not. You're trembling. Come over here and sit down."

He took hold of her elbow—Viola couldn't repress a smile at his serious, elder-brother bossiness—and led her to a seat which some optimist had set up in the hope of making the field into a park.

"Have my handkerchief," he went on prosaically. "It's quite clean, and yours is wet through."

Viola laughed again.

"Thank you," she said, and wiped her eyes like a ten-year-old, openly. "I'm quite recovered now," she added, with a wavering smile.

"Tell me now," he said, ignoring this, "was she bad to you, back in there? She looked as cross as the cats."

"No—oh, no, not a bit! I could have made a fight for it if she'd been cross. No—she—it was—oh, I can't explain, it's private; only I've done her a real injury by my carelessness—and she was so kind. ..."

He grunted incredulously.

"*You'd* done nothing," he began; but Viola cut in.

"Oh, I had! I knew what that rotten girl meant to do; she was in my charge. Oh, it was all my fault, every bit. And Miss Barr was as kind as could be. That's why I cried. It makes you, when you get a kindness you don't deserve. ... If you don't go away I shall probably begin again."

He ignored this. It was a way he had, Viola noticed, when he meant to get at a thing; he ignored everything else.

"Are you long here?" he asked suddenly.

"No, I only came this term. I've only been—why, it's six weeks—not six weeks. How absurd it seems!"

"What seems absurd?"

"Why, that you can—live so much—no, not *live*—change so much, learn so much—in less than six weeks. It's like—oh, I don't know—living in another world, an unreal sort of bad-dream world. Do you know what I mean?"

He nodded, rather grimly.

"I do, well."

There was suffering in his voice. Instantly Viola thought—the war.

"I *am* changed," she said impulsively. "I've got so narrow, so self-centred. I don't seem ever to think of anything but myself and the school, the school and myself. I never think what horrors other people have gone through—may still be going through—"

She broke off. Something in his face arrested her.

"What do you mean exactly?" he demanded in a voice low and repressed, but startled, apprehensive.

She answered nothing. She gazed at him, half fascinated, half alarmed.

"Did you mean—me?"

"I—yes, I suppose I did."

"Do you know, then? About me, I mean? Does everyone know?"

She stared frankly.

"Why, no—nothing special. I thought, when you said you knew how long time could seem, perhaps you meant—"

"I meant prison."

"*Prison?*" she whispered.

He nodded.

"I ought to be there now by rights," he said with a grim little half-laugh, "only I was one too many for them."

"But why? How did you—?"

He looked at her oddly—quizzingly, she thought.

"You never thought to speak to a convict, did you, now?"

"Why not?" asked Viola simply, "if it's a nice convict?"

He looked taken aback.

"Don't you want to know what I've done—why I was in prison?"

"No. Not unless you want to tell someone about it."

"Do you mean—it makes no difference to you?"

"Not the slightest," she affirmed stoutly. "I back my instinct," she added, laughing a little. "Whatever you did, or didn't, do, I'm sure you never did anything mean, nothing you're ashamed of."

"Indeed and that's true." He looked at her with eyes whose expression she could not quite read. "It was for Ireland," he added, quite simply. "The Black and Tans got me first. They—well, I don't think about that when I can help it. ... Then it was the English Government. I was five months waiting to be tried. I was—an unconvicted convict. ... I declare I'd almost rather the Black and Tans than the deadness of an English prison!" he exclaimed suddenly, with a restrained force that half frightened Viola. "I took a chance—a bare one!—and ran. I'm 'wanted' at this minute—to take my trial. That's why I call myself Hyde." Again he laughed, that short, grim laugh.

"And Mr. Glynn—he knows?"

"Joe's—ah, I'd never tell you what he's done! He's one you'd not meet in a century. ... I wasn't worth much when Joe took me in. ..."

He broke off. The note of suffering was as plain in his flexible voice as the darkness of pain in his grey eyes.

Viola laid her hand on his clenched fingers.

"I'm so sorry—so sorry," she whispered.

Like clouds before a west wind, the gloom left his face. The clever, sensitive mouth broke into a smile which was almost beautiful, and his eyes laughed into hers.

"Sure there's no need, now!" he said, "but—I'll not forget you said it."

And with a gesture so simple that it seemed as natural as speech, he raised her hand and kissed it.

"I brought you here to rest," he went on in self-reproach, "and here I've been bothering you with what's over and gone long ago! Tell me now," he continued, brushing aside her protest, "are you free this afternoon?"

She shook her head.

"No such luck! I go on duty at two."

"And where do you lunch?"

"To-day—I don't. I feed at school as a rule, and to-day I just couldn't. And I've had a row with my landlady, so I can't turn up there and demand food. And I don't want a café. But I meant to cut lunch," she added hastily, as he got determinedly to his feet. "This—the quiet and the air—will do me lots more good than lunch. I'll have a big tea."

"You've had quiet and air enough now," he said. "You've time to eat, too. Ah, go on, Beatrice, now, don't be silly! There's the café down in Howard Road beyond. Will you go there now?"

"Beatrice never did anything Benedick told her," laughed Viola.

"She did—in the end. ... I'll make a fuss if you don't, now. It's no wonder you feel tired if you go playing tricks like that," he scolded.

"I've no time."

"You have. It's only half-past one. Will you go, now?"

"Oh! All right."

She rose and pulled her hat over her tumbled hair. "Am I clean?" she asked, lifting her face as simply as a child.

"Mmmm—fair. It's lucky you don't use those powders and things, or you'd be in a fine mess. You'll do. Have you your purse with you?"

She laughed outright.

"How many sisters have you?"

"One. Why?"

"Nothing. Only—do you see that she has a clean face and a dry hanky and cash to pay for lunch when she goes out?"

He laughed too.

"I expect I do. Am I very bossy?"

"All Benedicks are. ... I've got loads of money, and I'll eat a gigantic meal. And—thank you, Benedick. You've cured me of—lots of things."

She hurried away over the wet, withered grass. Martin Hyde stood looking after her. Then with a sigh he turned away in the direction of Linden House.

"Where's the use?" he said half aloud. "Wouldn't a girl like that have scores after her without wanting one like me? God bless her!" he added with apparent irrelevance.

CHAPTER XVI
Things That Matter

Incongruous as the comparison seems, Miss Cullen felt, that misty afternoon, like a gambler who has staked his all on one throw. Lonely she had always been; but she had never before been an outcast. Now, she knew, she was that—unless Viola Kennedy stood by her.

"I think she likes me," she told herself, anxiously and wistfully, as, over the solitary lunch which she ate at home on her free afternoons, she carefully considered the coming festivity. "The great thing now is to make my rooms attractive to her—make her really *want* to share them with me. ..."

For a few moments she allowed her thoughts to dwell on that prospect. She would have a companion to face her over her lonely meals; there would be a young, fresh face to greet her in the morning when she returned from Early Celebration—a friendly voice to bid her good night. For Viola would be sent off to bed early, as became her youth, and leave her ugly old senior to the arid desert of Corrections. Already in fancy Miss Cullen mothered Viola.

"She must have my bedroom," she thought. "It's so much larger and quieter than the other one. And I'll see that she eats properly and goes to bed in good time. She's too young and pretty to be knocked about by this drudgery. I must look after her. ..."

Her face softened into the tenderness of motherhood—that selfless, brooding tenderness that some childless women feel so intensely and lavish on anything rather than nothing, when they know that children will never be theirs.

"She'll be like a daughter to me," thought the plain, patient, awkward woman. She felt a glow of humble thanksgiving that she had been given someone on whom to spend herself. Already she saw herself boiling water for Viola's hot bottle, making her change damp shoes—("girls are so careless")—giving her a hand with the hateful, interminable drudgery at the end of term. Planning denials and labours for herself, she was utterly, wholly happy. ...

Then she pulled herself up.

"Of course, I can't be sure that she'll come," she thought anxiously. "I must have everything very nice for her. Let's see, now, what do girls like for tea?"

She cast her memory back to those days (how distant they seemed now!) when junior members of the Staff had asked her out to tea. She vaguely remembered biscuits—fancy biscuits—and iced cake. She smiled a tender, indulgent smile as she thought of it.

"Just what children would like," she told herself. "Of course, they *are* only children. ..."

She got determinedly to her feet, resisting the temptation to a short rest before the fire, and dragged on her battered felt hat and hideous ulster. Then she took out her purse and rapidly counted its contents. An anxious look crossed her face.

"I thought I had more than that," she muttered half aloud. She hesitated; then, with an air of reckless defiance, she snapped her purse shut and put it in her capacious pocket. It was a look and gesture curiously reminiscent of the gambler.

"It would be worth *ten* shillings to have her enjoy herself!" she thought. Then, hesitating again, "Of course, there's the subscription to the Clergy Orphans—and the one to the Church Army—and Christmas charities coming soon. ... And I'd like to give the vicar something for the church. It could be done quite anonymously. ... If only I could be sure of my pension!" She sighed. "Still—if I could have her here, it would make me all the fitter to earn that," she concluded. "I think it's excusable extravagance. I'll do it."

And, with the air of a Napoleon, she sallied out to make her attack on the confectioners of Besley.

❦

Meanwhile Viola walked back to the school in a very different mood from that in which she had left it. The half-frightened, half-penitent child had given place to an older, gentler, wiser being in her. It was as if she had been enclosed in a tiny hollow sphere in which she futilely turned and turned; and, by that encounter in the wet, grey field, a window in her prison had been opened, allowing her to see, for one instant, into the lives and hearts of her fellow-men. Her eyes had a veiled look, like a visionary's, as she walked back up the drive, where the bare trees dripped slow beads of moisture on to the sodden ground. It was as if her heart, stupefied by routine into a sluggish sleep, had been touched into tender life by that quick gush of emotion for sufferings and ideals at which she could only guess. ...

"Penny for your thoughts," challenged Rowan as she entered the cloak-room and hung up her hat like a sleepwalker.

Viola started.

"Nothing doing," she replied with a laugh. As she spoke, she realised with pleasure that one of her colleagues at least would not send her to Coventry for her championship of the Staff pariah.

Miss Pearson looked round and smiled a slow, deliberate, meaning smile.

"You mustn't ask too many questions, Miss Rowan," she tittered. "When some people go out to lunch they like to be left alone afterwards."

Viola flushed.

"How odious she is!" she thought. Aloud she said, rather snappishly:

"Oh, nonsense, Miss Pearson! As if I minded! I went out to lunch at the Good Luck Café because I was sick of school dinner. Is *that* a crime here too?"

Miss Pearson coloured too. She opened her mouth to speak, then, markedly, closed it, with a little expressive grimace at the Staff. Viola felt her own rudeness acutely.

"I'm sorry," she said penitently. "I've had rather a trying morning, and I'm cross."

The silence said, more audibly than any words, that *that* old plea was no excuse to a Staff who all had trying mornings as a matter of course.

Viola realised that she herself had, by her incautious retort, slammed shut the door into friendliness which had been opened just a chink. Hurriedly finishing her small preparations she left the cloak-room, stuffy with damp clothes and oppressive with hostile emotions.

Back in the school atmosphere again, the episode of May Masters returned to her mind with renewed strength. How beastly the whole thing was—how sordid, how sickening. And, try as she would, she could not see how an atmosphere of which May's affair was an example, in which May was a popular and commanding figure, could be purified. May was an extreme case, of course; but May was admired by her schoolmates, always had a throng hanging about her, was a person of influence in both Upper and Lower school. That fact told its own tale.

As Viola was, rather despondently, revolving these thoughts in the solitude of the Staff Room, Miss Wilson entered with her slack, idle gait and nonchalant air. She seated herself in one of the wicker arm-chairs and watched, with a half-indulgent, half-quizzical smile, Viola's clouded face.

"Well, young woman—been putting your foot in it rather, haven't you?" she said at last.

"Mmmm—rather," Viola admitted ruefully.

"What's happening about the Masters kid?"

"Oh—is that out?" asked Viola with some annoyance.

"*Out*? 'Course it's out, my dear—thrill like that! Girls jabberin' about it all dinner-time. Public benefactor, May Masters."

Viola slammed the door of her locker and turned the key with a vicious click.

"Well—what's the solution?" she demanded, facing round on the ironic Miss Wilson. "It's a *damnable* thing to have happened. It looks as if all this watching and guarding and checking discipline was necessary after all—and I *know* it's all wrong!"

"'Course it's all wrong. If it hadn't existed, May would have met her youth *coram publico*, and all would have been well. As it is, they sneak about it, and lie, and get into corners and—there you are."

An eloquent shrug pointed the sentence.

Viola looked at her doubtfully.

"Then—do you think we're wrong to agree to carry out this system?"

Miss Wilson shrugged again.

"You can't split a system," she stated. "It's all or none—and you'll never get a Head like ours, or some of the Staff even, to try the 'free discipline' plan. They haven't the nerve."

"Well—but—with girls like these—it would be very risky, wouldn't it?"

"Risky? Oh, of course. Very risky. Liberty's a risky thing when first introduced. But it very soon pays, if you'll take the initial risk. ... If we'd had modern ideas here," she went on after a pause, "this would never— could never—have happened. As it is—d'you know that it's on account of those Linden House boys that we get that devilish dinner duty? Oh, yes, it is. The H.M.'s afraid that if we let the girls go out to play in the dinner-hour they'd sneak off and meet the lads. Well—to begin with, if they'd the chance to play tennis or hockey or even hide-and-seek, most of 'em wouldn't think twice about the boys. Some of 'em would, of course—say one in twenty, and that's putting it high. So, to save the ones, we herd the twenties into the Hall. What do they do? Look for excitement indoors— something to give 'em a thrill. Result—May Masters gets a following." She put up a thin hand to hide a yawn. "Oh, yes—wearin' business. ... Say, you comin' that weekend expedition with me some time?" she added inconsequently.

"Rather!" Viola caught eagerly at the friendly note. "When shall we do it?"

"This week-end suit you? We could get off on Friday night and come back latish on the Sunday."

"Oh, let's! Let's go off into the country somewhere—somewhere where there won't be any kids or Staff or rows—"

Miss Wilson's quizzical eyes surveyed her in amusement.

"Bad's all that?" she drawled. "Right, let's. I'll leave it all to you. You look as if you c'd deal with maps and time-tables and things. Only don't plan anything vigorous for me to do. Repose, that's the touch as far as I'm concerned."

The afternoon went better than Viola had feared. The Staff, most of them, now cast her pitying, even friendly, glances. They had heard by now of the episode of May Masters, and guessed that this new recruit had probably been "put through it" pretty severely and probably semi-publicly. More than one gave Viola a word of pity, and the general atmosphere was even genial. The fact that they saw Viola alone and *minus* her objectionable *protégée* probably was more responsible for their warmth than either they or she realised. None of them knew that all Viola's sins would have been forgiven easily, indulgently, if she had been a single unit instead of one of a pair of which the other half was anathema.

Though the afternoon passed easily enough, Viola found her thoughts straying often—to the interview in the Head's study, with the revealing conversation that followed it, with its pathetic alarming implications; to her own remorseful flight; to that meeting in the cool empty field. It was, of course, this last that held her most. What girl in her early twenties could have resisted the claim of the memory of a romantic youth who bore on him the marks of suffering for a poetic land, and who, at parting, had kissed her hand? Viola, engaged with a thrilled Fourth Form on a dramatised reading of "The Merchant of Venice," found her whole heart throbbing to the music of that magical "On such a night as this. ..." Though the mist of the morning had thickened to a fog which choked the air and dimmed the light to a smoky, sulphurous yellow twilight, for her (and, through her, for the children) the regal moonlight flooded an ancient garden where lovers wandered in the flower-scented dew. ...

Still in a dream, she led her last form down to pray; absently she followed her colleagues into the cloak-room and prepared for the street. Out of doors, the clinging fog, which made her fellows shrug their shoulders up to their ears and hurry along the ugly streets to their fires, with a hope of hot tea-cake lighting their gloom, affected her not at all. She trod the mean, dingy streets in a dream, and in a dream let herself into her ugly rooms.

❦

Miss Cullen, clad in a ceremonial garment of brown cashmere hideously adorned with green buttons, stood putting the final touches to the feast she had so lovingly prepared. Even to her eyes the sitting-room looked dull and stagnant. The plush "suite" and thick flock paper seemed dead, choked by the fog which they seemed to absorb as sponges absorb water. The Nottingham lace curtains, dry and harsh, were gritty with smuts before it had occurred to the lodger to shut out the insidious yellow vapour; the heavy rep curtains, flanking the lace ones, were limp with the moist atmosphere. In the grate the fire, economically piled with slack, smoked sullenly. Not even Miss Cullen's optimism could find that room anything but gloomily depressing.

"I wish I could have afforded a few chrysanthemums," she thought, taking a red and gilt vase from the mantelpiece and trying the effect of artificial poppies and dried grasses on the tea-table. "Still, these are nice and bright. ... Yes, I think they're an improvement."

She regarded the effect critically.

"Yes, distinctly more—festive," she decided, settling the grasses with a fussy finger.

Perhaps it was an improvement. Certainly nothing, not even that atrocity, could have made the general effect more deplorable. A plate of "lodging" bread and butter held one end. In the middle triumphed a yellow segment of "grocer's cake," splotched with raw cherries of an unwholesome purplish pink. This was flanked by two indescribably hideous glass dishes, one containing marmalade, the other raspberry jam of a curious shade of brownish purple in which glistened seeds palpably wooden. At the far end two garish china plates held the sugar biscuits with which Miss Cullen replaced the dainty *petits fours* of memory, and small cakes iced with pallid pink. A child of four, if unsophisticated, might have enjoyed that tea. Few others could even have faced it with equanimity.

Miss Cullen, sitting in the tight, hard gent's arm-chair by the sulky fire, regarded it with equanimity, even with tenderness, as one might the gaudy preparations for a children's party. She did not notice the flight of time. ...

A sound startled her—the muffled, dead *cling* of the warrior-guarded bronze clock on the black slate sarcophagus of a mantelpiece. She started and blinked, like one suddenly awakened from a dream.

"*Half-past five!*" Incredulously she looked at the heavy gold watch which, in these wristlet days, she still wore tucked into a solid waistband. "A quarter to six, really, then …"

She went to the window, parting the gritty curtains, and stared out over the grimy railings and depressed laurels. She even went to the gate and stood, the fog softly soaking her "best" dress, gazing down the road. The fog gave an air of mystery, almost of terror, to the little secret houses huddling in the narrow, straight road. Involuntarily Miss Cullen shivered. Vague fears, none the less terrifying for their vagueness, suddenly seized her. Standing there, alone in the mist, the line of brooding houses opposite, the shrubs silently dripping moisture, she knew, instinctively and certainly, that hope, for her, was dead. She turned back into the house.

"You may clear away, Mrs. Baker," she called in a voice surprisingly steady. "My friend will not be coming now."

CHAPTER XVII

Romance and Reality

Patience and humility are dull virtues when compared with the more dashing ones, like courage and generosity; but there is a patience which has in it the very soul of courage, and a humility which is generosity itself in a new dress. Miss Cullen, sitting over her work that foggy evening, displayed both. How deeply she was hurt, how bitterly disappointed, she would not acknowledge even to herself as, while steadily working with one part of her mind, she thought with the other of that lost afternoon.

With her usual rigid conscientiousness she went through the piles of books before her; even when a slow, reluctant tear welled up she just wiped it patiently away and went on working, choking back the flood of emotion which, she knew, seethed within her, ready to overwhelm her if she yielded an atom of her steady repression.

But at last the final book was corrected and marked, the mark neatly entered in her book, the last lesson prepared. She sat back in her chair, her head a little bent, the neat piles of work ranged before her, and allowed herself to think.

"It's not surprising," she thought patiently. "I'm so very—unattractive. ... She's always been so pleasant that I thought she really liked me. It was only politeness, I suppose. I can't offer her much, of course—not much that she'd care for. She must have so many friends, a pretty girl like that; it wouldn't mean much to her, my caring for her. ..."

She bit her trembling lip.

"It wasn't much to ask for," the current of her thoughts ran on. "Only to be allowed to look after her and help her a little. ... I shouldn't have wanted any return... They might have let me have just that much. ..."

The flood was rising now, rising fast. She could feel the quickened pulse in her throat and the threat of tears in her eyes.

"It isn't fair—oh, it *isn't* fair!" she whispered aloud. "Some people have so much—and I can't even be allowed to have one person to care for! She might have just *tried*. If she'd only just let me show her how much I could have done. I'd never have worried her. Only just done little things for her—she need never have noticed they were done. I wouldn't have intruded or been fussy. She might have given me a chance. ..."

Round and round, like a bird caught in a room, her thoughts circled, dazed, bewildered. The storm of emotion surged up higher and higher, nearing hysteria.

"Cruel—they're all cruel to me here," she thought. "She has seen it—sees I'm alone. She's like all the rest—can't bear to be in a minority. ..."

The hot, angry, bitter tears came then, streaming down her faded cheeks unchecked. Her mouth, set as in pain, twisted a little over the heavy, silent sobs that shook her lean body. Behind the flood of hysterical, passionate thoughts she knew that she was wronging Viola—knew that, whatever the cause, it was nothing mean, nothing self-seeking, that had kept the girl from her; but somehow it soothed her to feed the fire of her anger. It was easier to feel oneself cruelly, heartlessly slighted than merely forgotten.

Slowly the storm subsided. Tired, shaken, her head throbbing heavily, her throat aching, her breath still coming unevenly, she rose at last. She took out her handkerchief and blew her nose vigorously, wiping her eyes openly and pitifully.

"I've been a fool," she told herself bitterly. "I might have known that I could never hope to make a friend here. I've built my house on sand. ... Well, that's the last time. I'll never, never risk it again." She winced a little as she made the resolution. Better to make up one's mind to the continued slow ache of loneliness than to risk again the cruel pain of shattered hopes; but it was hard—hard! Folding her lips in the grim lines of silent endurance, she put away her handkerchief and drew herself to her full height.

"Never again," she said aloud, as, with her usual meticulous neatness, she set her hideous room in order. "Never again."

The words sounded horribly final in the stillness of the little room.

Of course, no thought of her engagement with Miss Cullen had entered Viola's head. The stormy incident of May Masters and the subsequent disturbing interview with the Head would probably have put it out of her mind in any case; but that meeting with Martin Hyde in the wet field left no room for any ordinary detail of life in her mind. It had been so sudden, so startling, and—yes, so romantic—so like the dreams that many girls have in secret and which die unfulfilled and forgotten.

Viola's sleep that night had been a rainbow maze of dreams in which Martin Hyde and Benedick were inextricably blended; only once or twice, like a black blot, a dark cloud more than an actual memory, did the trouble of the morning come to her mind. When she awoke and prepared for her day's work it was the awakening woman rather than the conscientious schoolmistress that was uppermost in her. Only, she was determined on one thing—that she would, with all her skill, keep her sacred thoughts secretly guarded from the prying eyes and vulgar jests of her three foes, Miss Parry, Miss Pearson and the satellite Fergusson. She flushed as she thought of the meaning glance that had accompanied Miss Pearson's sneer: "We don't want to be questioned when we go out to lunch."

"Vulgar little bounder!" she muttered, with an angry toss of the head. "Isn't it *like* her? I suppose if she'd been in my place we'd all have been hearing a highly-coloured version of her last 'affair.' She'd have turned it into a proposal. ..."

Then she pulled herself up.

"Isn't that exactly what you've been dreaming of all night yourself?"

It was as if a new voice had spoken the words. Viola, too, was developing a Second Self.

"Oh! I'm as bad as she is, every bit!" she told herself, blushing furiously.

"Isn't it *disgusting*! We can't meet a man without imagining ... It's this rotten, shut-in, unnatural life. ... But—he kissed my hand. He did kiss my hand. ..."

Viola went to school in a new mood that morning—a softer, gentler, happier mood, in spite of the troubled atmosphere which would, she knew, greet her when she got there. She was prepared for hostile and scornful glances—prepared, too, to make allowances for them, her whole mind sweetened by the emotions which had so lately swept her—emotions which comprised humility and penitence, as well as that deeper, lovelier emotion to which she could give no name.

Starting in this mood, she was naturally more interested, and even amused, than anything else as she looked round the mistresses assembled in the tiny cloak-room. She had definitely and voluntarily joined Miss Cullen outside the pale; she realised that; but she was not at all sure that all, or even many, of her colleagues wished her to be there. Miss Lexington looked grave, preoccupied, a little anxious, perhaps; Miss Parry frankly scowled; Miss Pearson looked, as usual, bored and sulky; Miss Moore was as abstracted as ever, Miss Reeve indifferent, Miss Wilson very faintly and cynically amused—in fact, Viola was almost sure that she caught the tremble of a wink in that immobile and ironic face. Miss Cullen had not yet arrived.

There came a tap, hurried, soft, insistent, at the door of the sacred cloak-room. Miss Rowan, as the nearest, opened it a modest six inches.

"Miss Barr has sent to say that she wants to see you, Miss Lexington— at once," she remarked, turning back into the tiny room.

Miss Lexington turned a countenance of dignified annoyance.

"*Now?*" she asked in a tone that said, "Is one *never* to be left in peace?"

Miss Rowan turned back to the door.

"So Mrs. Carson says," she reported.

Then Mrs. Carson's voice, agitated and excited:

"Yes, if you please, miss—at once, please."

Miss Lexington, in a silence more eloquent than words, departed.

"What's in the wind *now?*" said Rowan, resignedly, as she writhed into her tunic. "Always so beastly furtive they are in this place."

"Sure to be nothing at all," said Miss Reeve, fastening a slipper. "The H.M. loves alarms and excursions."

"Sh'd've thought she'd had enough of *them*, without inventing more," grumbled Miss Parry, anxiously scanning her nose in the mirror, powder-puff in hand.

Miss Fergusson snorted in affirmation.

One by one they left the cloak-room and reassembled in the Staff Room. No bell summoned reluctant Form Mistresses to their rooms. There was an atmosphere half of delightful stolen ease, half of uneasy apprehension.

"I say, it's five to," announced Rowan suddenly. "What can they be after? Fancy the H.M. forgetting the Heart-to-Heart bell!"

"Jolly glad she has," commented Miss Gilbert, swinging idle legs as she sat on the table. "Of all the idiotic institutions in this lunatic place, that's about the maddest. As if—"

She broke off. Miss Lexington, looking very grave and rather white, entered the Common Room.

"Miss Lovell won't be here to-day," she announced. She paused a moment, her keen eyes reading their faces. They all knew that something serious was to come. "You'll have to know sooner or later," she went on, "and I think it's best that you should know the truth of what's happened. The Head left it to me to tell you or not, and I think it's best to tell you. There'll be a dozen versions going about. It's not a thing we can keep dark. …

"Mrs. Carson had a rather alarming experience last night. She was in bed when she heard someone moving about the school. She called her husband, thinking, of course, of burglars. They came down together, and on the stairs they met—Miss Lovell. She seemed quite unconscious of them, like a sleep-walker. Except for shoes and a big coat, she was in her night-clothes. Obviously she had got up and put on the outdoor things in her sleep.

"They could not get her to go home or to come into their rooms. She kept moaning, they said—saying that she must be at school in time, or the inspector would get her dismissed. … They said it was terrible to hear her. …"

Miss Lexington paused abruptly. Her level, controlled voice had only just lasted.

There was a horrified silence. Then Miss Reeve asked:

"Where is she now?"

"She seems to have collapsed utterly at four o'clock or so," answered Miss Lexington. "They laid her on a sofa, and Carson went and roused up her landlady and a doctor. They fetched her away. She's still unconscious."

"Of course they've wired for her people," said Rowan.

"That's the tragic part. ... Do you remember my saying once that I knew more of the circumstances of all of you than any of the rest realised? That was quite true, but I was thinking of Miss Lovell when I said it. She—"

Again the quiet voice broke off sharply. Then, with an obvious effort, she went on:

"Nobody knows what that poor girl had to face. You all thought her cruel, hard as iron, I know—and so she was; but it was only natural that she should be. She had trouble of the worst kind to face. She—her mother is dead; she was killed in—in a horrible way—"

Miss Lexington gulped visibly.

"It's almost too ghastly to tell," she went on. "That poor girl! How she came through it I don't know. ... There was insanity in her father's family. It was he who—"

A horrified gasp came from the women who had known and disliked Miss Lovell. Miss Reeve alone spoke.

"It wasn't he—who—who killed—?"

Miss Lexington nodded.

"She—Miss Lovell—found them. ... The father is in an asylum, of course. She pays—I can't tell you how much—for him. She was devoted to him. And she has two small sisters to keep. You can guess how she felt over her position here—how much all this talk of dismissals meant to her—how much more even than the rest of us she dreaded those inquiries and upturns. Of course she, like a few of the rest of us, knew that to leave here was to end her teaching career—and her father and her two little half-sisters depended on her. ...

"Then—I think she began to be afraid—for herself. She had appalling headaches. Some of you must have noticed her sometimes, how tortured her eyes used to look, though she never dared admit how bad she was. She was afraid to go sick lest it should be made a pretext for her dismissal that she wasn't strong enough for her work. I—I can't bear to think what she must have suffered sometimes. ..."

"And we only thought how savagely ill-tempered she was!" murmured Miss Gilbert. "I remember saying that she loved to hurt people—"

"So she did; but it was like a tortured animal snapping," said Miss Lexington. "Well—we can't do anything for her now. Of course she'll have nothing but her savings. All the money she's paid into the Fund is gone, of course. I'm afraid, from what the doctor said to Miss Barr this morning, this is—the end."

"Oh!" cried Rowan, her eyes flashing, "how I wish we could make them suffer for it—the people who've driven her to this—those superior officials who robbed her of health and hope and—and reason, I expect—"

"It wasn't only them," said Miss Parry vindictively. "They wouldn't have worried her to this pitch if they hadn't've been set on—"

"Hush!" Miss Lexington interposed hastily. "It's no good blaming anyone now. The mischief's done. Only—it's a lesson. ..."

CHAPTER XVIII

Further Diplomacy

Somehow no one thought of telling Miss Cullen (who was unusually late at school, and finally appeared with sunken eyes that told of tears to anyone who cared to see) the reason for Miss Lovell's absence. Perhaps they thought she knew; some perhaps even thought that she had planned the catastrophe for which she was, at least partly, responsible; but the chief reason was that no one, or almost no one, was on speaking terms with her. She was neither hurt nor astonished; she just took the added coldness and barely veiled indignation as part of the day's pain, as an overdriven horse accepts the added lashes of a brutal driver. But to Viola—Viola, who had yesterday seemed so kind, Viola for whom she felt a love that even neglect and forgetfulness could not kill—to Viola she turned for that word and look of friendliness which made her load just bearable.

She approached the girl at lunch, when a Staff, unusually grave and subdued, sat almost silent in the Common Room, warming numbed hands and glancing over notes.

"Do you know you played me false yesterday?" she said, with her curious, stiff effort at humour, her voice ringing loud and false in the quiet room.

The Staff looked away, or exchanged glances full of meaning.

Viola flushed a little. Like the others, though perhaps with less virulence, she blamed Miss Cullen for the tragedy of last night. Always she had before her the sight of Miss Lovell's set white face and tormented eyes, and could hear the moans from those passionate red lips. How *could* Miss Cullen make talk in that foolish, affected, heartless way?

"I'm afraid I don't understand you," she said icily.

Miss Cullen winced almost visibly. To her accustomed ear there was no mistaking that tone. She shrank into herself.

"I expect you forgot," she murmured hurriedly.

With a slight, almost insolent, increase of emphasis Viola merely repeated her words.

"I'm afraid I don't understand you."

"Why—you—you said you'd come to tea with me yesterday. I dare say you forgot."

A little snort, half of contempt, half of wrath, came from someone. Viola thought it was Miss Reeve.

"Yes," she replied coldly, "I'm afraid I did."

"Oh, it didn't matter a bit—not a bit," said poor Miss Cullen hastily. "I—it—I was only in fun. But you'll make it up to me, won't you, and come another day?"

Viola murmured indistinctly. Angry as she was, the anxious, pitiful humility of the elderly woman was, as always, disarming her. She couldn't be cruel to her, whatever she'd done. Besides, what Lexo had implied in those few words—"It's a lesson"—was true. It was a warning against hasty judgment and unconsidered stabs. Yet—no, she couldn't, she simply *couldn't,* treat Miss Cullen just as usual. She ought not to expect it.

"That's right." Miss Cullen pounced on the indefinite mutter with the hope of the nearly desperate. "When can you come? You must fix a day, and *keep* it this time! Now, when shall we say? Saturday?"

"I'm afraid I can't fix a day."

"Oh, come, you're not as full of engagements as that! You can't make me believe that you are."

The wide, false smile and affected, pedantic, flippant tone put the last touch to Viola's indignation. She could only see the insincere mouth; the anxious, pleading eyes were hidden from her cold anger.

"I'm sorry, I can't make any engagement," she said frigidly, and pointedly turned to speak in a low voice to Miss Wilson, who sat next to her. Really, with Miss Lovell lying on the brink of death—or worse—and the blame of it partly, at least, at Miss Cullen's door, the woman's manner was incredible, unforgivable. She hardened her heart—though with an effort, as she saw, from the corner of her eye, the wound she had given and the immediate courageous recovery of her victim. Almost she repented—but no. The thing was too callous. It *was* unforgivable. With pain at her heart—that pain which sometimes does visit the executioner—she collected her books for the next lesson.

Of course the encounter had not gone unnoticed. No encounter ever does, even on a normal staff; and at Besley, where the currents and counter-currents were of such importance, its significance was enormous. If Viola had but known it, the pain she had inflicted on Miss Cullen caused an almost equal amount of triumph and hope to flourish in the bosom of Miss Parry.

"Cullen's done for herself now," she whispered to Miss Fergusson, with a glee that was too unholy and too out of place to betray to anyone of a finer texture. "She's not got a friend in the place now. I *thought* Miss Kennedy would find her out in time." And to herself she added: "And now's the time for me to strike."

It was a pity, she felt, that that decorum on which she was so strong forbade her inviting anyone to tea on this one day. It wouldn't be "good form" to do it, though; poor Miss Lovell, it was almost like a funeral, so depressing, and you couldn't, simply couldn't, do anything in the *least*, well, frivolous. Not that it did her any good, poor girl, for her friends to deny themselves their little pleasures, and it did seem a pity not to strike while the iron was hot; but no—with a final sigh she decided that she simply couldn't, in decency, ask Viola to tea to-day. These things are not done. If she had been a philosopher she might have reflected with profit, if not with pleasure, on the very different codes to which that elastic term is applied. It would certainly never have occurred to her that to, say, Miss Cullen, her aim in asking Viola at all would be among the things that are "not done." But that was a line of thought so little possible to Miss Parry that she spent her time instead in planning some means by which she could, without actually committing the enormity of asking Viola to tea, have converse with her, complete her detachment from the standard of Miss Cullen, attach her to her own banner, and extract in the process all possible information as to Miss Cullen's plans for the future and conduct in the past. If only tea had been possible, Miss Parry felt that she could certainly have done all this. She had a great belief in tea as a diplomatic agent. As it was, she must hit on something else.

It occurred to her almost at once—a plan to which no one could take exception, if it were put in a proper light—and she would take care that the proper light was shed. She joined the "dinner staff" in the Common Room after school and at once began her campaign.

"I don't feel that I can *beah* school dinnah to-day," she mourned. "Aftah that feahful tragedy, to sit and listen to the clammah would be simply *too* much. And yet I don't feel as if I could face eatin' alone. You're on dinner duty, aren't you, Margie?"

Miss Pearson nodded gloomily.

"And Trixie's gone home. What a pity! I thought perhaps. ... Now, Miss Kennedy, don't you agree with me that school dinnah reahlly is unthinkable today?"

"It is a pretty foul idea," Viola assented morosely.

"Well—won't you come out to lunch with me some-wheah? I want to go, but I do so dislike eatin' alone in cafés. Do be naice and come."

Viola considered the two evils rapidly. School dinner, with all the attendant din and stuffiness and horrid food, or a café with Miss Parry *tête-à-tête*. On the whole, the latter was the less.

"Yes, I'd like to," she assented listlessly. "I agree, school dinner would be impossible."

And so the ill-assorted pair hurried for hats and coats, Miss Parry ably concealing die triumph and delight that filled her breast. How neat! It put her in such a good light, so sympathetic and sensitive, and at the same time did the right work. She congratulated herself with perfect sincerity.

Skilled diplomat as she was, Miss Parry realised that the time at her disposal was too short for her to take the artistic method which her rather ticklish job required. In fact, had it been possible, she would merely have consolidated her position at this meeting and laid down the lines for future developments. But with certain ominous words of Miss Mortimer's, which she had kept locked in her most secret heart, hardly daring to remember them—that Damoclean sword of dismissal hanging trembling above her head—she dared not waste an hour. She must know. She must find out what was being actually planned by her enemies. In Viola Kennedy, late of that number, but clearly disillusioned now, she would find the source of information she so badly needed.

"Isn't it too *dreadful* about poor Miss Lovell?" she began, drawing off elegant gloves and picking up the menu card.

Viola, who had thought that the chief aim of this debauch was to avoid that terrible topic, shuddered a little.

"It's too dreadful to talk about," she said rather shortly.

"It is, isn't it? And yet, you know, Miss Kennedy, it's only typical of what's coming to all of us."

There was more real sincerity in her voice than Viola had ever heard there. She knew, almost instinctively, that Miss Parry was really, horribly afraid; though even then she did not guess that the elegant little lady had any reason, more than the general fear, for her alarm.

"Surely—" she began protestingly.

"Oh, I don't mean quite in the same way." Miss Parry recovered herself with an effort, and the refined voice came into play. "But it only shows, doesn't it, what this terr'ble anxahty can do. I mean to say, though some of us may not show ahr feelin's quaite laike her, we suffer equally as much in ahr hahts."

Her shrewd, anxious eyes scanned the girl's face eagerly. Would she take the hint—guess what was in her companion's mind? She must make sure.

"It's too dretful, isn't it, that one woman sh'd hev it in her pah'r to make so many othahs wretched?"

"You mean Miss Mortimer? I don't suppose she realises quite what it means to us."

"No, I *don't* mean Miss Mortimer!" Viola realised, from the change of tone, that Miss Parry was now coming down to brass tacks. "I mean someone who knows *exactly* what it is and what she's doin'—someone who's brought all this trouble on us—someone who doesn't mind sacrificin' all of us to save her own skin—"

"If you mean Miss Cullen," said Viola, her voice steadily cold, though she had turned a little pale, "I think she could say the same of others. I think she has been as cruelly driven and tormented as anyone—yes, even as Miss Lovell. I don't think anyone quite realises what she has suffered—is still suffering."

"Why—I thought—you yourself—" began Miss Parry in furious astonishment.

"I know. I did snub her, disgustingly. I've been sorry ever since. Oh, I don't mean that I don't, in a way, think she's responsible, partly at least, for poor Miss Lovell's tragedy; only I don't think she's as responsible as we want to make her. It's the system, chiefly, that's to blame. If it's a question of life or death, don't we all try to save ourselves, and the devil take the hindmost? Weren't some of the Staff doing the same thing to her?"

"I—see." Miss Parry's slow voice was full of meaning—a meaning which Viola entirely misunderstood. She thought she had actually done something, however little, to make Miss Parry see her enemy's point of view.

"It's horrible, ghastly," she went on, her voice shaking a little, "but mightn't it have happened to Miss Cullen just as much? And who'd have been to blame then?"

"I see that Miss Cullen has one very—er—*loyal* supporter," said Miss Parry, with a tiny sneering smile; and in that smile Viola read her mistake. Not in its entirety, for she still was incredibly blind to her own position in this elaborate game; but she saw that no words of hers—or of an angel—could make Miss Parry see herself as a torturer and Miss Cullen as a victim. With a little shrug she gave it up.

Miss Parry also gave it up. She saw, as she told Miss Lexington later, that Viola Kennedy was of no use to her in her campaign of self-preservation. Either she was too stupid to know what was going on between Miss Cullen and the Higher Powers, or too wily to betray her knowledge. On the whole, Miss Parry, having clear evidence of the girl's continued support of the foe, inclined to the latter theory.

"She knows which side her bread's buttered," she thought viciously. "She's banking on Cullen's influence with Morty."

And a kind of dismay swept through the little lady, shaking her with a sickening qualm. How *could* she find out her fate? What could she do when she had learned it?

"There's only one hope," she thought in desperation, "and it's a poor one! Somehow, by some dodge, we *must* get the H.M. to sack 'em both ... She knows we won't—*can't* resign. ... What will do it?"

Miss Parry held two interviews that afternoon. Though each was of a mere moment's duration, to her each was an important step in the furtherance of her schemes. To Miss Lexington she merely hissed, almost literally *en passant:*

"*Don't trust that girl Kennedy an inch.* She's in it up to the neck with Cullen and Morty—she let it out. She's out to save her neck when we all get notice to quit—and that's coming!" and was rewarded by seeing the grim set of the Staff Mistress's firm lips. Her other confidante was the Head herself, whom she caught just before the afternoon prayers.

"Miss Barr," she whispered hurriedly, "I've something—rather—well—embarrassing to tell you. You know that young Hyde, who came in here over that *disgraceful* business of Miss Kennedy and May Masters?"

Miss Barr flushed. Mr. Hyde's name was hardly one to recall pleasant memories.

"Yes?"

"Well—do you know that *after* that scene Miss Kennedy *ran* after him, and spent all her dinner-hour *alone* with him in the Brent Meadows? The whole town's talking of it. And, to make matters worse, she—well, you know, she's in the Town Dramatic Club, and her behaviour with him is—well! I'm not straitlaced, as you know, but *really*—! And, if you wanted proof, I've just heard from the President, Mrs. Atkinson, you know, that he's been forced to resign from the Club, it was so awkward for him!"

A short pause to let this sink in, and then:

"No wonder May Masters managed to dodge her!" Miss Parry added. "No doubt her eyes were occupied elsewhere."

Miss Barr looked anxious, perturbed, eager and piteous all at once.

"How very unfortunate!" she murmured. "I thought her quite a refined sort of girl. ... I don't quite know—I don't like—after school hours—"

"I know. But in a town like this—in our, well, *precarious* state—"

Miss Barr's eyes searched those of her assistant anxiously, helplessly.

"I thought I'd just warn you," murmured that lady. "It's becoming —serious."

And, having planted her seed, she retired to watch it grow. The soil was in beautiful condition. She had every right to expect the best results.

CHAPTER XIX
The Week-end

Becoming acclimatised to the peculiar atmosphere of suspicion and intrigue, Viola realised quite well that she was somehow becoming involved in a network of manoeuvres whose exact bearing she was too impatient to attempt to discover. Her own attitude she could hardly define even to herself. She saw quite clearly the two opposing camps—Miss Cullen *versus* The Rest; her instinct was naturally to side with the one against the many, and that instinct was strengthened by her faith in the honesty and simplicity of Miss Cullen; but she could not conceal from herself the fact that Miss Cullen had, in one instance at least, deviated from those principles which Viola had so much admired in her. After all, *was* there much to choose between her tactics and Miss Parry's? The one tortured a colleague to make her sign her own death-warrant, in order that she herself might escape; the other got someone else to sign the death-warrant of all her colleagues with the same motive. It is always horrible to witness a death struggle. Somehow it seemed worse when the weapons, and even the conflict itself, were concealed behind the mask of polite and commonplace existence.

"I say," said Miss Wilson to Viola on Thursday afternoon, "you still want that week-end away?"

Viola shrugged listlessly.

"I'm in Coventry," she reminded the other.

Miss Wilson regarded her with some curiosity.

"So you're catchin' the contagion, are you?" she asked.

"Can one escape it?"

"Oh, yes, with care. But you must take steps, of course—sort of mental disinfection. 'Specially you, because you're liable to be a bad case. You take life too hard, young Kennedy. You should cultivate cynicism, like me."

"Life *is* hard," argued Viola morosely.

"Course it is! D'you think I don't know it? But the harder you take it the harder it is. Come on, now, don't be an ass, my good girl. Where d'you think looks a good spot?"

"I thought Pendon looked all right from the map. There's a good big brown patch marked, and the general level seems to be about six hundred."

"Lord, I don't know what all that means. 'S long's it's quiet, and there aren't any kids or schoolmarms there, it'll do me. Is there a reasonable train?"

"Four-fifty. Just right."

"Good. Let's be dashing, and have tea in the town and take a taxi to the station. I don't mind blowin' an extra bob or two to do the thing in style."

Pendon, as a permanent abode, might have its drawbacks; but for a week-end resting-place for two tired women it was all that could be desired. After a single day of leisure, walking, air and calm, Viola blossomed out into something of her old fresh peaceable self—a self that seemed to shrink and die in the unnatural and morbid atmosphere in which she now spent her days.

"You know, young Kennedy, you're a fool to go in for this life," remarked Miss Wilson as she poured out the tea on Saturday evening, looking with something like envy at the bright eyes and glowing cheeks framed with curling tendrils of hair. "You want a nice healthy outdoor life and lots of kids. Why don't you marry a squire somewhere in the dark provinces?"

Viola laughed.

"I'd love to!—only 'nobody asked me, sir, she said'."

"They will, if you chuck teaching. If you stick to it they won't."

"Why not?"

"Because if they haven't got on to it before you start teaching, they never do. If ever you hear of a schoolmarm gettin' married (which is rare), you'll find the man knew her before, or only just after, she started. You chuck it while there's time."

"What about you?" retorted Viola.

Miss Wilson grimaced expressively.

"Me? Lord, I'd almost rather teach! I *couldn't* marry, not while there's crossings to sweep and a workhouse to live in. I'm a born spinster. You're not—you were born to marry."

Viola laughed again.

"You seem jolly sure!"

"I am," Miss Wilson asserted calmly. "I always am. You see, I'm a born outsider. I never enter into things or get intimate with people or anything like that, and so I see all there is to see."

"It sounds a bit—superior."

"Oh, it is!—and a bit cut-off, but I like that. 'Sides, it's the only line for me to take. I can't have emotions and things—not made that way—so I take an impersonal and intelligent interest in life instead. It's very amusing."

"Then—what about your teaching? Do you look at that in the same way? Are the girls just specimens for you to try experiments on?"

"That's about it," nodded the other. "I'm a specialist in life. Sometimes I find it interestin' in its early stages, but, I'm bound to say, not often. It's much more amusin' when matured."

"Do you like the job?" asked Viola bluntly.

"Teachin'? Only as a type of life. I don't know much about convents, but, apart from them, you get a quite distinct type of human female in the average girls' school. It's interestin' that way."

Viola was silent for a moment, Miss Wilson watching her clouded face with some amusement.

"Don't you like being a specimen?" she asked at last.

Viola looked up.

"Oh, *me*; *I* don't mind, only I should think I was far too ordinary to be a good specimen! I know what you mean exactly, and it *is* interesting if it wasn't so—beastly."

"Ah, there you are! You see, you feel things. I don't. I've trained myself not to."

"'Life is a comedy to those who think and a tragedy to those who feel'?"

"That's about it. I prefer comedy. I want to go on enjoying life, and to go on living; and if you feel things—well, first you get 'em wrong, and then you die."

"I think I'd rather," said Viola, "than—than not feel at all."

"'Course you would—you're a born feeler, as I said. But as a matter of fact you feelers get just as far wrong on the tragic side as we thinkers do on the comic. You make tragedies of trifles, and we make jokes out of—well, the semi-sacred, anyhow."

"Then, do you just teach because you like studying the human female in abnormal conditions?"

"No—not exactly. A year or two—three, anyhow—would show me all I want to know of her. Not that there aren't differences. This place, for instance, is worse than most, and you see the disease in an advanced stage, which is, of course, interestin' and instructive for a time. Same way, there's others which are better than most, and women there keep more or less—not quite, of course, that's impossible, but more or less—normal, and therefore dull. You don't often get so many things workin' to the same end as there are here. But they're all a type, and you get to know it in time. No, I teach because I've got a desire to live, and studyin' life doesn't bring in anything more solid than amusement."

"And—the job itself doesn't mean anything to you?"

"What—*teaching*? Good *lord*, no! Oh, I know what you're thinkin', my good girl—sin to let a woman like me have a hand in the sacred task of education. Isn't that it?"

"Not quite, but—something very like it." Viola flushed before the amused, cynical, friendly glance. "It *does* seem to me to be a very big job—I don't mean shoving girls through exams., of course, nor just making them able to earn a little bigger salary. I mean teaching them to *think*—to take a line for themselves, to see straight, to ignore parrot-cries and generalities—"

"And you really think that Besley, for instance, does all that?"

"No. Of course I know jolly well that it doesn't. If it, and other places like it, had done their job properly there wouldn't have been a war, for instance. And that's what sickens me, sometimes—that it *isn't* doing its job. Only I do think that one can perhaps do something, even in a hole like Besley; and then, in the next generation, these girls will be taking some steps to see that their children think still more—"

"And so *ad infinitum*? Well, don't let me crush your young optimism. I suppose it does get you through the job if you think you are likely to achieve something."

"Well—don't *you*? Honestly, now, shamming aside—don't you?"

Miss Wilson shook her head.

"My dear kid, I haven't an ideal left. Not one. My beloved Life has knocked 'em all out of me. I only have one aim in teaching—to get enough girls through exams, to make me useful, so that I can earn something while I can, because I know I shall never last till Pension age. My aim is to save what I can and get what fun I can out of the job while I'm doing it. And, like it or not, that's the aim of ninety-five per cent. of us. D'you think Lexo's got any ideal before her except her personal success? Or Parry, or Reeve, or Pearson, or any of 'em? D'you honestly believe they're out to reform the world?"

Viola was silent.

"Of course they're not! They're not supposed to be. They're not there to think; they're there as cogs in a machine for grinding out wage-earners. Some of 'em may have had ideals once—dare say Cullen had—but they've forgotten 'em years ago. If ever they remember them, it's either to sneer or to suffer. And that's the truth, for once. I don't often tell it, but now I have. And don't you forget it."

Viola pondered a moment. Then she burst out:

"But things *are* better—*are* improving! Not here, perhaps—"

"No, nor in one school in forty of this type! No, you chuck it, Kennedy. You'll break your heart and lose your looks, and you'll end, like Cullen, a tragedy. … Here endeth the first and last lesson."

Viola looked at her companion.

"I say," she said a little shyly, "just one thing more—it was decent of you to bother with me like that. I know it's jolly hard to talk out like that, 'specially when you're as reserved as you are. You've made yourself tired over it, too," she added remorsefully, noticing the grey pallor which had stolen over the other's face.

"Oh, that's nothing. That's been comin' on some time. That was why I thought of a week-end—thought I'd fob it off till the end of term, with luck. Shall, too, if I'm careful. I can't risk *another* breakdown. That'd mean no more jobs, not even at another Besley—if there is one—and no pension, and the dead loss of the ten per cent. levy I've paid into the Fund. Wish I could draw out that ten per cent. and use it for a year off!"

"But couldn't you? I mean, you'd get it back, wouldn't you, if you had to chuck teaching on account of your health?"

Miss Wilson emitted a little snort of derisive laughter.

"*Get it back*? Kennedy, you are *the* greenest lamb! Why, no one knows where it is—or any of the fund! There was a question asked about it a year or two ago, don't you remember? Or no, I s'pose you don't—I expect you were an innocent in the Sixth Form yourself then! But do you think that anyone would ever get any cash back once they'd handed it over to H.M. Government? Would anyone imagine they would?"

"Then why d'you pay the levy? It's voluntary, isn't it?"

"Just about as voluntary as most things of the kind. Pay it or get fired. My last Head told us that in so many words, when the idea came in. 'It's a voluntary subscription,' she said, 'but I may tell you that if you aren't willing to pay it there are plenty of other mistresses who are.' And she came as near winking as Heads ever do. She was quite a woman."

"But if you get ill and need it—?"

"What does that matter? I tell you the money's gone—Lord knows where, into paying for registers, I expect. I know three separate women who broke down, had to chuck teaching, needed treatment of one sort or another—sanatorium, one was, which costs the deuce of a lot. They were all optimists, like you, and tried to recover their subs. Their letters weren't even acknowledged. ... No, I can't afford to collapse. So on the whole, Kennedy, I think I'll get back to Besley and go to my bed for the rest of the weekend. I take it easy when I get like this."

"What is it?" asked Viola with concern.

"Heart. Had it for donkey's years. I hope to drop down dramatically some day and not get up again. Good plan."

"But can't you do anything—?"

"To cure it? They say not. Don't know that I would if I could. Don't worry over *that*, now, you silly infant!" she added, seeing Viola's look of distress. "Tell you I like it, as a final arrangement, and you have to pay a bit for these little conveniences. ... I'll be teaching the young idea on Monday morning, right as ninepence. Only you'll have to get me a hay-waggon or something to the station. They're sure not to have anything less rural in the way of a conveyance. And look here, I won't have you along. I can't bear company when I'm off colour. You walk back tomorrow, as you planned. I mean it now. I don't—want—you. See? I'm perfectly serious. Unselfish isn't a word I know, and I'm not going to learn it at this time of my life."

She quite clearly meant what she said. So, in the cold dusk of a winter evening, Miss Wilson departed in a vehicle that the Pendon inn called a fly and its occupant an ark, to spend the week-end, or what remained of it, in bed in her lodgings.

Viola slept that night like one drugged. The strong air and exercise did more for her than any drug could have done, for she came down next morning bright, fresh and vigorous, determined to explore the high ground about Pendon thoroughly well before starting on the eleven-mile walk down to Besley in the afternoon. She enjoyed, in a wordless rapture, the scent of the dead bracken and the cold, aloof freshness of the winter sky. She ate her dinner (the traditional roast meat and tart of an English country inn on a Sunday) with immense appetite, and, having disposed of it and sent her small case into Besley by a farmer's cart, set off at a swinging four miles an hour to cover the road to Besley.

It had turned very cold. Even her thick tweeds and the brisk pace at which she walked failed to keep Viola warm. Still, she enjoyed it—the rapid movement, the silence of the bare fields, the loneliness of the empty sky, where low, heavy, whitish clouds lay banked up on the brown, barren line of the horizon.

"Snow coming," she thought as she saw the slow, rolling advance of those clouds; and within half an hour her prophecy was fulfilled. Big soft flakes, the leisurely forerunners of a storm, began to drift idly on the cold air. The sky, overcast and gloomy, began to darken almost visibly.

The road, a mere track over the unhedged fields, became obscured as the snow began to lie. Viola, drawing out her inch-scale map at a questionable point, felt a sudden qualm as to her powers of getting back to Besley, not only by half-past five, the hour she had proposed to herself as a suitable one, but at any reasonable hour at all. She had postponed her start till too late. The sky was growing rapidly dark, and the electric torch she carried, though it served well enough for reading the map, or signposts, should she come on any, threw only a very limited light on the surrounding landscape. In fact, its small, concentrated ray was rather bewildering than helpful.

"They oughtn't to have marked this as a second-class road," she thought with a twinge of apprehension. "It's only a lane. ... I wish there was *some* kind of a boundary—hedge or wall or anything. ... Well, anyhow, the idea is to keep south by west, and strike the main road at this place where there's a letter-box marked. It can't be more than a mile. Wish I had a compass! Still, I ought to be able to keep a straightish line for a mile."

Needless to say, she did not keep a straight line. Few people, walking in new country in a whirl and flurry of snow, would. Viola plunged into holes full of wet snow, slipped on frozen puddles, blundered into hidden ditches, got soft snow into her shoes and down her neck, stumbled, swore, and grew thoroughly weary. As the sky blackened and the snow thickened she felt a stab of acute anxiety. Heaven only knew, she thought in a kind of angry alarm, what Besley would think of this escapade! Certainly it would not believe the truth.

After over three hours of stumbling and blundering, a line of telegraph poles met her weary eyes. The main road at last!—but at what point she had struck it she had no means of judging. She must just walk on and hope for a milestone or a signpost—or, better still, a village where she could get a very belated tea and, with a stroke of luck, raise some sort of conveyance.

The going was easier now. The snow had at any rate something solid beneath it, and did not suddenly drop into a hole to trap her tired feet.

But it is never easy to hurry in soft snow. Viola's feet seemed leaden. Her muscles protested at every step as she trudged doggedly on.

"*Fool*!" she said to herself viciously. "To-morrow's Monday, and I haven't got a single lesson ready. It must be half-past five, quite, and Heaven knows how far I've still got to go. ... Wish I hadn't walked so far this morning. ... What an ass I was to try to walk to Besley!—though it would have been ripping but for the snow, and I couldn't have foreseen that. ... Oh, *damn*!"—as a gust sent the swirling flakes down between her neck and the upturned collar of her wet coat.

It was then, just when things seemed blackest, that she heard the burr and buzz of an approaching motor-cycle.

"Good!" she thought in relief. "Now I'll get some idea of where I am, anyhow."

She walked out into the middle of the road, full into the glare of the approaching headlight, and waved violently.

"Can you tell me how far it is to Besley?" she shouted above the roar of the slowed engine.

"Besley? Why—*Beatrice*!"

"Oh! Benedick! Have you rescued me *again*!" she cried, between laughter and tears in her relief.

"What on *earth*—?"

"Oh, only my usual idiocy." Briefly she told him.

"Good Lord, you must have walked for miles! What *luck* I met you!" His tone was quite as fervent as hers. "You're soaked, too. Here, get in."

He helped her into the side-car of his machine. The sheer relief of sitting made her give a gasp that was almost a sob.

"You poor kid! Here, take off that wet coat." He held out a mackintosh and crammed her into it. "Now this scarf. ... That's better. We'll be in Besley in forty minutes."

The engine leapt into life. Viola, snuggling into the warmth and ease, felt that she could have cried with relief and gratitude. Forty minutes on a motor-cycle! That would have meant over four hours on foot, at the very least. ... She would have liked to go on for ever, whirling through wind and weather with this friend at her side.

The outlying streets of Besley came all too soon. Viola sat up and began to put herself into some kind of order.

"Please will you put me down at the station?" she cried above the roar of the engine. A sudden access of prudence had overcome her pleasure.

"Station? Why?"

"Oh—I can't explain." (How could one shout, above the noise of a motor-cycle, the exact construction that Besley would put on her arrival at her rooms, late on Sunday night, alone with a desirable young man with whom she had, apparently, been spending a gay week-end?) "Only please, *please* do."

"As you like," he grunted. "We're just there."

He stopped the engine and dismounted to help her out.

"You—*oh*! You *didn't*—oh, *Benedick*!"

"What's wrong?"

"Wrong?" she stormed, struggling out of the borrowed coat. "*Wrong*? And you've ridden all those miles—Oh, why didn't I think of it? I am *the* Gadarene pig. You'll get pneumonia or something—"

"Is it pneumonia? If I'd been to get pneumonia I'd have died young! No, but you will, if you don't get into a hot bath quick. Will you do that now?"

She held out the coat with shaking hands.

"I'll do—anything you like. You—I can't say thank you properly—"

"Ah, will you whisht?" he growled crossly. "Don't you know well that I'd do anything to please you, let alone a trrrifle I'd have done for anyone?"

"D'you expect me to believe that you'd have ridden miles and miles without a coat in this weather if I hadn't made you?" she scolded.

"Sure I like it. I've never liked anything so well—and that's the truth."

Something in his tone silenced Viola. She held out her hand.

"I'll try to say thank you properly later on," she murmured a trifle shakily.

"I'll come and ask ye to soon," returned Hyde imperturbably. "But now you're to go and get into a hot bath and away into your bed. And mind ye do!"

"*Well*!" gasped Viola, between gratitude, annoyance and amusement, as she watched his light dwindle. "Of *all* cool young men! *Ordering* me to do this and that and the other!"

But somehow she did exactly as she had been told.

CHAPTER XX
Buttons Off

Everyone knows the feeling of a second, quite separate, self waiting to slip on one's mind and heart as soon as the first had done with them. Sometimes it will not wait; and then there is a struggle, and sometimes the transference from one self to the other is so rapid that they almost coexist. That was what happened to Viola Kennedy as, stiff, sleepy, radiantly happy, bored, impatient and serene all at once, she prepared for school on Monday. Viola the woman and Miss Kennedy the schoolmistress co-existed, though they were quite different people; but the woman was uppermost, and thoughts of a soft, deep voice and laughing, friendly grey eyes filled her mental eyes and ears more than the pale countenances and fractious tones of her colleagues filled her physical ones. Yet, in the midst of her happy dream, she remembered the haggard face which had been her last impression of Miss Wilson, and anxiety for that courageous cynic banished her half unconscious visions as she entered the school premises.

"Well, the giddy whirl of a week-end off did *you* good, anyway."

The half friendly, half caustic words and tone which greeted her entrance to the cloak-room relieved her at once.

"Oh, good!" she exclaimed. "I was so afraid you'd be too knocked up to come to school to-day."

"Who's knocked up?" The anxious voice was Miss Lexington's. "For goodness' sake don't say someone's away."

"No, we're all here," answered Miss Reeve. "Why? What's in the wind *now?*"

"Oh, nothing much! *Only* Morty."

"*What!*" The consternation was general.

"Miss Lexington, she *can't* be here *again!*"

"Why, she was only here last week."

"Twice in a term! It's unheard of!"

"It's true, all the same. She's with the Head now. Heaven only knows what we're going to do about poor Miss Lovell's classes. Somebody'll have to give up their free afternoon, but there simply aren't enough on the Staff to go round this morning."

There was a new note in Miss Lexington's usually alert, decisive voice—a note which filled Viola with pity and a kind of fear. It was despairing, that was it—as if she, the gallant warrior of a hundred fights, was going to give up the battle, finding the odds against her too heavy. It was the first sign of that demon Old Age which would soon claim her.

What was in Miss Lexington hopelessness and fatigue was, in the majority of her colleagues, sheer panic. Terror, naked and unashamed, looked for a moment out of their eyes. For a moment only; for all were skilled by long apprenticeship in the art of concealing their emotions; but it had been there, and it made Viola feel physically sick to see it. She remembered Miss Lovell, driven by that concealed terror, into worse than death; she thought of Miss Parry, Miss Reeve, Miss Lexington, all faced with far worse than a fear of death—the fear of a lingering life in which they could no longer earn. She thought of Miss Cullen, driven by the same fear to involve her colleagues in this calamity. And she felt numbed and aching with the bewilderment and pity of it all.

Miss Lexington had already regained her control.

"We'll have to do what we can," she said with the calm of despair. "I haven't been able to see the Head, of course. Miss Reeve, you're free first lesson. You must take Miss Lovell's form—that's IVa. No one's free second lesson. Who's with the Sixth? Miss Cullen? Ah, well, then, of course, whatever happens, *you'll* be all right if you leave them and take Miss Lovell's IV Remove."

The scorn in her voice was quite open. A smile, bitter and only half concealed, ran round the Staff as Miss Cullen, anxiously smiling, accepted the stab. To Viola it was merely another pang, the pain one gets oneself when one sees one tortured creature rend another. White and sick, she hurried away. It was horrible, *horrible*, she thought passionately. Why, why,

why should life be made into a thing like that when in itself it was so warm and sweet?

On her way down to prayers, marshalling her form, she saw two figures at the end of a corridor—two figures whom she could not but recognise. It *was* true, then, all of it, all of it! For, if it were not, why should Miss Cullen be deep in anxious consultation with the dreaded Inspector while her colleagues trembled and raged in despair? Oh, it was all too beastly, she thought, between pity and anger and disgust.

"I must get away from here—I *must!*" she thought; and, inconsequently, embarrassingly, there swept into her mind the advice of last Saturday night—"You're born to marry. ... They will, if you chuck teaching. ..."

And then another memory, which made the ready flush sweep up over her face and neck.

"I suppose Parry began like this," she thought bitterly, furiously. "Am I going to turn out another Parry?"

And she slammed the door in her mind through which there had slipped that later thought.

It was a ghastly day—the kind of day which, in later years, one looks back on with a shudder, and wonders whether life was ever really as bad as that. Everyone was on the edge of collapse. Fear, fury, anxiety, helpless despair, gnawed at all the unfortunate women who, with calm faces and tormented hearts, went on their placid way, instructing the unconscious girls in the elements of what is mistakenly called education. What courage is theirs perhaps no one will ever know, those gently bred women who, fearing a future compared to which death would seem easy, yet carry on their accustomed round of work with controlled voices and unmoved mien. Only in their eyes could you see a hint of the seething torment of suspense and fear, and in their manner, alternating between a pitiful deprecation and a reckless defiance, read the story of prudence schooling nature.

It was, perhaps, worst for Miss Parry. The hint which had been dropped at the last inspection had been worrying her ever since; in this new visitation she read its fulfilment. Haggard under her composure, she came and went to and from her classes, marshalling all her powers in an attempt, which she knew would be vain, to prove her worth. And wherever she went, whatever she taught, Miss Mortimer appeared like a Vengeance, taking notes, making tiny caustic comments, wearing down her resistance by the sheer weight of persistent presence.

They all saw it, of course. Sympathetic though they were with the unhappy victim, each anxious heart felt an unquenchable moment of relief as the torturer fastened on her prey and left the others momentarily free. But not even to her colleagues did Miss Parry betray the dreadful close of the afternoon, when the executioner had delivered the final thrust—"Don't you think that you would do better to move on, Miss Parry? It seems to me that your lessons have got very *set*. One is apt to get into a rut if one stays too long in one school. *Twelve years*? Oh, but that's *far* too long for any mistress to stay in one school. I must see to that."

And out had come the inevitable note-book.

So it had come. The little lady, powdered and curled, in her elegant frock, saw her world crumble about her, and for a moment she was giddy and sick. But she called up a smiling commonplace, spoke of a new method of teaching French grammar, complained of the "reahlly *dreadful* weathah," and walked composedly down the corridor to the Common Room.

There, however, her courageous front broke down. After the stunning blow came reaction. The powder was ready to explode—and the match was forthcoming.

Most of the Staff were assembled in the Common Room as she entered, and the first words she caught came from Miss Reeve.

"... as strong a hint as she could well give! I'm expecting the sack any day after that."

The general murmur of indignant sympathy roused Miss Parry to make her great effect. She came slowly into the room, carefully laid her books down, and said, with the calm of despair:

"I'm not *expecting* it. I've *got* it."

The consternation amply fulfilled her hopes.

"*Miss Parry*! You don't mean it?"

"She hasn't dared?"

"Oh, Miss Parry, it can't be true! You *must* have misunderstood her."

"It's perfectly true. And now that Miss Mortimer's business here is done, I hope all the rest of you'll be left alone. You ought to be grateful to me—and, of course, to Miss Cullen."

She swung half round to face her enemy as she named her.

"*Especially* to Miss Cullen," she repeated, smiling a little.

Miss Cullen faced her, her mouth opening and shutting a little, silently, her eyes anxious, wistful, alarmed.

"*Me?*" she muttered at last.

"Yes—you. Wasn't it you who got her to come? Wasn't it you who fixed it with her to get me fired out instead of you—you, who ought to have left terms ago, who've been useless for years!"

She stopped, panting. Miss Cullen was silent, stunned.

"You see—nothing to say!" pursued Miss Parry in triumph. "You brought that woman here to save yourself—you know you did! It's you who've got me dismissed—just as it was you who've finished poor Miss Lovell. You knew what the future'd be like, and you got it for me instead of takin' your own medicine."

All the natural vulgar woman was out now—just as, one imagines, she comes out in a panic or in the face of death.

"I—I—didn't—" whispered Miss Cullen at last.

In the sudden silence after Miss Parry's strident voice the hoarse whisper was painfully audible. "I never—I didn't know—"

She looked desperately round the ring of stony, condemning faces. Suddenly she took a step forward.

"*You* know I didn't mean any—any harm," she whispered, appealing straight to Viola. "Say you believe me."

The agonised appeal was more than the girl could bear. She took the trembling, outstretched hand impulsively in hers.

"I'm sure you didn't," she replied in a clear voice that had a ring of challenge in it.

Miss Parry laughed, and the sound was not pleasant. The buttons were off the foils now with a vengeance.

"Very touching!" she sneered, "if only the effect hadn't been spoilt beforehand! Miss Cullen," she explained, turning to the circle of women surrounding the protagonists, "has been so kind as to interest Miss Mortimer in Miss Kennedy. She gave her quite a good character. Very useful—for Miss Kennedy."

"How dare you!" blazed Viola. "Miss Cullen has never mentioned me to Miss Mortimer. Miss Mortimer dislikes me—"

"Oh, that won't do!" rejoined Miss Parry with mock tolerance, like an elder in answer to a child's silly lie. "Miss Mortimer doesn't always lower her voice like Miss Cullen does when they have their little chats together. I know *quite* well what Miss Mortimer's report on you will be, Miss Kennedy. You were very wise, to see which way the cat was goin' to jump. I congratulate you."

"It *isn't* true!" Viola appealed to the little group about them. "It's *not* true, is it, Miss Cullen? You haven't spoken to Miss Mortimer about *any* of us, have you?"

Miss Cullen hesitated. Then she gently disengaged her hand.

"Yes, my dear," she said, in a new, quiet voice. "It's perfectly true. I am responsible for—all of this."

In a complete silence she moved to the door. The others fell away from her to right and left. Yet, despite her disgrace, her bearing was more dignified than theirs.

CHAPTER XXI

One Way Out

There was a moment's silence. All of them felt uncomfortable; some were scornful, some ashamed, some angry, some wrung with pity. Miss Pearson broke the silence first.

"*Well!* Of *all* things to do!" she said.

"I don't wonder!" cried Viola impetuously. "What could she do? She knew that you all hated her—well, at least were all trying to get rid of her. She hasn't a home, she hasn't saved much—who could?—"

"Why not?" interrupted Miss Parry, half aggressive, half defensive. "She's at the maximum, and it doesn't cost *her* much to live!"

"Of course it does!" Viola stormed on. "She has to live somewhere all through the holidays. She's got to pay out all the time, while the rest of us—well, most of us—simply go home. She's lost all she's paid in to the Fund—she'll never see a penny of that back. How *can* she have saved enough to live on decently for the rest of her life?"

Miss Parry had no reply. There lay, indeed, her own secret terror. With ordinary expenses, a few luxuries, and a loss of ten per cent. of one's salary, one cannot count on saving enough to live on for twenty, or more, years.

"Anyhow," she said, carrying the war into the enemy's camp, "*you're* safe enough. Whatever she's done to the rest of us, she's put *you* on velvet. It was worth your while to stand in with her."

"D'you think I'd stay, if the rest of you have to go? Or at all, after this? I'll do anything rather!"

"Hush. Listen." Miss Lexington's voice fell like cold water on the flame of their anger. Vaguely, half unconsciously, Viola wondered when the Staff Mistress had come in—how much she had heard. "There isn't the least use in talking like this. Whatever harm Miss Cullen could do us—or we her—is done. What we have to do now is to decide on our own future. If it's true that we're all doomed, I imagine that some of us will give up teaching—'*must*,' I should have said, not 'will.' We must just face it—the loss of our subscriptions to the Fund, the loss of our pensions, the loss of any market value our training and experience gives us. We must begin again—train for something else, if we can—anyhow, it's for each of us to decide. For the younger of you—those who are still low in the Scale—who haven't hopelessly expensive qualifications— it's easier. You'll get other work, better schools. You can't help getting something better! So, if I may advise, if you're still 'cheap'" —she laid a scornful emphasis on the word— "I should advise you to resign at once. Don't stop on here. You'll get *something* within a year; or at least you've got a good chance to train for something else. The rest of us—well, for myself, I can't afford the risk of resigning. If I'm told to go, I must—and begin again, at something else. But it's worse than useless to try to allot the blame. If you go back to the beginning of the trouble, it's not the fault of any of us—it's the fault of a system which forces a woman to go on teaching when she's no longer capable of doing good work. I doubt if any one of us would have resigned in Miss Cullen's place. It was too big a risk to take, and I'm sure she didn't realise that it was a choice between her resignation and our dismissal. We weren't to blame for urging Miss Barr to dismiss her—we did know that the choice lay between her and us, and we were in the majority. I don't know that we can blame her for using the only weapon left to her. I know that her position is desperate—*desperate*. We, most of us, are not hopelessly middle-aged yet; we can learn something new, and—" she hesitated— "well, since we're being frank, Miss Cullen's personal appearance is against her, in looking for new work, as ours is not. Don't be harder than you can help in judging her. ..."

She paused as if she had something further to say, but, flushing, she decided not to. Her habit of reticence checked the appeal which her heart prompted her to make.

After that homily, the Staff could not, openly at least, indulge in further combat. To do them justice, few wished to. Some situations, even in the dullest life, are so tragic that one cannot even have the luxury of a good wrangle. Almost silently they drifted away.

The afternoon was passed in an atmosphere of suspense and strain like that which precedes a thunder-storm. Miss Mortimer had now changed her tactics. Having, presumably, done her fell work with Miss Parry, she now had a roving commission which enabled her to stray from class to class, spending a scanty few minutes with each victim. Generally she said nothing whatever to these unfortunates. She merely smiled, pityingly, wrote in her dreaded notebook, and drifted out again. To Viola, taking one of the classes usually the portion of Miss Lovell, she was a little more expansive.

"Let me see, Miss Kennedy—is it Kennedy?"

Viola assented.

"You're new here, aren't you? I don't think I've had the pleasure of hearing you before."

Viola opened her mouth to retort, but closed it stonily.

"A very nice little lesson," cooed the Inspector. "Very pleasant indeed. I'm sure they're enjoying it tremendously—aren't you, girls?"

"Yes, Miss Mortimer," chorused twenty-eight dutiful voices.

"It's not my lesson," protested Viola, sulkily resentful of the enemy's patronage. "It's Miss Lovell's. I'm using her notes. It's her class really."

"Oh, are you losing a free time? That's *too* bad, isn't it? That means faulty organisation somewhere."

Viola reddened angrily. She was not going to be inveigled into even an apparent complaint.

"It can't be helped, if a mistress is ill. There are only just enough of us to go round, anyhow."

Miss Mortimer looked at her oddly, a warning, meaning look which Viola, boiling with indignation, chose to ignore.

"No doubt you've heard that Miss Lovell is ill—and why," she said, her voice rendered a little unsteady by the thumping of her heart.

"Oh, yes. Nerves, of *course*. I always said that it was the greatest mistake for a nervous subject like Miss Lovell to remain on this Staff. I told her so myself when I was last here."

Viola's eyes flashed. She dared not speak lest her anger should break through her control. So *that* was the cause of that pitiful collapse! Fear had been made certainty. And the woman dared to boast of it!

"I very much doubt, Miss—er—Kennedy," continued the Inspector, a new, steely note in her voice, "whether you yourself are quite—er—suited to this type of school."

"Oh! I'm leaving at the end of this term," said Viola shortly, coming to a sudden resolution. "It certainly does *not* suit me."

"Ah! Perhaps that's just as well," said Miss Mortimer with silky deliberation. "I'm sure you're—wise."

Viola left school in a turmoil of rage and pity and scorn. Through her mingled emotions she was conscious of relief—relief that this life of intrigue and suspicion would end in a few weeks. And she was also conscious of some other emotion. What? Regret? Something very like it, she thought, and inconsequently refused to analyse its reason, shutting the ears of her heart to a voice that was clamouring to her to hear and acknowledge it.

"But will a new school be any better?" she thought with some trepidation. "Is this just normal school atmosphere, all beastly suspicion and insincerity and hidden hatred? Will it always be like this? Shall I become like that too?"

Her youth rose in laughing scorn of the idea; but something within her—something that had been born in her since she came to Besley—whispered a warning that made her shiver a little. Middle age very quickly swamps youth.

She went home through the town, visited the library and a few shops, and then turned down towards her rooms. She had fallen into that dreary, introspective mood which often follows on anger and excitement, and she walked slowly, idly noticing the streets—the lighted shops, the blazing facade of a cinema-hall, with now and then something beautiful—a few lingering leaves, golden within the radius of a street lamp, like magic fruit blossoming out of the lamp itself; or a coster's barrow reflected in a puddle, looking like a tiny enchanted sea of rainbow colour. She was so absorbed in her thoughts, so lost to reality, that it did not even startle her when a hand relieved her of her books and bag, and a voice beside her said:

"Good! I wanted to meet you. I want to know when you'll let me come and see you. I want to ask you a question."

It all fitted into her dreamy mood. It *was* a dream, she felt—one of those happy dreams in which everything comes right—dreams which so seldom come true.

"I wanted to see you, too," she said. In a dream you may allow yourself to think thoughts and say words which, in the life of everyday, you must repress ruthlessly. "I wanted to tell you that I'm leaving."

"*Leaving*! When?"

There was real consternation in Martin Hyde's voice—yes, and grief.

"Beatrice, don't go. I—I can't go on in Besley if you aren't here."

Viola's heart leapt and her throat became oddly constricted, as if she were going to cry. But it was not that. The dream was coming true. ...

"I've—I've got to. I—oh, Martin, I don't want to go—not if—"

She broke off. She knew now exactly where she was—knew, too, that she had hopelessly given herself away. For a moment of sickening silence she writhed in the knowledge. Then:

"So you *do*—I hoped you might, some day," he said quietly.

"Might—?"

Let *him* speak out now!—if he wanted to, if she hadn't made a ghastly mistake.

"Might care, of course. You know that well."

Viola bit her lips hard, trembling with a quite new emotion. This was unlike any dream. It was reality.

"I—I—you—" she faltered out, frantically trying to control and judge the emotions that swept her like a storm.

"When I saw you, over that row in the school back there," said Hyde, with a jerk of his chin, "I knew how 'twould be—for me. And I said then that it wasn't fair for a man like me, living as I'm living, to hope for it. But—well, I'm selfish by nature, Beatrice, and I—I grabbed at the chance. A better man would have left you. I—well, I wanted you too much. I suppose I loved myself more than—anything. I made up excuses. I said

I'd had the bad times, and it was my turn for the good—though God knows that no bad times could count against—what I was hoping for! So—I followed you into that field. And then, when I saw you, helpless and crying there alone, I—I knew I couldn't stop. So I told you a bit about myself, so that you'd know what like I was—outside, anyway." He gulped like a schoolboy, and then, like a boy, the eager words flooded out again. "When I left you that day, I knew *I* was for it! But that made me think—and I thought most about you. I knew you ought to have the best, and I knew I wasn't *that*! And so—well, I meant—I said I wouldn't see you again if I could help it. Because I knew you couldn't care, and—I couldn't bear just to meet you and say how-d'you-do, and—"

He broke off. Viola laid a shaking hand on his arm. She could not speak.

"Well, I cut that acting stuff because I couldn't bear to hear you saying those things to me—What?"—as she made a tiny movement of surprise—"didn't you guess why I'd chucked it? That was why. And then I thought of some other fellow—Andrews or some chap like that—speaking those things to you. ... Jealous, of course I was jealous! I cursed myself for every kind of a fool—yes, and I acted like one, too, till Joe got on to it, and he said—well, he said I was a fool and a coward to give in before I knew. He said—ah, well, sure it's no matter—"

"I guess, though! He said it was a bit rough on me, not to have the chance to say—to say—if I cared—"

He nodded, and squeezed the hand on his arm against his side.

"Still, I didn't think it was possible you should care two pins, and I—well, I kept funking it. But then—Do you believe in an angel guardian?"

The question was so unexpected and his voice was so serious that Viola wanted to laugh. She murmured something incoherent.

"I used to think mine had forgotten his job, luck's been against me so often. And that Sunday, when I was out trying to—to forget you, Beatrice, because it hurt so damnably to remember—ah, sure, never mind!" (as she stole soft, consoling fingers into his)—"well, when the snow came I fairly cursed! And then—"

"Then I threw myself violently at your head," put in Viola.

"Then I decided I'd—find out," said Hyde, a trifle grimly.

"Well—have you?"

"Haven't I?"

"You haven't asked me a thing," Viola pointed out.

"Do I need to? 'By my sword, Beatrice, thou lovest me!'"

Viola took the cue.

"'I protest I do love thee,'" she answered, only half audibly. "'I love you with so much of my heart that none is left to protest.'"

CHAPTER XXII

Scandal

Miss Barr sat at her desk as usual—no, not quite as usual, for now she made no attempt to simulate, even to herself, that her head and hands were busy with its contents. Her hands—those pretty, fluttering, useless hands of hers—lay idly in her lap; and in her head there buzzed, like heavy, useless moths, a few heavy and useless thoughts. It was of no use to plan, now; of no use to scheme an active line of attack or defence. If it had been useful, she could not have done it. She was too beaten, too weary, too dead. She had no hope left; she was too numbed and apathetic even to despair.

There came a knock at the door—a hesitating knock. Automatically Miss Barr pressed her knob. She felt no interest at all in her visitor; she was beyond even annoyance.

Miss Lexington entered and crossed straight over to the desk. The two pairs of eyes met—woman speaking silently to woman, rank and order gone. Without invitation, Miss Lexington, the scrupulous, meticulous Miss Lexington, sat down opposite her chief. Still neither spoke.

At last Miss Barr broke the silence.

"I suppose this is the end," she said dully.

"For some of us," Miss Lexington corrected her.

"No—for the school, I meant."

Miss Lexington looked at her curiously. For her, just then, the school did not exist apart from its Staff.

"The school?" she queried vaguely.

"Yes—the school—*my* school. I—" Her voice died away. Her lips continued to move silently, as if she were still speaking. Then her voice became audible again. "I … The school. … Do you think they will close the school?"

Miss Lexington looked at her gravely, concern in her face.

"I don't know—I should think not—"

"I don't mind anything, so long as they don't close my school. If they send someone else, someone *good*, to put it right again. It used to be a good school, Miss Lexington."

There was a half questioning, half appealing note in her voice.

"We had some very nice girls here once. We used to get really quite good Results. ... It was the war that spoilt our girls, wasn't it? Yes, the war. ... It will recover, don't you think?—If they only give it a chance. If they only don't close it."

Suddenly Miss Lexington realised that in all her eight years' acquaintance with the Head she had never known her.

"I didn't know you felt about it like that," she said gently.

Miss Barr raised slightly surprised eyes.

"*Didn't know I cared about the school?*" she asked, half incredulously. It was as if a mother had said, "You didn't know I cared about my child?"

Miss Lexington was silent. She saw suddenly, as if by a revelation, that this woman, weak, despised, futile, had had in her life a selfless ideal which perhaps none of them could rival.

"I'm sorry. I didn't know," she muttered, in unwonted humility.

"But *of course* I cared! ... I haven't known *what* to do, Miss Lexington. I've tried to do my best, but I know I've been wrong. I see it now. I ought to have consulted you. I—I didn't want to. It was *my* school. But I see it now. At one time, you know, I sacrificed everyone and everything else to the school. You told me so, you remember." Miss Lexington did remember—a stormy interview in which, taking up the cudgels for the overdriven Staff, she had made that very protest in those very words. "You were right. I saw it after you'd gone. And I determined that I would not do that again. So, when Miss Cullen began to—to fail, I tried to see things more widely, more from other people's point of view. I remembered so well how your voice had sounded when you told me that I was sacrificing my Staff to the girls. It was true, I had pampered my own ideal at the expense of you all, and I felt that I had perhaps even destroyed your feeling of devotion to the school by my own want of—of proportion. So I thought I'd give

Miss Cullen a chance. … And then, later, I saw how terrible it would be for her to have to leave. … Miss Lexington, I couldn't do it. I know you've all felt that I ought to ask her to go, and I honestly have tried to do it. I've even sent for her, meaning to—to ask her to resign; and each time, when I saw her there, I—I just couldn't do it. It seemed too cruel. … I know I was wrong. I see it now. I've been hard in the wrong place and weak in the wrong place. I've meant to do my duty, both by the school and by the Staff; and first I sacrificed the Staff to the school, and now the school to the Staff. You can't blame me more than I blame myself. …"

Her voice trailed away. Miss Lexington found nothing to reply. It was too true to be comfortingly denied, too serious to be put lightly aside. At last—

"They won't close the school, I feel sure," she said with a quiet decision that gave her hearer hope. "It's too big, serves too large an area. No, I'm sure that the school's safe, Miss Barr, as far as that goes. The question is—are we?"

Miss Barr sat up. There was a spark very like triumph in her eye.

"Do you really think so?" she asked eagerly. "Do you honestly believe that the school will get over it and—and go on?"

"I feel sure it will. Only I expect there'll be big changes in—in organisation."

As she dropped the hint, Miss Lexington fixed her eyes anxiously on her superior. How had she taken it? Did she understand that her own fate was probably the reverse of that of the school, that she would never "get over it and go on"?

Whether she did or not, she gave no sign. A peace, which had been a stranger to her for long past, now filled her whole being and beamed from her eyes. Vaguely, half unconsciously, she answered.

"Changes—oh, yes, of course. Big changes," she murmured happily.

Miss Lexington hesitated, and then took the plunge.

"Have you thought what you will do?" she asked bluntly.

"Do? About what?"

"Why, about—everything." At the last moment her courage failed her; she simply could not answer, "About your own future."

Miss Barr sat up and drew her chair to the desk in quite her old manner. Her one great anxiety, the future of the school, settled, she became her usual self, the Head Mistress of Besley High School, arbiter of fates, ruler of destinies.

"Oh, of course, on certain points I'm quite decided. To begin with, Miss Cullen must go. I've been weak, very weak, about her in the past, but she's had every chance now, and she must go. Miss Mortimer quite agrees with me. As a matter of fact, she told me that she had advised the County Authorities, after her earlier visit here, to ask Miss Cullen to resign."

"*Miss Mortimer!*"

Accustomed as she was to duplicity—or diplomacy—or perhaps they are the same thing?—Miss Lexington was startled. She had not expected that the tool would be discarded quite so soon, even though its use was now over. There was a cynicism about that speedy rejection that almost shocked her.

"Yes," Miss Barr continued, "I imagine that they will write at once and give her half a term's notice. So that clears the ground, doesn't it? Once she's gone, we shall be able to get on."

Miss Lexington said nothing. *Could* it be, she wondered, that Miss Barr was really so infatuated as to think that, the incubus gone, all would be well? Did she really not know that it was too late—months too late? Did she not see the cloud that threatened to overwhelm both her subordinates and herself in disaster?

"Yes," the Head babbled happily, "our way will be clear then. And then—"

"Yes? And then?"

The inexorable blue eyes met the hesitating, deprecating, furtive grey ones.

"Why—don't you think—I mean, we shall be all right then, shan't we? Or do you think—?"

Miss Lexington said nothing, in words. She allowed her scornful, steely look to speak her mind.

"Miss Lexington, what do you mean? Do you think—are you afraid that—that—further steps may be necessary?"

While the Second Mistress was yet framing her thoughts, impatient, turbulent thoughts, into words, a hurried tap came at the white door.

"Oh, dear!" sighed the Head, quite in the old manner. "Who *can* that be? I never seem able to have a *minute* to myself."

And, in that sentence, she undid completely all that she had unconsciously achieved in winning her colleague's sympathy and even admiration. Miss Lexington had no use, especially at this juncture, for the graceful trimmings of Headship.

"It sounds like Miss Parry's knock," she said coldly.

"Ah, perhaps it is. I think we'll just ask her to come in. She gives very shrewd advice sometimes."

Miss Lexington sat stonily silent as the knob was pressed, the door opened, and Miss Parry's entrance effected.

"Miss Barr, I felt I *had* to come to you at *once*," breathed the new-comer, plumping down unceremoniously in the nearest chair. "And I'm so glad Miss Lexington happens to be here. I've just heard *the* most scandalous thing."

She paused for breath.

Miss Barr eyed her a little nervously. She did hope that Miss Parry would not say anything—anything indiscreet. Miss Lexington was so—well, one had to be so careful with Miss Lexington. She took such hard, uncompromising views of the simplest matters. ...

"Yes?" she said a little stiffly.

Miss Parry hitched her chair a little nearer—the true gossip's gesture. Instinctively Miss Lexington backed hers a corresponding distance away. Useful—necessary, even—as the alliance with Miss Parry had been, it had always had these moments when it so much offended her taste that she wondered whether it were worth it.

"You remember my tellin' you," began the little lady with hoarse, eager volubility, "that everybody in the town was talkin' about the way Miss Kennedy simply *pursued* that poor boy at Linden House—Mr. Hyde? Oh, yes, Miss Lexington" —seeing that lady's look of incredulous disgust— "it's quite, perfectly true. Mrs. Atkinson told me she'd noticed it, and the poor boy absolutely had to give up the Dramatic Club, that girl made it so awkward for him. ... Well, that was only the beginning."

She paused dramatically. Even Miss Lexington, consistent hater of gossip, felt mildly interested as she noticed the glistening eye and eager manner. Obviously something tremendous was to come.

"I had to go round to Mrs. Holmes's on business last night," pursued Miss Parry with unction, "and I happened to say, in a friendly sort o' way, you know, like one does to these people, that I hoped she'd got a new lodger in Miss Kennedy's place. (She went to live with Miss Wilson, you know. Moved in last Monday night.) Well, you should've seen Mrs. Holmes look! 'Whoever or *whatever* I get,' she said, 'I can't get worse than that Miss Kennedy.' That's what she said. 'It was well for her,' she said, 'that she gave me notice, because if she hadn't've done it herself I'd have given it to her.' So I said, 'Oh, Mrs. Holmes,' I said, 'don't say that. She's only young,' I said, 'and you can't expect old heads on young shoulders.' She just *looked*. '*Any* girl's old enough to know right from wrong,' she said, 'and when it comes to ridin' out at night on a young man's motor-bike, that is *not* right,' she said, 'and I won't have it.'"

Miss Parry paused to draw breath, her glittering eyes scanning her companions' faces eagerly. Miss Lexington looked contemptuous, even bored; but Miss Barr had a half dubious, half shocked expression that was more promising.

"Surely Mrs. Holmes's gossip—" began Miss Lexington.

"Oh, it's true enough! We all knew it, all of us at the Dramatic Club. Ask Miss Reeve," she added, with a gambler's recklessness risking the result if she were taken at her word. "And it isn't only Mrs. Holmes who talks. It's her neighbours, and the shop-people—why, even our own girls!"

"Dear me!" murmured Miss Barr, much perturbed; "That's most undesirable—*most*."

"Isn't it? 'Specially when it was Miss Kennedy who let May Masters behave in that scand'lous way at Linden House. People will talk, won't they?—put two and two together. ... And that's not the worst."

Again she paused dramatically. Something in her attitude, the attitude of a cat licking its lips over a particularly pleasant fish's head, infuriated Miss Lexington. She put up a polite hand to conceal a simulated yawn. The gesture had its desired effect.

"Last week-end," began the narrator, in suitably impressive tones, "Miss Kennedy went away."

"With Miss Wilson," put in Miss Lexington in a tone of faint disgust.

"Yes. She *went* with Miss Wilson, of course. We all knew that—we were meant to know it. What we were *not* meant to know, and what I learnt by the merest chance, was that Miss Wilson came back alone on the Saturday night, and that Miss Kennedy arrived, late on Sunday night—*in Mr. Hyde's side-car.*"

"How do you know?" Miss Lexington almost snapped the question out.

"Oh, it's true enough! Miss Wilson was in bed in her rooms all the Sunday; and my landlady's brother saw the rest, so of course he told her, and she told me. And—I've got another proof of it, if you don't believe that; Mr. Masters, May's father, saw them, and told Mrs. Atkinson."

She threw a triumphant glance about her. Mr. Masters, a Governor, already furious on his daughter's account, to learn such a thing! Even Miss Lexington looked taken aback: Miss Barr's expression was one of horror.

"Miss Parry, how terrible!" she whispered. "I can hardly believe my ears. What a thing to happen, on top of everything else! ... A whole day later—alone with a young man, with whom her name has been linked. ... You're *sure* there's no mistake!"

"Positive." The little lady shut her mouth tight and nodded her head decidedly. "I don't repeat what I can't prove, Miss Barr."

This, Miss Barr knew, was true. It was this which had given Miss Parry such value as a communication file.

"It's a thing which calls for immediate action," said the Head, sitting very upright and adjusting her expression to that of the Woman of Affairs—almost the stateswoman. "I shall send for Miss Kennedy to-morrow, as soon as she arrives. If she cannot deny, categorically, what has been said, she must go—at once, if necessary."

"The Education Authority—" began Miss Lexington.

"I have no need to consult them when the question is one of—er— Tone on the Staff," replied Miss Barr. "That is particularly stated, you may remember, when Staff are engaged."

Miss Lexington was silenced for the moment. Then she said:

"But of course you'll give her a chance to explain? I mean—it seems so unlike Miss Kennedy, of all people, to behave like that."

"Ah!" Miss Parry's voice was full of meaning. "You haven't seen her out of school, Miss Lexington, like I have. If you'd've belonged to the Dramatic, you'd have known. It was most embarrassin'. I'm not straitlaced, as you know, but I—well, I didn't know where to *look*! He, poor fellow, he did put up a fight. As I told you, he resigned. But you know how it is—if a girl *hunts* a man, and doesn't mind *what* she does—!" She shrugged expressively. "And there was that time, after he'd been here with Mr. Glynn—I told you about that, Miss Barr—"

"Yes, I remember. Yes, it certainly is—" Miss Barr blushed faintly. "I will see Miss Kennedy in the morning. I quite see that I must *act*—act very firmly."

She shut her mouth with a snap. In the gesture she showed her thought: "You think I'm weak about dismissing incompetents. You wait and see!"

Miss Lexington, with a tiny shrug, rose and took her leave. After all, it didn't much matter if Viola Kennedy had to leave. There was still hope for her elsewhere. Her own problem remained unsolved.

CHAPTER XXIII
The Victim

In the midst of all the alarums and excursions of the week, most people had allowed Miss Cullen to slip into the backs of their minds, where she remained, a mere painful impression. Just as one may imagine that, in the full horrors of a plague-swept town, the sufferers have a lurking hatred for that faulty drain or contaminated water which has been the immediate cause of their tribulation, but are too much occupied with the results to dwell on the cause, so did the majority of the Staff feel to Miss Cullen.

She knew it, of course. She had, in that one short time of plain speaking in the pleasant, familiar Staff Room, read it in their scornful, angry eyes and bitter tones. She knew, too, that never till merciful Death claimed her—perhaps not then—would she be able to forget those contemptuous eyes or forgive herself that she deserved their scorn. Like others on the Staff, Miss Cullen's eyes were opened, and she saw herself in a new and terrible light.

She went straight to her lodgings after the day of that moment of appalling disclosure. She had not meant to go there—she had no active volition left, it seemed, but acted like one stunned or sleepwalking; but her feet had carried her over the accustomed ground, up the familiar street, in at the shabby door which for six years had stood to her for home, and was to be her home no more. And now she sat in the dim, firelit room, thinking.

How had she come to this pass? Where had she begun to leave the path of duty and honour which she had walked from babyhood? She looked back over her life. Mary Cullen playing in the Vicarage garden with her little sister Ann. Even then the younger Ann had been the leader, the one to plan games and get into mischief, while Mary, patiently plodding after "little sister," had invariably cleared up the mess and taken the blame of the mischief. "You ought to have given little Ann a better example. You are the eldest."

School at Miss Jennifer's, with Ann rapidly acquiring the smattering of everything offered to her, while Mary worked steadily on the small material she could get. Governesses for them both; Paris "to learn the language," both working hard now, with the knowledge, impressed on them from home, that both must earn, and that dear papa was so ambitious for his two clever daughters. Home again. The Dean, who had called Mary brilliant and christened her Minerva, but who had preferred to laugh with Ann—the Dean, speaking of College as the indispensable factor to a successful career "nowadays."

So College had followed. Ann at Newnham, because she "wouldn't have Mary eternally fussing after her," and Mary at Somerville, beginning at twenty-two to please herself and to make her own friends, but not very good at either because she was unused to such things, and because that label of brilliancy, which she secretly cherished all the rest of her thwarted life, here put her automatically into a coterie of the "clever" and debarred her from the friendship of the pretty and the ordinary—the friendship which, at fifty-four, she was still wistfully trying to make with girls of the same pretty and ordinary type. It was here that Mary Cullen had learned to scrape back her hair, to use "sensible" steel-rimmed glasses, to protrude her jaw, to wear hideous clothes, to despise dress and frivolity, to affect a firmness which she could never possess. Here she had been finally set in the mould into which life had early poured her fluid character.

But it was also here that she had first found an ideal on which to set her earnest devotion. Sitting now in the dark, she looked back on that fervent young ideal with wonder that it had become so obscured. "Education" had been a war-cry to her then, a cry rousing her soul, calling to her to throw herself into its service. In Education she had seen the salvation of the world. "If people are educated, really educated, there will be an end of trouble. There *must* be." That had been the thread of argument with those young enthusiasts of thirty years ago, as it was still the thread of argument with Viola Kennedy.

"And we were right," thought the faded woman, dwelling calmly and gravely on the memory of her dead self. "Only, as we got absorbed in teaching, we forgot the meaning of education."

Yes, that had begun early. In her very first post Mary Cullen had learnt that ideals which do not show immediate commercial results are not wanted in the world of schools. Get the girls through; teach them what examiners will expect them to say; cram into them the opinions of the textbooks. Original thought? Certainly not! What can you be thinking of? These questions have answers, and the girls must know those answers; they are all to be found in the textbooks. ... Get them through, get them through. ... And then, later, "Miss Cullen is such a successful teacher. She always gets good Results!"; this, said so often that its sound overwhelmed the tiny, fading voice that asked, plaintively, "Is *this* Education?"

Changes again. A new generation, whose ways Mary Cullen had never understood—could never understand. Girls speaking a new language, thinking new thoughts in a new way. Education? Oh, yes, useful as far as it goes—you can't get a good screw without passing some rotten exam. or other. Get them through, Miss Cullen, get them through. ... But examinations changing too; examiners getting hold of her forgotten theory that to be educated is to be able to think; textbooks no longer of supreme value; knowledge now of less importance than intelligence—and too late, now, to go back to the old ideals. Set, now, in the text book rut. Miss Cullen's Results are getting very bad. You must get better Results than that, Miss Cullen. Get them through. Examinations are so important nowadays, for good posts.

What a muddle it all was! All doing the same thing with a different aim. How could a woman steer her course right when she had no guiding star to set it by? And then:

"Ah, but I had one once. I had an ideal, and I threw it aside. I left it for success. If I'd kept to my old College ideas I should have been all right now. It's my own fault."

And yet—was it quite as simple as that? Wasn't it rather that no one quite knew what they did want of that talisman Education, or even quite what it was? Was it, as the more idealistic teachers and examiners thought, the power to think, to show what was in one? Was it, as employers thought, the power to write English, to spell, use a typewriter, do accounts, perhaps read French? Was it, as the girls thought, a key with which to open the golden door to a salary, to be thrown away as soon as the door was opened? Could one give it, or help anyone to get it, when no one knew what it was?

"It wasn't altogether my fault," thought Miss Cullen, brooding in her chair. "How could I know first that Education meant getting through examinations out of textbooks, and then that getting through examinations meant—education?"

For a few minutes longer she dwelt on that; then she came down to a less abstract problem—the problem of her own career.

"It's all due to the same thing," she told herself in grave condemnation. "It all comes of throwing away ideals for success. That set me wrong in my work, and now it's set me wrong in my life. I ought to have seen it last term—last year—years ago. I ought to have seen that I didn't give what I offered, that education was better without me. I oughtn't to have let my fear for the future make me do what I knew was wrong. 'Consider the lilies of the field. ... Are not five sparrows sold for a farthing. ...' I ought to have thought of that. I'm not a practical Christian, or I would have thought of that. Has my religion been a sham, too? It was certainly a great sin to pretend to do what I knew I couldn't do. They say one sin leads to another. That's how I've got to be what I am—treacherous, deceitful, grasping, cruel, selfish ..."

She brooded on the picture. Even Miss Parry might have thought it highly-coloured; but Miss Cullen, seeing herself with the cruel eyes of self-reproach, thought it painfully accurate.

"If only I'd trusted more, had more faith! But I can't expect to have my future cared for now, not after I've rejected the promises and taken my future into my own hands. And what have I made of it?"

What indeed? The practical question seemed to act as a sudden spur on Miss Cullen's reminiscent and passive mood. She sat up with a start, clutching the arms of her chair, looking with wide, terrified eyes into the dark room which suddenly seemed typical of her dark future. With an almost superstitious terror clutching at her heart, she got up and with trembling fingers lighted the gas.

The cold light glared down on the orderly, ugly room; but it did nothing to dispel the black fear in Miss Cullen's heart. She sat looking with new eyes at the room in which she had lived and suffered for six years. It was as if she were trying to read into the stiff furniture, the battered books, the tawdry ornaments, some new meaning—to find among them some clue for her guidance. They stared back, stolid, immovable, inimical.

"What am I to do? Oh, God, what am I to do?" she whispered aloud; and her voice was like the voice of a stranger.

She must go, of course—at once, if possible. She could not live on at Besley High School now that they knew her for what she was—now that she knew herself. What then? She had an instant vision, sickeningly clear, of herself answering advertisements, trudging round agencies, waiting with desperate hope for a letter that never came. She saw herself vainly writing to a remote Board to plead for that precious ten per cent. of her salary which she had paid in, year by year, to a Fund for Superannuated Teachers which had never been known to benefit a soul. She saw her tiny savings dwindling, shrinking, month by month and year by year. She saw herself ageing, weakening, but never attaining the desired goal of Death.

"If only I could die now—*now*," she thought with a frantic longing that was near despair.

Ah, what a solution that would be! Death would be—the end. No need to plan and struggle then; only to accept, humbly, what comes. No responsibility after death. Grief, remorse, might be hers, the wages of her life; but these would be hers in life too, and, after death, when she saw things aright, and saw that they were one's due, one could surely find peace, even pleasure of a sort, in the working of perfect justice? Oh, and to be at peace—alone—no one but oneself to reckon with! Like a lost traveller in the desert who dreams of water, Miss Cullen dwelt on the thought of death.

"I have suffered all my life," she thought. "Need I struggle on any more? Must I go through that long, long agony of failure and want and unloved old age? Would it matter to anyone if I—ended it? No one would care, no one need know. I could do it secretly, disappear. ... It would be the best way out for every one—for the school, for Ann, for me. ... Oh, and so easy compared with life!"

She played with the idea, tantalising herself with it; but all the time she knew that she would never do it. The habit of stern duty, of self-abnegation, had too firm a hold on her. Never would she take the coward's way out.

"I don't deserve to escape like that," she thought, and a heavy sigh escaped her laden heart. "No, God knows best. If I am to have my punishment here, it will be for the best. I must just endure it, and—and hope that I'm making up. I will take everything, everything—scorn, dislike, age, loneliness, whatever comes. It will be best, whatever it is."

And, with the decision, peace came to her at last—the patient, enduring peace which she had hoped for as the best that death could offer.

"I will take everything as it comes," she whispered. "I will do nothing of my own accord. I won't struggle. Whatever comes I will accept."

A knock at her door. It was so like a direct reply, a messenger summoned by her resignation of herself to her fate, that she felt a moment's fear, as of one who receives a supernatural reply to question or prayer. Perhaps that was exactly what it was; for the letter, with the well-known crest of the Stamborough Education Committee, was the first stage of her punishment. Reading it, the death sentence of her teaching career, she lifted a face transfigured by faith and a penitent's gratitude.

"So soon!" she whispered. "Then I *am* forgiven. I can bear anything now."

CHAPTER XXIV

And the Rest

These three letters will tell all that it is now necessary to know. Number One has no formal beginning. It reads:

Glad to hear that you took my advice to heart. You were never cut out to teach, and you'll be a sight happier and better educating your own young than breaking your heart over instructing (which, as you sagely pointed out on that week-end of ours, is a bit different) the young of Besley. I liked the looks of your young man. I quite saw Parry's point of view. You'll both (I mean you and him, not you and Parry) take life too hard, but I believe that's the way you Feelers enjoy yourselves, especially when there's two of you to help each other do it.

No, I don't in the least know what's become of poor old Lexo. Enigma to the end! Reeve, as perhaps you heard, really did go and train as a superior parlourmaid. Rather sporting of her, I call it—as Rowan would say—and I believe she's very good at it. She'd look the part, so efficient and neat. She says it's a lady's life compared with Besley, which of course it could well be. Parry, after a figurative and most becoming funeral in which Fergusson was chief mourner, and the elegy "It's rather hard on me" was constantly intoned, has gone to help a cousin keep a boarding-house—I beg her pardon, a Private Hotel, of course—where she seems happy enough, so there must be plenty of male guests. She'd be rather good as the elegant hostess with a Sad Past of deluded hopes (unspecified)—don't you agree? She'll be having her wedding in the papers soon, I'll bet my bottom dollar.

Of course you heard that the Head had been shot out too? She never expected it, I gather. She gave us a harangue on Hope, Ideals, Old Times, Carrying on the Torch, in such approved style at the end of term that we all thought she must have fallen on her feet and got a job; but she hasn't—hasn't even tried to, as far as I can make out. She's pinning her hopes to—what do you guess? THE FUND!!! Wonderful, isn't it, such optimism. She'll end like the lady in Dickens—"Bleak House," I think, but you'll know—who expected a judgment "shortly—on the Day of Judgment."

The rest of us jog on. We were too unimportant to get sacked; besides, it looks bad to get in a whole new Staff. But Rowan's leaving, and Baldwin, and of course Gill was, anyway; so I expect to become Staff Mistress at any moment. Funny thought.

Yes, on the whole, I'm glad you're out of it. You wouldn't enjoy the remnants as I do. Yes, I do—a Staff of Newton, Pearson, Jervis, Moore and Me fills me with delight. It must be—well, bracing at least, for the kids. By the way, one Rhoda Stein mourns you deeply. I won't give her your address unless you say I can. I know what these schwärmerei girls are.

Good luck to you, young Kennedy, and forget us all as soon as you can.

The second writer is a lady whom you have heard of by repute only. She is, you see, more or less successful, and had therefore no place here except as a "noise off."

Dear Mary,

What a very extraordinary state of affairs you seem to have landed yourself in! I had no idea that, with all your expensive training, to say nothing of your many chances, you were not making at least a moderate *success of your career; but I gather from my friend Gertrude Mortimer that this is so far from being the case that you were actually* dismissed *from your post at Besley! Of course I know that Besley is a very poor type of school and that probably you did not care for your work there, but it seems to me that that made it all the more important for you to give them of your best. Surely one can do more good (from an* idealistic *point of view, which I believe yours used to be) in a school of a low standard than in a really* good *school. In any case, it was clearly your* duty *to do your best. Besides, when at your age you deliberately selected a school of that type, you surely knew what you were doing, and that, if you did not like it, you could not change. You must have known that you would never get another post. You seem to have had no forethought, no consideration for your future. You have*

certainly played your cards very badly, first to get into a school like Besley at all,
and then to leave before you reached Pension Age.

If, as I understand, you left a year ago, and have not so far got other work, I
suppose it will be best for you to come and share my tiny home. It is not, I think,
a really good arrangement, certainly *not as a permanency, but you are welcome*
to come for a time, if necessary. I am, of course, by no means a rich woman, but
I do not wish you to feel that I grudge you a home. You will, no doubt, be able to
contribute something towards household expenses, and do a little to help in the
actual management of the house, and for the rest, as I say, I do not grudge you
what I can afford to give.

Please let me know in good time if you think of coming to me, as, should it be
soon, I must put off some dear friends who had planned to give me the pleasure
of a few weeks' visit.

Your affectionate sister,
Ann Cullen.

She also writes the third epistle, some months later.

Dearest Gertrude,

Indeed I do congratulate you, most warmly, *on your news. You have made*
a splendid *success of your life, and it is so pleasant to have one's capabilities*
recognised. You seem to have done a real public service in making a clean sweep
at Besley, and your rapid promotion proves that others, more influential, *have*
taken the same view.

How sweet of you to congratulate me *on getting the Stamborough district!*
Of course it will be easy, now that you have done so much there. And how even
sweeter *of you to inquire after my poor sister! Yes, she is* still *here; I can hardly*
turn her out, you know, and though of course it is a great hindrance to me in
many ways to have her with me for so long, I try to bear my burden contentedly.
She keeps out of the way as much as one can expect, I suppose, and she does do a
certain amount to help in the house, but—well, as we are such close *friends, I*
can say to you *that I do find her, socially as well as financially, rather much of*
a dead weight at my heels. She is, of course, quite unaware of this. She is very
happy—perfectly contented to "sit back and take it easy" on her small savings!

I suppose you cannot tell me of any Home or Sisterhood where they would take her in for what she contributes to this household—twenty-five shillings a week? Of course she could not expect luxury for that, but she can hardly expect that, can she, after making such a mess of her chances? I am afraid she could not afford to give more. She seems to have saved very little. She is, of course, a bad manager in every respect.

But never mind my little worries! I am used to shouldering responsibilities and burdens. I hope that you, in your new glory, won't forget those of us who are still struggling along in the old ruts! Keep a "plum" for me when you are in real authority at Head-quarters! And, dearest girl, I do most sincerely hope and believe that that time is not far off. Now that you have shown by your fearless and masterly handling of the situation at Besley what you are capable of, I feel sure that even greater promotion is in store for you. ...

Miss Mortimer, spreading marmalade on her toast, smiled gently as she came to that. Poor Ann, always so *obvious*! *Of course* greater things were in store for one of her ability. And why, ... Why, in the name of common sense, should she bother about Ann Cullen and her tiresome, futile, hideous sister? She had made her own way, by her own brains and energy, and so must Ann. As for the sister—well, she might thank her stars she had *any* sort of a refuge to go to—though to live with a resentful Ann, running Ann's house and keeping oneself in the background, must be rather worse than penal servitude. ... Yes, a rather dreadful way to drag out one's life. Still, it was only what inefficiency deserved. ...

She dismissed them from her mind—trifles, to ponder which would be to confess herself a weakling, sentimental, unfit to climb the iron ladder that led to the barren goal at which she aimed. Yes, Besley had served her well. She felt a glow of something very like gratitude to Besley for its inefficiency.

That is, so to speak, Besley's justification. Surely you cannot wish for more than that?

Afterword

When *War Among Ladies* was published in 1928, the school story
wasn't new. The genre is sometimes dated to Sarah Fielding's 1749
The Governess; or, the Little Female Academy – also regarded as the first
full-length novel written for children. Skipping forward a couple of
centuries, Scott's take on the school story puts the pupils in secondary
position. Though we encounter these girls along the way, by far the
most significant characters are those who occupy the background in
most novels about schools: the often-warring teachers.

While the teaching staff in *War Among Ladies* have varying levels of
affection and respect for one another, different degrees of competence
and interest in their work, and the whole spectrum from naivety to
cynicism when it comes to their pupils, they have one thing in common:
their careers, and their independence, could end at any point.

One reason for leaving the profession could be marriage. All the
teachers in Besley are referred to as 'Miss', and that is because women
would be expected to leave the profession if they got married (as
happens with Miss Jessop). The Sex Disqualification (Removal) Act
1919 had purportedly made it illegal to disqualify anyone 'by sex or
marriage from the exercise of any public function' but, in practice, this
legislation was not enforced when employers chose to apply a policy
whereby married women were disqualified for many jobs – or had to
leave their role if they did tie the knot. This 'marriage bar' covered
doctors, nurses, lawyers, accountants, clerical workers in banks – and

teachers. A House of Commons debate in 1921 concluded that the government could not interfere and compel a local authority to employ a married woman. The few challenges in court in the 1920s met with very limited success, and the marriage bar wouldn't be lifted in teaching until 1944.

The economic reasoning was supposedly that married women could benefit from their husband's financial earnings and didn't need to 'take' the role from a man, while unmarried women required their own income. An even more sexist, underlying view was openly stated by a senior British judge in 1925: 'The duty of a married woman is primarily to look after her domestic concerns and it is impossible for her to do so and to effectively and satisfactorily act as a teacher at the same time.'

At Besley, though, it is not the prospect of marriage that looms as the chief reason these women may have to leave teaching. Rather, it is being seen to be incompetent. A schooling system, in which failing one subject means a pupil fails in them all, foments a toxic culture of feuding, with each teacher ready to blame others to save her own skin. And at the heart of *War Among Ladies* is the devastating portrait of French teacher Miss Cullen, widely considered to be the most incompetent and certainly the most vulnerable. Our first encounter with her is not prepossessing:

It was an odd face, as so many faces are when you look into them. The skin, reddened and rough, and slack now from want of exercise and years of unhealthy life, stretched tightly across the high, narrow forehead, where no stray line of hair softened the angularity, and sagged beneath the eyes and long, weak, protruding chin. The mouth, set a little open, smiled perpetually, anxiously.

The portrait hits many familiar notes of how unmarried women were often depicted in the period (and, indeed, in almost any period of literary history) – witchlike, with the pointy chin, and nothing

redeeming in the way of beauty. But what makes Scott's depiction
a little less offensive is that the reader is shown beyond the 'hideous
home-made' outfit of 'brown casement cloth' (a self-imposed uniform
that Miss Cullen alters on 1 May and 1 October, regardless of the
weather) and outdated hairstyle (that doesn't require a mirror). The
reader already sees that the eyes are 'uneasy, alarmed, defensive', that
the mouth is anxious. Scott's writing is always perceptive, and there is a
sympathy beneath the unkindness.

Miss Cullen is respected by neither teachers nor pupils, and the
results of the French Grammar test are the reason that only four
students pass that year's exams. 'For the paper was a modern one, and
Miss Cullen taught by the methods of thirty years ago.' The period
was seeing a shift away from rote-learning to methods that encouraged
pupils to respond more inductively to the questions presented to them:
'conundrums that demanded original thought and not the reproduction
of textbooks'. (Ironically, few of the girls learning this new way would
be expected to use these skills professionally, where women still most
commonly undertook routine clerical jobs where original thought would
have been frowned upon, if they did paid work at all.) With little scope
for workplace development or further training, teachers like Miss
Cullen were left to rely on any training that they'd received in decades
past. And yet we learn late in the novel that Miss Cullen herself had
emerged from Somerville College – one of the University of Oxford's
first two colleges for women – with the view that 'to be educated is
to be able to think'. Exams are finally catching up with her youthful
idealism, several decades too late.

Alongside this educational shift was one of discipline in schools –
away from "all this dogmatic 'Do this,' 'Be silent,' 'Sit straight', 'Don't
speak' business," as newcomer Viola puts it. Miss Cullen clutches on
to this shift to excuse her own inability to control a class, though the
reader and everyone else can see through the facade.

It is a mortifying depiction of a desperate, sad, lonely woman. Today, a teacher who is overwhelmed by the requirements of the job might, a few years from retirement age, decide to retire early. In 1928, this was not an option.

The School Teachers (Superannuation) Act 1918 set out the rules by which pensions could be given to teachers; it was amended in 1922 and 1924 to allow contributions from the teachers themselves. Unlike today's pension laws, where even brief periods of work can mean a corresponding pension in retirement, schoolteachers would only qualify for pensions if they had been employed 'for not less than thirty years in recognised or qualifying service'. Alongside this government provision, the Teachers' Pension Scheme was set up in 1923 – referred to as 'the Fund' by most of the teachers in the novel and which, in the reflection of one, 'had never been known to benefit a soul'. Similar rules applied in terms of the length of service needed for qualification.

In practice, this meant Miss Cullen would have to work right up to her retirement age. Early retirement would mean forfeiting everything, as is Miss Cullen's common refrain. If she loses this job and "I failed to get a position for four years, that I should have to forfeit my pension and all that I have paid in to the fund". More than pride or spite, it is financial necessity that motivates everything Miss Cullen does in *War Among Ladies*. When she makes her list of pros and cons about whether or not to resign, she recognises that everything and everyone is in favour of her going – except for the solitary 'con' – "I cannot afford to go." That was all. There was nothing else to say.' Single working women lived precarious lives in many ways. Paid less than their male equivalents, often denied mortgage applications without a male guarantor, accorded little respect by a society in which a woman's marriageability was still seen as her most significant characteristic. This indignity about pensions is a final kick in a lifetime of sustained kickings.

But did the Act and the Fund have no caveats? Scott uses another teacher, Miss Wilson, as a mouthpiece for the difference between the theory and the practice of teachers' financial situations. While the 10 per cent levy paid into the pension fund is supposedly voluntary, Miss Wilson points out that "If you aren't willing to pay it there are plenty of other mistresses who are". And while the 1918 act makes provision for those who 'become permanently incapable through infirmity of mind or body of serving efficiently as a teacher in a recognised service' to be 'grant[ed…] a gratuity', and 'the Fund' supposedly made similar provisions for repaying levies, Miss Wilson laughs at anybody who trusts this:

> Miss Wilson emitted a little snort of derisive laughter.
> "*Get it back?* Kennedy, you are *the* greenest lamb! Why, no one knows where it is – or any of the fund! There was a question asked about it a year or two ago, don't you remember?"

If she is referring to a question in the House of Commons, it's not clear exactly which it is, but teachers' pensions were the subject of many written and spoken questions in the 1920s and subsequent years. Many of these related to technicalities and special cases, but also concerned the number of teachers receiving pensions – for instance, in 1925 Lord Eustace Percy, then the equivalent of the education secretary, could tell the House that 14,360 teachers had received pensions under the 1918 Act.

Viola Kennedy enters the school in the middle of the oncoming catastrophe facing Miss Cullen individually and the school as a whole. Rumours of closure are circulating, as are suggestions that some teachers will, or at least should, be fired. The staffroom has an inexact hierarchy, not based entirely on how long a teacher has been in her role, but certainly taking this into account. The new staff like Viola, the 'meek new-comers', are 'positively struggling for inconspicuous seats and earnestly hoping that no one would say to them: "Friend, go up higher"' – a reference to Luke 14, where Jesus advises humility: "When you are invited, take the lowest place, so that when your host comes, he will say to you, 'Friend, move up to a better place.' Then you will be honoured in the presence of all the other guests." Honour is seldom bestowed in this staff room.

Viola's idealism is much like Miss Cullen's was, decades earlier. When asked what she thinks about teaching, she echoes some of the same mantras:

> It *does* seem to me to be a very big job – I don't mean shoving girls through exams, of course, nor just making them able to earn a little bigger salary. I mean teaching them to *think* – to take a line for themselves, to see straight, to ignore parrot-cries and generalities.

She still feels driven to give her pupils the best literature, wanting to avoid Charles Lamb's essays (which are chosen simply because there are plentiful copies of them), and worried that they will be obliged to learn Rudyard Kipling's 'If' (written in 1895, published in 1910) and Leigh Hunt's 'Abou Ben Adhem' (1834). Though she doesn't explain her distaste for them, it is possible that she doesn't believe their sentiment of stoicism would instil a 'real love of books' in her pupils, advocating instead for R.L. Stevenson's *Treasure Island* (1883) or a retelling of the tales of King Arthur. The poem that does move her pupil Rhoda, with the line 'There is sweet music here that softer falls / Than petals from blown roses on the grass / Or night dews on still waters', is from Tennyson's 'Song of the Lotos-Eaters' (1832). Scott does not tell the reader the title, and perhaps we are supposed to recognise it.

In the hands of a different novelist, the introduction of a new, naive, hopeful teacher might be Miss Cullen's saving grace. And there are initially suggestions that Viola Kennedy and Miss Cullen could become firm friends, and Miss Cullen will find an ally in her final years in the profession. But Scott is too clear-eyed to allow *War Among Ladies* to find that last-minute reprieve. Rather than 'saving' Miss Cullen, it is

❧ ❧ ❧

Viola who finds herself being dragged down into the worldview of her colleagues:

> She had realised, in that brief space of time, that they were not normal, any more than the trapped animals to whom she had compared them. She *knew*; for she, too, was no longer normal. Perhaps she never again would be quite normal, quite her old self, as convicts are, they say, never quite the same after their years of unnatural life are over…

A clue that Viola might yet be saved is that, in the narrative, she keeps her first name while the other teachers are referred to as 'Miss' and their surname. The narrator is acknowledging that her identity has not yet been dismantled: 'Viola the woman and Miss Kennedy the schoolmistress co-existed, though they were quite different people; but the woman was uppermost'. And it is into marriage that Viola escapes, to protect that 'normality' – the remnants of her literary ambitions being that she does so in the guise of a character from Shakespeare's *Much Ado About Nothing*.

Eleanor Scott's dedication to *War Among Ladies* is to 'the man in the train between Newton Abbot and Exeter who declared to the Author that all teachers had too much pay, too little work, and too much leisure'. Perhaps teachers still encounter men in trains (and elsewhere) who say such things. If nothing else, Scott's take on the school story, and her sad story of Miss Cullen's fate and Viola's crushed naivety, show how untrue the allegation has always been.

Simon Thomas

Series consultant **Simon Thomas** created the middlebrow blog Stuck in a Book in 2007. He is also the co-host of the popular podcast Tea or Books? Simon has a PhD from Oxford University in Interwar Literature.